ALL'S FAIR IN LOVE AND WAR

Sir Thomas's mouth descended, cutting off Amica's speech. Then, as he gently and thoroughly kissed her, she gave way, putting her hands up around his neck and holding him. When he lifted his head, she sighed and smiled.

"I will allow you to court me, Thomas of Reed."

"I do not ask for your permission," he replied with a soft smile, setting her away, "when Sir Eric has already given me his." He bent and picked up the basket. "Make certain that you are ready to receive me when I come for you this afternoon." He put the handle in her open fingers. "I will not court you in an untimely or disorderly manner. No battle was ever won in such a way."

Amica's eyebrows lifted. "You think courtship a battle, my lord?"

He turned and began to walk away, calling back, "Only a fool would think otherwise, my lady."

Books by Mary Spencer

Fire and Water
The Coming Home Place
The Vow
Honor

Published by HarperPaperbacks

Harper
Monogram

Honor

⊷ MARY SPENCER ⊷

HarperPaperbacks
A Division of HarperCollinsPublishers

This is a work of fiction. The characters, incidents, and
dialogues are products of the author's imagination and are
not to be construed as real. Any resemblance to actual events
or persons, living or dead, is entirely coincidental.

HarperPaperbacks   *A Division of* HarperCollins*Publishers*
                    10 East 53rd Street, New York, N.Y. 10022

Copyright © 1996 by Mary Spencer Liming
All rights reserved. No part of this book may be used or
reproduced in any manner whatsoever without written
permission of the publisher, except in the case of brief
quotations embodied in critical articles and reviews. For
information address HarperCollins*Publishers,*
10 East 53rd Street, New York, N.Y. 10022.

Cover illustration by Donna Diamond

First printing: March 1996

Printed in the United States of America

HarperPaperbacks, HarperMonogram, and colophon are
trademarks of HarperCollins*Publishers*

❖ 10 9 8 7 6 5 4 3 2 1

*This book is dedicated with much love
to the memory of a very special lady
whom I had the great honor of calling
my "second mom,"
and whom I feel the loss of more each day.*

CAROL JUNE BOWDEN
JULY 15, 1938 – NOVEMBER 23, 1994

One of the best things about writing is making so many terrific friends, and in this regard I think I've been especially lucky. I'd like to thank a few new friends who've helped keep me sane these past several months, especially after Carol's passing.

Special thanks to Suzy Winschel at B. Dalton's for always being so kind and supportive, to Vickie Denney for making me grin every time we talk, also for sharing a love of romance and the romance industry, and to all my buddies on America Online, the wonderful ladies in the Romance Writers' Group and everyone who hangs out in the Writers' Club. I'd try to list all you folks by screenname, but that'd be a whole other book.

Prologue

"Forgive me, my lord, but the leech says she'll not live much longer. You must come now if you wish to see her."

Duncan Selwyrn, lord of Sacre Placean, pulled his fascinated gaze from the red, wriggling body of his newborn son, whose angry cries filled the chamber as he protested being given his first bath, and gave his attention to his steward.

"Has the priest finished with her, then, Alfred?"

"Aye, my lord."

"Do you see my son?" Duncan turned to watch as the two women attending his heir lifted him from the water. "Is he not magnificent?"

"A fine, healthy boy, my lord."

"She meant to defeat me," Duncan said, clasping his hands behind his back, "but I am the victor. I have had my son off her, and there was naught she could do." He chuckled. "'Tis sweet to think on. She is a foolish woman, and has ever been." His smile relaxed. "But no more after this day."

Alfred gave no reply, but stood away from the door when his master strode past and followed behind as Duncan Selwyrn made his way to another chamber far down the hall.

The physician and priest moved away from the bed when he entered, revealing the young woman lying there.

She was as pale and still as she had been when the steward had left her, and when his master strode toward her, Alfred stole into the shadows on the opposite side of the bed.

The lord of Sacre Placean sat beside the girl, setting his hand to her forehead to push back several strands of her fine brown hair. His touch caused her eyes to open.

"My son," she whispered. "Please."

"He is being cared for," Duncan answered. "You must have no fears for him."

"Fears," she murmured. "I have done naught but fear for him these past many months." She drew in a shuddering breath. "I pray God will be merciful, and will let him die now."

Duncan laughed softly. "God has spited you, foolish woman. You have given me a healthy son, who will live long after you have passed this day."

Her next breath was more difficult to draw; she struggled to keep her eyes open.

"Let me see . . . my son. Please. Only once . . . "

Duncan stroked her forehead with gentle fingers. "Before you die, Alys? I will let you do so, but you know the price. You must tell me where she is."

Her eyes shut on a weak sob. "No."

He kept stroking, calmly, gently. "Then you will die never seeing him. It is sad, Alys."

Another sob; her eyes cracked open to let tears seep out.

"Please."

His fingertips brushed over one temple, down to her ear, which he caressed tenderly. "I shall have to tell him that his mother did not want to see him very badly. I shall tell him that she cared more for her pride than for him. Is that what you want?"

She tried to turn from his touch.

"God will keep him," she said tearfully. "And God will save Amica."

"God did not save you," Duncan told her, "and He'll not save your sister, whether you reveal where she is or no. I shall find Amica, on that I give my solemn vow. Best to tell what you know, Alys, than to go to your grave silent and never knowing the face of your son."

"Nay," she whispered. "You will never find her. I wronged her badly in life. I'll not do so in death." With an effort she met his gaze. "She is safe from you, Duncan Selwyrn. I have made certain of it."

Duncan's hand stilled, resting upon her cold cheek. "Certain?"

She drew in another difficult breath, and her eyes drifted shut once more, just as her words began to drift, softer and lighter as the breath left her. "You will never find her. You have my son, but you shall never have her. God save . . . "

For many days after, all those who served in the castle of Sacre Placean spoke of little but their lord's strange and violent reaction to the death of Lady Alys. Duncan Selwyrn was a man of strongly contained emotions; he was as famed for his calm, imperturbable manner as he was for his lineage, which was counted among the most ancient in Britain, stretching as far back as those Celts who had lived on the land before even the Romans came. Yet he had nearly cursed the stones down from the walls when Lady Alys died, and had almost killed one of the stable lads when it had been discovered that Lady Alys's maid, Jennie, had taken a horse and left Sacre Placean only hours before her mistress's death, though why such as that should enrage him none of the servants could say. They had not been allowed to speak to Jennie, or to Lady Alys; the two women had been kept abovestairs for the past many months, just as the other lady and her maid had always been. No one in the castle knew much about any of them.

It was all very strange, but those who served Duncan Selwyrn knew better than to whisper long behind their lord's back. Alfred the steward, who had been present when the lady died, spoke of the matter once on the morning afterward, in the kitchen as he ate a bowl of boiled oats. All those present gathered close to hear the softly spoken words. He said little, in truth, and what there was gave no reason as to why the master had gone so mad.

"She died very suddenly," was what Alfred said, leaning against a wall and eating his meal. "It was peaceful and easy. The lord was beside her, and she died with a smile on her lips. 'Twas a contented smile. Peaceful. And that was all."

1

"Grandfather? Grandfather, can you hear me?"

Amica leaned closer and stroked her grandfather's brow with gentle fingers.

"Grandfather?"

With a murmur of annoyance he woke, blinking at her.

"Mmm?"

"I am sorry to disturb you, but I must go to the river and you have not yet eaten."

"I do not hunger," he said. "And you should not go to the river alone."

"I know." She slipped her hands beneath his pillow to pull him up. "You must eat some of this broth, else your strength will never return. Come, now." Lifting his heavy body higher, she tucked another pillow beneath him. "'Twill only take a moment. Please, grandfather."

He pursed his lips at the spoonful of broth she

offered and turned his head. "I've no taste for food, and naught will return my strength to me." With an effort he lifted his hand to push the spoon back into the bowl on her lap. "Let me die in peace, I pray."

"You will not die. You will be well again, and soon. If you would only eat . . . "

"'Twill make no difference. Amica," he said her name gently, seeing how she compressed her mouth. "You must cease this pretending, and prepare yourself. I would not leave you if 'twere but my choice, but naught can stay the hand of God. Soon I will depart, and you must make yourself ready."

Lowering her head, she set the bowl on the small table beside his bed.

Andrew Fawdry took his granddaughter's hand and squeezed it with the small strength he had left.

"All will be well," he murmured. "The king will receive my missive and send someone, and you will be safe. Selwyrn shall never have you."

She lifted her eyes and gazed at him with defiance. "I'll not leave you. The king may send his whole army, but I'll not go!"

Andrew Fawdry's mouth tilted into a wan smile. "'Tis good to hear you speak with fire, lass. I have prayed God that you should know courage when I am gone." The smile faded. "You must remember all I have taught you, Amica, and never let your many fears show. No matter what is inside you, girl, you must master yourself and not give way. 'Tis all that may save you one day. Never forget it."

"You will *not* die," she repeated stubbornly, pulling her hand free. "'Tis but foolishness you speak, and I'll not stay and hear it." Rising, she took up the bowl of uneaten broth. "I must go to the river and do the washing, else 'twill not get done."

"Nay, Amica, do not. Wait until the king's men arrive. 'Twill only be another day or so."

Color rose in Amica's cheeks. "It cannot wait, grandfather. The bedclothes . . . there are none clean." She quickly turned to take the bowl back to the fire, where she knelt to pour the uneaten broth into the pot hanging there.

Andrew swore beneath his breath, then said, "It matters not."

"It does. I'll not have you lying in a dirty bed." She took up her hair linen, covered herself and tied the cloth beneath her chin. "I shall not be long," she promised, returning to his bedside to kiss him.

"'Tis dangerous," he said, worry thick in his voice. "Don't go."

"I'll be careful, and will be back before the sun touches your bed." She pointed to the place near his feet where the late afternoon sun shone in through the window each clear day during the spring. "When I return," she said, smiling into his worried face, "I will wake you, and you shall eat. Until then, dear," she bent to kiss his cheek once more, "rest."

The three men on horseback sat side by side in the midst of the road, gazing in three different directions.

"There is naught here," said Derryn Thewlis, "and the road grows worse. It cannot be farther on."

"Aye, we've missed it," Stevan of Hearn agreed. "None but thieves could live in such as this. I say we go back." He looked at the man sitting in the middle. "We missed the place, surely."

Thomas of Reed contemplated the condition of the road before them, realizing what the pits and rocks and ever narrowing width told about how seldom used it was; more, about how few people inhabited the area to give it any care.

"We will go on until there is no more," he said, "and then we will turn toward the river."

The men on either side of him groaned loudly.

"You cannot think she abides here," Derryn argued. "'Tis impossible."

"No one in the village knew of them," Stevan put in. "They cannot have lived here and none known of it. Our lord must have been mistaken—"

His words were cut off by Thomas's hand gripping the collar of his tunic.

"Our lord is never mistaken," Thomas said quietly, lifting the smaller man from his saddle as he dragged him close, "and we will go on toward that place where he sent us."

With one hand Stevan kept control of his nervous steed, with the other he sought to loosen the fist that threatened shortly to stop his breathing. "Of course, Tom," he rasped. "You know full well I meant no disrespect to our lord of Reed. I should never do such a thing."

Thomas frowned, and his fingers tightened.

"Give way, lad," Derryn advised affably, leaning over to thump one of Thomas's massive shoulders. "Sir Eric will be angered if you kill one of his best men, and you'll regret having slain one of the few men on this earth who'll ever name you friend. Give way, I said." He hit him again, harder this time, the sound of his gauntlet-covered fist making a loud *thwack*.

With a breath, Thomas opened his fingers and released Stevan, who gasped with relief.

Straightening in his saddle, he fingered his throat and glared at the man beside him. "You're a fine fellow," he complained. "When will you learn that a man may misspeak himself every now and again? I meant no disrespect to our lord. I revere Sir Eric as dearly as you."

Thomas's brow lowered. "I meant you no harm, but we will go on as our lord bade us." Taking up his reins, he set his steed into motion.

Derryn and Stevan glanced at each other, shook their heads, and dutifully followed behind.

Half an hour later they stood in the midst of a thickly treed forest, watching as a woman—the first sign of human life they'd seen that morn—set her washing down by a wide, shallow river and knelt to begin her work.

"She must be a witch," Derryn whispered. "I've heard there are such living in dark places like this, descended from those who were before William's time."

"Celts," Stevan murmured with awe. "True Britons."

Thomas looked from one to the other with incredulity. "You are fools twice over. She's naught but a woman doing wash."

"A woman living here?" Derryn asked, swinging a hand at their surroundings. "How could she do so without aid from some unearthly source? No one else has dared try it, 'tis clear."

Bewildered by this sentiment, Thomas looked about at the heavy forest. It was true that the land was wild and pure, as yet untamed by human hands, yet there was nothing strange or untoward about it. His ears caught the sound of the Irish Sea a quarter mile or less away; it filled the forest with a soothing, steady thrum, as well as with the tang of salt. "'Tis a goodly place," he said. "Peaceful and calm. 'Twould be a simple thing to make a life here."

Stevan shuddered and rubbed his arms. "'Tis dark and damp," he muttered. "The sun barely gives light through these trees. Even the horses are unsettled."

As if to prove this fact, Thomas's own mount, Maelgwn, moved restlessly, tugging at the reins in his master's hand and pawing the moist ground.

"Very well," Thomas said. "The two of you stay with the beasts. I will go down to speak to the woman."

"Nay, wait." Stevan set a staying hand on Thomas's arm. "You'll frighten the lass off with that scowling face. Let me go instead."

The scowl in question deepened. "You speak falsely," Thomas stated. "I do not scowl."

"Let *me* speak with her," Derryn countered, running his fingers through his long black hair to straighten its disarray. "I've a way with women." When his companions stared at him, he smiled pleasantly. "Well, 'tis but the simple truth. God knows *my* face would never scare a maid away." Continuing his grooming, he began to brush the dust from his tunic. "And, sorry to tell, but you do scowl, Tom lad. Especially at women. S'truth, you could scare the Fiend himself back to Hades with but one of your fierce looks."

"Cease your preening, Sir Peacock," Thomas advised, taking one of Derryn's hands and slapping Maelgwn's reins into it. "'Twill be lost on the horses."

The girl appeared younger than he'd thought from a distance, and, as he moved ever closer, not unpleasant to look upon. She was bent over her work, vigorously washing a bed sheet in a bucket of soapy water. She hummed quietly as she worked, and took no notice of Thomas, who stood on the opposite bank, watching as she first rinsed the sheet in the wide, gentle river, then spread it upon a rock to dry, then took up another piece of her wash and pushed it into the bucket with the soapy water.

He remained silent, waiting for her to notice and address him, but she merely continued her work, so that he at last cleared his throat and said, loudly, "You girl. Attend me."

Her reaction was so violent that Thomas was unexpectedly startled, and immediately angry for being made to jump in surprise like some kind of timid whelp, so that when she had gasped and thrown her wash aside and stood to gape at him, he couldn't help but frown at her, despite his every effort not to.

The next moment the foolish creature lifted her skirts and started running for the trees, giving Thomas no choice but to follow. She was the only person they'd seen all morn, and his only chance thus far of finding the lady he sought. He wasn't about to lose such a chance for naught but a female's foolish fears.

The river was wide but thankfully shallow—though Thomas knew he would have pursued the girl across the Irish Sea if she'd thrown herself into it—and he crossed it quickly, oblivious to the soaking his boots and clothing took. Even more quickly did he close the distance between himself and the girl, though she ran swiftly, with admirable speed and direction. He shouted twice at her to stop, but she flew headlong, heedless, until Thomas came right behind her and reached out a hand to grip one of her arms. Still running, she jerked violently, stumbling and sending both of them rolling heavily to the wet ground, where she ended up on her back and where Thomas landed face down in mud.

His anger thus inflamed, and keeping a firm hold on the struggling creature, Thomas lifted himself up, shook the mud from his mouth, and shouted, "Stupid girl!" just as his eyes opened and beheld the most stunning face they'd ever before known.

He had seen many beautiful women in his life; indeed, was not his master's wife, Lady Margot, widely praised as the most beautiful woman in all England?

And at both Belhaven, his birthplace, and Reed, his home, there were more than a few women, whore and lady alike, who could well be described as pleasant to gaze upon. Not that he'd ever wasted time gazing at them, of course, but, being responsible for the men in his lord's army, he had striven to understand what it was that made good men behave as fools. He'd quickly learned that a beautiful woman was both a nuisance and a source of trouble, as much an enemy to the order and obedience of fighting men as any better trained army would be. Unlike other men, Thomas had found himself oddly immune to a woman's beauty.

Until now.

He had been born to poverty, to a woman who'd died too quickly for him to remember and to a man who'd used him as a handy source of relief for his misery and anger and, because of that, Thomas had learned to dream. It had been his one secret pleasure as a child. He had dreamed outside of slumber, during the day hours, during every moment he had been able to call his own. His dreams had been as important as breath to him; he had lived from them. Nothing had ever affected him so deeply.

Until now.

She was like his childish dreams. Beautiful, perfect, unreal . . . he didn't know why, couldn't even make himself think on it. She lay before him, blue eyes wide with terror, her long, golden brown hair, now freed of the linen cloth that had covered it at the river, tangled and dirtied in the damp earth, her face liberally smudged with dirt, yet she was so perfect that Thomas was stunned . . . for about the space of five seconds, which was the longest he'd ever permitted himself to suffer such an affliction before.

Suddenly, he was flooded with an inexplicable dread,

and, without thought, sat up and away from her as though she were about to do him some great and terrible harm. Almost at once the dread faded, to be replaced by a fury that any woman, no matter what she looked like, should wrest such foolish behavior from him.

"*Stupid* girl," he repeated, more than ready to vent his wrath on her. "Why did you run? I meant you no—"

Thomas never even saw her reaching out to grasp the fallen branch lying nearby; he only felt it when she began to whack him about the head, repeatedly, putting a surprising amount of strength into the matter for such a small, slender being.

"*Cease!*" he shouted, snatching the branch away. When he made the mistake of releasing her so that he could use both hands to snap the offending weapon in two, the girl leapt up from the ground. But Thomas was faster and, catching her by one ankle, threw her roughly to the ground again, where she lay face down, panting and clawing at the earth as if she would dig a hole to escape him.

Angry, Thomas tossed the girl onto her back and straddled her struggling body, squeezing his knees tightly against her waist to still her movements. He took her tiny wrists in his much larger hands and pressed them into the dirt above her head.

"I mean you no harm." He said each word tightly, striving to contain his fury. "I seek one who lives in this place and require direction, that is all." When she turned her face away, he released one of her hands and grasped her chin, forcing her back to him. "You will attend me, wench, and answer. What is your name? Where is your dwelling?"

She said nothing. Indeed, her only response was to clench her teeth and breath noisily through them, as if she were in great pain and could not draw in enough air.

Thinking perhaps he was crushing her, sitting atop her, Thomas lifted himself slightly onto his knees.

"There," he said. "Now, tell me your name. And look at me," he added with greater aggravation. "I have said I will bring you no harm."

Still she gave no answer, but kept her eyes shut and her teeth clenched and shook her head, so that Thomas lost his temper altogether.

"*Do as I say!*" he demanded. "Answer me, girl!"

She kept shaking her head, and her body began to tremble mightily, and tears seeped out of her closed eyes, and her heaving, panting breaths turned into heaving, panting sobs.

Shocked to his very core by such a reaction, for he could not fathom why she should behave in such a way, Thomas once again felt overwhelmed by a strange and uncommon dread. Once again he moved away, lifting himself off her body and kneeling beside her.

"Are you ill, woman?" he asked, peering at her more closely. A thought came to him, and he muttered, "Ill in your mind, I vow. A madwoman. 'Tis just my fortune." He squeezed the wrist he still held, feeling the throbbing of her blood in the veins there, and leaned a little closer, tilting his head back and forth to better observe her strange behavior, her clenched teeth and tightly shut eyes. "Mad, aye," he stated with more certainty. "Or mayhap simply . . . feeble in your mind?" He tried to speak more gently. "Can you not speak? Eh, girl?" When she only lay there, weeping and trembling, Thomas touched her forehead with his fingertips, meaning to soothe her. "Come, I did you no harm. Speak to me, if you can, and I shall let you go. I am sent by the king to seek out a lady who is known to abide in these parts. She is called Amica of Lancaster, and is under her grandfather's care, one known as Sir Andrew Fawdry. Have you seen or known of them?"

The girl stiffened and made a gasping sound, then her eyes opened wide to stare at Thomas.

She had, he thought, beautiful eyes for a lackwit. Large and blue as the sky above, and still filled with terror.

She had long since ceased struggling to be free, though her trembling went on, and Thomas freed her completely, releasing her wrist and sitting back on his heels.

"There. You are free." He lifted both hands up to prove the fact to her. "I shall not lay a hand to you again if you will not flee. Do you know of Amica of Lancaster?"

She opened her mouth, first to draw in a breath, then to form a word, as if she would speak to him.

"Aye?" Thomas encouraged, inclining his ear. "Tell me."

For several seconds she struggled, drawing in breath and forming silent words. At last, with a sound of dismay, she stopped and shook her head.

"Tom!" Derryn called through the trees. "Is all well? Where are you?"

The girl sat up at once, but Thomas put a hand on her arm.

"Stay," he said quietly. "They are men under my command and shall bring you no harm. Do you understand me?"

She nodded and drew her arm free of his touch.

Keeping his gaze upon her, Thomas lifted his voice. "Here! Come and bring the horses."

"God's my life!" Stevan declared when he came through the forest and saw the girl sitting silently on the ground. "She's a beauty!"

"Who's a beauty?" Derryn asked, coming behind

him and leading both Maelgwn and his own steed along. "The witch? Ah, by the rood, 'tis the truth you speak." He frowned deeply at Thomas. "You should have let *me* speak to her. It does you no good to speak to a beautiful woman."

Thomas spared him a brief glance. "'Twill do you no good to speak to this one, either. The wench is dull-witted."

"Never say so," Stevan said, moving to kneel beside Thomas. "Ah, that's a pity, poor little lass." When he reached out a hand to touch her cheek, she flinched. "God's teeth, she is fair beyond words."

"Is she?" Thomas pushed Stevan's hand away. "Leave her be. She fought me like a devil before this. I do not want her overset again."

Derryn moved closer as well, coming to a stop when the girl glanced at him sharply.

"Does she know where our lady can be found?"

"Do you, girl?" Thomas asked. "Do you know of the lady Amica of Lancaster?"

She frowned, but nodded slowly.

Thomas let out a breath of relief.

"And can you take us to her? Can you show us where she abides?"

Glancing with distrust at the two men beside him, she nodded again.

"God be praised," Thomas murmured, holding out his hand and pulling her to her feet.

2

It was impossible to make her hands stop trembling; even more impossible to halt the need to draw breath through her mouth in order to give her body the air it demanded. It was humiliating, making such loud, gulping sounds with every breath, but Amica knew very well there was nothing she could do but wait for the terrors to pass before her body would become her own again. Still, she was thoroughly embarrassed, and kept her eyes forcibly on the path ahead, not wishing to see the curious expressions on the faces of the three men who followed behind.

The king's men! Why, in the name of Heaven, had she had to make such a fool of herself before the king's men? Grandfather would be so disappointed when the scowling giant who'd accosted her told him the full of it, of how foolishly she'd behaved. God's mercy, she thought, glancing at that particular man as he drew closer and walked beside her, if she could only find her voice she would ask him—nay, she would plead with him not to speak of the matter, for Grandfather had little life left and should not be made to spend it saddened and worried over her many weaknesses.

If she could only find her voice . . .

"You suffer some distress?" the giant asked, causing Amica to lift her head.

She would not have called him comely, as she would have said of the other two men, but there was that about him which drew the eye. He was a big man, very tall and quite broad; she knew first-hand how strong he was. His hair was blond, almost white, and long enough to brush his shoulders. Dark gray eyes met her gaze steadily, intensely, but without any visible emotion held in them. Indeed, not only his eyes, but his entire face, seemed emotionless, as if it were made of stone instead of flesh, as if he possessed no soul to harbor feelings.

She tried to speak to him, to say the word *no*, but the only sound that came past her disobedient lips was an unintelligible croak.

"Cease worrying the girl," another of the men said, the beautiful one with the long black hair. "Can you not see she's afeared of you?"

"Stop scowling at her," said the other, a bearded, red-headed man whose elegant dress told Amica that he was either a wealthy man or of very high birth.

"I do not scowl," the giant told them. "I'm doing naught to frighten her."

But, as if he took their words to heart, he slowed his pace and moved away, so that Amica walked alone again.

The man was dying—Thomas knew it the moment he set sight on him. Sir Eric had warned him that Andrew Fawdry might have little time to live, and Thomas and his men had ridden hard to reach this place, to make certain that Amica of Lancaster would not be left alone and vulnerable should her grandfather die too soon. And yet, though he'd expected to find the famed knight abed and ill, he'd not been ready for the sight of the man whose many lauded feats and adventures had made him one of Thomas's heroes. It made Thomas shudder and pray silently to God that his own life would not find a like end. He'd rather be run through with a sword, he thought, than to waste away to almost naught.

Andrew Fawdry gazed at him out of red, swollen eyes, and slowly lifted a thin hand from his bed.

"You have come, at last," he murmured. "I have prayed to God that you would come soon. I am weary."

Knowing what the effort to greet him cost the man, Thomas quickly took Andrew Fawdry's hand and, holding it, sat on the stool the girl had placed beside the bed. "I am Thomas of Reed, my lord, and have come with my men—" he nodded toward the small table where the girl had made Derryn and Stevan sit and where she was presently putting out food and drink, "—at the king's and my master's command. My master, Sir Eric Stavelot, lord of Reed, bade me greet and wish you well, and to tell you that he should have attended himself, save my lord's lady is heavy with child, and there is naught that could draw him from her side. He begs you will understand."

Andrew Fawdry smiled, though the effort was weak. "Eric Stavelot . . . aye, he is a good lad, a good man. I knew him when he was but a child, and have known his father, Garin, oh, for many and many a year. 'Twas I lent Garin aid when he stole Elaine Bowen from her father's house. And 'twas I kept her father and uncles at bay while he forced her to wife. Ah, he was a strong-willed lad, was Garin. We had many fine times together."

He closed his eyes, still smiling, and dozed. Thomas waited patiently, and when a minute or two had passed, Andrew Fawdry woke and gazed at him directly.

"She is Amica of Lancaster? That girl?" Thomas asked, glancing to the fire pit in the middle of the room where the girl stood stirring the contents of a cooking pot that was hung over the flames.

"Aye, she is my granddaughter."

"Amica of Lancaster," Thomas said, resigned to the fact. He'd hoped that she was naught but a serving girl, that Amica of Lancaster would suddenly open the door to the small cottage and enter and explain that she'd been out picking flowers, or whatever it was that women liked to do on spring days. "She is feeble-minded?"

"Nay, not that," the older man murmured, "though 'twould be more merciful if she were. Nay, Amica is cursed with fears."

Thomas frowned. "Fears?"

"Aye, she suffers badly, not in the common way others do. Did you frighten her earlier?"

Thomas gave a curt nod. "'Twas not by intent, but she did seem . . . afeared."

Andrew Fawdry made a mournful sigh. "She was born a timorous lass, but when her terrors overtake her, ah, then my poor, sweet girl suffers badly. 'Tis as if she is possessed by a spirit, and cannot help herself. E'en her voice leaves her, and she cannot speak until the fears have passed."

"She has a voice, then?"

"Oh, aye. Give her time, be gentle and patient, I pray, and you shall hear it. 'Tis pretty as her face, to hear. Very pretty . . ." He dozed for another minute or so, and when he woke, he looked at Thomas as if for the first time and said, "You are dirty. Amica will be displeased to have you muddy the dwelling."

"She is the one who muddied me," Thomas told him, "and she is the one who must clean me." At Andrew Fawdry's questioning look, Thomas clarified, "My clothes, and boots."

"Ah. Amica muddied you? Did she?"

"Aye, she ran from me, and I gave chase. She fought me when I caught her."

A spark of hope lit Andrew Fawdry's eyes. "Amica? Fought you?"

Thomas rubbed his temple, where a lump was swelling. "She struck me several blows with a branch."

"God be praised, 'tis the first time she's ever done such as that." With an effort, Andrew Fawdry turned his head to watch his granddaughter as she filled a small pitcher with wine. "She appears to have taken no harm from you, save to be muddied as well."

Thomas saw the emotion that filled the man's face as he watched the girl. 'Twas clear he loved his granddaughter.

"I do not strike women without cause, nor bring them harm," he said. "My master bade me never to do so."

"Sir Eric," Andrew Fawdry whispered wearily. "If any can keep my girl safe, 'tis the lord of Reed. I charge you, Thomas of Reed, get her to him as quickly as may be. Do not let Duncan Selwyrn have her."

"I'll let no one steal her away," Thomas promised. "My master bade me take her to Reed, and that is what I will do."

Andrew Fawdry drew in a long breath and shuddered. Thomas gripped the man's hand tightly.

"Kill her first . . . before ever letting the lord of Sacre Placean have her." He held Thomas's gaze. "Swear to me that you'll kill her first."

"I make no pledge to any man save my lord of Reed," Thomas replied. "He bade me take her to Reed, and I will do as he commanded."

"Selwyrn will do all he can to have her. He searches for her, even now, be certain of it. You must take all care in your travel."

"I will take care. Do any but my lord and the king know of this place, that the girl is here?"

Having drawn another breath, Andrew Fawdry answered, "The maid . . . Alys's maid . . . she managed to escape that devil, and found her way to my brother's home. 'Twas he who came to me, and he who took my missive to the king. He was the only one who knew, but the maid . . . Alys may have guessed where I'd hidden Amica, and may have told the maid. I do not know." He squeezed Thomas's hand with his small strength. "If she knows . . . if Selwyrn finds her . . . God save you, and God save Amica, for he'll not stop . . . until he finds her or dies."

"Who is Alys?" Thomas asked. Sir Eric had told him to beware of Duncan Selwyrn, the lord of Sacre Placean, but he'd said little else. Thomas didn't even know why Amica of Lancaster was being pursued, or why both his master and the king sought to keep her safe.

"Alys is my granddaughter," Andrew Fawdry whispered, his eyes drifting shut. "Alys of Lancaster. Amica's sister. She is . . . dead . . . and Selwyrn wants another . . . "

Thomas felt the hand in his go slack, and he leaned closer. "My lord? Sir Andrew?"

A small, gasping sound made Thomas turn his head, but before he could see who stood beside him, a tiny fist struck his shoulder. Amica of Lancaster glared at him, then put both hands on his arm and shoved until he stood. She shoved again until he took a step away from the bed, then she turned back to her grandfather and sat on the stool. Tenderly, she took her grandfather's hand and pressed it to her cheek. With her other hand she stroked his brow.

Thomas stood behind her for some time, listening to the soothing, murmuring sounds she made to the dying man and wondering what her voice sounded like, and why she would not speak when she no longer had any reason to be afraid. Her actions were very gentle, loving, and Thomas watched with fascination as her slender fingers smoothed several strands of hair from her grandfather's pale face.

He seldom indulged in daydreams any longer, for he thought it an unseemly practice in a man of three and twenty years, but for a few brief moments, as he watched her, Thomas let himself imagine that he was lying on the bed in Andrew Fawdry's place—not dying, certainly—mayhap simply sleeping . . . and that her fingers were stroking through his hair. No woman had ever touched him in such a way, and it did look most pleasant . . .

"I'll not leave him."

With a shake of his head, Thomas realized that the girl was looking at him, that she had spoken to him. He blinked, met her blue-eyed gaze, and said, "What?"

She flushed deeply. "I'll not leave him."

She'd begun to tremble again, Thomas realized, and he felt himself scowling.

"I would not willingly leave a dying man alone," he told her, feeling unaccountably angry. "My master would upbraid me were I ever to do such a thing. Your grandfather will die soon, and we will bear him company until that time and make our prayers to God to receive his soul, unless Duncan Selwyrn discovers us. If he should, we will go."

Her nostrils flared and her lips flattened as she strove to speak again, and Thomas was aggravated that he should find her, in that moment when she should have looked like a snorting horse, which was what she sounded like when she drew in a breath, so perfectly beautiful. After a moment's struggle she managed to declare, "I'll *not!*"

He gazed at her steadily. "Hear me well, woman. You will stay when I bid you stay, and you will go when I bid you go. Until we reach my master's home, you are under my hand, and will obey me."

Her lips pressed together more firmly, and she began to shake her head, which only made Thomas angrier.

"Aye, lady, you will. I give you warning, for I am a man of short patience. Your grandfather has said you are not feebleminded, and if you would be wise, then fashion yourself into my obedient hound until we reach Reed, and obey my every command. I am vowed to keep you safe, and whither you aid me in this or no, I do not care. That is the way it will be."

Her trembling became something fierce, so that Thomas knew a foreign, unwanted desire to put his hand upon her delicate shoulder and speak to her more softly, but she turned away and gripped her grandfather's hand, bowing her head low.

Thomas thought perhaps she wept, for her shoulders shook, though it might have simply been her fears overtaking her. He had never known anyone before who suffered such an affliction. Terrors, Andrew Fawdry had named it. Whatever it was, he did not like it, and was wary. Women weren't to be trusted, and this odd, timid female much less so.

3

"'Twas a fine meal," Derryn Thewlis said as he set his empty bowl in Amica's outstretched hand. "I thank you, my lady."

He followed these words with the same charming smile he'd already bestowed upon her half a hundred times in the two hours since he and the other men had arrived, and Amica sighed wearily. Ignoring his efforts to dally, she turned to Stevan of Hearn and put her other hand out to receive his bowl, only to have that man instead grab her hand and gallantly press his lips to her fingers.

"Indeed, my lady," he said, grinning when Amica angrily snatched her hand away. "'Twas truly a feast."

Thomas of Reed, sitting beside the red-headed man and drinking the last contents of his bowl, made a grunting sound of disapproval. "'Twas naught but soup and bread," he stated when he'd finished. He added the bowl to Amica's load. "Do not make more of it than it was to turn the girl's head. I'll not allow such foolishness on this journey. Wait until we achieve Reed before making asses of yourselves."

The other men chuckled and Amica turned to carry the bowls to the bucket where she would wash them.

"You possess no heart, Tom," she heard Derryn Thewlis chide his master.

"Mayhap," was the calm reply.

"I've ne'er seen a man less courtly than Thomas of Reed," stated Stevan of Hearn, but this comment only drew another grunt out of the blond giant.

Amica listened to their conversation as she continued her chores, though she had little interest in the things they spoke of. The effects of her terrors had passed more than an hour earlier, and her body was her own again. Her voice had returned, the trembling had ceased, and she was no longer afraid of the three strange knights. Indeed, what she mostly felt for them was anger, and dislike. The thought of spending many days and nights in their company while they journeyed to Reed was an unpleasant one, especially if she had to endure the winks and smiles and trifling manners of the two handsome men. Perhaps the scowling giant was unkind and crude, but at least he would not subject her to such foolishness. In truth, Amica doubted that he would subject her to much at all, if he could save doing so. He seemed to have taken her in as much dislike as she had him.

She was *not* going to leave Grandfather to die alone, she thought determinedly. She feared Duncan Selwyrn more than any other living man, but she would rather face him again than leave before her grandfather was properly buried. Andrew Fawdry would have no priest to perform his last sacrament, no coffin to rest in until the Day of Resurrection, no funeral mass, or sermon. All Amica had to offer this man whom she loved more than any other was a meager shroud that she'd sewn from the tattered remnants of two old surcoats, and a decent burial in God's earth, and the promise of her prayers. It was little set against the grand, public funeral he would have had if he'd not hidden away with her in this dark forest, but it was what Amica could give him, and she would not leave until she had done so, no matter what Thomas of Reed said or did.

Thinking of that, she lifted her eyes to glare at the man, only to find that he was already looking at her. His expression was hard and set, as if he knew her thoughts and would challenge them. Aye, he was hard, she thought. Like the lord of Sacre Placean, he would have his way, or no way at all.

Her grandfather shuddered powerfully and moaned. Snatching up a clean cloth and dampening it in her bucket of water, Amica went to him and smoothed the cooling cloth over his forehead and cheeks.

"Rest easy," she murmured. "All is well."

A large body bent over her from behind, enveloping Amica in warmth, and a hand moved around her to press against the pulse in her grandfather's neck. A moment passed, and then Thomas of Reed straightened and said, "'Twill not be much longer. Is there a place you have chosen for his burial? Would you have us prepare it?"

The words filled her with a sharp dread. "Nay, not yet." She turned to look up at him. "Can it not wait?"

He gave a very slight nod. "It must be soon, however, for we will leave immediately once he is buried. Have you made yourself ready?"

At her grandfather's insistence, Amica had packed the few garments she possessed a few days earlier. She pointed to the spot where the leather bag sat near the door. "That is all I have."

"Nothing more?" He sounded amazed.

"Nothing more," she replied, and returned her attention to her grandfather.

The night passed slowly, each hour seeming longer than the one before it as Amica maintained a bedside vigil.

She was not entirely aware of how the three knights occupied themselves, though she heard them murmuring from time to time, speaking in deep, serious tones, and heard them coming and going, as well. At one point Derryn Thewlis brought her shawl and set it over her shoulders, and Thomas of Reed was there often, leaning over her to feel her grandfather's neck. The last time he did this he asked whether she had yet said prayers for the benefit of Andrew Fawdry's soul. When Amica silently shook her head, Thomas of Reed went down upon his knees beside the bed and prayed. When he finished he stood and gruffly told her to wipe her face, which was the first moment that Amica realized she was crying.

Half an hour had passed since then, and Amica knew, by the change in her grandfather's breathing, that there would only be a few minutes more. Kneeling beside his bed in the place where Thomas of Reed had been, she held his hand and kissed him, then tried to pray. It seemed impossible to think of the words. She closed her eyes and strove to recall her religious instruction. Just as she began to remember, Thomas of Reed spoke behind her.

"Riders approach. Come with me now."

Amica twisted in her kneeling position to look at him. "Riders?"

He strode toward her, the bag she had packed clutched in one hand. "It can only be Selwyrn's men. Who else would enter a place like this in such darkness? Come and I will hide you."

"My grandfather!" she protested as his other hand closed over her arm.

He dragged her up off the ground and pulled her in the direction of the door.

"I cannot leave him!" Amica struggled against his

iron strength. "He is dying!" She began to hit his rock-like forearm with a small, impotent fist. "I'll not go! I do not want to leave him!"

"Be quiet!" Thomas commanded angrily.

Amica kept struggling, and lifted a foot to kick him. "I'll not leave him! He is dying even now!"

Thomas of Reed jerked her around to face him. "You will obey me, woman, else I will—*oof!*"

Amica's knee struck its sensitive target, and Thomas of Reed doubled over, unwittingly pushing her away. She fell backward; and the sight of Thomas's hand flying out to catch her was the last thing Amica knew for some time.

She awoke in darkness, her head throbbing, to find herself gagged and tied to a tree. Her body ached, and she moaned and lifted her head. How long had she been here? Fear rose as her dazed mind grew clearer. She could hear sounds . . . not far, sounds of horses and men, of fighting. And she could smell— Smoke? Twisting, Amica gazed into the darkness and saw flames.

She screamed a denial into the cloth that bound her mouth, but the fire leapt more fully, consuming the small cottage. She saw the dark figures of men fighting in front of the flames, but couldn't make out who they were, or how many.

The fighting went on a long time. Amica heard men shouting and screaming and longed to free her hands so that she could cover her ears. Leaning against the tree, she gave way to the shaking that possessed her, and wept with fear and misery. She thought of being taken captive by Duncan Selwyrn and knew that she would rather be dead than live under his hand.

She didn't even know that Thomas of Reed had come until he was kneeling before her, cutting away her bonds. The forest was dark as a cave at night, but the light from the fire revealed him. His expression was grim and rigid, his skin was covered with dirt and sweat and some few streaks of blood, his hair had been singed by the flames. Concentrating on his task, he did not look into her face until he removed the cloth from her mouth, but then his eyes met hers, and held them.

He tossed the cloth away and Amica gasped at the relief of being freed. Thomas of Reed took her face in both hands and examined her more closely.

"You have taken no harm?" he asked, turning her face to the light of the flames to better see her.

Amica disliked Thomas of Reed—she disliked any man so hard and cold—but in that moment the touch of his big, rough hands flooded her with relief and gratitude. Weeping, she set her own hands over his and pressed hard, pressing his human touch into her flesh to make herself know that she was alive, that there was no need to be afraid. This man had kept her safe and would keep her safe.

Thomas of Reed stared at her with a stunned expression. His hands fell still against her cheeks, his gray eyes widened, and his mouth parted. Then he blinked and the expression disappeared, to be replaced by one of irritation.

"You weep more than a newborn babe," he stated, and touched his thumb to a tender spot on the side of her head. When she winced, he frowned. "You struck your head on the table when you fell. It does not seem too great an injury, but it will pain you a day or so. Mayhap 'twill serve as a reminder to obey me without question while we journey to Reed."

"My grandfather," she whispered.

He ran his thumbs over her cheeks with surprising tenderness, drying her tears away. "I do not know if Andrew Fawdry still lived when the fire began. There was naught to be done. Selwyrn's men—"

"They *were* Duncan's men?"

"They bore the colors of Sacre Placean. They kicked the wood from the pit when they did not find you within. There was naught that could be done, but they are dead now, and sent to their judgment in the same fire that has given your grandfather's soul flight."

"You killed them?"

Pulling his hands from her face, he bent to take her in his arms, lifting her from the ground. "Aye, we did so."

"Duncan was not among them?"

Thomas strode quickly through the trees, carrying her away from the flames and toward the river.

"I have never seen him, and so I cannot say, but they were fighting men, not noblemen. I cannot think that the lord of Sacre Placean would have come to such a place as this himself."

"Nay," she said softly, "Duncan would not."

They neared the river, and Amica saw Derryn Thewlis and Stevan of Hearn standing by the water's edge with the horses.

"We will take no chances," Thomas told them as he set Amica on Maelgwn and mounted behind her, "but will ride through the night. How is your arm, Stevan? Will you be able to ride long?"

"It does not bleed so much, now," Stevan replied, and Amica thought he sounded as if he were in a great deal of pain. "I've kept pace with better men than you, Thomas of Reed, never fear."

"If you slow us, I will leave you," was Thomas of Reed's reply, and Amica was shaken anew by the coldness of the man.

"You could not be Thomas and do otherwise," Stevan of Hearn said, chuckling, as he turned his steed and followed his master into the night.

4

They did not travel on the poor road that led to the edge of the forest, as Amica thought they would, but instead followed the river, riding in and out of the patches of trees and shrubs, so close to the water's edge that the horses' hooves splashed water up onto their clothes. It was dark, save for those rare, brief moments when the thick clouds gave way to the light of the stars and moon, and their progress was made slower because of it. Derryn Thewlis rode ahead at Thomas of Reed's command, finding a path through the darkness and keeping a watch for any more of Duncan's men. Stevan of Hearn rode somewhere behind, Amica hoped, though she did not know with certainty, as Thomas of Reed had kept his word and not so much as glanced backward once to see if the badly injured man still followed.

Wet and cold, Amica shivered, then sneezed, and Thomas of Reed uttered a low curse before taking the reins of his steed in one hand and tucking Amica more closely against himself with the other.

She was not really more comfortable being held against Thomas of Reed's hard body and prickly chain mail armor. The tension in him was a palpable thing, and the tautness of his muscles made him about as soft as a rock. His arm, especially, gave discomfort, for it held Amica so tightly that her ribs ached from the force. And yet she was glad for the warmth he provided, and so gave no resistance.

Exhausted from the long vigil with her grandfather, Amica let her tired eyes drift shut. Weary as she was, she did not believe she would be able to sleep against a pillow as hard as Thomas of Reed's chest, or with the jarring and jolting that came from the huge, laboring beast upon which they rode, so she was surprised when, several hours later, she felt herself being pulled down to the ground, and woke with a start to see that a dawning sun was filling the sky with a soft, yellow light.

"Where . . . ?" she began as Thomas of Reed set her on her feet.

Ignoring her, he looked at Derryn Thewlis, who still sat wearily upon his even wearier looking steed.

"Find Stevan," he commanded in a tone that reminded Amica of a hunter commanding a hound. "Search no longer than a half hour's time before returning."

Derryn nodded and turned his horse about. In another moment he disappeared among the large, thick-leaved oak trees that forested their resting place.

Taking his own horse by the reins, Thomas of Reed walked away, leaving Amica to stand alone and take in their surroundings. It was very different from the damp, green forest she and her grandfather had lived in, drier and more sparsely wooded, even though the river they had been following still flowed close within sight, narrower now than it had been.

"Come and sit," she heard Thomas of Reed say

behind her, and she turned. He had taken his steed toward a group of trees that would provide a good shelter against sun or rain, and was unsaddling the beast with easy, expert motions.

Amica pulled her shawl more closely about her shoulders. She felt weary, too weary to move quickly, and wished to stand where she was for a few minutes and gather her thoughts. But Thomas of Reed lifted his head and gazed at her as if she were some unimaginable apparition, as if he could not believe such a person as she existed, though Amica knew very well he was simply unused to people who did not jump at his bidding.

"Come," he repeated, "and sit." Tossing the horse's saddle to the ground, he went so far as to lift a hand and point at the base of a particular tree. "There."

Amica had known many kinds of men during her ten and eight years and had learned much of them. Some men were good, gentle and kind, some were hard and severe as a harsh winter. Some were wise, some bitter, some timid, some bold. A few were wicked and cruel. Many men—most—were a little of all, save the few who were wicked and cruel. What Thomas of Reed was, Amica wasn't entirely sure. Yet. It would come to her after a time, she was certain, for the nature of men could rarely be hidden long and Amica had ever had a sense for such things. But for now she would take no chances, and would be as obedient as Thomas of Reed had advised she be. There was no wisdom in resistance, and she had long since learned that those who are weak and timid have little but their own wisdom to save them from those who are stronger and bolder.

A moment later, sitting upon the cool, slightly damp ground beneath the tree, Amica tucked her skirt beneath her legs and said, "Will we stop here long, my lord?"

"For some few hours," he replied, giving his attention to wiping the sweat from his horse's body with a thick cloth. "It is safe as any other, and the horses require rest before going further."

Well, Amica thought, *he cares for the horses at least, if not for his men.* Gazing at the place where Derryn Thewlis had disappeared, she wondered if Stevan of Hearn had yet been found, and, if so, in what state. If he had been lost, or if he had died, would Thomas of Reed be distressed? As if she might find the answer to her question by looking at the man himself, Amica glanced once more at Thomas of Reed, and was surprised to find that he was already watching her, the thoughtful frown she'd seen before set on his face. Their eyes met only briefly before he lowered his gaze and again gave his attention to his steed.

"What will you do if Stevan of Hearn cannot be found?" Amica asked, surprised at herself for being so bold.

He did not look at her again, but replied, "I do not play such games as that. 'Tis the fool's way to waste his time guessing at what may or may not be."

"But 'tis the wise man's way to prepare for any happening, either well or ill."

"A wise man," he said, "is ever prepared. He need waste no time worrying and wondering o'er what may befall him. And," he added tersely, "I do not care for a woman's useless prate. Hold your tongue and give me peace."

Amica's eyes widened with surprise at his sharp words, and she couldn't contain the small, angry gasp that escaped her lips. She longed to tell Thomas of Reed what she thought of his crude, churlish behavior, and cursed the weakness that made her too timid to do so. But if she *could* tell him, oh, she would, indeed, tell him *exactly* what an insensitive, unkind, unfeeling . . .

"Girl, do you hear me?" His words broke into her angry thoughts. Amica lifted her head and saw that Thomas of Reed was looking at her, holding his steed's reins. "I told you to rise and come. I must take Maelgwn to the river."

She folded her hands in her lap. "I am weary, my lord, and would remain here."

Thomas of Reed's mouth pressed into a thin line, and the tanned skin of his face darkened. When he spoke, his tone was one of tight control. "There was a man under my command once who disobeyed me," he said. "It has been so long that I do not remember his face or name, but I should know him if I saw him, I think."

Amica found it increasingly difficult to breath, and she clenched her hands to keep them from trembling. "H-how so, my lord?"

"He developed a most unusual twitching," Thomas replied, and lifted a hand to one eye. "Here. I was given to understand that the affliction would never leave him."

"But . . . why?"

"He questioned my command," Thomas stated, "and so was punished."

Amica swallowed loudly. "But . . . was your master not angered with you for such as that, Sir Thomas?"

An expression of bewilderment crossed Thomas's features. "Nay, why should he be? I am his constable, and his men are under my hand to command and discipline as I will. I am a just man."

"Just?" she repeated softly, both frightened and curious. "To punish one who merely questions you?"

"To punish one who questions my command, aye."

Memories of Duncan Selwyn, of being forced to do his bidding without question, surged through Amica, and she began to shake. She clenched her teeth to keep them from rattling and shut her eyes, willing herself to calm.

She could hear Thomas of Reed approach her, but could not move to avoid him. She heard him kneeling, and felt his fingers on her chin, lifting her face. Squeezing her eyes more tightly shut, she jerked free of his touch.

"I would never harm a woman apurpose. I have told you this before, and I do not speak falsely." He took her hands in his and held them firmly. "You shake like one possessed," he stated in an amazed tone. "You are the oddest female I've e'er known, and I've known many and many an odd female." After a few silent seconds, he said more gently, "I did not mean to overset you. Maelgwn thirsts and so must drink, and I am vowed to keep you safe. 'Twould be a sorry fool I am to leave you here, even though the river is close. And," he added, "you are dirty. 'Tis but the truth," Thomas insisted when she opened her eyes and glared at him. "Look at your clothes, if you doubt me. And if you could but see your face, you would shriek and howl as ladies do when they're dirtied."

With a gasp, Amica furiously pulled her hands free.

"S'truth, I swear it."

"Oh!" Amica said, yearning to slap him.

"Your hands shake, yet," he said. "'Tis a sorry affliction you've been cursed with, Amica of Lancaster. What the lord of Sacre Placean wants you for, I cannot think."

"Oh! You—!"

"You've not lost your tongue this time, at least," Thomas said, rising to his feet and holding out a hand to her. "Come, lady. We must take Maelgwn to the river, and you must clean yourself, as must I, for I am quite as filthy as you are."

Amica gazed stubbornly at his outstretched hand.

"I will carry you, if I must."

Without another word, Amica rose and followed him to the river.

*   *   *

This was bad, Thomas told himself as he watched Amica of Lancaster rinsing her long, unbound hair in the river. This was very, very bad, and he would not suffer such foolishness, especially not from himself. He'd never before been troubled by a woman, and he'd not fall prey to one now, certainly not to such a one as Amica of Lancaster. 'Twas her beauty that turned his head, and only a fool would let himself be snared by something so false.

And yet, he thought, tilting his head to better see as she drew her fingers through the long, wet strands of gold and brown, hers was surely not a common beauty. The smoothness and purity of her skin, her gently jutting cheeks and small, slightly upturned nose, and her large blue eyes, set beneath curving brows, suggested noble birth. Hers was far beyond the ordinary beauty of other women. She reminded him greatly of his master's wife, the lady Margot, who had always seemed, to Thomas, more angel than lady. As Lady Margot's beauty was unearthly, so was Amica of Lancaster's. He had heard tales before of Helen of Troy, and had scoffed that a mere woman could cause countries to war with one another, but now, seeing Amica of Lancaster, letting his eyes wander to the swell of her breasts, and further still to the curve of her hips, Thomas began to wonder if perhaps he'd not fully understood the matter.

Her head dipped lower as she continued her rinsing, causing the thin garment she wore to pull more tightly against her small, round bottom, and Thomas felt his traitorous body harden at the sight.

"God's teeth," he unwittingly muttered aloud, shifting to relieve the discomfort of his body even as visions of a naked Amica of Lancaster made it that much worse.

"My lord?"

Thomas's head snapped up. She was gazing at him from where she knelt by the river, her wet hair held up in her hands and a look of concern upon her face.

Clearing his throat, Thomas tugged at the hem of his tunic and glanced longingly at the cold, clear river water.

"'Twas naught," he said, praying that she'd not notice his arrant arousal. "Finish your task, that I may have my turn. I would wash this filth from me."

"I do not stop you, my lord. There is water aplenty for two and many more."

A feeling of disdain for the foolishness of women's logic rose up in him, quelling, to Thomas's relief, that other unwanted feeling.

"You would make a poor soldier," he told her, "to give Duncan Selwyn such an advantage."

Understanding lit her clear blue eyes, and her mouth formed a silent, "Oh." Bending over the river once more, she squeezed the water from her hair, then deftly braided the heavy wet mass into a long, single braid. When she had finished she sat upon her knees and said, "I will lend you aid, my lord, and then you need not cease your watching."

Thomas stared a moment before comprehending that she meant to bathe him, to wash the sweat and dirt and blood from his face and neck and hair.

"I . . ." he began, then stopped and wondered why he should be so afraid to let a woman—any woman— touch him. He was not, after all, a boy.

Tugging one last time at his tunic, he strode forward and knelt beside her. The ground was only slightly damp by the river's edge, for the water ran deeper here, and Thomas laid his long sword carefully on the ground, within his easy reach. Giving Amica of Lancaster a look of full warning that she do naught to anger him, Thomas turned so that he rested upon his back, propped up on his elbows, and hesitantly offered his head for washing.

Her face, with an expression slightly amused, loomed over him, and he saw her lift one hand to touch his cheek.

"You were cut," she said, frowning and touching a tender spot by his ear. "Here. 'Tis bloodied, but does not look too dirty." She moved to examine him better, and Thomas felt his chest tighten.

"Let me wash your hair, first," she said, pushing her fingers into Thomas's hair, not seeming to notice that he stifled a groan. "'Then I will see to the rest."

One hand dug deeper in the fine blond strands, while the other scooped up a handful of cold water. Rising up to pour the water over his head, she innocently lifted her breasts above his face, and Thomas openly stared. Welcoming the redeeming effects on his senses, Thomas did not flinch when she poured the cold water over his scalp, but said, "Your hands shake, yet."

"It takes time for them to calm," she told him. "I cannot make them do it."

Her fingers tangled in his hair, gently rubbing, and Thomas fought the urge to close his eyes with pleasure.

"'Tis a strange affliction," he said.

"So you have said, my lord."

"Does it not seem so to you?"

Intent upon his hair, she gave a tiny shrug, and Thomas's eyes followed the slight lifting movement of her breasts.

"I have always had it and so have become accustomed to it, much as I have grown accustomed to being a woman." She poured more water over his hair, then began to squeeze out the excess. In another moment she sat back on her knees, took up the hem of her surcoat, wet it and began to wash his face. "Here is another cut," she said, dabbing at a spot on his neck. Her face took on a look of concern as she concentrated on removing the dried blood, and Thomas, consumed by an unexpected rush of pleasure at being cared for by such gentle hands, gazed at her and wondered, with some confusion, at what strange things she made him feel.

"Why does the lord of Sacre Placean pursue you?" he asked.

Her ministrations ceased, and she met his gaze directly, her eyes wide with surprise. "You do not know?"

Despite the fact that his heart had begun to hammer painfully the moment she'd looked at him, Thomas felt a surge of irritation.

"I do not ask questions for which I already have an answer."

She sat up. "You were sent by the king. Surely he told you why. You *must* know."

Her words made him feel foolish, and when he realized how foolish he must look, lying there before her as if he'd naught better to do than loll about with a maid all the day, he also felt furious. Turning over and kneeling by the river, he scrubbed his face with the cold water, then shook his hair and picked up his sword. Standing, he said, "'Twas my master who sent me, at the king's command."

"But, surely he gave you reason—"

"He did not," Thomas told her, "and I do not question my lord."

She seemed thoroughly amazed by this. "I have never known a man who obeyed his master so readily, without question. Is he so dear to you, then? The lord of Reed?"

"He is," Thomas replied at once, sheathing his sword. "I owe him my life."

Gathering her damp skirt with one hand, Amica began to rise. Thomas put his hand beneath her arm and lifted her. When she had gained her feet, she said, "Your lord must greatly prize you then, Thomas of Reed."

"He does."

"What man would not?" she replied with what sounded to Thomas like sadness. "Duncan Selwyrn would give a fortune and more to possess such obedience."

Thomas made a sound of disdain. "Loyalty bought with gold is as worthless and shifting as so many grains of sand." His fingers tightened about her arm, and he searched her wary eyes. "Why does the lord of Sacre Placean want you?"

A look of revulsion crossed her beautiful features. She replied, quietly, "For obedience."

The sound of horses approaching stopped the question on Thomas's lips.

"Come." He released her and strode to where Maelgwn grazed. Amica followed without question, and in another moment they had returned to the shelter of the trees.

Thomas pressed Amica against the trunk of one and shielded her with his body.

"Can you ride Maelgwn without a saddle?"

"Yes," she whispered, and he could hear the fear in her voice.

The next moment Derryn Thewlis rode into view, leading along the horse that carried Stevan of Hearn, who was slumped precariously over the beast's back.

With a smothered oath, Thomas strode forward. Reaching Stevan, he lifted up his massive arms.

"Tom," Stevan muttered as Thomas pulled him from the steed. "I told you . . . I could . . . keep pace with you."

Cradling Stevan in his arms, Thomas took him toward the trees. "Aye, and so you have. What of it?"

Stevan cursed and with a weak hand clubbed Thomas across the head. "I'm no babe to be carried!" he shouted.

The small blow did nothing to Thomas, and he kept walking. "Nay," he said as he laid Stevan on the ground, placing his head in Amica's lap as she knelt to receive him. "You are naught but a braggart." With a frown he felt Stevan's damp, fevered brow. "And a knave," he added as he lifted the injured man and nodded a request at Amica to help him remove Stevan's tunic. "And so will I warn this lady who succors you."

"Lady?" Stevan murmured, opening his eyes a little.

Amica smiled and stroked Stevan's hair while Thomas, scowling, examined his wound.

"But you're wrong, Tom," Stevan whispered as he gazed worshipfully at Amica.

"I am never wrong," Thomas replied distractedly, carefully wiping blood from the deep cut in Stevan's flesh.

"You are," Stevan said faintly, closing his eyes. "She is an angel."

5

It was growing dark by the time Amica woke from her much needed slumber. Dazed, she sat up, blinking and looking about.

Stevan of Hearn lay not far away, sleeping peacefully now after suffering his master's ministrations. Thomas of Reed had skillfully tended the wound, Amica had noted with some surprise as she'd held Stevan's head and tried to soothe his misery. From the ease with which he had cleaned and bound Stevan's arm, it was clear that he had done such work before.

After delivering Stevan to the camp, Derryn Thewlis had unsaddled his steed and tossed a blanket to the ground, wearily throwing himself down after it. He'd slept soundly through all of Stevan's moans and protestations, and continued to slumber deeply when Amica finally gave way to Thomas of Reed's insistences and lay down to sleep. Now fully awake, Derryn squatted beside a small fire, drinking from a cup and tending two roasting rabbits, the delicious smell of which made

Amica's empty stomach rumble with want. He was gazing directly at her, smiling.

"Good eve, my lady," he greeted, sounding much the better for the sleep he'd had.

"Good eve, Sir Derryn," Amica replied, yawning and running a hand over her hair to brush away the few small leaves that had clung to her. "Where is Sir Thomas?"

Derryn nodded to the place beside her, and Amica turned to find Thomas of Reed lying only inches away. In slumber, with his features relaxed and his constant scowl gone, he appeared younger, and his countenance was much like an innocent boy's. Amica regarded him for a silent moment, looking at him closely and seeing, for the first time, the number of scars that marred his skin. His overlong hair fell lightly across his cheek, and Amica nearly lifted a hand to sweep it back. She did not, however, for she knew that it was unwise to touch a slumbering warrior, no matter how innocent the touch or how deeply he seemed to sleep. Rising quietly to her feet, she went to join Derryn beside the fire.

"Sir Stevan looks to be sleeping peacefully," she said, settling before the warmth the flames provided.

"Aye," Derryn said. "His fever has lessened. He'll be whole in a few days' time." He offered her his cup and Amica caught the faintly sour scent of wine. She gratefully took a sip of the bitter drink and passed it back to him.

"Not if he's made to ride as hard as he was last eve," she countered.

Derryn shrugged. "Stevan's not a babe. He'll do as he must, or die."

A look of disdain crossed Amica's features. "He'll do as Thomas of Reed tells him, sir. That is what you mean."

"Aye," Derryn agreed affably. "We have sworn fealty to Sir Eric Stavelot, the lord of Reed, and he has commanded that we obey Thomas of Reed as faithfully as we would obey him. There is no mystery in that."

"Nay, there is not. The mystery is why Sir Eric should choose such as Thomas of Reed to lead his men. He is hard driven, is he not? I wonder that he allows himself the mercy of such deep slumber."

"Tom's not a martyr, my lady," Derryn said with a chuckle. "A more practical man I've ne'er known. Indeed, he thinks those who make themselves suffer for no good reason are fools. And any man who would deprive himself of sleep when he need not do so is certainly a fool."

"That is so," Amica conceded. "I suppose I believed, since he asks so much of his men, that he would ask much of himself."

"And so he does," Derryn said, bending to refill his cup from a wineskin that lay on the ground. "Thomas of Reed is a worthy man to obey. His men trust and respect him and would follow him straight into the Fiend's realm with never a fear for his ability to bring them out again."

Amica looked at him with disbelief. "You can say such as that when he left Stevan of Hearn, wounded, to fend for himself? When he sent you to find Sir Stevan— a man *he* is responsible for—rather than going himself?"

Regarding her with some surprise, Derryn replied. "Aye, I can say such as that, and readily. Such actions only prove my words. Tom gave our lord his solemn vow that he would deliver Amica of Lancaster safely to Reed, and his vow is a matter of honor, as it is to any just, righteous man. Having given it, how then could he leave your side? For any reason?"

"You are as capable as he of giving protection," she argued. "And I am not so valuable a person as Stevan of Hearn, I trow. Certainly not to Thomas of Reed."

Both Derryn's eyebrows rose at that. "You are modest, Amica of Lancaster, or have never seen your reflection to speak such words. But that is beside the matter. Did you think it slight of Thomas to leave one of his own behind? He has been my master and friend these many years, my lady, and I know him well. I can promise 'twas no easy thing for him to leave Stevan. The care of his men is Thomas's first concern, and has ever been.

"And as to being capable," he went on, turning the stick upon which the rabbits hung over the flames, "I would advise you to wait until we achieve Reed before saying that any man is more capable than Sir Thomas." He grinned at her. "If you still believe then that I am such a man, I will be greatly honored, indeed."

Amica's stomach rumbled suddenly and loudly, and both she and Derryn laughed.

"It has been long since we have eaten," he said, passing her the wine cup again. "Drink more of this to ease your hunger. 'Twill not be much longer and we shall eat. Tom bade me wake him when the sun had fully set. We needs must be on our way soon after that."

"'Twill be dark soon," Amica said, gazing at the sky through the trees. "Do Duncan Selwyrn's men pursue us yet?"

"There is no way of knowing. We rode far last night and were not followed, but we have stayed in this place for many hours now, so that if Duncan's men do seek us, we have given them a small advantage. Tonight we shall ride long again, and try to take the advantage away."

Amica shivered helplessly at the thought of being

overtaken by the lord of Sacre Placean's men; Derryn, seeing it, said, "Do not fear, my lady. No harm will befall you while we live."

"Will it take many days to reach Reed?"

"Some few," he admitted. "We must keep away from the open road and from towns. That will make the journey slower, but safer. We shall do what we can to assure your comfort, my lady, though I fear 'twill be little enow."

His charming, practiced manners made Amica smile. "You are chivalrous, Sir Derryn. But I do not care so much for comfort. I am grateful to be rescued from the lord of Sacre Placean, and will be content with whatever else befalls me. I expect nothing more from any of you, certainly not from Thomas of Reed."

Chuckling, Derryn turned his gaze to where Thomas lay sleeping. Amica could clearly see the affection on his face.

"Ah, Tom's a good man and a good leader, but s'truth he has no great love for women, nor for men who are ever dallying with women, either."

"So I have understood, my lord," Amica said. "Indeed, he has made himself very clear about such matters."

"He cannot help himself," Derryn said. "'Tis his nature to be wary of what he does not understand. My lord, Sir Eric, says he was ever thus, even as a child."

"As a child?" Amica repeated. "Thomas of Reed has been with his lord so long, then?"

Derryn took another sip from his cup. "Tom was my lord's squire when he was but ten and two, and has been with him ever since. Tom is as the lord of Reed's son. Indeed, Sir Eric has made him his heir."

"His heir? But, does not the lord of Reed have children of his own? Or is Thomas of Reed his bastard, in truth?"

"Thomas is no bastard. His mother and father are long dead, but he is of lawful birth. My lady of Reed has given our lord three daughters and is expecting a fourth child shortly, and they have all been provided with an inheritance, for my lord is a wealthy man, but Thomas has been with him since he was a boy, and Sir Eric has ever loved him. He wanted to adopt him as a true son, but Tom would have none of it."

Amica shook her head in confusion. "Why? 'Twould be a great honor to be made the son of Sir Eric Stavelot."

"S'truth," Derryn agreed. "But he does not feel worthy to bear my lord's name, and so will not accept it."

"Is Thomas of Reed such a proud man, then?"

"Proud?" Derryn said thoughtfully. "Mayhap, though I have never thought him so. He is a stern master and a demanding friend, but I can think of few men I admire more. He is the only man I've e'er known who means those few words he speaks and does those things he declares he will do. He is neither vain nor boastful, but knows his limits and the limits of others." He looked at Amica directly. "Tom respects limits," he said. "I find that wise in a man, do not you?"

Amica opened her mouth to say "aye", but stopped when Thomas of Reed said, irately, "You are bothersome as chattering jays. Can you not keep quiet?"

Amica and Derryn turned toward Thomas, who was sitting upright, wearily rubbing his eyes.

"We'll be quiet, Tom," Derryn promised. "Go back to sleep. You've not had much, yet."

"Nay." Thomas rose stiffly to his feet, brushing leaves from his tunic. "'Tis just as well. We must go soon, else we give Selwyrn's men too much benefit." Moving sleepily, he stumbled toward the fire and sat beside Derryn, who pressed the shared cup, filled newly with wine, into his master's hands.

Thomas drank deeply, then gave the cup to Amica.

"I have decided what we must do," he stated, "to keep those we pass from commenting on a lady traveling in the company of three men, but none of them her husband or relative. Selwyrn's men will be asking after a beautiful woman, and we must do all we can to allay notice."

"Aye," Derryn agreed, "but there is naught we can do to alter Lady Amica's beauty, save cover her with a veil."

"That is true," Thomas said. "But a woman so covered, unless she were a nun, would only cause more notice, and the lord of Sacre Placean would expect such as that."

"Duncan is a suspicious man," Amica said softly. "Because he is so false himself, he expects deceit everywhere he turns, and so is prepared for it."

Thomas nodded. "He will be searching for it, and if we do as he expects, then we make ourselves simple prey in this hunt. But there is one thing he'll not be seeking, and that is a married woman who travels only with her husband and his men. Such a woman, though she might be reported as very beautiful, might not draw forth interest from the lord of Sacre Placean."

Derryn and Amica stared at him.

"Especially," Thomas went on, "if that woman's husband possessed proof of their marriage. Proof that would satisfy any curiosity."

"A marriage contract?" Derryn guessed, his lips tilting into a smile. "And who better to write such as that than a priest?"

"Very good, Derry," Thomas said approvingly. "You have always had a quick mind."

"I do not understand," Amica said. "What can you mean, my lord?"

"I mean," Thomas replied, "that you are about to become a wife, my lady."

"Wife?"

"Aye. My wife. We shall wed as soon as we are able to purchase parchment and ink to write the contract. It shall be fully lawful, do not fear."

Several moments passed before Amica could make her lips move.

"Nay, I— I cannot— I—"

Thomas of Reed's brow lowered. "Aye, but you will. It shall be as I have said until we reach Reed, and then the marriage will be annulled."

Amica started shaking her head. "I cannot, my lord. I cannot . . . "

He made an angry sound. "You can. You will. It shall only be for a few days' time, and only to keep you safe until we reach Reed. After that we shall gladly part ways."

"But, my lord, you do not comprehend me," Amica insisted. "I cannot wed you."

Thomas's face grew hard. "Woman, you try me sorely. I have said how it shall be. Do not speak of the matter more."

Her hands began to tremble, yet Amica managed to argue, "There is no priest, sir. It cannot be done without a priest who is willing to wed us."

Rising to his feet, he said, "Stevan is a priest. Or was a priest, once. He shall write the contract and wed us, and only God may judge us once the deed is done."

6

It was not a real wedding, of course. That much Amica was able to find comfort in.

They had once again ridden through the night, and had only stopped when the first hint of the sun glimmered in the sky. Thomas of Reed had made Stevan of Hearn lie down, and had tended to his wound, and Derryn Thewlis, winking at an exhausted Amica, had turned his horse about and ridden off. She was too weary to care where he went, and gladly lay down in the place Thomas of Reed pointed to. When she woke several hours later, it was to find Stevan laboring over a piece of parchment, writing as quickly as his wound would allow and muttering to himself about the foolishness of his task.

Amica had argued with Thomas of Reed, or had tried to do so at least.

"There is no sense in this," she had said. "Why can we not simply pretend to be wed? Why must we have a ceremony?"

Scowling, he had replied, "'Twould be false to say

we were wed if we were not. 'Twould be lies, and I cannot abide falseness in any form."

Amica had never known anyone more honorable than Thomas of Reed, and she could not decide whether it made him a better man or simply a fool; whether it gave him an advantage over lesser men or left him prey to those who harbored no such honor in their souls. Duncan Selwyrn would have used such a desire for honesty as a weapon, first to torment Thomas of Reed and at last to destroy him. But Duncan's soul was filled with treachery and deceit. He would never be able to see what other use honesty might serve.

Having accepted Thomas of Reed's explanation, Amica was not surprised, when the false ceremony was performed, that he repeated each vow with manifest integrity. She stood beside him, holding his hand and obediently repeating the words she was directed to say, and wondered what Thomas of Reed would think were he to know that, despite his desire for the truth, the ceremony was wholly a lie. They were not wed, even when 'twas all done, but he bent over her and quickly gave her the kiss of peace, on her cheek and not her lips, and when he lifted his head she saw clearly that he believed her to be his wife. The thought in no way made him happy, she saw as well, for he looked deeply uncomfortable to have to suffer such a thing.

"'Tis done," he said, taking the contract Stevan had prepared and rolling it up to place inside his tunic. "We'll have it annulled the very hour we arrive at Reed. My lord, Sir Eric, will know how to manage it."

"'Twill only be easily annulled if it is not consummated," Stevan warned.

Amica grew warm at the words. Somewhere behind her, she heard Derryn Thewlis coughing, trying desperately to control his laughter.

"'Twill not be consummated," Thomas of Reed stated, his tone cold enough to freeze Hell's fires. "Of that you may be sure. Let us have no more of this foolishness. We've a long ride ahead. Tonight we will find a decent inn to shelter us, and decent food to fill our bellies."

He held out a hand to Amica to help her mount Maelgwn.

"Come, lady."

"Lady *wife*," Derryn corrected lightly as he walked past them to mount his own steed.

Thomas of Reed said nothing as he helped her to mount, but when he had swung up behind her, he muttered, "Derry is right. You are my lady wife, if only for a few days. You have taken a vow of obedience, and so must obey me."

"Have I not obeyed you these past two days?" she asked, angered by what he implied.

"You have done well, thus far," he admitted, prodding Maelgwn forward. "But women cannot go long without causing trouble of some kind, and so I would remind you, do not give way to temptation, for I may punish you now, if it pleases me, as is a husband's right."

"You are not my husband."

"Not for long, may God be praised. Yet for now I am, and so I tell you, heed my warning."

"You would not lay a hand to me," she insisted, clenching her hands in her lap to control their treacherous shaking. Duncan had beaten her more times than she could remember, indeed, he had greatly enjoyed doing so, for her tears never failed to excite him. The memory made Amica's mouth tremble, and she pressed her lips together.

One of Thomas of Reed's hands suddenly pressed over both of hers, covering and holding them.

"Nay, I would not," he said solemnly. "'Twas wrong of me to speak thus, and so do I beg your pardon. I would never beat you, Amica of Lancaster. You may be certain of my words, for I do not speak falsely."

The Black Bull Tavern was the kind of place Thomas despised. It was damp, filthy, and thoroughly rank. The smells of urine and unwashed bodies were strong enough to make a man sick, and the smoke from the fire pit was so thick it burned both eyes and throat and made the already bitter ale that was served there taste of ash. Most of the patrons were lewd, low-born creatures who drank heavily, spoke loudly and fought with one another for the slightest offense or for none at all. The women in the place, almost all of whom were whores, were so foul that Thomas wouldn't have set a finger on one to save his life. Derryn already had one of them in his lap, and was smiling and dallying with her while she wiggled relentlessly and gaped at him with a toothless grin. If Stevan hadn't felt so ill from his wound, Thomas knew he'd have latched onto another such disgusting creature, for he and Derryn were ever craving the small comforts that a woman's body—any woman's body, no matter how filthy—could provide. Over the years, Thomas had had to suffer through many such nights, enduring Derryn and Stevan's unfortunate weaknesses. He should not have done so, he knew, but they were the only friends he had, and so he accepted and suffered their defects, though he certainly did not approve of them.

The only fortunate thing about the Black Bull was that it had a private chamber that Thomas had been able to hire for the night, where even now Stevan slept, trying to recover from their hard day's ride, and where they all would find their rest as soon as they'd eaten whatever viands the Black Bull was able to offer. He had told the innkeeper to bring them clean food as soon as possible, and had displayed enough of both gold and displeasure to cause the man haste, yet an hour had passed and naught but ale had been brought them. Thomas was nearly out of patience. He did not care so much for his own discomfort; it was Amica of Lancaster's suffering that angered him.

She was sitting on his lap, just as completely as Derryn's whore was sitting on his, but Amica of Lancaster did so out of fear. When they had first entered the tavern she had somehow managed to draw the attention of a particularly crude drunk, who had not only spoken to her in a very coarse manner but who had also dared to set a hand upon her arm, causing the wretched woman to take up a shaking so fierce that she nearly collapsed from it. Thomas had quickly taken care of the matter, making certain that the fool would be able neither to touch anything nor to speak for a long time, and he had sternly told Amica of Lancaster that she had nothing to fear, for he would not allow harm to come to her, but she had only continued to tremble, and shake, and stare at him as if she would shortly burst into tears.

At last, fully annoyed, Thomas had picked her up and put her in his lap, though he'd been more than a little tempted to turn her over it instead and make her cease her foolishness, and had held her tightly to make the shaking stop. It hadn't done much good; she'd clutched him with both hands and begun to weep. What foolish creatures females were. Duncan Selwyrn must be the greatest idiot alive to risk his men over a woman.

He ran one hand slowly over her back, feeling, even

beneath the thick cloak that he'd bought from one of
the villagers they'd met outside the tavern, the small-
ness of her bones.

Were some women so small and frail, then? Thomas
wondered, mapping the curve of one shoulder with his
fingers. He remembered the way she had knelt above
him as she'd washed his hair the day before; he remembered gazing at her breasts.

Thomas glanced toward Derryn and his whore,
observing the toothless girl more closely. Yes, that was
what he had seen of women. A creature like that, with
breasts large and slack and loose beneath her clothing.
He had never been compelled to caress such women, as
he knew other men enjoyed doing, not even while he
had been engaged with one in sating his physical needs.
The idea had always seemed quite unpleasant. Strangely,
though, he did not find the thought of touching Amica
of Lancaster unpleasant. Her breasts were small and
firm, or had seemed so the other day. He wondered
what they looked like . . . felt like. Pressing his palm flat,
he moved his hand down the smooth bow of her back
and wrapped his fingers around her waist. He marveled
at how tiny it was, how delicate she was in every way.

Amica of Lancaster had ceased her tears, and with a
long, weary sigh settled more fully against him.

"'Twill not be much longer, now," he heard himself
saying, and wondered why his voice should sound so
thin.

"I am sorry to be so foolish," she said, sniffling.
"Truly, my lord. I beg you will forgive me."

Her soft, quiet words worked on Thomas like a
bucket of hot coals poured over his head. One moment
he was merely irate, and the next he was furious. He
wanted to kill someone. He wanted to make every man
who frightened her and made her suffer extinct.

"I . . . I think perhaps it is because I am so hungry," she whispered apologetically. "I will not be so foolish as this later, I vow. I am so sorry, my lord."

He would kill the cook, he thought blindly, gripping her. The innkeeper—aye. He would kill the innkeeper first and then the cook. And whoever else had caused her to suffer so much hunger that she'd been made to cry over it.

"Tom."

Derryn's voice was dim in the red haze of Thomas's fury. He barely heard it.

"Tom."

Thomas turned and saw that Derryn was gazing at him as if he were seeing a madman.

"What?" Thomas demanded, angry at being distracted.

"Where do you go?"

"What?"

"Where," Derryn said slowly, "do you go? Are you taking your lady wife to your chamber? Did you not wish to sup, first?"

It took a moment before Thomas realized what Derryn meant, before he realized that he was standing with Amica of Lancaster in his arms and that he meant to take her somewhere better than where she presently was.

"I—" he began, not certain what to say and fully bewildered at his own behavior.

The innkeeper and his wife approached their table, their arms laden with wooden boards filled with meats and bread.

"Forgive me, my lord," the innkeeper said, puffing breathlessly as the food was set down before them. "You did say clean food, good sir, and so I had the cook kill two young chickens and bade her make fresh rysbred from the good flour. And there were parsnips, sir, and parsley and eggs and cheese. Enough for an arboletty."

Thomas gazed dumbly at the egg tart and struggled to gather his wits. Amica of Lancaster felt light in his arms; she had lifted her tear-streaked face and was looking at him. Why in the world was he standing?

Embarrassed, he sat back down and put Amica away from him, seating her on the bench in front of the food.

"Thank you," Thomas mumbled to the innkeeper, who beamed at him. "You shall be recompensed."

"A pleasure, my lord," the innkeeper replied while both he and his wife bowed repeatedly. "'Twas naught but our great pleasure. May you and your good lady wife enjoy our simple fare."

They were too hungry to engage in conversation as they ate, though Thomas said, as he split the chickens, "We will put enough aside for Stevan. Save the best parts for him."

"Oh, it is *wonderful*," Amica murmured around of a mouthful of rysbred.

"Food always tastes better when one is hungry, does it not, my lady?" Derryn said, grinning and winking and earning a deep scowl from Thomas, who upon hearing Amica's words had begun adding more chicken to her pile of food.

The moment he was certain she had eaten her fill, Thomas stood, taking Amica's arm and pulling her to her feet.

"Drink no more wine this night, Derryn, nor ale. Come to the chamber in three hours' time."

His arm about the girl at his side, Derryn shook his head sadly. "You are generous, as always, Tom."

Thomas made a scoffing sound. "You could tumble every maid in this village in three hours' time, and would, most likely, if you did not need to keep your eyes open more oft than that this night."

Derryn laughed, glancing at Amica with slight embarrassment. "I shall be in the chamber as you have commanded, my lord."

Amica wrapped the food they'd saved for Stevan in a linen square and Thomas filled a tankard with ale. Carrying their burdens, they traversed the steps to their rented chamber in silence. It was a large, simple room, clearly meant for sleeping with several pallets strewn about on the floor. In one corner a solitary table stood, atop which a lone candle put its small light into the darkness.

Thomas relieved Amica of the food she carried. "I bade the innkeeper to bring fresh water," he said, nodding toward a bucket and a bowl near the door. "Prepare yourself for sleep. I will wake Stevan."

Amica obediently did as she was told. Kneeling beside the bucket, she unlaced and removed her cloak and set it aside. As she poured a small amount of water into the bowl for her use, she heard Thomas of Reed speaking softly to Stevan, bidding him to sit and eat.

Longing for the comfort of a real bath, Amica washed her hands and face, then removed her shoes and leggings and rinsed her feet and legs. When she was finished she took the bowl, carried it to the room's only window, and tossed the water out to the ground. Replacing the bowl on the floor beside the bucket, she sought the pallet that was hers, found her bag and dug through it, at last pulling out her comb.

The men murmured quietly back and forth, filling the chamber with the comforting sound of words while Amica unbraided and combed her long hair.

It would be good to sleep, she thought, watching Thomas and Stevan. She was very tired, and now that her stomach was full, Amica knew she would sleep deeply and well. For that, she was glad. She had not let herself think of her grandfather yet; had not let herself grieve. There had been no time for it in the past two days, and now she was too weary. Only vague thoughts came to her as she at last lay down on her pallet.

That Stevan of Hearn had once been a priest was one such contemplation. She had realized earlier, by the richness of his clothing, that he might be of high birth, and when he explained that he was indeed the second son of a wealthy lord, Amica had at once understood how he had come to be in the Church, for that was the common fate of many second and third and fourth sons. To please his parents, Stevan had striven to accept the vocation that had been forced upon him, but, after a number of years, had failed.

"I was a terrible priest," he had explained that afternoon when they stopped for a short rest. "I could think of naught but women. Day and night, during prayer and mass and even communion. But it was not merely a lust of the flesh, my lady. I dreamt of a family, of having a proper home with a wife and children. I wanted all of that so badly, 'twas all my mind could seize upon."

"But how did you manage to leave the Church?" she asked. "'Tis not easily done, as I have heard."

Stevan smiled and sighed. "I begged my father to help me. He was against the idea, having paid the Church so much gold to take me and knowing how much more it would cost to make them let me go. And 'tis always well for a family as ours to have a son in Holy Orders, to guard against ruin if there's any trouble with the Church. But I was fortunate, for my youngest brother, Edmund, had always wished to become a priest, and was more than glad to do so. I promised my father that I would repay him whatever it cost to free me of my vows, and he finally agreed to help me."

"And that is how you come to be in service to the lord of Reed?"

"Even so. I was fortunate, indeed, that he accepted my vow of fealty, for I have been under Thomas's hand ever since, and thus have been content."

The sound of water sloshing in the bucket caused Amica to open her eyes, though she hadn't even realized she'd closed them. Stevan was lying down again, she saw as she gazed through the dim light of the room, and Thomas of Reed was bent over the bowl that sat on the floor, vigorously washing his face.

He was the cleanest man she'd ever met, and the most habitual, as well. She had only met him a few days before, and yet she already knew much about him. Like her, he would remove his shoes and wash his feet, just as he had done each time before he had sought sleep. Unlike her, he would put his boots back on after a few minutes and would sleep in them. Before he lay down on his pallet, he would kneel and pray, and after that, he would remove his sword and set it carefully nearby, within easy reach should he happen to need it.

Amica's gaze followed as Thomas of Reed stood and took the bowl to the window to empty it, and stayed upon him as he knelt beside his pallet, crossed himself, and softly murmured his recitation. When he finished he removed his sword and set it beside his bed, but then, when she expected him to lie down and seek his slumber, he turned and gazed at her.

He seemed surprised to find her awake. "Will you sleep, Amica of Lancaster?"

"Yes. Good night, my lord."

"'Tis cold," he said, rubbing his arm, "and I gave the

extra blanket to Stevan. If you wish it, you may sleep here with me."

His invitation was so fully grudging that Amica nearly laughed. He must think, since he believed them to be wed, that he now had a duty to assure her comfort.

"I shall be fine as I am, Sir Thomas, I thank you."

"That is well. Good night, then, my lady. God keep you."

"And you."

Lying down, he pulled his one blanket over his large body and immediately closed his eyes. With a soft yawn, Amica continued to watch him, though her own eyes felt increasingly heavy.

He was handsome, she decided, though she had not thought so at first. She liked his face, with all its angles and scars. There was nothing hidden in it, nothing false. She liked his dark eyes—they were surely his most attractive feature. She liked the way he'd held her in his lap this night, so gently yet surely, for he'd made her feel safe and warm. And his hand, as it had glided over her back, had been soothing. It was a strong hand, big and scarred like the rest of him, yet it had given gentle comfort and she had been grateful. How strange, she thought, as she drifted into sleep, that she wasn't afraid of him. She had believed, after Duncan, that she would never feel safe with a man again.

7

He had not had the dream in more than a year, and had been foolish enough to hope that he would never suffer it again. Even as his mind cast him back to that time of terror and helplessness, Thomas struggled to make himself wake. Yet it all seemed so clear and real, as if he were there again, in the hut he had shared with his father, cowering on the floor as his father raged and threw everything he could find. Thomas huddled by the table, praying that the drunkard would pass out before he ran out of things and started throwing fists instead. He tried crawling closer to the door, for if he could only get outside he could run away, and if Sir Eric were in the village, he could find him, and all would be well.

"You're naught but a bastard! Did you know that, boy? A stupid, filthy bastard!"

His father picked up his empty tankard and beat against the table as he spoke each word.

"Your mother was a whore! Spread her legs for the whole village!"

The tankard flew at Thomas. He covered his head and felt the sting as the heavy metal struck his hand. But even the pain of that couldn't stop his fury, or his angry words.

"My mother wasn't a whore!"

It seemed so real, but his father moved slower in the dream than he had then, coming toward Thomas with his hands outstretched.

"You'll say it. Before this night is done, you'll tell the truth about the slut that bore you."

"Nay!"

"Aye, God's my life, boy, you will."

"I'll not! I'll not! I'll—"

"My lord!"

Amica's frightened voice penetrated his dark hell with a blinding brilliance, and Thomas bolted upright, fully awake and breathing harshly.

"My lord . . ." Her voice was filled with worry. From the corner of his eye he could see her sitting beside him, one hand wavering anxiously near his shoulder.

He could not speak, but breathed laboriously through his mouth, trying to control his shaking body and put his mind in order.

She touched him, finally, setting her hand upon his arm—a tentative, uncertain action.

"Go . . . *back.* . . . Sleep," he managed, biting each word out tightly, embarrassed that she should see him in such a weak, defenseless state.

But she didn't go. Instead, she shocked him completely by setting her arms about his neck and holding him as if she would calm his shaking.

"I suffer such dreams," she whispered. Hugging him tightly, she moved her hands soothingly over his back and shoulders. "I hate and fear them. 'Twill pass but shortly, I vow."

He had never been held by a woman before. Not like this. When he'd been a boy, indulging in his daydreams, Thomas had often imagined his mother holding him, loving and comforting him after one of his father's beatings, and when his master had married the Lady Margot, Thomas had learned how gently a woman's touch could sooth away a young boy's misery and anger, though, in truth, he had suffered little of either once Sir Eric took him under his care. But none of these maternal embraces, either imagined or real, could compare to what Amica of Lancaster was doing to him now.

She was pressed full against him; he could feel her breasts against his chest, and her long, unbound hair tickled the skin of his face. He didn't know why his breathing would not lessen. In sooth, the movement of her hands upon his back only seemed to make everything worse. His heart pounded furiously in his ears, and his chest—his entire body—felt painfully taut. He turned his face toward her, breathing in her clean, feminine scent. Without thinking of what he did, he lifted his hand to touch her hair.

Startled, she pulled away, and Thomas felt a bewildering sense of loss. He made a quick fist, capturing a quantity of the fine strands in his grip, keeping her beside him.

"My lord," she whispered.

He barely heard her.

"'Tis soft," he murmured with surprise, relaxing his fingers and pushing them deeper into the cool, silky mass. "I have never . . ." With a frown of concentration, he lifted his other hand and set it on the other side of her head, running it through her hair as well.

Amica sat very still through his exploration, torn between amusement and confusion. Had he never touched a woman's hair before? she wondered. How strange that would be, for he was a man—a fine, healthy man—and well past the age of boyish exploration. And yet he touched her so gently, with such wonder and curiosity, that Amica knew it must be so. He grew bolder after a moment, reaching back and drawing the weight of her hair forward, over her shoulders.

"'Tis great in length," he stated, measuring it against his arm before he threaded his fingers into the strands at the base of her neck, touching her scalp with his fingertips and causing Amica to close her eyes against the pleasure of his touch. Oh, Duncan had never touched her like this, so gently, so carefully. She had not known that a man could do such a kind and pleasant thing. How was it that Thomas of Reed possessed so tender a touch when in all other ways he was so hard? Amica opened her eyes and gazed at him. His own eyes were intent upon her hair, his expression one of great interest. And then, suddenly, he looked up. And stilled. His hands fell away and they sat staring at one another.

After a moment, feeling inexplicably embarrassed, Amica said, "You will sleep better now. Such dreams seldom come twice in a night." She saw his mouth twist into its usual scowl. "I shall return to my bed now."

He set a hand upon her arm. "You tremble. Do you suffer your affliction? Are you afeared of aught? Of me?"

Afraid? Amica thought. Nay, she was not afraid. She didn't know why she trembled.

Thomas spread his fingers wide and ran his hand over her arm, up to her shoulder.

"You are chilled," he said. "'Tis from the cold that you shake."

"Nay, I am not—"

"Fetch your blanket. You will sleep here with me."

"But, my lord—"

"My master would be angered were I to let you fall ill ere we achieve Reed. Go and fetch your blanket."

"Nay, my lord, I would rather—"

With a sound of aggravation, Thomas took Amica by both shoulders and pressed her down onto his pallet. "Stay," he commanded, then got up and went to fetch her blanket. In another moment they lay side by side and Thomas arranged the thick wool blankets about them.

"If you were a soldier under my command," he told her, "I would have already punished you for such disobedience." He roughly tucked the blanket beneath her.

"I'm *not* a soldier beneath your command," she replied angrily.

"May God be praised," he muttered, lying back fully. "You are only my wife, and are disobedient even so."

"I am also not your wife," she insisted. "We are not legally wed."

"We are, for we spoke aloud our intentions before witnesses, and you know as well as I that that is enough to bind us legally, whether 'twas a proper ceremony or no."

"You do not understand," she began, turning toward him even as he set a hand on her shoulder and turned her back, away from him again.

"Go to sleep, woman. I'll not waste time listening to you prate when I might be slumbering. I can only thank a merciful God that you've not yet managed to awaken Stevan with your silly chatter. And cease that . . . that wriggling. Lie still!"

"I only mean to make myself comfortable." She twisted just enough to glare at him. "This pallet is too small for us both, or you are too large, more likely. Let me return to my own bed. I was not cold, as you seemed to think."

"Nay," Thomas said, scooting away from her disturbing softness. His loins had begun to ache moments after he had lain beside her, and her every movement made the ache that much worse, until Thomas wanted to clench his teeth or swear aloud. "There, I have made room for you. Now be quiet and go to sleep."

Amica tried to do as he commanded. For several long minutes she lay on her side, staring out into the chamber, and tried to make herself sleep. His breathing, like hers, was loud in the darkness—uneven, unrestful. Awake.

Knowing that he did not sleep, she asked, "What did you dream of this night?"

His sigh sounded weary. "I dreamt of my father."

"Your father?"

"Aye, my father. And that is all."

He spoke the words in a hollow tone, empty and without emotion.

Amica was too wary to press him further. She listened to his breathing, instead, fixed upon it, and as each breath he drew deepened and became more relaxed, so did her own, until her eyes drifted shut and she fell asleep.

So deeply did she sleep that she could not fully wake when she felt him curl up against her. To her great shock, he tossed one heavy arm about her waist, then began nuzzling her. Muttering, he buried his face in her hair until he burrowed through and Amica could feel his breath hot upon her neck. He made an irate grumbling sound, as if he had not found what he sought, and then his hand moved, pressing against Amica's belly and causing her to draw in a sharp breath. The sound of it made him stop for a brief moment. Then, still grumbling, he moved closer, pushing his hips against her buttocks so that Amica felt, with unmistakable recognition, his rampant state of arousal.

"My lord," she whispered, hating the weak, shaking quality of her voice.

He paid no heed, but kept muttering and pressing his face through her hair, moving his head back and forth. She felt his lips against her skin as he spoke his vague words, and his nose, which sniffed at her as if to discover what she was.

"Sir Thomas!" Amica whispered more loudly, afraid to move even slightly lest she arouse him more.

"Hmmph!" The sound was sharp and annoyed. He was clearly dissatisfied with his search.

"Please, my lord," Amica begged. Lifting a hand, she touched his arm with her fingertips, but that only caused him to tighten the grip he had on her.

"Mmm." His tone was lower, thoughtful, and he began to move the hand that was still pressed against her belly.

Amica gasped out loud when his fingers touched her breast.

"No," she said firmly, wrapping her smaller fingers around his hand and tugging. "Cease this."

He grunted and pulled his hand free and settled it more firmly on her breast.

"My lord, this is unseemly," Amica insisted quite loudly, unable to believe that he didn't hear her.

But he must not have, for he only gave a contented sigh, pressed his face deeply into her hair once more, and fell still.

Amica waited for him to do something more, to do what she'd come to expect of a man when he was in such an aroused state. But he didn't pull her onto her back or try to draw her skirts up. He simply lay still, with his hand upon her breast, and held her as if she were some child's toy; something to comfort him while he dreamed. A few minutes passed, and he began to snore.

The realization that he was asleep almost made Amica laugh, and she let out a breath of relief. Pulling his hand from her breast, she set it firmly at her waist. He was very warm, sleeping against her, and for that Amica was glad. It had been a long time since she had been so warm at night. She closed her eyes and let herself slide back into slumber, and did not wake from it when Thomas's hand drifted back to resume its place at her breast.

An hour later, Derryn stared down at the sleeping pair in amazement. If he hadn't seen it with his own two eyes, he never would have believed it. Even seeing it, he wondered if he might be dreaming. He had known Thomas of Reed since they were both ten and six years of age, and had never known him to share a bed with a woman, much less to touch a woman if he could keep from doing so. Yet here he was, curled around Amica of Lancaster like a cat curled around a blanket. Why, he was actually *hugging* the woman. Derryn shook his head in disbelief.

Lifting a foot, he nudged Thomas between his shoulders.

"Tom, wake up."

With a grunt, Thomas lifted his head.

"Hmmm?"

"'Tis time. Three hours have passed."

"What?" Thomas sat upright and, with a moment of confusion, looked about. Amica of Lancaster was asleep beside him, he saw as he began to rub at his sleep-ridden eyes.

"Three hours have passed," Derryn repeated. "'Tis your turn to keep watch."

His years of soldiering rose up in Thomas, and he quickly became alert. "Very well. I'm awake. Go and seek your rest."

Derryn's wide smile was lost in the room's darkness. "You have been keeping Amica of Lancaster warm in this cold night, I see. I shall be glad to take your place and offer her the same comfort."

Thomas scowled. "Why do you speak thus? She is no whore."

Derryn chuckled. "I never said she was. I but jest, for you clearly consider the woman your wife in truth. Had you gotten any closer to her, lad, you would have been bound to her for life." He cocked an eyebrow and regarded Thomas with growing interest. "Or have you, already?"

Thomas pushed to his feet. "Have I what?"

"Enjoyed the pleasures your lady wife has to offer." Derryn cast a glance at Stevan's slumbering figure. "Come now, Tom. With Stevan in the room? Could you not have waited until there was a place more private?"

Thomas gave Derryn a look of complete bewilderment.

"Your words have no sense to them, as ever. I merely shared warmth with the woman. It is no more than you and Stevan and I have shared on cold nights."

"Ha!" Derryn exclaimed, lowering his voice at Thomas's sharp look. "If you ever got so friendly with me, my lord, as you were with Amica of Lancaster just now, you would find yourself a eunuch, shortly, I vow."

"What do you chatter about, idiot? I have never set so much as a finger to her. I did naught but share a pallet and some blankets, and that only as I had to. She was as troublesome and noisy as she ever is, and there is no pleasure in that. Now cease wearying me and get to bed."

Derryn made to kneel beside Amica but a strong hand on his tunic pulled him back up.

"Not there," Thomas said sternly. "Go to your own pallet."

"But 'tis cold!" Derryn protested. "And there are no more blankets."

"Take the extra blanket from Stevan, then, but leave these two with the woman."

"I'd rather leave myself," Derryn replied, smiling at Thomas's angry look. He might not remember the way he'd been wrapped around Amica of Lancaster's lovely person, Derryn thought, and he might pretend to disdain her as he disdained other women, but there was something there, brewing beneath that scowling visage that Thomas himself probably wasn't aware of. And how could it not be, when Amica of Lancaster was so lovely that even a monk would be tempted to sin?

"Of course, my lord and master," Derryn said mockingly, giving Thomas a slight bow. "I shall take myself to bed at once."

He went to fetch Stevan's extra blanket and promptly arranged his pallet to his satisfaction, fully aware that Thomas watched him the whole while. Ah, it felt good to lie down, to close his eyes. Derryn smiled as he felt slumber tugging at him, and thought, in his last coherent moment, that the next few days, as they journeyed toward Reed, were going to be most entertaining indeed.

8

The great hall of the castle at Sacre Placean was a place of ancient beauty. Rich tapestries depicting the Selwyrn history adorned the walls, and throughout the hall priceless treasures gave testament to the family's wealth and accomplishments. Along one wall the various armor worn by Duncan Selwyrn's ancestors were displayed; useless protection by the standards of the day, certainly, yet they bore proof of the widely lauded Selwyrn bravery and so were given their place of honor. In the chamber's far corner, upon a finely crafted table of oak, sat the most precious among the Selwyrn possessions: a crude bowl made of stone, a scepter, a splintered, decaying bow lying beside two equally poor arrows, a javelin with a long metal blade at its tip, and a battered drinking vessel made of gold.

Sitting not far from these objects, in an overlarge, throne-like chair that had once served as his great great grandfather's seat of judgment, the lord of Sacre Placean gazed lovingly at the sleeping babe he held in his arms.

"All dead, did you say, Ivar?" he asked softly, in the same lilting tone he had earlier used to soothe the child to sleep.

Standing before his master, Sir Ivar shifted nervously.

"Aye, my lord. All dead, I fear. The dwelling was burned to the ground, and as none have returned to Sacre Placean, I can only believe that the bodies of those whom we could not find were lost in the blaze."

"Lady Amica?"

"There was no sign of her, my lord, nor of the knight, Andrew Fawdry."

Lifting a hand, Duncan stroked the soft cap of hair on the baby's head.

"'Tis a handsome color, is it not, Alfred?" Duncan asked of his steward, who stood beside him. "'Tis golden brown, like Alys's." He smiled. "Like Amica's, as well. She will be pleased when she sees how greatly he favors her."

"Aye, my lord."

Standing, careful not to wake the babe, Duncan passed the infant into Alfred's waiting arms.

"Take him to his nurse," Duncan instructed. "Make certain his guards are in their places to watch over him while he sleeps. In another hour I shall retire to my own chamber. Fetch that girl from the north tower, if she has not yet managed to kill herself, and have her washed for my pleasure. After last night I fear she will have quite an unpleasant smell about her."

With a nod, Alfred carried the child toward the stairs. Duncan watched until his steward had passed out of sight, and only then did he turn his attention to Sir Ivar.

"You have searched Lancaster?" he asked.

"Yes, my lord, though there has been no sign of either Lady Amica or her grandfather."

"You were not so foolish as to distress any members of her family, I hope?"

"Nay, I was careful, my lord, as were my men. It is certain that they all believe Lady Amica to be here at Sacre Placean, recovering from the rigors of childbirth and grieving too deeply over the sudden death of Lady Alys to answer their missives about the birth of the child, although they are grateful that you, in her stead, were so kind as to send replies. Of course, they are gladdened to know that the lady Amica has at last given you an heir, and they anticipate a visit to pay honor to the future lord of Sacre Placean as well as to yourself, my lord."

Clasping his hands behind his back, Duncan grew thoughtful. "They understand that Alys died of the fever, then?"

"Yes, my lord. And they understood the need for her immediate burial, though they were saddened, certainly."

"Certainly," Duncan echoed. With lowered brow he moved toward the table that bore his family's inherited treasures and stood a long while, staring at them in silence.

At last Ivar cleared his throat. "Perhaps, my lord, as I have been able to find no sign of her, the lady Amica perished in the flames?"

"Nay." Duncan shook his head. "She is not dead. The old man has her hidden away somewhere. Andrew Fawdry is not for nothing a man of fame. I have seen him lead men into battle and can attest that he is a shrewd and crafty soldier." He smiled grimly. "He would know of a way to hide Amica from me."

"But he could not have killed so many men, my lord," Ivar said. "There must have been others to lend him aid in keeping the woman."

"That is so," Duncan conceded. "Let us only pray that he did not appeal to Henry, for if the king should learn that Amica was not at Sacre Placean, then my son were suddenly made a bastard, and that I will not allow. I would take the child's life, first—aye, and with mine own hand—than ever see the name of Selwyrn stained with such a blot."

A shudder trembled down Ivar's spine, and he bit his tongue to keep it still.

Duncan took the golden scepter and held it up, gazing at it worshipfully.

"This scepter belonged to one of my most honored ancestors," he murmured. "Cadwaladyr the Beloved. He was the Arch-Druid of his tribe, and this was the symbol of his wisdom and power. He ruled here, at Sacre Placean. The Sacred Places, as the Druids knew them to be, and it is so now as it was then. There is power here, in this place, in everything that lives on this sacred ground. No king on this earth has ever been able to bring his men upon it except they die. Did you know that, Ivar?"

Ivar found his master's intent stare upon him, and, unable to speak, stiffly shook his head.

"Verily, it is so." Duncan set the scepter down gently. "And do you know why?"

Again, Ivar shook his head.

Duncan approached him slowly, speaking in a soft voice.

"Because the spirits in the earth have ordained it to be, just as they have ordained that Selwyrn be the name of those who rule their earth. Not only Britain," he said, "but the full earth. Do you understand?"

Knowing better than to naysay the lord who owned his fealty, Ivar replied, dutifully, "Aye, my lord Selwyrn."

"My son shall be the rightful king of England," Duncan whispered when he had drawn close to Ivar. "Any child of Amica's will be considered an heir to the throne. Even Henry knows this, just as he knows that he can never stand against Sacre Placean and keep his throne."

"But . . . the lady Alys . . . "

"Is dead. Amica of Lancaster is the mother of my

son." Duncan's hand lifted to Ivar's bare throat, which he stroked with his fingertips. "Find her, Ivar. Find her soon and bring her back to this place where she belongs."

Ivar swallowed loudly. "I have had my men searching everywhere, my lord. I tell you, there has been no sign of her."

Duncan chuckled. "No sign of a woman so beautiful and rare?" he asked with disbelief. "It is impossible for her to go without notice wherever she may be. I have seen men, strong and healthy, faint from the mere sight of her."

"That is so, my lord Selwyrn, but no one has seen a woman of rare beauty, save for one who travels with her husband."

Duncan's eyebrows rose with interest. "With her husband and no one else? Is there no old man with them?"

"Nay, lord. There are only two knights, in service to the man."

"No maidservant?"

"Nay."

"That is uncommon, do you not think, Ivar?"

"Aye!" Ivar squeaked as his master's hand closed around his throat.

Duncan's eyes grew dark, and his lips curved at the edges into a solemn frown.

"Did you let her slip through your fingers, Ivar? For something so stupid as a false husband?"

Unable to speak, Ivar desperately shook his head. Duncan squeezed tighter.

"Find my wife, Ivar. Find her and bring her back to me, else I'll carve her name on your flesh and leave you with nothing more than that to comfort you on your journey to Hell."

9

"What place is this, my lord?" Amica asked, as they rode through the gates surrounding the village and grand castle they'd been riding toward for the last several hours.

"Belhaven," Thomas replied. "It is the place of my master's birth."

"Is it not also your place of birth, my lord?"

"It is."

"You will be glad to see your own people then, if only for a night."

His arm tightened about her waist.

"I have no people. They are all gone."

But as they rode through the handsome village of Belhaven, Amica wondered if Thomas of Reed spoke the truth. People on all sides hailed him, lifting their hands in greeting and shouting for others to come and greet him as well. By the time they reached the castle, a large crowd had gathered. Ignoring them, Thomas set Amica upon the ground and then dismounted. Only when he had handed Maelgwn over to a waiting servant did he solemnly begin to greet the people around him. Keeping a hand about Amica's waist, he extended the other and gripped those held out to him.

"Tom, well met," said a man of an age with him.

"Samuel," Thomas acknowledged him with a nod as he turned to others in the crowd. "Alex. Brian."

Amica had begun to tremble at the sight of so many unknown faces, and with a hand kept her own face covered with the hood of her cloak. Soon his acquaintances began to demand of Thomas who she was, and he replied, simply, "This is my wife," to which the entire crowd responded with loud cheers.

"Thomas has a wife!" someone shouted. "Let's see her, Tom!"

"Aye!" shouted another. "Show us your bride!"

"Is she a beauty, Tom? Or is it her ugliness that she hides?"

Thomas's arm tightened about her and Amica knew he felt her shaking. She pressed her face against his chest and gripped his tunic.

"Get back," Stevan said angrily from beside her, having dismounted as well.

A hand reached out to pull at her cloak, and Amica gave a little squeal.

"Do not," Thomas said in a stern voice, "or I'll break your arm, John. Leave my lady be. She is timid and you are all noising and crude."

"Don't let them frighten you, my lady," Derryn said from somewhere behind her. "Tom was a mischief maker when he was a lad, and most of these were counted amongst his gang of troublous knaves."

"Derry . . ." Thomas warned.

"You see that they still hail him as their leader,"

Derryn went on. "More trouble, that's what they're looking to make."

The thought of Thomas of Reed behaving in any way less perfect and proper than a saint almost made Amica laugh, but the sound of a voice of authority stopped her.

"I am one who can speak of this lad's poor behavior. He was ever a thorn in my flesh before my son took him away from Belhaven. A troublous knave, indeed."

There were few people to whom Thomas went down on his knee. His master, certainly, and his master's lady. The king, also, and a few certain members of his master's family.

Hearing now the voice of his master's father, Thomas lifted his head and sought the face of Sir Garin Stavelot, the lord of Belhaven.

"My lord," he murmured, surging forward. When he went to his knee before the tall, golden-haired giant, he took Amica with him.

"Thomas." Garin Stavelot spoke the name with love, and Amica felt the man's big hand settle upon them. "You must ever be as you are, but will you never learn to greet me as you should? I do not want you on your knee."

Ignoring him, Thomas took the lord of Belhaven's hand and kissed the back of it reverently.

"My lord," he said again. "I praise God that I have seen you once more. Have you word of my master?"

Pulling her face from its hiding place beneath Thomas's arm, Amica peeked at the lord of Belhaven. She had heard much of this man, and knew much, for Garin Stavelot was the son of her grandfather's former master, and her grandfather had spent many a night recounting the adventures they had once shared. The lord of Belhaven was a handsome man, she saw, with long blond hair and eyes of blue. His son, Eric Stavelot, was accounted throughout all of Britain as a giant, so that Amica was not entirely surprised to find that the father, as well, was exceedingly big.

"Eric is well, Tom, and pleased to have another daughter delivered safely of his lady, hale and hearty. The messenger arrived only yesterday with the blessed news."

"May God be praised," Thomas murmured fervently, so unlike the man Amica had come to know that she twisted her head to gaze at him. Her regard drew his eyes, and, after a moment of bewilderment, he suddenly seemed to realize that she was bent and helpless beneath his arm, her legs awkwardly pressed upon the ground on which he knelt.

Scowling, and tugging at the hood of her cloak to keep it over her face, Thomas rose to his feet, drawing Amica up, and turned his frown upon the lord of Belhaven.

"This is . . . Amica," he stated uncertainly, at which statement both he and Amica waited for some kind of reaction.

The lord of Belhaven drew nearer, placing one hand on each of their shoulders.

"Your wife," he said. "So you did proclaim, Tom, and so I gladly heard. You have given my heart great joy this day, lad, and shall give my lady's heart joy, for you are as our son's son. May God be praised." Bending, he kissed Amica's forehead through the cloak. "Daughter, be welcome here," he murmured. "Belhaven shall be as your home." He set an arm about Thomas's shoulders and hugged him fiercely. "I do not know why Eric said naught of this, but it does not matter, for this night we shall celebrate. This night," he said, drawing away and grinning, "we will give thanks to know that our Tom has at last taken to himself a wife."

*   *   *

"I want to tell him," Amica said stubbornly, crossing her arms over her breasts. "He should know, and my grandfather would have desired it."

"Your grandfather would not have desired anything that might cause you harm," Thomas told her wearily, wishing the woman would give way and leave him in peace. They'd been arguing from the moment they had been left alone in their chamber, and naught had come of it save a throbbing in the back of Thomas's skull. He disliked being in Belhaven; arguing with a stubborn female only made being there that much worse.

"Surely you cannot think that the lord of Belhaven would ever do me harm? The father of your own sainted master?"

Ignoring her caustic tone, Thomas walked to the chamber's one window and flung the covering aside. He couldn't very well deny that she had reason to be angered. He felt a little angry himself, as well as bewildered. This was not the welcome he had expected from Sir Garin, who had always before been privy to every one of the king's secrets. Thomas had expected, nay, even depended upon, Sir Garin knowing more of this matter than Thomas himself did. That he knew nothing, had not even been expecting Thomas to bring Amica of Lancaster to Belhaven on their journey toward Reed, made Thomas feel rather lost. Worst of all, Sir Garin and his wife, Lady Elaine, were joyously happy over the news of his marriage. Even now they hurried to arrange a feast for the eve. Thinking of it, Thomas groaned and lifted a hand to rub that place in the back of his head where it felt as if someone were striking him with an axe. Sir Garin and Lady Elaine had ever treated him with love and kindness. What would they think when

they discovered that this wedding they meant to celebrate was naught but a counterfeit?

Amica moved to stand behind him. "My grandfather
saved his life many times over. For that alone Garin
Stavelot would be required to lend me every aid. I have
naught to fear from him."

"I do not know why my master gave him no warning
of our arrival," Thomas told her, "for surely Sir Eric
knew I would bring you to Belhaven when we passed by
it. But he did not see fit to do so, and I shall not do
more than he. 'Tis clear the king wishes no one to know
of you, and so we will go on as we have done. You shall
be nothing more than my wife until we reach Reed."

"But I am not your wife!" she protested hotly. "I am
Amica of Lancaster!"

Angry, Thomas spun around, grabbing her by the
arms. "And what is *that*, woman? I have no knowledge
of you. Sir Garin knows naught of you. You do not
seem to exist, save to the king, who wants no one to
know of you, and to Duncan Selwyrn, who pursues you
as though you were a thief. What, then, are you, that
you should want to make such a boast of it?"

Her bottom lip began to tremble, and her eyes filled
with moisture.

"N-naught. I am naught, and have ever been." A tear
slipped out of one eye and slid down her cheek. "But
my grandfather was worthy. I would have him mourned
by a man who loved him well. I would have him
mourned . . . "

A sob stopped her words, and Thomas stared as she
began to cry in earnest. He released her as if she burned
him, and took a step away. Amica bowed her head, covered her face with both hands, and wept helplessly, her
sobs shaking her slender body. These tears were vastly
different from those Thomas had seen her shed because

of her fears. These tears, born of her grief and loss and his thoughtless cruelty, made his heart ache with remorse.

"I . . ." Thomas began, wondering what he should do. He had led men into battle, had faced bigger armies than his own and enemies stronger than he was, yet had seldom known fear; but this—this small, weeping woman who grieved so deeply for her grandfather— was more terrifying than anything he'd faced before. He wished, with all his heart, that Derryn or Stevan were there in his place.

"Am-muh . . . Ama-hum . . ." He couldn't even get her name out of his mouth. She began to sway and, afraid she might fall, Thomas did the only thing that seemed to make any sense: he bent and picked her up. Her arms went about his neck and her face pressed against his shoulder and Thomas stood there, holding her, cradling her in his arms, and felt even more terrified.

Moving to the bed and settling Amica firmly on his lap, Thomas sought to ignore her wretched tears and tried to think of what to do. He had seen Sir Eric console his wife before, and also his daughters, when they'd been overset. Doing his best to recall exactly how his master had gone about the matter, Thomas set out to soothe Amica of Lancaster.

Lifting a hand, he tentatively patted her back, mur- muring, "There, now. There, there."

She drew in a loud breath, gave a sob and a hiccup, then settled once more. Her crying lessened slightly, and Thomas felt encouraged.

"I'm sorry," he murmured. "You loved him, and he was a fine man, worthy of much love and such honor as you would give him. I wish you could speak of him to Sir Garin. Verily, I do."

"He . . . was the . . . only one," she managed tearfully.

"The . . . *only* one . . . my whole life. Now he's gone . . . gone."

Thomas understood what it was she tried to say. He, too, had had only one person in his life to love him, at least when he'd been young.

"I'm sorry," he said once more, unable to think of anything else. Sir Eric had always kissed the lady Margot whenever she'd been distraught, and she had never failed to calm, but the idea of kissing Amica of Lancaster—any female—made Thomas's stomach turn.

He had been kissed twice in his life. The first time he'd been ten and five years of age. Sir Eric had caught him contemplating one of the prettier serving maids at Castle Reed, and had shortly thereafter taken him to visit one of the village whores, a woman old enough to be mother to both of them. What followed had been quite pleasant until the woman, in her excitement, pulled Thomas's mouth down to hers and kissed him fully, thrusting her tongue past his lips. The foul taste of her unclean mouth and rotted teeth had finished the matter before Thomas could. He'd gone away from her humble dwelling disgusted, unfulfilled and miserable and had to suffer his master's laughter and relentless jests all the way back to the castle. Later that night he'd sought out the pretty chambermaid and finished with her what he'd started with the whore, though he'd refused to kiss her when she'd asked it of him.

The second time had been some years later, while he'd been mounted upon a tavern whore with whom he'd nearly finished. At the moment of his release, the crazy female had wrapped both her hands about his neck, squeezed as if she would choke him, and pulled his mouth down to hers and kissed and bitten him, using lips, tongue and teeth until his own lips and tongue had bled—the sight of which had given the

madwoman her own satisfaction. He'd had cuts and
bruises around his mouth for days and had sorely suffered the taunts and jests of his men.

Since that time, he had not kissed a woman, and had
no desire to do so, despite the fact that Sir Eric and
every other man he knew seemed to enjoy the activity a
good deal.

And yet, he thought, lowering his eyes to gaze at the
wet and unhappy face pressed against his shoulder,
Amica of Lancaster's lips looked very pretty and soft.
She kept her mouth clean, he knew, for he had come to
know something of her washing habits, and she was
possessed of all her teeth. He wondered, in an indiffer-
ent manner, what it would be like to set his mouth over
hers. It might possibly be enough to make her cease her
tears and, as he was the cause of those tears, it was his
duty to do everything he could to make amends.
Indeed, she might even expect it of him, though that
thought made him frown, for he had never known
Amica of Lancaster to be forward or lacking in propriety, and if Derry or Stevan were here, in his place, she
surely would not welcome such caresses from them. Of
course, they were neither of them her husband, as he
was, and neither had the right to touch her, as he did.
That truth, for some unknown reason, filled Thomas
with relief, and without further reflection he took her
chin in his fingers, tilted her face upward, and put his
mouth on hers.

His first thought, after a moment passed and as
Amica went utterly still, was that she was in no way
repulsive. His second thought was that her lips were,
indeed, quite as soft as they looked. His third thought
was that he wasn't doing this correctly, for he had seen
many men kiss women and had always noted that some
kind of movement was involved. Having ever been the

kind of man who strove to do things to the best of his ability, Thomas pressed his mouth against hers a bit more firmly and tried to duplicate the movements he had seen others make.

And that, for some time, was the last coherent thought he had.

Amica's thoughts flew away the moment she realized what Thomas of Reed was doing. When he set his lips over hers, she stiffened with shock and terror, unable to do anything save wait, frozen beyond movement, for the pain she knew would follow.

But several moments passed and there was no pain. He did not put a fist in her hair and pull until her eyes filled with tears. He did not set his hand against her throat and squeeze until she lost consciousness. He didn't even press his fingernails into her arms until she squealed from the pain. All he did was sit there, holding her, his warm mouth laid against hers, and was still.

Amica didn't think she'd ever been more surprised by anything in her life, but then he began to move his lips over hers, gently and carefully, and her surprise ascended into complete wonder.

It lasted a long while, it seemed, though Amica could not have said how long exactly. As each moment slipped by, so did her terror slip away, and she began to feel, instead, a curious heat low in her belly and an odd tingling in her breasts. She felt numb all over, so that when he at last lifted his mouth away she couldn't even open her eyes to look at him. They both sounded as if they'd been running, and she could feel his breath, hot and rapid, against her face.

He made a sound, somewhere between a curse and a groan, and stood, letting Amica fall back on the bed. Her eyes flew open and she saw Thomas stalking back to the window, both his hands fisted in his hair.

"My lord?" she said, and was amazed at the weakness of her voice.

He kept his back to her and said nothing. She wondered if he was going to pull his hair out, his fists strained so hard, and then, all at once, he let out a loud breath and his fingers relaxed and his hands fell to his sides. Still he gazed out the window, and Amica said again, "My lord?"

He looked at her over his shoulder.

"What?"

"Well, I . . . "

"Why do you look at me so?" he demanded. "Have you never been kissed before?"

Amica gingerly touched her lips. "I do not think so."

The words seemed to soften him, and he said, less gruffly, "You were crying, and I wanted you to stop. That is all. There was naught else to it."

"I see."

Silence passed. Thomas turned his gaze back out the window, and Amica cleared her throat and murmured, "I am sorry, my lord."

"Nay," he said abruptly. "I am the one who should speak words of apology. I did not mean to . . . offend you, my lady."

Offend? Amica thought. What a strange word to use. He had not offended her. Not in the very least.

"I will leave you to rest. Lady Elaine has said that she will send a bath. Be pleased to use it as you will. I shall bathe later."

He walked toward the door, but Amica leapt off the bed and ran in front of him.

"Please, my lord, I would not stay here alone."

Her eyes were filled with fear, Thomas saw, and he wondered, with a stab of regret, whether he had done that to her with his unskilled kiss.

"I cannot abide to be alone in a castle chamber," she went on, setting a hand on his arm. "Please let me accompany you, Sir Thomas."

Frowning at the tiny hand that stayed him, he said, "I mean to go to the village. You cannot desire to go there."

Her expression brightened visibly. "I would be glad to, if you will allow it. I shall not put myself in your way, I vow. Please, my lord, I beg you."

Thomas didn't want to be in her company, not until he could make some sense of what had happened to him a few moments ago. His head was still buzzing as if it were a hive filled with angry bees, and the rest of him—well, in truth, the rest of him felt as if it were on fire, a state of being that distressed him to no small degree. He was not in control of himself, as he always was, and he disliked it. She was the cause—Amica of Lancaster—and he liked that even less.

"I will not be vexing," she promised pleadingly. "You shall not know I am there."

Her hand, he thought, was a miraculous thing. 'Twas small and white and pretty, yet while it lay soft upon his arm it held him utterly powerless. He could not do other than give way, and so, though he dreaded her nearness and what it did to him, he said, in a low voice, "You may come."

10

The small dwelling was nearly empty. A ring of rocks that had clearly served as a fire pit lay in the middle of the room and a pile of dirty straw took up one corner; near the ring of rocks one lone, simple stool sat. It was a dark, chilly place, long untouched by human warmth, and Amica shivered and moved closer to where Thomas stood.

"What place is this?" she asked softly.

His gaze moved slowly about the dwelling. "I lived here once."

She shivered again and whispered, "Oh."

"After my father died, my master wished to burn it to the ground, but I would not let him."

"Burn it?" Amica rubbed her arms with her hands. "Why should he have wished to do such a thing? It is not so poor that it cannot give shelter."

"It will never again give shelter. That is not why I wished to let it stand. It is mine, and so long as I live, I shall keep it, simply to see it and to . . . remember." He looked at her. "My mother and father both died here. I spent my childhood here. This is more a smithy than a dwelling place, for I was forged here, just as steel is forged by fire."

His eyes and words seemed haunted to Amica, and she felt an overwhelming, bewildering urge to give him comfort, though for what, she did not know. This place held bitterness for him, that much she could see in his face and hear in his words.

She looked about the room. "It is almost empty. One would have to sleep on the ground to use it as shelter."

"Aye," he agreed solemnly. "'Twould make a better lodging for sheep or cattle than men. Everything of use was taken away by the villagers. 'Twas well, for I wanted none of it."

"The little stool . . . ?" she asked.

"'Tis kept here for me, they . . . the villagers make certain of it. I gave it away many times but always it is here when I return." A shrug lifted his shoulders. "I have been glad of it. Sit, if you desire to do so."

"Oh no, I would rather not. Please, my lord, do not let me disturb you. You must do as you wish." Moving forward, seeing his troubled expression, she pressed, "Did you wish to sit for a time? I will be very quiet."

"Nay." He frowned. "'Tis foolishness to come here. I will stop doing so, in time."

He would not look at her, but kept gazing about the room as if he would find something he sought. Amica remembered the dream he had suffered the night before.

"Your mother and father," she said, searching his face even as he searched the dwelling, "have been long dead?"

"My mother, aye, since I was a child. I do not remember her overmuch."

"And your father?"

"He died when I was ten and four. No one has lived here since that time."

"You became squire to Sir Eric then?"

"I was my lord's squire before that time. For two full years I had taken care of him."

"You were not with your father, then, when he fell ill?" She thought perhaps his dreams were weighted with guilt.

"Ill?" Thomas repeated. "He was not ill."

"Oh. Was it an accident, then, that caused his death?"

"Nay," he muttered, moving around the room. "Or mayhap it was. I do not know."

"You do not know?"

"Nay, I do not know how he died. Sometimes I wonder . . ." He stopped his restless pacing and rubbed at the back of his neck. "I come here and try to remember what happened, but I do not know that I ever will. It seems very clear at times, but never clear enough. He was found here." He pointed to the corner where the pile of straw was. "Here. He had struck his head upon the table, or so it seemed. I do not know if he fell, or if he was pushed, or if it was the table or some wielded instrument that did the harm."

"You were here?" she whispered.

"Yes."

"But you do not remember what passed?"

He began to look troubled again. "Nay." He cast his gaze about the room. "It will come to me one day. I believe it will."

Amica let out a breath that sounded loud in the small dwelling, and then she, like Thomas, fell silent. A few moments passed before she spoke. "My father died four years ago. His passing meant little to me, for my sister and I were his bastards and he did no more than acknowledge and endow us with suitable marriage portions. I grieved for him as best I could, though I had not seen him above a dozen times in my life."

Glancing up, she saw that she had Thomas of Reed's full attention. He had ceased to look troubled, and now looked only thoughtful and that, for some odd reason, made Amica continue speaking.

"My mother died when we were young, and upon my father's passing my sister and I became the wards of Duncan Selwyrn, the lord of Sacre Placean."

She seemed to have stunned him, for Thomas of Reed's eyes widened and he said with disbelief, "Duncan Selwyrn is your *guardian?*"

"He was," she replied truthfully.

"Yet you run from him," he said, "and the king himself gives countenance. How can this be? If he is legally your guardian, he has every right to pursue and hold you." Thomas set a hand to his head. "And my master—even my master lends you aid! He could be punished for it, for breaking the laws of England!" He glared at her accusingly.

Amica's voice drifted to a trembling whisper. "Duncan held me nearly four years. Was that not enough? I was as his prisoner. I passed over the threshold of Castle Sacre Placean and did not again feel the warmth of the sun until the day that I escaped." She took a step toward him. "Four years, my lord. The days were endless. I would have killed myself if I could have only found a way."

"Those," he said sharply, "are truly the words of a woman. Weak and foolish. God's feet!" He ran a hand through his hair in exasperation. "What of your sister? Was she kept a prisoner, as well?"

She flushed deeply before answering, "No. Not as I was."

"Your grandfather said she died."

Amica nodded. "Yes."

"By Selwyrn's hand?"

She spoke so softly that he almost could not hear her. "I do not know."

The feeling Thomas had known the night before, the one that he would shortly need to kill someone, welled up in him, but he reminded himself that Sir Eric knew more of this matter than he, and that if Selwyrn had, in truth, harmed an innocent maid, Sir Eric would certainly deal out justice.

"Come. Let us walk in the village. I must think on the matter."

He strode past her and into the sunlight and Amica obediently followed. Several villagers hailed Thomas as they made their way, but he responded with little more than nods and grunts. At last they came to the village well, where several of the young men sat, relaxing and conversing. When they caught sight of Thomas they stood and greeted him heartily.

"Well met, Tom!"

"Tom, lad, how have you fared of late?"

"Bring your wife forward, Tom, let us see her!"

"Aye, let us see her!"

Stopping in the midst of them, Thomas said, "Fools. She is only a woman, not some fine steed to be admired."

He felt Amica press close behind him, trembling, and when she slipped her small, shaking hand into his he instinctively wrapped his fingers around it. In his agitation over her recent revelation, he had forgotten how timid she was. As well, she no longer seemed afraid of him, and if Thomas had not seen for himself how her fears could overcome her, he would not have believed she was possessed of them. But she *was* possessed of fears, and now she suffered them because of his own stupidity. Smothering a curse, he turned and enfolded her in his arms.

"By all that's holy, Tom, she's a beauty!"

"Aye, a great beauty, indeed, lad. Well done!"

"How did you ever come to be so blessed, Tom?"

Blessed? Thomas thought vaguely, wondering if his childhood friends had lost their minds. This was marriage they spoke of, after all. And, yet, an odd feeling of possessiveness overcame him at their open admiration of Amica, and his hand moved to pull the hood of her cloak over her face, to hide her from their eyes, only to find her hair, instead. Glancing down, he saw that her head was bare of a proper covering.

He briefly considered telling her that she was a bad wife to go out so indecently clad, also that he would not countenance such a lack of propriety from her again, but somehow he could not, and said, instead, "Yes, she is very beautiful." Which was, he decided, no more than the simple truth.

"Kiss her!" someone shouted, and they all began to shout.

"Aye, kiss her, Tom!"

"Kiss your lady wife!"

Thomas saw Amica's eyes widen. He frowned, thinking that she had naught to fear from him and that he had every right to kiss her if he pleased. She was his wife, and a man might kiss his wife if he wished to do so.

"My lord, you must not . . ." Amica began in an admonishing tone, which was a great mistake, for it only made Thomas feel stubborn.

He set one hand against the side of her face to hold her still, ignored the shocked expression in her eyes, and lowered his mouth, determined that he would kiss her for as long as he pleased, or at least for as long as the villagers cheered, which turned out to be much longer than he had hoped.

11

"*Cease your worrying* and come to wash my back. The water has grown cold and I would be out of it."

Amica reached the chamber's one window, glanced outside of it briefly, turned sharply about and walked back toward the door.

"Can you not wash your own back?" she called out, directing the words over the screen behind which Thomas of Reed sat bathing.

A deep, masculine *huh!* drifted past the screen, and then Thomas said, "A wife should do such as that for her husband. If a man cannot expect his woman to attend to so small a duty, then he cannot expect much from her at all."

Having reached the door, Amica turned and began back in the direction of the window.

"I am not your wife," she reminded him.

"You are. Do not argue truths with me, for thus does a woman's tongue grow wearisome. Come and wash my back."

"You did not do the same for me," she charged, reaching the window and making her turn. "Indeed, you did not even offer to do so."

"A man does not lower himself to such menial tasks. It is for a woman to do, and you did have maids to attend you."

Amica gave no answer to this, but continued to pace until Thomas said, in a warning tone, "My lady . . . "

With a sigh, Amica put her steps in the direction of the screen. "Very well. I will do it, but no more after this, for I am neither your wife nor your serving maid. Set your towel about you, sir."

He was sitting in the large wooden tub that Amica had earlier used to bathe in, his broad, muscular arms and shoulders gleaming with water and his white hair lying wet across the top of his back. He had arranged a large towel about his waist and sat forward.

She first pulled up the sleeves of the chemise she wore, then put her hand into the jar of potted soap set nearby on a stool and scooped some out.

The moment her hands touched him, Thomas rested his forehead upon his hands, which were folded on his indrawn knees, and closed his eyes.

As she set to washing his back, she said, "You should have a squire to tend you."

"Hmm," he intoned. "I have never had a squire."

"Never?" She was truly amazed.

"No."

"I thought every knight who achieved such stature as you kept for himself a squire. 'Tis your right."

"I have never wanted one." He sounded very relaxed. "He would ever be underfoot, and I could not abide such as that."

Having finished, Amica pulled her hands from him

and made to rinse the soap from her hands, but Thomas sat up quickly and looked back at her.

"Did you not miss a part?"

"I do not think so, my lord." She glanced at his glistening skin. "Indeed, you appear most clean."

"But it did not seem as if you did much," he protested. "Do it again, and be thorough about it."

"But—"

"Although you are but a woman, surely even you can do a proper job of washing a man's back."

She was tempted to throw the jar of potted soap at him, but scooped up another handful of the stuff and slapped it on his back.

"You are a most foolish man, my lord," she said as she began to scrub his skin rigorously. "Foolish and stubborn."

With a grunt of satisfaction, Thomas leaned forward once more, closing his eyes and resting his forehead upon his hands. "Be thorough this time," he reminded her.

"I was thorough last time," she said, but he gave no reply. They both fell silent, and the sounds of soapy water and her rubbing joined the sounds of the hot fire. After a moment, Amica felt Thomas relax and she leaned forward to glance into his face.

He looked as content as a happy child with his mouth relaxed into a slight smile and his face possessed by a look of intense pleasure. Perhaps a child was not the right creature to compare him to at the moment, she thought, for he reminded her very much of a pleased, purring cat, and Amica realized, all at once, as her hands slowed their motion to a more gentle kneading, that Thomas of Reed was starved for such as this . . . for a gentle touch. A caress. The idea softened her heart and stilled her anger, for she knew what it was to hunger for kindness, for gentleness. Splaying her fingers wide, she glided her hands over the hard, smooth muscles in his shoulders, massaging gently. He nearly moaned with pleasure, and Amica smiled. She had learned much of Thomas of Reed in the past few days, but what she learned now was the most important of all. Despite his hardness and strength, the boy he'd once been yet lived in him. A lonely boy, mayhap, motherless, frightened, denied, and aye, as bitter as the man.

She made his washing last a long while, for understanding what it was he truly craved she saw no reason to deny him, and it pleased her to make him happy, though she could not begin to understand why that should be so. He thoroughly disliked her. Amica shuddered anew when she thought of the way he had looked at her in the village before he kissed her, and during the feast that the lord and lady of Belhaven had given in their honor, when he'd been made, by Sir Garin's stern request, to kiss his lady wife for the benefit of those assembled. Each time, as he had bent over her, his eyes had been alive with fury and anger, and Amica had been more than a little afraid. And yet, his kisses had been as gentle as the one he had given her to stop her tears— gentle and wonderfully pleasant—so that she had felt almost lost when they had ended. What Thomas of Reed had felt, Amica could not fathom. She had assumed he would be relieved to have such false embraces brought to an end, and yet he had looked even angrier afterward than he had before. Perhaps, she thought, cupping warm water in her hands and pouring it over his soapy skin, she had done it all wrong. Perhaps her kisses were horrible and gave him a great disgust, and that might verily be true, for she had found Duncan's kisses fully disgusting while he had clearly enjoyed them a great deal.

"There," she said, standing and handing him a dry towel. "You are pure as the Virgin's heart."

With a sigh, he straightened, stretching. "Thank you," he murmured, taking the towel.

Amica moved around the screen, leaving him to dress. She was ready to start her pacing again, but Thomas's voice stopped her.

"Your hair is still damp," he said, and Amica wondered how he could have possibly taken note of that while he'd been in his tub. "Go and stand by the fire. I'll not have you fall ill before we reach Reed."

With a laugh, Amica moved toward the fire. "And after Reed, my lord?"

"After Reed," Thomas said, walking out from behind the screen, dressed in clean leggings and a tunic, "I will not care whether you take a chill or no. 'Tis of no matter to me then unless my master should suffer by it."

Amica stood with her back to the flames, exposing her long, unbound hair to the heat. "Ah, your master," she said. "Of course. My life only has value if it has any value to him."

Thomas strolled to a table where a decanter and two goblets were set. "It has value to yourself, or to others. It simply has no value to me."

"You are kind, my lord," Amica said mockingly, and took the goblet he held out to her.

"I am honest, as I told you I am. Drink all that I have given you. Mayhap it will calm you."

She took a sip of the rich wine, and afterward said, hopefully, "Mayhap."

Drinking his own wine, keeping his eyes on her pale face, watching the way her eyes moved about the chamber as if it would cause her some harm, Thomas knew that nothing, save leaving the castle, would calm her. She'd been nervous and tense from the moment they had returned from the village, even through the merry feast that had been given in their honor.

"You did very well this eve," he told her suddenly, thinking of how well mannered she was. Though she'd been ill at ease and timid, she had never once embarrassed him. Indeed, she had behaved exactly as any high-born lady might, much to Thomas's relief. If he must have a wife, even for a short time, he would far rather have one like Amica of Lancaster, who knew how to eat properly at table and who answered every question sent her way with polite deference. If the truth be known, Thomas had actually felt rather proud of his temporary wife.

"Thank you, my lord," Amica said. "The lord and lady of Belhaven are kind, indeed. 'Twas an honor to accept their gracious hospitality. 'Tis clear that they love you well, and count you among their family."

"They are the kindest people on God's earth," he said with honest affection. "You have pleased me well this night by pleasing them. It will go hard with me when they must learn the truth of our marriage."

"Yes, it shall, I think. I can understand now why my grandfather loved both of them so, Lady Elaine and Sir Garin. Did you know that he was godfather to their eldest son, Sir James? My grandfather was, I mean."

Thomas shook his head.

"Well, he was," Amica said, setting aside the empty goblet. Leaning back, she closed her eyes and began to run her fingers through her hair, separating the strands to let them dry more rapidly.

Hearing the sadness in her voice, thinking of how mornfully she had wept over her grandfather earlier, Thomas said, "I will tell Sir Garin about his death in the morn. I give you my solemn vow that I will do so."

Lifting her head, Amica gazed at him with a shining gratitude that took Thomas's breath away. The fire shone behind her, making a halo of her hair and outlining her body through the chemise she wore. The image worked powerfully on Thomas, for her arms were lifted, her fingers yet tangled in her hair, pulling the thin garment away from her body so that he saw her most clearly.

"Oh, my lord," she whispered. "Thank you."

What followed after this thoroughly confounded Thomas. He could only believe, during the days that followed and as he considered the matter, that his body had been so often aroused by Amica of Lancaster during the time that he'd known her that he reached for her out of some overwhelming, undeniable, *maddening* need.

She was in his arms before his mind acknowledged the fact, and when the shock of this melted away in the more demanding heat of his desire, he realized, albeit dimly, that she was there willingly.

This was not like the other kisses they had shared. There was no tentativeness or newness attached to the experience, so that his mouth moved over hers knowingly; there were no others to watch them, to distract them. To make them stop.

Her mouth opened beneath the force of his, and the moist heat he found there made him groan with pleasure. She made a sighing sound in turn, then lifted her hands and set them about his neck. It was that—the touch of her fingers on his skin—that made him lose the already uncertain grip he had on his control.

His hands moved over her clumsily, with desperation, caressing, discovering, pressing her tightly against his aching, needy self. Untutored as he was, he did not know how to be gentle. Everything about her—the curve of her waist and hips, the delicateness of her bones, the softness of her breasts—was a revelation. He did not realize that he was being rough; he only knew one way to use a woman and that way was direct and practical. He wanted her, he would take her. There was nothing else to it.

He heard himself saying her name as he took her down to the floor. "Amica." The word sounded breathless and pleading and bewildered him, briefly. Pressing her to her back and pushing her knees apart, Thomas knelt above her. He tried to look at her, to see her face, but he felt mindless of all save the goal of fitting his body into the warm, blessed woman's place between her legs. Grasping the hem of her garment, he pulled her skirt up to her waist, then set his hand to the laces of his leggings. Tugging at them, he put his mouth to hers once more, thinking vaguely that he had never kissed a woman while he was inside of her.

And then he froze. All at once and completely, he fell utterly still. A moment passed before he realized why, and then he knew what it was. Lifting his head, he stared into her face and saw the tears that he had tasted on her lips.

"Wha—? Why do you . . . cry?"

Her mouth trembled, and Amica shook her head.

Thomas tried to calm his breathing, to gain control of his body's demanding urge to assuage its need. It was with shock that he realized what he wanted to do to her—what he'd been about to do. To *her*.

"God's mercy," he whispered, sitting back on his knees, drawing in deep breaths. "God's mercy, you are a *witch!*"

With a sob, Amica set one hand over her mouth. With the other she tried to tug down her chemise to cover herself.

Thomas scooted farther away, staring at her with all the horror he felt at what he had almost done.

"God above," he said, gaining his feet and stumbling to the nearest wall, which he leaned against for support. Amica lay where she was, just as he had put her with her knees pushed apart and her legs exposed, weeping and shaking her head.

"Amica, stop. Please, I beg it . . . "

She went on crying as if she didn't hear him. Thomas ran his hands through his hair and shuddered. "I have never done such a thing before. Never." He drew in a harsh breath. "'Tis clear that you have bewitched me, that you have cast some sorcery upon me, just as you must have done to the lord of Sacre Placean. Oh, aye, that must be so," he said when she stopped shaking her head and looked at him. "For such as that he had good reason to lock you away, else you would cause much trouble, just as you have done. I can only thank God you did not cast your wiles upon Derryn or Stevan, for they might have more easily been ensnared." His gaze hardened with his words.

She said nothing, but lay upon the rushes with the firelight playing over her still form. The hand that had covered her mouth relaxed and drifted to rest upon her throat, but she remained silent, giving no defense so that, in Thomas's mind, she gave truth to his words.

His expression became one of disgust. He pushed away from the wall and strode toward the chamber door. "I will find another place to sleep."

Amica sat up quickly. "No!"

Thomas heard her rise to her feet, but he was already at the door and opening it.

"Don't leave me alone!" she cried. His last glimpse of her before he shut the door showed him an image he would carry throughout the night, as he sat alone in the dwelling he had once shared with his father, one with Amica's arms stretched toward him and her face filled with terror. He did not lock her in, though she must have thought he did. All the way down the hall he could hear her crying after him, calling his name and pounding on the door, begging him not to leave her alone.

12

The valley that spread out below them was wide and long and very beautiful. Neatly mapped fields, freshly tilled and planted, promised to yield rich crops in the coming harvest of late summer. Further on, a town that had spilled outside its former walls gave evidence to the land's prosperity, and beyond this sat a large, quite magnificent castle.

Lifting her face to the warm afternoon sun, Amica knew a deep sense of pleasure. How different this was from the wild, cold, hilly lands of Sacre Placean. She wondered, for the first time since their journey had begun, whether she was far away from Sacre Placean now. She hoped she was, though it didn't really matter. Duncan would not care how far she went, and she would not be safe from him forever until either he, or she, was dead.

"Is it Reed, my lord?" Amica asked, seeing the answer in Thomas of Reed's face.

"Aye," he murmured, his attention fixed on the large castle in the valley. "It is Reed."

Derryn reined in beside her. "He'll not be fit company for the rest of our journey, my lady. Not until he's set eyes upon our lord and made certain he is alive and well." He grinned at Thomas's scowl. "He has been Sir Eric's squire since he was but a lad, and no matter what title he may carry, he shall ever be so, worrying o'er our lord's care and comfort. 'Tis the truth I speak," he insisted when Amica lifted her eyebrows in question. "You shall soon see."

"You are a fool, Derry," Thomas told him. "Your speeches waste the day away, as ever, when we might already be nearing home." He glanced at Amica. "And my lord's present squire is naught but a simpleton. Someone must keep an eye open to make certain the boy performs his duties well." Setting his heels into Maelgwn, he started the horse toward Reed.

Amica nudged the mare Sir Garin had given her and followed. Derryn, she heard, set his pace a short distance behind, as had been his custom since they left Belhaven. Despite the fact that Stevan of Hearn had had to remain in Sir Garin's and Lady Elaine's care until his wound had better healed, Amica had felt secure.

The two men were fierce guardians, so much so that Amica had begun to feel a little sorry for those few innocent people who dared to look at her with even the slightest curiosity. Thomas of Reed, especially, had become impatient, gruffly informing every stranger they met that he did not like his wife being stared at and offering to throttle anyone who did so. More than one foolish man who'd tried to peek beneath Amica's cloak in those taverns in which they stayed had found his face hammered by Thomas of Reed's large, heavy and thoroughly unrepentant fist. It was frightening to watch him in such a moment, for he carried out the violent deed calmly, with no emotion whatever showing upon his face. And Derryn Thewlis was just as bad, if not worse, standing to the side and watching his friend pummel complete strangers with a nodding approval.

"Why do you not stop him?" Amica had asked him once, trembling badly at the sight of such violence.

Derryn had merely set his arm about her in a comforting gesture and replied, "I'm not such an idiot as that. There is only one man on this earth who could make him stop, and as our lord of Reed is not here, we must simply let Tom do as he pleases. Never fear," he added, grinning at her with his easy charm. "He'll not kill the fellow."

It seemed a harsh punishment for nothing more than simple curiosity, she thought, and it was strange that Thomas of Reed should feel obliged to do such a thing when he disliked her as greatly as he did. She supposed, however, that he did not protect her so jealously for her own sake; he merely fulfilled the task that his master had given him and, as with everything regarding his master, he sought to do the task as best he could.

He had made his opinion of her clear during these past days since they had left Belhaven. He had as little to do with her as he could, he spoke to her only when necessary, and he stayed close by her solely for the sake of her safety. At night they shared the same chamber, yet they might as well have been in different countries, for Thomas of Reed seldom did so much as to let his eyes fall upon her. Always he was taut, always hard spoken, until Amica began to wonder if she had imagined those times when he had been gentle and kind. She knew that she should hate him, in turn, but she did not. He was the only man, save her grandfather, with whom she had felt truly easy, and despite his anger and coldness, that remained the same.

And despite his dislike, he had not been cruel to her.

Not even on that night when he had left her alone in Castle Belhaven, when she had felt the old fear that she had always known with Duncan. He had returned a few hours after he left and put her to bed, lifting her from the chair where she'd fallen asleep beside the fire.

He had asked her why she had not sought the bed earlier, but she had given no reply, for how could she tell him of what Duncan had done that had taught her never to sleep in her bed at Sacre Placean? Such things were not spoken of. She had not willingly slept in a bed even long after she had left Duncan; it had taken Grandfather many weeks simply to convince her that she would not be attacked while she slumbered. Even so, she had not slept well until Thomas of Reed had come. Indeed, it had only been since then, during these few days while she had shared a chamber with this man who so disliked her, that Amica had at last known again what a deep and peaceful rest was.

On the day they had left Belhaven, he had kept his promise and told Sir Garin about her grandfather's death. Amica had not known what to do when the lord of Belhaven had come out of his working chamber, where Thomas had asked to speak with him, and, oblivious of everyone else present, strode purposefully toward her, his face so taut it seemed made of stone, and took her in his arms and held her tightly. His voice had been thick with anger and grief. "Andrew Fawdry was as fine a man as has ever walked God's earth. He was my friend, and so was I honored to call him. For whatever reason he did not turn to me in his troubles, I do not care. His suffering will not be left unavenged, and thus do I make my vow before God and you."

"He would not trouble you," she whispered. "It was never his wish to involve you in the matter, for he loved you and would not bring you harm."

"He should have turned to me! I owed him more than I could ever repay."

"It was not so simple, and is not still. Only the king may stand against the lord of Sacre Placean, and even he must move with caution, for Duncan holds much sway among the nobles, as you know. I pray God that your son, the lord of Reed, will not be made to suffer for lending me aid."

Sir Garin's arms had tightened around her. "Never fear for Eric, my lady. Duncan Selwyrn would curse the day he e'er thought to menace him, should he be so foolish as to try." Then he added, solemnly, "Selwyrn's days are few, now. Cherish that thought and believe it."

Amica had lifted her head. "But, my lord—"

"Do not fear. I will do naught without the king's permission. And no one shall learn of this matter from my lips. Until the king deems it wise to reveal the truth, you shall be known in Belhaven as the wife of Thomas of Reed." With a smile, he added, "Were that it was so! 'Tis time and since that Tom found himself a pretty wife to keep that scowl from his face, and he would have to search the world over to find another maid as pretty as Amica of Lancaster."

Despite Sir Garin's great kindness and warmth, Amica had been too shy to tell him that she was certainly not the right woman for such a task, for she only seemed to make Thomas of Reed's scowl thrive, and since they had left Belhaven, she had somehow managed to do it quite often.

The horses moved more quickly as they neared the valley, as if knowing by instinct the final destination of their long journey. Thomas of Reed, Amica saw, was leaning forward over Maelgwn's neck as if he would set the steed racing full out toward home. But he didn't. He kept up a steady even pace all the way through the valley, past the fields—where the workers stopped their labors to lift their hands and voices in greetings that were ignored by Sir Thomas but answered cheerily by Sir Derryn—all the way past the town walls and through the town, where the townspeople called out to them and were ignored and then greeted in the same manner that the field workers had been. He even controlled the pace as they neared the bridge that led into the castle's outer courtyard, but the moment Maelgwn crossed the bridge, one of them—either the horse or his master—gave way to desire and they galloped the rest of the way, right up to the steps of the great hall.

There was a good deal of excitement in the inner bailey when Amica and Derryn arrived. People swarmed around Thomas of Reed just as those at Belhaven had done, but he paid them no heed. Shoving Maelgwn's reins into the hands of a soldier who had tried, without success, to greet him, Thomas swung his gaze around and found Amica. In another moment he had pushed past those surrounding him and put his hands on Amica's waist. As he pulled her to the ground, he shouted over the chorus of voices, to Derryn, "Take care of the horses and greet the men. I will come to inspect them in an hour's time."

Amica's feet never touched the ground; Thomas carried her up the steps of Castle Reed and through the doors that were held open by two pages, into the great hall.

"Welcome home, my lord," one of the boys said, to which Thomas replied, "Where is my lord of Reed?"

"He is abovestairs with the lady Margot—"

"Thomas!"

Striving to gain her feet, for she was held under Thomas's strong arm like a bag of grain, Amica lifted her head to see the source of the childish voice that greeted him.

"Thomas is home!" another voice cried, and the next thing Amica knew three young girls sitting by a fire dropped their needlework onto the rushes and were flying in her direction, or, rather, in Thomas's direction.

Instead of letting her go, Thomas hitched Amica up higher in his arm, putting her bid for freedom at an end, and strode forward.

"Elizabeth," he murmured gladly, going down on one knee to catch the girls as they threw themselves at him. "Katy." He kissed each child soundly. "Ellie. Little sweetings."

"You've been gone such a long time!" the eldest, a tall, dark-haired child of nine or ten years, declared.

"And I have missed you all very much," he replied, hugging all three of them at once and unwittingly giving Amica the slight freedom she'd sought. Pushing mightily, she struggled to the floor, where she landed with a *thunk* on the rushes. She sat, legs awry, trying to gather her breath as well as to manage the shock of Thomas of Reed's sudden and complete tenderness with the children.

The younger girls, one blond and quite fair and one a small child of very few years who was as dark as the eldest, both began to babble at once.

"We have a new baby!"

"Why have you been away, Thomas?"

"Who is the lady you've brought?"

Reaching out a hand to grasp Amica's arm, Thomas said, "Not all at once, sweetings. Only give me a moment to—"

"*Tom!*"

The thunderous voice that filled the hall demanded attention, and got it. Every other voice fell silent and, as far as Amica could tell, every head lifted toward the stairs, from where the voice had sounded. Hers certainly did, and when she saw the man who stood there, it became impossible to turn away.

He was a giant. A great, dark, *huge* giant. He made every other man Amica had ever seen, including Thomas of Reed, look frail.

"Tom, lad," he said, his voice filling with warmth and a smile growing on his dark, heavily scarred face. "You have done well, as always. Welcome home to Reed."

Thomas had pulled Amica nearly to her feet, but at the sound of his master's voice, he dropped her back onto the rushes again.

"My lord," he murmured, moving toward the stairs down which the lord of Reed descended.

Amica had envisioned this moment many times during her journey to Reed. Having heard Thomas of Reed speak of his master so often and with such love and devotion, she had expected him to greet Sir Eric Stavelot with something like godly reverence, much as he had greeted the lord of Belhaven. But it was not like that at all. He didn't even go down on his knee, but embraced him heartily and pounded his back just as loudly as his master pounded his, and then, after a moment, he took Sir Eric by the shoulders, held him away and looked him over quite thoroughly.

"You are well?" Thomas demanded in what seemed to Amica an impertinent tone. "You have taken no harm while I've been gone? And Lady Margot is well?"

The lord of Reed laughed. "Aye, Tom, all is well. No evil has befallen us in your absence."

"Siegart has attended all his duties?" Thomas pressed, his searching gaze moving minutely over his master's clothes as if to see whether he was properly dressed. "He has not been slack? You have not had to worry o'er any matter? He has seen to your horse and armor? And has served you well at table? He has given Lady Margot no cause for distress?"

Sir Eric patted Thomas's shoulder in a fatherly manner and said, "I promise you, Tom, all is well. Siegart has done all you have taught him, exactly as you commanded. S'truth, the poor lad lives in fear of any failure, lest he should call your anger down upon his head. Now, be easy. All is well."

Thomas looked unconvinced. He glanced toward the stairs. "Lady Margot?"

"Is hale and hearty, and feeding our new babe. You shall see them both shortly, I vow, but first, be pleased to present Lady Amica to me."

He seemed to have forgotten that she existed until that moment, but at his master's words Thomas swung around to gaze at Amica with a confounded expression. When he saw her sitting on the floor, he scowled and moved toward her.

"You loll about on the rushes when the lord of Reed comes to greet you?" he whispered angrily as he pulled her to her feet. "Have you no manners whatever?"

"I—"

"You tremble," he muttered, and pulled her close, leaning to speak in her ear. "There is no man on this earth whom you can trust more than Sir Eric Stavelot. If you have trusted me, then so much more may you trust him. Do not be afraid."

But she was afraid, for Sir Eric Stavelot was alarming to gaze upon. His darkness and size and fierce features were enough to daunt the most courageous woman, let alone one so timid as she.

Swallowing, Amica gripped Thomas's arm and whispered, "Do not leave me. I beg you."

"You are foolish. No harm will come to you."

Amica flashed a look in the direction of the puzzled

lord of Reed, who now held two of his daughters, one in each strong arm. The children certainly had no fear of the man, she saw, though he looked as if he could easily crush them with but the slightest effort.

"I give you my vow," Thomas went on, pulling her fingernails out of the flesh of his arm. "No harm shall come to you at Reed. I will not allow it."

He spoke the words so solemnly that Amica turned her gaze on him, staring. And she believed him. He had proven himself to be a man of his word. Striving to remember all of her grandfather's admonitions about being strong, Amica let out an unsteady breath and released Thomas completely.

"Very well," she murmured, letting Thomas take her elbow to lead her forward.

"Amica of Lancaster," he said as they drew nearer, "this is Sir Eric Stavelot, the lord of Reed."

Her voice deserted her, but Amica managed a timid bow.

"My lady, I am deeply honored to meet you. You are welcome at Reed."

"Thank you," she whispered, her eyes lowered.

"She's very pretty, Father," the eldest of his girls stated softly, to which the lord of Reed replied, "Yes, she is. These are my daughters, Lady Amica. Elizabeth," he set a hand on the girl's head as she nestled against him, "and Kathryn," he lifted the second girl, more delicate than her dark-haired sisters, higher in his left arm, "and Eleanor." The youngest laughed when she heard her name.

Amica's trembling began to fade, and she smiled at the children.

"I'm glad to meet you all," she told them, then said to Sir Eric, "They're beautiful."

"They are indeed," he stated, not without a little

pride. "I regret that my lady is not here to greet you as well. She is yet abovestairs with our newest daughter. Ah, Jace." He gave his attention to a handsome man who strolled toward them with a languorous gait.

"My lord," he greeted before turning to Amica. "And Thomas," he said without looking at that man. "You have returned."

The sound that came out of Thomas was part word, part growl. "Jace."

"Amica of Lancaster," said Sir Eric, "I make Reed's troubadour known to you. Jace is his name, though you may call him whatever you wish." He grinned. "He'll answer to nearly anything."

Not understanding this comment, Amica simply stared, but the handsome jester smiled and moved forward, bowing to capture her hand and carry it to his lips.

"My lady," he murmured, his eyes filled with appreciation. "I am honored. Your beauty is . . . inspirational."

"Jace," Thomas said again, a warning in his tone.

"I must write a special song to extol it," the jester went on, adding, more softly, "and you, my lady. I shall pray that we will be blessed with your glorious presence for many, many days."

He would have kissed her fingers once more, but Thomas reached out and took Amica's hand away.

"I did not bring her all this way merely for you to dally with her," he informed the older man. "Go woo the serving maids, as is your habit."

The lord of Reed seemed surprised by these words, but the jester only smiled the more and nodded. "I will dally indeed, but with these lovely young maids." He looked at the children. "It is time for them to practice the lute, and I think my lord wishes to be rid of such troublous creatures." His easy grin flashed at Sir Eric. "At least for an hour or so."

With a laugh, Sir Eric gave his daughters over to the jester's care. "Oh, an hour, at least, Jace. Only make certain they do you no harm. Such troublous creatures as they are, after all."

"Father!" Elizabeth protested, blushing and glancing at Amica as she obediently followed Jace and her two sisters.

Sir Eric smiled after them before turning back to Amica and Thomas.

"'Tis well," he said, "for we have much to speak of. Let us go to my private chamber, where no others may hear, and I shall send a servant to bring wine. After such a long journey, you are both full weary, I vow."

13

The look on Sir Eric's face as Thomas's account of their journey came to a finish had Amica shaking again. He looked as if he would gladly kill someone and enjoy every moment of it.

"Andrew Fawdry may look down from heaven and be content," he said from where he stood, quite stone-like, near the chamber's one window. "If he ever wished for Duncan Selwyrn's death, he will have that wish fulfilled."

"Sir Garin has already claimed that right, my lord," Thomas said.

A terrible smile formed on the lord of Reed's lips. "Aye, Father would know how it is best managed, s'truth. Selwyrn would truly know fear. But," he added, looking at them directly, "he will not be allowed to do anything. The king will so decree it. Selwyrn must be handled with all care, very quietly, and none but us must know the truth of any of this. Others will wonder and ask questions, but they must not be given an answer.

Understand this well, for 'twould be a simple thing to bring danger upon ourselves by misspeaking even a word. Lady Amica,"—he nodded at her—"you will remain at Reed until the king believes it safe for you to leave. You must have no fear that Selwyrn will be able to touch you here, for even he is not so foolish. Thomas, I charge you with the lady Amica's safety. Set as many guards as you need, secure the castle in any way you see fit, but make certain of it at every moment."

"I will do so, my lord."

The lord of Reed's face relaxed. "Aye, I know you will, lad. You have done well in every task I have set for you, and especially now, in bringing Amica of Lancaster to Reed safely. I am well pleased, Tom."

His master's praise seemed to work a miracle on Thomas of Reed, Amica saw, for his face grew pink and his gaze fell to the floor and the corners of his mouth tilted upward in a slight smile.

"And now," said Sir Eric, his tone becoming brisk, "give me this marriage contract that you want annulled and go tend to your men. I would speak with Lady Amica alone."

Thomas hesitated, glancing at Amica, who silently pleaded with him not to leave. It occurred to him, suddenly, that this would be the first time they had parted company for more than a few minutes' time since leaving Belhaven.

Amica sat rigidly in her chair, her pale face filled with panic.

"Tom?" He could hear the surprise in Sir Eric's voice at his hesitation. He had never disobeyed his master before. It wasn't in him to do so now, nor, he believed, ever.

Rising from his chair, he pulled the document out of his tunic.

"Here, my lord."

"Very well. You may go."

"Yes, my lord." Thomas made a bow, then turned toward the door. He stared at Amica for a long moment. "I will see you at table this eve, my lady," he said, willing her to believe that all would be well. Another moment passed before he resolutely forced his feet into motion, and then Amica and the lord of Reed were alone.

Despite the trembling of her hands, Amica lifted the goblet she held and drank deeply of the wine. When she lowered the cup, it was to find Sir Eric smiling at her.

"I am fearsome to look upon, I know," he said.

"Oh no, my lord," she began, horrified to think that she had offended him.

With a chuckle he waved away her words. "My lady, do not. I have lived with myself for many and many a year, and know full well what I am. But, despite my monstrous appearance, I beg you will believe that I mean only well for you, and would never bring you harm. How could I do so, especially to the granddaughter of Andrew Fawdry, whom I loved well?"

Amica reddened. "I am timorous, my lord. I pray you will forgive me."

"Timorous?" he repeated. "Aye, I can see that it is so. I was not without knowledge of this, as the king gave me warning."

Amica looked at him with surprise. "The king?"

"Aye, the king. He recounted his memories of you often while I was at court with him, and with much love."

"With love? I find that hard to believe, my lord."

"What, that your own cousin should love you? 'Tis not so difficult a thing to imagine."

She almost smiled. "He did not seem to bear Alys or

me much love when his father sold us to the lord of
Sacre Placean four years ago. Indeed, he did not seem
to care at all, just as none of our family cared."

Sir Eric moved to sit in the chair that Thomas had
vacated.

"He was not then the king, my lady. What could he
have done to stop his father from selling your wardship
to the man whom your own father had already chosen
for your husband? At least Henry Bolingbroke, may
God rest his soul, gained Selwyn's agreement to wait
until you had aged two years more before he took you
to wife."

"Yes, at least there was that," she replied. "Duncan
found that to be quite unpleasant. He could not take his
anger out on the king, but found another victim on
whom to vent his rage. Those two years brought me little comfort, I promise you, my lord."

Sir Eric shifted uncomfortably in the chair and
cleared his throat. His gaze fell upon the marriage contract that he yet clutched in one hand. With a grim
smile, he tore the paper in two.

"This is a matter easily cared for." Rising, he went to
the hearth and tossed the strips into the fire. "There.
Your marriage to Thomas of Reed has been annulled."
He returned to the chair. "Poor Tom, believing that he
had wed you."

"He did believe it," Amica assured him.

"Aye, that is so, for he'd never have done such a
thing otherwise."

"I tried to tell him, to stop him, but he would not listen or let me explain."

"'Tis well," Sir Eric told her. "No one must know
that you are wed to Selwyn, Lady Amica. Not until the
king has found a way to bring him disfavor in the eyes
of the other nobles. He is too highly regarded to be

publicly disgraced without cause. The king would lose
all the support he has gained for his battle with France.
You must confide the secret of your marriage to no one,
not even to my lady wife, whom you will shortly come
to know."

Amica felt as if her stomach had turned to ice. "I
understand," she whispered.

"Nay, you do not." He set a hand over hers and gently squeezed. "The king means to grant you an annulment if you can but give him just cause."

"*What?*"

"Verily, it is so."

"If I can—!"

"If you can give the king good cause, he will grant
you an annulment, and you shall no longer be wed to
the lord of Sacre Placean. The king especially wants to
learn the truth of the lady Alys's death, if you know any
of it. If Selwyrn had aught to do with it, then the king
will more clearly have a way to bring him down."

"I do not know how Alys died," Amica said truthfully, "though I am certain Duncan was the instrument
of it. But if there is any just cause for annulment, it will
be the life I lived under Duncan's hand. If the king
knew the truth and yet did not release me from my marriage vows, then he possesses neither heart nor soul!"

"Very well," said the lord of Reed. "You must have
no fear in all you speak, for the king has declared that
you tell me what passed while you and your sister
lived at Sacre Placean. All of it, my lady, barring no
unpleasantness. If 'tis hard to speak of, then so much
the better, for so much more will I have to tell our
king and thereby gain the freedom you say you so
desire."

"I do desire it!" she cried.

"Then speak the truth to me, my lady, and speak it

fully. Other than the king, no other living person shall
hear from my lips the words you say. On this I give my
solemn vow."

"But if I speak, if I tell you all that happened, fantas-
tic as it may seem," she hesitated, "will you believe
me?"

"I will not disbelieve you without good cause. That is
all I, or any man, can do."

"It is not easy to speak of." Her voice fell to a thin
whisper. "Duncan is a cruel and sometimes perverse
man. I feel great . . . shame."

"I can only tell you once more that no other living
being, save the king, shall hear from my lips of what
you speak. I regret that there is no other way. If you
would be free of Selwyrn, then you must speak."

She was silent, so that he thought perhaps she considered the matter and would tell him what she had
decided, but when she opened her mouth to speak, she
did not say *yea* or *nay*, but simply began her tale.

"You know much of me, already, my lord, that my
father was John Beaufort, the earl of Somerset and son
of John of Gaunt. My sister, Alys, and I were born of his
mistress, our mother, Jehanne Fawdry, the only child of
Andrew Fawdry and herself a bastard, the outcome of
one of my grandfather's adventures." She met his gaze.
"My father was a bastard as well, one of John of
Gaunt's many, before he was made legitimate, by command of the king, along with his brothers and sisters.
But that you know, for he was also made the earl of
Somerset at that time. I only mention it because Alys
and I found the idea such a comfort as we grew. We
thought perhaps, having known what it was to be as
stains in the history of such a great family, that he
would one day do for us what his father had done for
him. We dreamed of becoming his children in the light

as well as in the darkness, but John Beaufort paid little heed to his bastard daughters. His family was kinder, even my revered grandfather. I have but few memories of John of Gaunt, but those that I have are good. I am not ashamed to have been descended from such a man, though I have often wished that I had not been born into such a noble lineage."

"It is the noblest family in all of England," Sir Eric murmured, almost sympathetically, it seemed to Amica. "Your ancestors are kings and queens, dukes and duchesses, every manner of noble and holy man."

"Oh yes," she agreed. "All the way back to Athelstan of England. I have been reminded of that fact daily, almost, for the past four years, my lord. There is only one other family line in England that descends farther than my own, as best I know, and that is Duncan Selwyrn's. His family ruled this land before mine, and his family, so he asserts, shall one day rule again."

Sir Eric's eyebrows rose. "Will it? The king would find that interesting to know, I vow."

"Yes, I have often thought my cousin would be amused to hear of it. It is what Duncan wanted me for. To bear him noble heirs. He was great friends with my father, and from the day of my birth, he begged him to let us be betrothed. It would have been much better had he chosen Alys," she said, and gave a sigh, "but Alys was born with a mark, here," she touched a place on her arm, near her shoulder, "and Duncan would not have her for a wife, though she did not know that until the day he wed me. But I am before myself, I think. Let me tell you of the days we spent at Sacre Placean before Duncan wed me, and then I shall speak of what came after."

"Drink a little wine, first," Sir Eric told her. "Your hands tremble."

"Oh," Amica said with some surprise, as if just noticing. She obediently lifted the goblet and drank. When she set the goblet aside, Sir Eric asked, "Is it so bad, then?"

She regarded him solemnly. "You must judge that for yourself, my lord."

He nodded.

"We were sent to Sacre Placean shortly after my father's death. Duncan had petitioned the king to gain custody of our wardships, which were honorable, in truth, as my father had seen fit to let us marry without shame, at least. The king, my uncle, agreed to Duncan's request, for my father's family could do no more than see us well settled, while my mother's family was not allowed to do anything for us. You can see the difficulty, can you not, my lord? We are bastards, yet of noble blood. We were desirable for marriage despite our illegitimate birth; indeed, Duncan Selwyrn was not the only man who sought to wed either of us. Though my grandfather, Sir Andrew, wished to have Alys and me, he could not, for we were far above him, or so it was declared by those who decide such matters."

"You are cousin to the king of England," Sir Eric said. "You are descended from—"

"Kings and queens," she finished dolefully. "I shall never forget it, I promise you." She folded her fingers together in her lap. "Duncan did not truly want Alys at Sacre Placean, but he understood my father's family perfectly. Not only would he rid them of one unsightly stain, but of two. He promised that he would remain faithful to his vow, and would wed me in two years' time and, as well, he would find a suitable husband for Alys. The family was pleased and the king, my uncle, was pleased, and so we were sent to Sacre Placean.

"'Twas autumn when we arrived at our new home, and a lovely day, as I remember," she said wistfully. "The sky was very blue, it had just begun to grow cold in the afternoons. It was so beautiful, but I did not make myself take any special notice of it. If I had known that I would not touch the earth with my feet again for four years after that day, or feel the sun on my face, I certainly would have done so.

"We did not realize for many days that we would not again be let outside of the castle. At first, Duncan said that he wished us to become accustomed to our new home before we met any of the villagers, or that he feared the increasingly cold weather might make us ill. For the first week we were allowed to go anywhere inside the castle that we pleased and to speak to anyone we met. Duncan told his servants that I would one day be their lady and that they should treat me accordingly, even while I was not yet his wife. This pleased me then, just as it should please any girl of ten and four. Indeed, for those few days I began to believe that I should fall in love with him, for he was very handsome and always softly spoken and his servants obeyed him readily, which I took as a sign of reverence, though, in truth, 'twas merely that they feared him.

"We took our meals in the great hall that first week, though they were not the festive occasions we had been accustomed to when we had visited our father's home. But they were pleasant, especially after hours of our own company, and Alys and I looked forward to sitting on either side of Duncan at each meal, listening as he spoke, in that soft, even voice that I was to dread in coming days, of his family, of the history of the Selwyrns, of Celts and Druids and ancient, mystical times."

Amica stopped for a moment, gathering her thoughts. "I should mention, I think, that Duncan understood that I lack bravery. It did not seem to displease him. My sister, Alys, though my twin, was much the opposite. She was bright and strong and brave.

Hard, perhaps, in some ways. We shared very little save the day of our birth. In truth, we did not even look alike, so that people often declared amazement that we should be sisters, let alone twins. I admired Alys for her strengths. She was all that I wished to be, even with the hardness. Duncan found her attractive as well. I knew, from those very first days, that Alys would seek him out. She wanted him, and told me, most plainly, that she meant to be his wife in my stead."

"How so?" Sir Eric asked with some surprise. "Did she not understand the legality of the betrothal between Selwyrn and you?"

"Oh, she did, surely," Amica replied. "She simply did not care. Alys did not care for boundaries of any kind, you see. She was brave, as I said. Such things meant little, or less, to her.

"On my last day of freedom—I did not know it was the last, then—she told me this, that she meant to charm Duncan to wed her, instead of me. I was quite angry, though she knew well the way to daunt me. She screamed until I was nearly deaf from it, saying wild things, that I had ever been the blessed one, the one born with beauty and countenance, and that she—she who had all those things that *I* had so wanted and admired—had been made to suffer for it. Ah, God above," Amica said with a miserable laugh, "if we had only realized what was to come, neither of us should have dreamed to say, even to think, such things.

"Duncan came to my chamber that night, just as I had prepared for sleep. It was not fitting that he should be there, I told him, but he paid me no heed and sent my maid away. I was not afraid of him then, thinking him a gentle man, but, being as I am, I was yet wary. Seeing my fear, Duncan spoke gently, in his soft way. He asked me whether I understood that we could not be wed for two years, and I replied that I did. He asked if I knew that my uncle, the king, had demanded that this be so, and again I replied that I did." Amica lifted her hands, pressing her knuckles beneath her chin as if she might pray. Her gaze was distant as she spoke. "My father, Duncan told me, had not wished for such a delay in our marriage and, had he been alive, never would have made us wait to become man and wife. If my father had not died, he—Duncan—would even now be sharing my bed. But as he could not yet claim his rights as my husband, he would take that place which my father had left empty. For the next two years, until we wed, he was going to be my father. And I"—Amica closed her eyes—"was to call him such. I was to call him 'Father.' I was always to call him 'Father', never failing."

"God's mercy," Sir Eric whispered.

Amica let out a breath. "I could not believe he would ask such a thing of me, for I had no idea then of what evil possessed him. I laughed, I think, though I truly cannot remember. I told him that I could not call him by that name, that such was foolishness. He said that I would do as he told me to, that he would not countenance disobedience of any kind from his—from his little daughter."

Sir Eric swore violently under his breath, and when Amica glanced at him he said, "Such men are the vilest on earth."

"Yes," she whispered. "Yes, he was. He is. I soon knew that very well. That night, when I would not do as he bid me, I learned how cruel Duncan could be, how heavy his hand was in punishment."

"He beat you?"

Amica nodded. "I had never been struck in such a way before, and was so stunned that I did not react quickly, so that several minutes passed before I did as he commanded. That was the first of many lessons I had in how to obey Duncan Selwyrn. I came to learn more quickly what it was that he wished of me, so that I might obey at once and not be made to suffer more. I learned, most especially, that I must always address him in that manner, calling him Father, for if I failed he would be unforgiving in my punishments."

"My lady," Sir Eric murmured, "do not." He put out his hands and took both of hers, unlacing them so that Amica saw where her nails had dug deeply into the flesh on the back of each.

"After that night," she went on, "Duncan declared that I should no longer be allowed to leave my chamber, not for any reason, until the day that we married. My maid was allowed to come and go, to bring me what I required in food and drink and other things, though, poor thing, she was as much a captive in Sacre Placean as I, at least for the short time that Duncan let her live."

"He killed her?" Sir Eric asked. "Or had her killed?"

"He killed her," Amica replied. "A few months before we wed. He had told me to remove my clothing while she was present and I did not obey quickly enough. When he realized that I had hesitated because of her presence, he killed her, quickly and carelessly. And while she lay on the floor dying, he pleasured himself with me on the bed. The sounds she made as she died excited him greatly. I was sick after he left, and she lay there on the floor through the night, dead, with no one but me to grieve for her. And I being such a sorry creature, how much she would have hated to have had no one else!"

"Amica," Sir Eric said softly, and she noticed for the first time that he had drawn nearer to her, and now held her hands upon his own knees. "This is hard, and you have done well and bravely to speak as you have.

You must tell me, in truth—did Duncan Selwyrn possess your maidenhead before you wed him? If he did,"
Sir Eric added quickly, gripping her taut fingers, "then
the marriage may be annulled with no further word. It
would have been a breach of the agreement he made
with your uncle, the king, had he done so. Only tell me,
and no other save the king shall know of it."

Amica could not meet his eyes, but she curled her
fingers around his. "I almost wish he had," she whispered. "Nay, Duncan did not do that until we were fully
wed. He did . . . other things. My lord," her voice broke
on a sob, "I beg you will not ask me to speak of them. I
can speak of all else, save that."

"Have no fear," he murmured, bending closer, lifting
a hand and stroking her hair gently. "I tell you now, I
swear it, Duncan Selwyrn will never have you. I think
now of my own daughters. If any man had done such to
them, I would slay him by my own hand, and gladly.
God damn me to Hell's eternal fires if I would not do as
much for you, Amica of Lancaster."

Weeping, she nodded. A minute passed while she
cried, head bowed, striving to control herself. Sir Eric
continued to stroke her hair with tender care, and then
he wiped at the tears on her cheeks with the backs of
his fingers.

"There," he said. "There, now. These are things long
past that we speak of. I would not have you so overset
by the memory of them. Shall we stop for a time? We
may speak later, if 'twould be easier."

"No!" Amica said vehemently, drawing in a sobbing
breath. "No, I will never—after this, I will *never* speak
of these things again, please God!"

"Gently, then," he soothed. "In your own time, my
lady. I am here, at your will. There is no hurry."

She took in a long breath and sniffed. Her wet lashes

were lowered, her gaze held upon the giant hand she clutched, which made her own hands seem so tiny. Her breathing, though strong and heavy, calmed.

"Alys became my maid, after that. I had not set eyes on her in more than a year, since I had become a prisoner in my chamber. She came the next day, bringing me food. It seems odd to me even now, but we had little to speak to one another. She told me that I had been made to suffer because of my own faults and weaknesses, and that if I had only been stronger, Duncan should have admired me, just as he admired her. Duncan loved her, she said, while he despised me and would set me aside and wed her in my place."

"Faithless shrew!" Sir Eric declared angrily.

"She loved him," Amica said, "though I could scarce believe it, knowing Duncan as I did. But, though I have oft wondered if I did not go mad during those endless days while I was locked away, and am yet mad now, I do remember Alys. She could not have loved a man whom she did not believe loved her in turn, and so I can only think Duncan had continued his kindness toward her, and never showed her that part of himself, that evil part, that I came to know so fully. It must have been so, for on the day Duncan and I wed, Alys was as one turned to stone, and stood beside me as witness before all his people as if she had no life in her whatever. That day, after all the days she had chided and cursed me, she said not a word."

"You were wed before his people?" Sir Eric asked sharply. "'Twas a public wedding? 'Twas well known of in Sacre Placean?"

"Oh yes. I shall never forget that day, for it was the only time in nearly four years when I left the chamber which had become my constant hell. Duncan declared that our marriage be known of, for, though he meant to keep me locked away, he would never countenance the thought that his heir be rumored a bastard. A wife, wed before all his people, would stop such whispers as that."

"Especially if his heir would one day be king," Sir Eric put in.

"Yes. Even so. My duty before we wed was to bring him pleasure, in any manner that he saw fit. My duty after we wed was to bear him a son. In a way, it was a blessing for me. He ceased to beat me as often, for he did not wish to chance harming any child I might have conceived, and he ceased to visit so many surprises upon me, for fear that I might miscarry from the shock."

"Surprises?"

"Did I not mention them yet?"

"Nay."

"Oh." Amica let out a weary sigh. "Duncan loved those most of all, and I hated them most. They were his favorite form of evil. He would wait until I slumbered, and would creep, silent until he sprang, flinging himself upon me and screeching wildly. I cannot tell you how vile such as that was. How horrible. I went for days at a time, afraid to sleep, but he would wait until I could no longer keep awake, and then he would spring, when I had fainted from weariness. I could not make him stop this torture, for it delighted him. My only defense was to forsake my bed and sleep in a chair, where he could not terrify me so greatly."

"God's feet," Sir Eric muttered. "The man is insane."

"Aye, that is so," she agreed, "yet his madness does not rule him, as it might another. Or, mayhap, it rules him, yet it is not such a wild madness that he cannot bend it to his will."

"Perhaps not," Sir Eric said thoughtfully. "Many of his cruelties ceased after you wed him? He no longer required you to name him 'Father'?"

"Nay, he did not. Instead, he declared that I must evermore call him 'Master', for he was my master, in truth, and should be named as such. I did as he said, without care. I knew well to obey him after living two years beneath his hand.

"As to his cruelties, I would not say that they lessened, merely that he became more careful not to harm any child I might carry. In truth, I think he strove to find more evil methods to torment me, as he could no longer use my body as he pleased to feed his perverse desires. He began to enjoy tying me to my bed for long hours, often throughout the night and often with my legs tied and my feet hoisted up upon one of the bedposts."

Sir Eric gave her a looked that was equally puzzled and dismayed.

"It was because," she said, "he believed I should more easily conceive if I were kept in such a position, once his seed was in me. After many hours, however, it only served to set me in a very great agony, as you might imagine. He much enjoyed keeping me bound in various ways, on the bed, in a chair. It was as if I were an object to be kept waiting, unmoving, for his pleasure, like a child's toy that might be put away when it is not being played with. He had long since had chains put into my chamber walls, for the purpose of binding me there when I had somehow displeased him. Once we were wed that particular punishment was withheld until the day that my monthly flow began. Those were my worst days at Castle Sacre Placean. Duncan was always so angry to find that I had not yet conceived. For a few days, then, until he would again attempt to put a child in me, he had no care, not even for my life." She shuddered.

"Did you ever try to escape on your own, before your sister helped you?"

"Oh, yes, I did," she said quickly. "Twice I tried to escape out of my chamber window, but each time I was stopped, and then Duncan had it covered with mortar. 'Twas very dark, after that. And, then, later, I was ever being tied and chained, so that it became impossible." She bit her lip. "But I should have found a way. Alys would have, had she been me."

"A heartless female such as that would," he said dryly.

"Alys was hard of heart," Amica admitted, "and yet she saved me at the cost of her own life, and possibly that of her child's. I did not understand her love for Duncan, but in the end, she loved me better."

"What happened to turn her from him?"

"I cannot know for certain what particular thing it was, for many circumstances changed once Duncan and I were wed. He began to be less kind to Alys than he once had been, which dimmed her love, I think. As well, she and her maid, Jennie, were made to care for me, and Alys could not for long ignore Duncan's cruelties when she saw the results of them with her own eyes each day. At first, she urged me to be strong, to stand against him." A mirthless laugh escaped Amica's lips. "That did not last long, for she tried to stand against him, herself, and the next day came to my chamber with her face much bruised. Next she promised that she would find a way to make him release me. If she could but conceive his child, he would surely put me aside and take her to wife, for I had proven myself useless in the matter of giving him children. But, though Alys claimed to share his bed as often as he shared mine, she did not conceive, either. In truth, my lord, I do not think the fault was ours. Is it so impossible that Duncan should have been the barren one?"

"It is indeed possible," Sir Eric told her. "Fully possible, for his lineage is so tightly bred that many unnatural results, such as that, may have been born in him. But your sister did conceive a child, did she not? Duncan's child?"

"Not Duncan's," Amica replied. "Alys did not tell me who the father was, but it was not Duncan. When she realized it would be impossible with him, she sought another to sire her child. She still believed that once Duncan thought she carried his heir, he would send me away and take her to wife."

"But he did not," Sir Eric stated.

Amica shook her head. "Nay, he did not. He was pleased, of course, about the child, but he told Alys that he would not take her to wife, that she was marked, and not beautiful enough to be anything more than his whore. She would remain at Sacre Placean and bear him children, but I should be counted as the mother of each one. This, as you might imagine, horrified her completely."

"Yes, I do so imagine it."

"He began to keep Alys in her chamber more often, so that she understood what her future was to be. Once her body began to show that she was with child, she would never again be free, for Duncan could not have his people know which of us had truly borne the child. She came to me, then, and told me her plan."

"She did arrange your escape, then," Sir Eric said thoughtfully. "The king had wondered how much truth there was in that part of the tale."

"It is all truth," Amica said with a touch of anger. "Alys made it all possible, knowing full well what Duncan would do to her when he discovered me gone. She found a way to get a missive to our grandfather, Sir Andrew, and made a way as well for me to steal out of the castle on the night he came for me. And 'twas she who stayed behind, even when Grandfather and I pleaded with her to come away, to keep Duncan from discovering my absence until the following morn. She is the only reason that we were able to ride far enough to escape the men Duncan sent after us. Knowing my *husband*," she said the word hatefully, "as I do, I can only imagine how he made her suffer for such duplicity. Only the presence of the child spared her death, then, but he killed her, I believe, once the child was born."

"But why would she not go with you? Surely she knew what Selwyrn would do."

"She knew," Amica admitted. "But she believed herself shamed, for she had willfully lain with her own sister's husband. A bastard child would have been accepted, but not that." Her voice grew softer, as if she could not bear to speak the words. "She would have been fully shamed before our family. Alys was proud and strong, and could not have borne such a stain."

"I understand," he said. "I am, myself, bastard born. My father was a base murderer, my mother naught but a child when she gave me life. I know something of shame."

"How can you say such things!" Amica stared at him. "I have met your father. Sir Garin Stavelot is no murderer! And your mother, Lady Elaine, could have been no child when she bore you!"

"Sir Garin and Lady Elaine adopted me. I was born just as I said. I am a bastard by birth."

Amica kept staring.

"'Tis not well known," he said. "I do not speak of it much."

"Certainly. You would not wish to distress them— Sir Garin and Lady Elaine."

"Nay, I should not. Just as I do not wish you to be distressed in any way at this time. My lady, I believe, with all the honor I possess, that your marriage to Selwyrn will be annulled. I give my oath that that will be my recommendation to the king. I give equal vow that I shall use any power I wield to encourage the king toward that end. As I live, you shall be freed from Duncan Selwyrn."

She felt breathless, as if she'd suddenly fallen on the ground and was stunned by it.

"My lord," she murmured gratefully. "Sir Eric."

"It shall be done."

She wanted to go down on her knees to thank him, to weep, but he held her fast and said, "Tell me what I may do to make your stay here easy, my lady. Your time at Reed may be long, but I would have you be happy."

For a moment, his words bewildered Amica. "I do not . . ." she began, then stopped, feeling lost as to what he meant.

Sir Eric smiled gently. "It has been long since you have been treated with the deference your birth decrees, but such as that will return to you in time. You must never fear, while you are at Reed, to make your wishes known, however slight, however great. Here you shall be treated as what you are."

"The king's cousin," she said.

He nodded. "Aye, even so. 'Tis what you are, whether you wish it or no."

"Yes." A faint remembrance of what it had once meant to be Amica of Lancaster briefly shadowed her thoughts. "Yes," she said more firmly, "that is so. I was taught it from my cradle. But I am weak, and weakness is not valued in my father's family. I wish Alys had lived, instead of me."

"Nay, never say such as that. 'Tis a great folly to curse life."

"Yes, my lord."

"All will be well," he promised, kissing her hands soundly and rising from his chair, pulling Amica to her feet. "I will write the king at once and send a messenger on his way to London in the morn. Tonight, we shall have a feast celebrating your arrival, and Thomas's return."

The thought of sitting through another public feast made Amica's heart pound with fear, though she merely said, "Oh."

"And you must let me know, when you've had time to think on the matter, how we can best make you comfortable at Reed. For now, let us go abovestairs, so that I may make my wife, Lady Margot, known to you. She has much anticipated your arrival, and has had our finest chamber made ready."

Obediently, Amica let the lord of Reed lead her toward the door, but before he had opened it, she pulled her hand from his arm and said, softly and hesitantly, "My lord . . . "

Sir Eric looked at her. "Yes, my lady?"

She twisted her fingers together. "There is one request I would make of you."

"Anything," he said, grinning into her face as he lifted her chin with his fingers. "Do not be afraid. Anything you ask of me, I shall do all in my power to grant it."

"Anything, my lord? It may seem quite . . . odd."

"Anything," he declared. "I vow it by all that is holy."

14

"The priest's lodgings!" Thomas slammed his tankard of ale on the table. "'Tis naught but madness! You jest, surely, my lord."

Calmly cutting into a slab of roasted meat, Sir Eric cast a mild grin in Thomas's direction. "Nay, I do not jest. Lady Amica has made but one request of me, and that is it. I have already had the dwelling prepared."

"'Twill not be safe," Thomas countered, then turned his scowl upon the young man who stood nervously beside the long table. "Our lord's meat was not properly prepared," he stated with impatience. "See how he is made to cut it himself? Must I remind you yet again that such is your duty, not his!" Turning back to Sir Eric he looked past Amica, who sat between the two men in a stunned silence, meekly eating her food, and said, "She would be kept more safely in the castle, proper."

"Leave Siegart be," Sir Eric chided. "He is a good squire and does not treat me as a child." He winked at the trembling lad before adding, to Thomas, "As another of my squires was used to do."

Thomas began to cut his own meat with quick, angry strokes. "When you will behave as a child, you will be treated as one. My memory is not so short, my lord, as to forget the many times you and your crazed brothers did all you could to seek out every manner of foolish destruction. I was hard put with the lot of you, God save me."

"Bah!" said Sir Eric. "Worrying as an old hen, you were, Tom, and still are. Ever worrying. And dour as a monk at Lent." He nudged Amica with an elbow. "Never a frivolous man, is our Tom. Can't even enjoy a good fight, by the rood! Not e'en when 'tis his own quarrel!"

"And may God be p-p-praised," declared his wife, Lady Margot, who sat on the other side of her husband. Leaning forward, she smiled at Amica. "T-Thomas has kept my l-lord whole these p-past many years. He'd n-never have d-done it himself!"

Amica managed to smile at the beautiful lady of Reed, though only barely. She was thoroughly shocked at Thomas's unseemly behavior toward Sir Eric. If any other man had dared speak to the lord of Reed in such a contentious manner, he would probably even now be throttled by Thomas of Reed's own hands.

"My love, you ever take Tom's side o'er mine," Sir Eric complained teasingly. "'Tis not fitting in an obedient lady, I vow."

"Aye, and s-so I shall do," Lady Margot told him, "so l-long as he keeps you alive and well. Tom has the right of it, L-Lady Amica. My l-lord and his brothers are given to much childish behavior, on occasion."

"Especially when they're all together," Thomas put in. "And I still say she should be kept safely in Castle Reed."

"Lady Amica will reside in the priest's lodgings

while she remains at Reed," Sir Eric said. "So have I given my vow, and so it will be. As to her safety, make yourself easy, Tom, for you have the keeping of it and may do all you please to be satisfied that it is complete."

"Of course," Thomas grumbled. "'Tis *I* who must lie awake nights, wondering if every latch in Reed has been properly set, as ever." He shoved a piece of meat into his mouth and chewed violently.

"Select a guard," Sir Eric continued in his usual pleasant tone. "Make every necessary action."

Thomas swallowed before warning, "The castle gates will need to be kept shut and locked at all times. Mayhap the village gates, as well."

"So be it," agreed Sir Eric.

Thomas scowled. "None will be able to come or go without being given leave by the guards. The merchants in the village will be angered with such as that."

"Then they may answer to me," Sir Eric told him. "Do what you must, Tom. I require that Lady Amica be kept safe and comfortable. I will make certain of the comfort, and I require that you make certain of the safety. That is all there is to the matter."

With a sound of complete vexation, Thomas applied himself to his food, eating it with silent purpose.

He was full angry with Amica of Lancaster. Was it not enough that she had been so troublous on their journey to Reed? Must she make his life here, in the place he called home, a hell, also?

"I would have you choose another to take this duty," he said suddenly, surprised to hear the bellicose words that came from his own lips.

Amica stiffened beside him and a moment of silence passed throughout the hall before Sir Eric said, in an odd tone, as if he could not believe what he'd heard, "Tom."

"I would have some time of my own," Thomas went on. "A few months, to travel and do as I please."

"What?" said Sir Eric, just as Lady Margot said, "But, Thomas, you have only j-just c-come home to Reed!"

"Have I not served you well?" he demanded, turning to face his master. "Have I ever before asked anything of you? Can you not grant me this one request?"

Sir Eric stared at him so hard that Thomas felt proud of himself for holding the gaze.

"Nay," said the lord of Reed, loudly, clearly. "I do not grant it. Be silent. Do not speak another word of the matter to me this night. I will not suffer such as this from you."

Thomas drew in a breath through his nose that sounded loud to him—so loud that he thought the entire hall must have heard the dissent behind it. It was impossible for him to disobey Sir Eric, and so he made himself look at his food again. Beside him, Amica shook so badly that he wanted to clamp a hand on the knee that knocked against his leg just to make it stop.

"Eat, Thomas," Sir Eric said in the cold silence of the room. "You will escort Lady Amica to her dwelling when we have done."

Thomas briefly closed his eyes, fighting the urge to naysay his master. When he opened them once more, he did not let himself speak, but obediently began to eat. Slowly, the room filled with noise as those around him, save Amica of Lancaster, began to speak, and as Jace, sitting off to one side of the hall, plucked a pretty tune on his lute.

"Fair one who holds my heart captive with thine eye," Jace sang loudly, merrily. "Whose gracious smiles impart secrets of paradise. Give me hope to cherish, for without I perish. Fa la la la la, fa la la la la."

Thomas scowled at the troubadour, who returned the look with a wide smile, and thought to himself that there was nothing he would like better in that moment than to strangle the singing jester.

"It is this way," Thomas said, striding through the gardens as Amica followed behind, struggling to keep pace with him.

"So far from the castle?" she asked breathlessly.

Thomas turned so suddenly that she ran right into him, their bodies making a *thud* as they collided.

"Oh!" She jumped back. "Forgive me, I—"

"Did you not wish to be far from the castle?" he demanded.

She stared at him, blinking, before she replied, "Yes."

"Then make no grievance to me now, if you find the place farther from the castle's comforts than you wished it might be. Reed was not built to satisfy you, Amica of Lancaster."

"I did not think it was," she murmured.

His jaw tightened, but he said nothing. Turning on his heel, he continued moving through the gardens until they came to a small clearing where a half-timbered dwelling sat. Though it was early evening and not yet dark, light shone through the building's two front windows, and Amica could see a hearth alight with flames. Her eyes moved upward, to the red tiled roof.

"It has a chimney," she said with some amazement.

"Of course it has a chimney," Thomas replied with impatience. "Did you think my master would lodge you in some hovel without heat?"

"I did not. But neither did I expect a dwelling such as this. 'Twill be good to have a hearth set in a wall again, and not have to worry about stumbling o'er a fire set in the midst."

Thomas thought of the humble dwelling she had shared with her grandfather, and said, simply, "That is so."

"This is where the priest lives?"

"Priests," Thomas corrected. "The dwelling was built to lodge two. There are two bedchambers above." He nodded toward the second floor. "Two study chambers, as well."

"It is large for just one person," Amica said. "I shall feel fortunate, indeed, to have it to myself."

"You will have servants with you."

"Nay, I need none, and have asked the lord of Reed not to press me in that matter. I am well able to care for myself, and wish to do so."

Thomas's expression grew foreboding. "I will speak with him. You must have servants to bear you company, to fetch and carry and tend the house."

"I am able to care for myself," she repeated. "I wish to do so. I have promised Sir Eric that I will attend meals with the castlefolk in the hall, so that he may be certain of my well-being. And I will not be entirely alone even while I am here. You will set guards nearby, will you not?"

"Aye, I shall do so," he muttered. "I am half tempted to set one inside the dwelling, to make certain of you."

A smile tugged at the corners of Amica's lips. "To make certain of me?" she repeated, then laughed. "I know you hate me, Thomas of Reed, yet, even so, you cannot think I would leave Reed of my own free will. That I would sneak out in the dark of night and seek my own fortune?"

"I do not know what to make of you, Amica of Lancaster," he told her solemnly. "And my regard should hold no meaning for you whatsoever. I am done with being bewitched. But if you would know, I bear you no ill will. 'Twould be a great folly to waste a moment in such a worthless effort. You exist only as a thing to guard and keep safe, and as my lord has bade me do so, I shall."

Flushing, Amica looked away, just as the big wooden door to the dwelling swung open. Two serving maids came outside, looking distraught when they saw Thomas and Amica standing there.

"My lord!" one of them said while the other made a bow toward Amica and murmured, "My lady."

Thomas regarded the women. "You are Maida, from the kitchen, are you not?"

The girl, who looked to be younger than Amica, tugged at the cloth that covered her red hair and replied, "Yes, my lord, Sir Thomas. And this is my cousin, Margaret. She serves in our lady's bedchamber."

"Sir Thomas," Margaret nervously made a bow to him, too. "My lord."

"Your duties at the castle keep you fully occupied through each day?" he asked.

The girls exchanged brief glances before replying that they did.

Thomas nodded, still gazing at them thoughtfully. "All is well within?"

"Oh yes, my lord," Maida assured him. She showed him the broom that she clutched in one hand, and patted the cloth that was tucked into her skirt. "'Tis all clean and ready. We lit the fires and changed the bed linens. My lady should be very comfortable. 'Tis a fine house."

"Aye," Margaret added. "A very fine house, my lord. And there's fresh water for my lady, and plenty of wood for the fires."

"Thank you," Amica said gratefully. "You are kind."

With expressions of shy pleasure, the girls smiled.

"You may return to the castle," Thomas told them. "Tell the chamberlain, Sir Lowell, that I would speak with him in the morn."

Maida almost dropped her broom. "The chamberlain, my lord? But I could not speak to him so bold, without permission. He would have the kitchen clerk send me off."

Thomas scowled at the girl. "He will do no such thing. If he dared try it, when I had sent you to him with a message, he would shortly thereafter find himself the one sent off. You have my word as the constable of Reed. Do as I have said and have no fear."

Maida made another quick bow and Margaret did the same, and they kept bobbing up and down even as they backed away toward the castle. "Yes, my lord," Maida said, and then both girls turned and rushed away.

"They're afeared of you," Amica said when they'd gone.

Thomas made a snorting sound. "Should they not be? You were afeared of me, once."

"Aye, once I was so," she admitted softly.

"But no more?"

Amica lifted her face. "No more, my lord."

His scowl deepened, and Amica amended, "Perhaps—sometimes—I am." Her voice dropped to a murmur. "You are not always kind."

"No, I am not," he said gruffly. "Let us go inside and see the place."

The dwelling was more than Amica had expected it might be. Every modern comfort had been provided: the floors were not only set in clay tiles, but were covered also with Spanish carpets; six windows held

expensive glass panes; the dwelling's two levels each
had a magnificent hearth fitted with ornate stone
hoods; the two bedchambers contained large beds with
feather mattresses, and throughout the dwelling there
were tables and chairs, more than enough to make
Amica thoroughly comfortable. It was, in her opinion, a
house fit for royalty.

"Oh, look!" she cried, circling the single room of the
lower level. "I wondered at how it could be so light
here, though the darkness falls so rapidly outside.
Look." She pointed to a large wooden beam set in the
wall, of a height that neared the top of her head, where
four large iron wrought lamps set with glass bowls were
putting out a steady light. "It is nearly bright as day!"
she exclaimed, lifting a finger to touch one of the bowls,
only to have her hand caught and held by Thomas.

"'Tis hot," he warned. "You will burn yourself."

"Oh." She pulled her fingers free. "Thank you. I did
not realize. I've never seen such as this before. They are
not candles."

"They're oil lamps," Thomas said. "My lady of Reed
will not countenance candles, for she detests the smoke
they make. This oil comes from Denmark, and burns
very cleanly, as you see."

"'Tis most wonderful!" she declared. "They give
such clear light."

"Hmmm," Thomas agreed lazily. "All of Castle Reed
is fitted with them. You will not try to light them yourself. I will have someone here to do it each eve before
the daylight begins to dim."

"But surely 'tis not difficult," she countered. "I am
certain I can do it."

"You will not," he told her. "I do not permit it. Be
wise, my lady, and heed my word."

Amica began to feel angry. "I shall ask the lord of

Reed. He will certainly grant me permission to light my own lamps!"

He made a scoffing sound. "My master will naysay me directly, lady, as you have heard this night, but he will not naysay my commands. You may ask him if it pleases you, but 'twill do you no good. If my lord of Reed understands that I have said such a thing will not be, he will not go against my word."

Amica was truly astonished. "Never?"

"Seldom," he replied. "From the time that he made me his constable and put the care of his men into my hands, he has only twice revoked commands that I have given, and those not because he disagreed with my decisions, but because he felt them too lenient in their dealings." At Amica's questioning gaze, he went on, "I am a hard master, but not always so cruel as you think me. The first time Sir Eric saw fit to correct my command, I had declared that one of my men, who had stolen the possessions of those left dead on a battlefield, should be whipped and jailed. Sir Eric sentenced him to death. On another occasion two men under my command were sopped with drink and defiled the maiden daughter of a villager. I decided they were to be whipped and then hung until death in the village square. Sir Eric declared that they should be drawn and quartered, instead, and so, to the villagers' satisfaction, they were."

"God's mercy," Amica whispered.

"I, also, being accountable for the actions of my men, was rightfully punished. I was whipped and left shackled in the square for a full day's time."

"Oh, my lord." She touched his forearm. "How terrible it must have been."

He stared at the hand on his sleeve. "'Twas my just due for allowing such misconduct among my own men."

"But what they did was in no way your fault!"

"Everything my men do is my responsibility. If I am not accountable to them, for them, they would not follow my command. Since that time, no man serving under my hand has behaved with a moment's disregard. And, save the one time that a man openly defied me, which I have told you of before, none have been disobedient."

"Oh, the one who developed the, ah . . . twitch?" She pointed at a spot near her eye. "Here?"

"Even so."

Amica swallowed. "I see. Then, my lord, I am persuaded to be obedient in this matter of the lamps. However, shall I douse them at night, when I retire? If I do not learn how to handle them, they will burn through the darkness."

"You need not worry o'er the matter. One of my men, whichever may be guarding you in the night, will quench the lamps."

Amica nodded and moved away, surveying the room's finely crafted furnishings. "Have there been priests living here? Sir Eric said nothing, but I would not like to have uprooted them."

"Nay, Father Baruch and Father Wade moved into the castle more than two years past. Sir Eric and Lady Margot had new quarters built for them there, thinking 'twould be easier for them to be cared for. Also, 'tis much nearer the chapel, and they need not go out in poor weather to do their good work."

"I am glad," Amica murmured, her attention given to inspecting the contents of a small closet. Thomas watched her for a moment, then moved to settle into a chair near the fire. Wondering at himself, thinking that he was a fool to stay in the company of the one who had so thoroughly taken hold of his senses, he nevertheless put his booted feet toward the flames and let himself rest.

Amica lifted her head at the sound and, seeing him by the fire, realized how weary he must be. Why had he stayed? she wondered. Surely he must desire the comfort of his own bed over her company.

"It smells as if there is wine warming in this pot," she said, walking around his chair to look into a small kettle hanging on an iron arm attached to the fire hood. The pot was set just far enough away to keep from becoming too hot. Amica peered inside of it and smiled. "Aye, 'tis wine, and smelling of spices. How kind of Sir Eric to provide it."

"'Tis my lady Margot who required it, most likely," Thomas told her. "She is not known to let guests at Reed go without, and has acquired no small fame for her hospitality."

"Indeed," Amica murmured, stirring the wine with a small ladle. "Would you have some, my lord?"

"I will take a small amount." She could hear the hesitation in his voice.

Amica pulled two brass goblets from a shelf. "Maida and Margaret are excellent workers. Even the cups are clean." She ladled warm wine into each vessel and handed one to Thomas, then took the other and settled into the chair beside him.

"You are not much given to drink," she stated, which caused Thomas to lift his eyebrows. "I noticed that this is so while we journeyed," she explained.

"Does it not say in God's holy book, 'They also have erred through wine, and through strong drink; they err in vision, they stumble in judgment'?"

"Aye, this is so," she replied.

He looked at her fully, and Amica was struck by the solemn beauty of his gray eyes.

"I have thought long on the matter," he said. "It does not seem right for a man in charge of other men to drink overmuch." His expression grew slightly troubled. "The word of God warns against such a man losing his judgment, and I could no longer lead men if I was not able to judge wisely. Do you not think this is true?"

She was surprised that he should ask her such a question, that he should care what she thought.

"I do think it true," she said. "And I think that you are a good and wise man to understand such things."

"Not more than half an hour past you called me unkind," he reminded her.

"And you, my lord, agreed that that was so."

Drinking his wine, he looked away. After a moment Amica asked, uncertainly, "How is Sir Stevan? Have you had any word regarding him?"

Grateful for a reason to pull his thoughts away from Amica of Lancaster's striking beauty—which, in Thomas's unhappy opinion, had become his mind's unwholesome and constant occupation of late—he said, "Nay, not yet. I sent two of my best men on their way to Belhaven shortly after I left you with my master. Stevan will not welcome their escort, for it will go hard against his pride, but I bade them stay with him every moment while they journey back to Reed. 'Tis not safe for a weakened man to travel alone on the open road, even one so well skilled at fighting as Stevan. If I had not had so many matters to attend here at Reed, I should have gone back for him myself."

Thinking of what had passed earlier between him and Sir Eric, Amica thought that he must have wished, very much, that he had ignored whatever pressing matters had held him at Reed and had instead turned back for Belhaven before Sir Eric could make him stay to watch over her.

Clearing her throat, she commented, lightly, "I did not see Sir Derryn at table this evening. Is he well?"

Thomas recalled the last instant when he had seen Derryn, soundly sleeping on his bed in the chamber they shared with Stevan in the soldiers' quarters, and almost smiled.

"He slumbers, and will do so for another day, at least."

"That is long," Amica said, tilting her head with curiosity. "He did not need such long slumber while we journeyed."

"'Tis something strange in him," Thomas explained. "He will go for many days with little sleep. Indeed, I have known him to go two and three days and nights without rest while we were engaged in a siege or held fast in a battle. Then, when all is well, he . . . fails, I suppose you might say. He stops."

"Stops?" Amica repeated.

Thomas sat forward, trying to think of the words to explain it better.

"It happens sometimes without warning, though he usually waits until he's at least found a bed. He cannot seem to help himself, but falls into a slumber so deep that naught will rouse him from it. Once, I found him lying face down on a battlefield, after the battle had ended. I tell you, lady, my heart near fell into my feet, for I thought him dead, or gravely wounded."

"Oh, aye," she murmured with sympathy.

"But he was only asleep, praise God. I did all I could to wake him, even so far as to striking him with the flat of my hand across his cheek, but 'twas to no avail. I carried him to our tent and set him on a pallet and there he stayed, snoring loudly, until two days later, when he sat upright all at once and demanded a cup of water."

"But how strange, indeed!"

Thomas nodded, "Aye, 'tis so. I have often wondered at it."

"Has he not sought the help of a leech?" Amica asked, sipping her wine.

"In the past, he has, but he grew weary of their powders and potions, and none of them helped, i'faith. 'Twas naught but misery for him."

"'Tis no evil spirit, is it? But how could it be, for he is a fine and good man in every way."

Hearing her speak of Derryn with such obvious affection caused Thomas a feeling that he couldn't define. Rather than try, he looked at her sharply, and said, "Do not go setting about to bewitch Derryn, Amica of Lancaster, as you sought to bewitch me. I will allow no man of mine to face the king's wrath over naught but a woman."

The ire that Thomas of Reed ever seemed to call forth in Amica rose high, and she said, angrily, "Why do you think so ill of me? I have done you no harm. I did not ask to wed you, I did not ask to be in your company. I have asked naught of you!"

"You are a witch," he threw back at her. "You enslave every man who sets sight upon you."

"Oh!"

Drinking down the rest of his wine, Thomas set his goblet aside with loud force. "But you will not count any of my men as your victims. I would give you over to Duncan Selwyrn by my own hand rather than let you cause division among my men. Heed me, Amica of Lancaster, for I swear by all that is holy, by God above, that this is so."

All color drained from her face, and for a horrible moment Thomas thought she might swoon. The cup trembled in her hand, then dropped to the floor. She stood, looking dumbly at the red wine that had spilled on the lovely surcoat that Lady Margot had given her to wear.

"I am sorry," she mumbled. "Sorry. I will . . ." She looked about, as if she would find some source of help.

Thomas rose to his own feet. "It is no trouble, do not be so foolish." He put a hand out to take her arm, to push her back into her chair. "I will attend to it . . ." The words came to a halt when he felt how she trembled. Smothering a curse, he pulled her into his arms. "Do not," he said, pressing her hard against him. "Do not do this."

He felt her lips moving against his shoulder, and she made a sound, "S-s-s-s-s."

"Sorry, aye," he muttered, lifting a hand and pulling the covering from her hair. "You are sorry, and so you should be." Dropping the silk cloth on the floor, he set a hand over her braided hair, and clumsily stroked. "There is no cause for such foolishness as this."

"You!" she managed, tightly, accusingly. "You!"

"Nay, not me," he countered. "You are not afraid of me. I do not know what you fear, but 'tis not me. I am the one who is afraid. Of you."

Releasing her, he moved to the nearest window. Setting his hands on the sill, he bowed his head. "God save me," he murmured, as if he prayed, "'tis true. I am afraid of you. I have never been afraid of a woman before. I do not even understand how it can be."

"It can not be," Amica said, staring at him with full amazement. "It is not true."

"It *is*," he insisted woefully. "I am like one possessed. I can think of naught but you, day and . . . night. My food tastes of you, and my drink, be it no more than water. Every word spoken to me seems dull unless it comes from your lips. Today, after I left you with my master, I could barely keep from returning to make certain that all was well. I have never done such as that before." He groaned aloud, the sound filled with remorse and misery.

"My men have ever come first in my thoughts, and today, having just returned after so long an absence, they should have been my utmost concern. But they were not. I do not even think I greeted them well. Nay, I know I did not." Lifting a hand, he rubbed at his eyes. "I found myself staring into their faces and not knowing their names, like some maddened idiot. I looked at them, but saw only Amica of Lancaster, and if Derryn had not spoken for me, bringing me back to myself, I should have been shamed before every one of them. God's mercy! How have I come down to such as that? 'Tis low and dishonorable. 'Tis worse than death! Indeed, I would prefer death than to be . . . *enslaved* by any woman."

"And especially by me," Amica whispered, wiping away the strange tears that flowed freely down her cheeks. She could not fathom why the sight of him so troubled and unhappy should make her weep. "I know you would rather hate than desire me."

He turned to her, his expression filled with gloom. "It is not a matter of love or hate or any kind of human feeling. It's only *wanting*, do you not understand?"

Dumbly, Amica shook her head.

"By the rood!" he burst out, exasperated, as angry with his own inexperience in discussing such matters as with her inability to understand what he meant. "I am become no more than an animal, sopped with lust. I want to have you—in bed." Her look of shock enraged him even more. "Or on the floor, or in the middle of the road. *Anywhere*, i'faith. I do not seem to care for comfort. I only," he drew in a breath, filled with self-loathing, "I only want you." He set a hand against the door, leaning there and closing his eyes. "God save me," he said wretchedly. "How has this happened? What shall I do to be rid of it?" He set his forehead against his hand. "I've never been so beset."

Amica folded her hands and pressed them against her stomach. "Thomas, please . . . "

He groaned in reply.

"I'm sorry," she whispered. "My lord, I did not mean to—beset you. I thought you hated me."

"Nay, it's me." His words were muffled against the wooden door. "I have tried to hate you, since that night in Belhaven. I have tried to keep away, to treat you with indifference and disdain, but it has been to no avail. I am cursed beyond all reason. 'Twas worse when we were wed, for I knew I could do as I pleased with you—claim my rights as a husband—and not be persecuted for it. You will never know how long those nights were, my lady, as we journeyed here from Belhaven. I vow, 'twas the Fiend himself whispering in my ear to have you then. Only the thought of being shackled to you for life held me back." He lifted his head, staring at the door. "If it had not been for that, if I had taken you in my madness, in my lust, we should still be wed." He shuddered, as if the thought were too unbearable to contemplate.

"Is that why you wished to leave Reed? And why you did not wish to be made responsible for my safety here? Because you were afraid that you might . . . "

He nodded. "Aye, that is why. I am afraid of you. Afraid to be near you, even while I cannot seem to help seeking you out. I have not been master of myself since that night in Belhaven, verily, since before then. Mayhap," he said hopefully, "now that I no longer have the right to do as I please as your lawful husband, I shall be returned to myself. My sense of honor has ever been strong in such matters. Mayhap 'twill be so now, and there will be no more madness. I shall pray that it will be so."

"I, also, my lord," Amica promised. "You will not

believe me, but I have not bewitched you. I know nothing of such things."

His scowl began to form on his lips. "That is not simple to believe. I have never felt such as this before. How could it be, if not for some evil sorcery?"

Amica lifted her hands in a helpless gesture. "My lord, I promise you, I have done naught."

His eyes moved over her figure, from top to bottom, then back up again. "Are you cursed, then? Did not Duncan Selwyrn lock you away because of your beauty? Because he thought you had bewitched him and might do so to others?"

"Nay!"

"And has not the king himself been enchanted, even to the point of such foolishness as keeping you safe at Reed, by my master's hand, until such time as he may fetch you and make you his leman?"

"He has not given me aid for that purpose!" she told him. "In all the years that the lord of Sacre Placean held me captive, I never set sight on King Henry, on *either* of the kings. How should he have been enchanted, as you so clearly think?"

"I do not know. I only know that you have made my life miserable, from the moment I set sight on you. S'truth, you are so beautiful that even a tale of it, even a breath of it, would make any man desire to gaze upon you with his own eyes."

"*Beauty!*" she spat the word out at him, full of hatred and venom. "As God above is my witness, I curse beauty! I curse the day I was born with such a face as this! Four years I suffered because of it. Four years I lived in darkness because of it. But no more!" She withdrew the eating dagger that was secured at her belt. "If Duncan had only given me such a weapon then, I would have killed first him and then myself. Now I wish to live!" She took a step toward Thomas, who looked at the knife she waved about with keen interest.

"Amica—"

"Why should I not live?" she demanded angrily, thrusting the knife toward him as if she might hand it to him. He put out a hand to take it away and she stepped back. "I was buried in Sacre Placean, but now I *will* live!" Turning, she moved swiftly to the lamps that glowed brightly on the far wall. Leaning close to the nearest one, she peered at the dim, leaping image of her own face reflected there. "I will live," she repeated, "but no more with this."

She had lifted the knife and slashed her cheek before Thomas could even understand her intent. The next moment he sprang toward her, shouting her name and slapping the knife away just as she had set it to her chin.

"God's mercy! Are you mad?" He put a hand up to press against her bleeding face, but she shoved it away.

"Aye! Just as you are!" she screamed. "'Tis my own face, and I shall do with it as I please!"

Weeping, she lunged toward the place where the knife had fallen on the floor, but Thomas set his hands about her waist and lifted her high up in the air, holding her over his head.

"Cease this foolishness!" he demanded wrathfully. "Cease! Else I'll hang you out a window by your heels! I would never bear such as this from any man beneath my command."

That only made her angrier.

"I'm not one of your men!" she screeched so loudly and furiously that it made Thomas's ears ache.

"God's feet," he muttered, heading for the stairs, still holding her over his head, her arms and legs flailing and the blood from her face dripping down onto his hair and clothes. "She's surely no witch." He climbed the stairs one at a time, slowly and surely, ignoring the knee that she stuck in his eye. Raising his voice above her shrieks, he said, "She's too foolish and feeble in her mind to be one!"

He tossed her on the bed in the first chamber and pushed her onto the pillows when she flung a fisted hand at his belly.

"Be still," he commanded, sitting beside her.

"Leave me be!" she shouted back.

He ignored her. Holding her down with one hand, he gripped the nearest corner of the bedsheet and ripped a large section of it free with one strong tug. Then he loomed over her, putting most of his weight on her slender body to keep her still and pressed the strip to her bleeding face.

"Calm yourself," he told her, his head near her own. "I'm of a mind to punish you for such foolishness, anyway, but you are weary, and overset, and I think I may in some small way be responsible for what has happened, so I will not."

Breathlessly, angrily, she replied, "I wish for you to leave me in peace."

"I will not do so this night," he said, pressing the cloth against her skin a little harder. "Not after this madness you have shown. What did you mean to do? Flaw your beauty?"

"Aye. I would remove it. Forever."

"You might have done so," he admitted. "You will bear a scar from your folly, I think. Does that give you some measure of peace?"

Tears welled in her eyes. "Yes!"

He wiped the tears away with his thumb. "I am sorry, then, for it will be a small measure. You will still be very beautiful. Indeed, you will still be the most beautiful woman I have ever seen. The scar will not take that away."

Closing her eyes, she sniffled loudly.

"I am not practiced with women," he said more softly. "I do not understand their ways, their thoughts. My words angered you this night, but it was not meant to be so. Had I known that I would wound you so badly with my ignorance, I would never have spoken thus. I beg that you will forgive me."

She uttered a sob and lifted a hand to touch her forehead, as if she had a terrible ache there. "It matters not," she said miserably. "All you said was true. I am cursed. *Cursed*, all my life. Weak and timorous. With this face. Why did God let me be made in such a way?" She looked at him, pleading. "Why?"

Thomas stroked her hair. "I do not know."

Another breath helped to calm her. "Even you hate me. I try not to be troublous, yet I always am. Why must it be so?"

He scowled. "You are not troublous. Save when you become crazed. Then you are, in truth, most vexing. I must make certain that you are never in possession of an eating dagger again."

Weary, her eyelids drifted downward. "I wish I were more like you, Thomas of Reed. I do not know how to be strong. 'Tis fitting that you should despise one such as me. I despise myself, as well."

"I do not despise you, neither do I bear you this hatred that you continually speak of."

Amica felt heavy with sleep, and her eyelids shut altogether. "I do not hate you, Thomas of Reed," she whispered. "You are the only man I am not afraid of."

Lifting the cloth a little and looking at her bloody, swollen cheek, he said, "You are not afraid of me, yet I fear you more than the fiercest army. 'Tis very strange."

She yawned. "Aye, 'tis indeed."

"I am going to stay in the next chamber this night," he said. "I will not let you harm yourself again, as you have done. Never again, Amica. And you will not be alone in this place. 'Twas foolishness to think I would let you be so. You shall have Maida and Margaret to tend you, and my men to watch over you. There will never again be anything for you to fear."

"I know," she said with a long sigh.

It was not a lie to say that he would sleep in the next chamber, for Thomas did, in truth, mean to do so. But he could not leave her side until he was certain that she was fully asleep, and after that he could not leave until he had bathed her face and inspected her wound and made certain, to his satisfaction, that it would not bleed again. He dabbed at the wine stains on her skirt, as well, for he thought she would be upset if she woke and saw them, though, in truth, his efforts did little more than cause the stains to seep and widen. With fresh water, poured into the chamber's basin, he washed Amica's blood from his hair and face and tunic. And then, just as he meant to go, she began to whimper, so that he had to calm her, holding her hand. Once she latched onto him, however, she did not let go, nor lessen her grip so that he might free himself, and as it was late, and he felt more than weary, Thomas sat beside her with the intention of staying only until the moment that her hold on him grew slack. But it never did lessen, and at last, expended beyond care, he lay down, with sword and boots on, fully clothed, and, pulling a cover over them both, fell soundly to sleep.

15

"*Elizabeth, k-keep the stitches* very s-small, love. See how L-Lady Amica does it?"

"Yes, Mother." Elizabeth obediently leaned toward Amica to observe the corner of the tapestry that Amica held up.

"'Tis not such a good example, is it?" she asked, smiling at the girl, who grinned back.

"Nay," Elizabeth replied honestly, "'tis not." She giggled when Amica winked at her.

Lady Margot stopped mid-stride, turning to her eldest daughter with full surprise. "Elizabeth!" she said, mortification heavy in her voice.

Amica and Elizabeth burst out laughing, and Lady Margot gave them a measured look of reproof. "A fine p-pair of jesters you m-make," she said. "That t-tapestry will ne'er be f-finished, I vow, if those who ply the needles do n-naught but make m-merry. Leave the foolishness to Jace, if't please you, and t-tend your work."

"But, Mother, 'tis such a fine day," Elizabeth coun-

tered. "Must we waste all of it on needlework? You did
not make Katy and Ellie labor on it."

The babe in her arms whimpered, and Lady Margot
hitched her tiny daughter higher, rocking her back and
forth. "Ellie is t-too little to d-do such work," she
answered. "And Katy's eyes are weak. You know that
she c-cannot do such f-fine sewing and not suffer an
aching head later. And," she added quickly as Elizabeth
opened her mouth to argue, "the tapestry is for Kenric
Willan, as your g-gift to him this c-coming Michaelmas.
'Tis only right that you labor on p-part of it with your
own hand, before I give it over to my l-ladies to finish."

Both Amica and Elizabeth dropped the heavy cloth
into their laps and stared at her with equal expressions
of surprise, though Amica's was one of gladness while
Elizabeth's was filled with fury.

"Kenric Willan?" Amica repeated.

"Why did you not tell me!" Elizabeth demanded
angrily, her dark eyes flashing with accusation. "I never
should have touched it had I known, save to rend it!"
With a shove, she pushed the tapestry from both her
and Amica's lap and sent it to the ground.

"Elizabeth!" Lady Margot scolded. "That is enough!
N-Never let your father hear you speaking thusly, else
you'll f-find yourself abovestairs with neither f-food nor
c-company for a day and a night. Kenric Willan is a fine
young m-man. He has done n-naught to deserve such
scorn."

"I hate him!" Elizabeth declared, stamping her foot
and crossing her arms.

Lady Margot made a *tsking* sound, shaking her head
at her eldest child's furiously unhappy expression.

"You are young, yet," she said more gently. "You
have n-naught to fear of Kenric Willan or any other
m-man, as your father and I have oft t-told you. Has

your father not p-promised that, when you come of age, you will n-not be made to m-marry any man you do not wish to? Including Kenric Willan?"

Amica reached down to pull the tapestry back up to her knees. Dusting the fine wool cloth, she asked, "You are betrothed to Kenric Willan, Elizabeth?"

"Yes," the girl replied sourly, glaring at the tapestry. "I hate him," she repeated. "He pushed me in the mud when I met him, and then he laughed!"

"He did n-not push you into that m-mud puddle," Lady Margot corrected patiently. "You fell in on your own account, and he tried quite valiantly to p-pull you out."

"He laughed the whole time!" Elizabeth returned hotly. "And I never would have fallen in if he'd only let me see his bird! He shoved me back when I tried to look at it!"

"He was t-trying to keep you from being b-bitten," Lady Margot said. "That bird had n-not yet been well trained, and you behaved j-just as if it were one of our own b-birds here at Reed." She looked at Amica. "Kenric only m-meant to keep her safe, I'm certain of it, but he is a rather l-large and clumsy boy, and he d-did push Elizabeth a bit harder than was n-needed. And, to be fair, he did try to pull her out at once. Poor K-Kenric, he t-tried to apologize to her often while we remained at court that season, but Elizabeth would have n-none of him. I felt most sorry for the b-boy. He was a little afraid of her, I think, though he is six years older and so m-much larger than she."

"Aye, I know Kenric Willan very well," Amica said. "He is in truth quite shy, and rather clumsy, just as you say, but he is a good and gentle lad, Elizabeth. I am certain he would never want to bring you harm apurpose."

Elizabeth looked at her more closely. "How do you know him, my lady? He is one of the king's cousins."

"He is one of my cousins, as well," Amica told her. She smiled into Elizabeth's angry countenance, recalling how vulnerable she, too, had felt at being betrothed at such an early age.

"'Twas the k-king's desire to see our families m-more closely related through m-marriage," Lady Margot said with a sigh. "My l-lord could n-not naysay him, though he d-did secure King Henry's p-promise that our children will be free to d-decline any arrangements he has declared f-for them when they are of age. 'Tis n-not that we should be against Elizabeth wedding Kenric if she w-wished it, or for any of our daughters to wed those l-lads whom Henry has chosen for them, but I have n-never wanted them to wed for any other p-purpose than the desire to do so."

"Oh yes!" Amica said quickly. "How good you and Sir Eric are, my lady, to love your children so well and to think so kindly of them." She smiled at Elizabeth again. "You see, all shall be well. You need not wed dear Kenric, though he is, I vow, a good lad. I have not seen him in many years, but unless he has changed greatly, he was always used to be so."

"Why have you not wed, Lady Amica?" Elizabeth asked, bending to take up the tapestry once again and pull it reluctantly upon her lap.

"Elizabeth!" her mother cried once again. "Your t-tongue is as f-free as a rudderless ship."

"But she is so beautiful!" Elizabeth protested. "I have seen all of Father's men gazing at her as if she were a sweet and they would like to eat her up. Even Thomas looks at her so!"

Amica's face grew hot with embarrassment.

Lady Margot seemed momentarily at a loss for words. "God's m-mercy," she managed at last. "Elizabeth, l-love, why do you not go and f-find your sisters? I believe J-Jace has them out in the bailey, playing with the d-dogs."

Grateful for her reprieve, Elizabeth leapt to her feet. "May I practice my archery, Mother? I shall not let Ellie touch my bow or any of the arrows. I promise!"

"Yes, but p-please do m-make certain of that," Lady Margot told her. "I do not want her s-stabbing Jace in the l-leg, as she did last time."

Giving her solemn vow that she would do so, Elizabeth ran out of the garden. Lady Margot turned to Amica, who, still red-faced, was carefully inspecting the tapestry.

"Forgive Elizabeth's thoughtless p-prattling," Lady Margot said gently. "She did not m-mean to be so rude."

Amica lifted her face and smiled. "Nay, I know she did not, nor ever would. She is young, yet. I took no offense, my lady. And 'twas a likely question. 'Tis indeed odd for any woman to be unwed at such an advanced age." Which was only the truth, Amica thought, despite the fact that she was indeed wed.

Lady Margot looked at her consideringly. "I m-must speak in truth," she stated. "I have often wondered the s-same. I p-promised my l-lord that I should ask no questions of you regarding your circumstances, and so I will n-not, yet I too f-find it most amazing that you are n-not wed. I do not think there is a m-man in all of Reed who does n-not gaze upon you with dreams in his heart."

"My lady!" Amica protested.

"N-Nay, 'tis so," Lady Margot insisted. "Even our T-Tom, who has n-never, that I can remember, looked upon a grown woman with anything more than d-disdain."

"He does not look upon you with disdain," Amica countered.

"Bah!" Lady Margot scoffed lightly. "I have b-been

as his m-mother these past many years, and would have f-fostered him, in truth, if he had b-but permitted it. I meant that he does not look at women of his own age with anything m-more than disdain. Save you, of course." She glanced at Amica, grinning. "I d-do believe our Tom has been smitten by you, my dear."

The words were so foolish that Amica didn't know whether to laugh or weep.

"My lady, he is not, I promise you."

"I c-cannot think of what else it m-might be," Lady Margot told her. "I have never seen him seek out the company of a woman before, as he does yours—"

"But, my lady, he doesn't! If he seeks me out, 'tis merely to make certain of my safety, as his lord has bidden him."

Lady Margot chuckled. "And having made certain of it, why then d-does he linger?" she challenged. "It has n-never been his way to loll about, m-making idle speech. It has gladdened my heart to see him so often in your company." She looked at Amica with a glowing expression. "I hope you will not be angered if I s-say that I have begun to harbor a hope that, p-perhaps, you m-might feel kindly toward him."

"My lady—" Amica began, mortified.

"Oh, I realize that he is n-neither handsome nor charming, as m-many other men may be, and that he sometimes appears to be without f-feeling, but it is there, deep within him. He suffered greatly when he was a child, and l-learned to hide his heart, to k-keep from b-being hurt."

"I have wondered on that," Amica admitted quietly. "When we were at Belhaven, he took me to the dwelling he had shared with his father, and told me something of his father's death. It seemed that the memory pained him, or what little of it he recalled."

Lady Margot nodded. "Aye, and so it should. Thomas's f-father was a brute, a drunkard who b-beat him often. He had n-nearly beaten Thomas to d-death on the night that he himself died."

Amica nearly dropped the tapestry onto the ground again. "God's mercy! Thomas told me he was there when his father died, but he did not say that he had been beaten. It is no mystery, then, that he cannot remember how his father's death came about."

"Indeed, and if my l-lord had not gone to the dwelling in search of T-Thomas, he surely would have died. He came very n-near d-death even so, after Eric carried him back to Castle Belhaven, so b-broken and bloodied, poor boy!" She shook her head. "I have seldom seen my l-lord shed tears, but for f-fear of losing his Tom, he did, and beseeched G-God on his knees to make him live. When the p-priest came to administer a final sacrament, Eric cursed him and threw him out of the chamber, b-barring him from entering again under threat of d-death, which threat my lord readily would have c-carried out with his own t-two hands, I vow, for he was in such a state. He would n-not let Thomas die, and stayed by his side through the n-next two days and n-nights, commanding, m-most sternly, that he l-live." She smiled. "Even in that, Thomas was obedient."

Amica felt the sting of tears in her eyes. "May God be praised."

"Aye," Lady Margot agreed. "You m-must see, then, that Thomas has a rare and w-wonderful heart. He is a m-man worth many. Oh, indeed he is. When T-Thomas gives his love, it is a wondrous gift, strong and everlasting. When he g-gives his loyalty, it is wholly and without fetter."

"Yes," Amica whispered.

"These are things that no amount of g-gold can purchase," Lady Margot continued. "I have often thought, nay I have known, that the w-woman who is blessed with these g-gifts—should Thomas ever find a woman whom he may t-trust them with, for they are really himself—will be a woman most f-fortunate."

Such thoughts were not foreign to Amica. She had wondered, often, what it might be like to be the possessor of such faith and love as Thomas of Reed was capable of giving. How different life would be with such a man than it had been with one like Duncan Selwyrn. Without thought, Amica touched the scar upon her cheek. She had been the one to put it there, yet Thomas had taken the blame of it, and had told his master that she had somehow slipped in the priest's lodgings, and that he had not caught her in time before she had torn her face on the edge of one of the tables there. Sir Eric had accepted the lie without question, though he had looked very knowingly at the sharp cut on her cheek and said, "How fortunate that it is so even and clean, more like the cut of a knife than the ragged tear a wooden table might cause. It will heal with little left to show for it." Then he had added, rather severely, as he kept his eyes upon her, "Do not let it happen again, Tom, else I shall be sorely angered." In that moment, filled with shame for her wretched, foolish behavior, Amica had been more than a little grateful to Thomas of Reed. She had not wanted him to take her blame; she knew she should not have let him do so, and yet she was grateful that he had, for she could not have faced the lord of Reed otherwise. They had never discussed the matter, she and Thomas. She had been too aware of what it would cost him, even if she should try to speak her thanks.

"Does it g-give you p-pain, my dear?" Lady Margot asked, bringing Amica's thoughts back into the garden.

"I shall m-make a new pot of ointment this afternoon and add m-more camphor this t-time."

"Oh no, my lady," Amica said quickly, lowering her hand. "There is still some left from the last pot you made. It has proved most soothing and in truth there is no longer any pain."

Lady Margot nodded with satisfaction, leaning forward to inspect the nearly vanished wound. "'Twas a f-fortunate thing that it d-did not mar your face m-more permanently. Even s-so, your beauty would have remained to enchant every m-man who sets eyes upon you. Indeed, I will f-feel a little s-sorry for dear Thomas, should he one d-day win your hand. He will ever be j-jealous of his lady being stared at by so m-many men." She laughed, and Amica, despite her desire to naysay the lady of Reed, found herself laughing, too.

"You are in good humor, I see."

Both ladies looked up to see Thomas standing just inside the garden courtyard, dressed in his armor, his sword held in one hand and his helmet in the other. His white-blond hair was damp, sticking to his sweaty, dirt-streaked face. He gazed back at them questioningly.

"Aye, and w-why should we not be?" Lady Margot asked. "It is a beautiful summer's d-day and all is w-well." At that moment, Lady Gwendolen Stavelot opened her tiny mouth and emitted a squeal of distress, drawing her mother's attention. "Save with this l-little one," she said, "who is probably w-wanting to be fed. Hush now, little Gwen."

Thomas strode across the courtyard, frowning as he gazed at the child, whose mouth opened once more to give a louder cry.

"You have disturbed her slumber with such noisome laughter," he accused, dropping his sword and helmet and reaching to take the tiny bundle expertly into his arms. Cradling her, he walked slowly about the yard, speaking softly. "There now," he murmured. "There now. Did they wake you, my lady? They are loud and rude, are they not? So cruel, disturbing your sleep. There, there."

Lady Margot cast a glance at Amica. "Thomas seems to think n-no one can do as w-well for my children as he."

"She no longer cries," Thomas stated, which was true, for the baby had quieted in his arms. "It is too bright a day to have her out of doors for so long a time. The sun will harm her eyes. She should be inside, near the fire." He bent his stern eye upon his master's wife. "And taking her nourishment, i'faith," he said, in a tone that indicated Lady Margot was more than a little remiss in her duties as a mother.

"This is s-so," she agreed readily. "But who will b-bear Lady Amica company if I go indoors?"

"Oh, my lady, I am well enough alone," Amica assured her.

Thomas, still walking slowly with the child, scowled. "I was not aware that she required company every moment of the day. Indeed, I understood that she did not wish it."

"It is inhospitable to speak as if L-Lady Amica were not p-present, Thomas," Lady Margot chided, standing and holding her arms out for the baby. "I shall s-send one of my ladies to b-bear you company, my lady."

"Nay, nay," Thomas said, setting Lady Gwendolen in her mother's arms as if she were made of some delicate, airy substance. "I will bear her company." He sounded as if it were a great sacrifice to make.

Lady Margot looked at him with mock surprise. "You, T-Thomas? I had n-not thought of that." She gave Amica a knowing grin. "I had s-supposed you to be busy with your m-men."

He spent a moment tucking Lady Gwendolen's blanket around her face before replying, "Nay, we have finished our practice. A messenger has just arrived, announcing that Stevan of Hearn will follow within the hour. I did not wish to greet him while attired in such a manner."

"Sir Stevan is arriving at last!" Amica said happily. "I am so glad, my lord."

Something like a smile briefly touched his lips.

"Aye, 'tis good news. 'Twill be good to have Stevan back at Reed."

"So it w-will," Lady Margot agreed. "We m-must have a feast in his honor. He has been gone so much l-longer than we had thought. My lord will be m-more than pleased."

Thomas nodded. "I would appreciate that, my lady. A feast to give Stevan welcome. It would mean much to him." He seemed, to Amica, to speak the words almost shyly.

Lady Margot lifted herself on her toes to kiss his dirty cheek. "I will g-go and put it in order right away."

When she had gone, Thomas collapsed on the bench beside Amica, closing his eyes wearily.

"You seem fit this day," he stated in the blunt manner that Amica had come to know so well.

"Aye," she said lightly, turning her attention to the tapestry on her knees. She could think of little that she enjoyed more than spending time in his company. Although she had come to love the lord and lady of Reed and all of their beautiful daughters, it was Thomas of Reed alone with whom she still felt comfortable and relaxed. "I am. You have been laboring with your men?"

"Battle practice," he said, rubbing his eyes. "They have all done well, may God be praised. I cannot think of another army that would care to meet my men across a battlefield."

"They are well trained," she agreed, drawing her needle through the cloth. "You are very dirty, my lord." She eased the statement with a tiny smile. "With Stevan returning this day, would you not rather go and tend to your bath than to sit in this garden?"

He stretched his legs out, relaxing. "I will sit a moment and take my ease. I feel very weary today."

The admission surprised Amica, for Thomas seldom spoke of any personal weakness. "You are not falling ill, are you?" She felt a genuine distress at the thought.

"Nay," he said, though the word sounded troubled. "'Tis simply that we have trained so oft this past week, and I do not sleep well, as you know."

She knew very well. He spoke of his sleeplessness often enough, and of the cause of it.

"Sir Evrain was here earlier," she said after a moment of silence passed. "He said that you put those two soldiers to work in the stables for what happened yesterday."

"Aye, and so I did. If they will behave as crudely as cattle, they will labor with the cattle."

Amica's needle fell still. "But 'twas not their fault that I am so foolish as to be frightened when they merely wished me a good day. I do not see how you can punish them for such as that."

He made a scoffing sound. "They did more than frighten you, or have you forgotten that I was a witness to the encounter? 'Twas the way they looked at you, lewd and unmannerly—"

"But I did not even see their faces!" she protested.

"I did," he said curtly. "The lecherous knaves. I should have done more than knock their heads together and cause them to work in the stables for a month.

They were fortunate to escape without a more fitting punishment." He folded his arms across his chest. "You shook for more than half an hour's time. And wept." His hands curled into fists. "For that alone I should have beaten them senseless."

"'Twould not have been just," she said.

Thomas gave no reply, but merely sat beside her, making an angry grumbling sound until Amica said, more gently, "I did enjoy seeing the forest. 'Twas the first time I've been outside the castle gates since I came to Reed. Thank you for taking me there, my lord."

The set line of his mouth relaxed. "'Twas the only way I could think of to make you stop that cursed weeping. And I did think that you might enjoy an outing." He began to look embarrassed. "God's truth, you've walked every bit of the gardens inside the castle walls a hundred times over or more."

She laughed. "Not so much as that, surely! Though mayhap you would know better than I, for you have walked with me often enough."

"As my lord would wish," he noted, "for he did charge me with your safety."

"Aye, that he did."

Amica thought of what she had so recently learned about Thomas. She longed to speak of it, to tell him that she knew about his father, and to give him comfort, though he would not want it from her. Indeed, he would most surely become angered, for he was a man who hid his need for kindness and gentleness, a man who could not openly accept it from others.

"Sir Eric loves you well," she murmured. "I understand fully why he sought to make you his heir."

"He should not have done so," Thomas muttered, lifting a hand to rub wearily at the back of his neck. "I resisted him in the matter as long as I could, but at last gave way, just as he knew I would. He is the most stubborn man on God's earth, I vow."

His sigh almost made Amica laugh. "I believe, my lord, that Sir Eric would say very much the same of you."

The sudden smile that Thomas gave her was more blinding than the sun. Amica felt a sharp pain in her chest, and her thoughts scattered just as if she had, in truth, been momentarily blinded. Blinking, she strove to collect herself as she heard him reply, "Aye, that he would. We argued long and fully on the matter for many years. I only gave way when it was understood that if Lady Margot gives him a son one day, then I shall no longer have claim to the title, or to any of my lord's properties. For now," he said, leaning to retrieve his sword and helmet from the dirt, "I will be content to hold Reed and its treasures for my lord's children and grandchildren, and will keep them safe against any who would try to wrest it from them, should my lord, God forbid it, pass away."

With another sigh, he turned to Amica. "I should go now, I think. It is . . ." The words faded away, and the expression he saw on her face caused him to release his sword and helmet and let them slide back down to the ground.

"Why do you look at me so?" he asked.

"I do not know."

"You are not becoming ill?"

"Nay."

"You look most . . . strange." Gently, he touched the scar upon her cheek, running his fingers over the length of it. "This heals more each day. It does not pain you?"

"Nay."

He frowned, gazing into her eyes with increasing worry. "Then why do you stare at me so?"

"I do not know," she said again, and lifted her own hand to touch his chin with her fingertips, noting the tremor that ran through him. "Your face is wonderful. I see it in my dreams, sometimes."

His hand fell still, warm against her flesh. "Why should you? I am no handsome man."

Amica thought of Duncan, of his handsome face which she had come to hate. She slid her fingers upward to touch a scar beneath one of Thomas's eyes. He was not handsome as Duncan was, and yet, she thought she loved the sight of his face better than anything else.

"I find you very beautiful," she said, hearing with some bewilderment the breathlessness of her words. She wondered what she meant by them, why she had said them.

His eyes filled with confusion and hunger. "You dally with me," he whispered, drawing nearer. "You seek to bewitch me."

"I do not know how. I begin to think I am the one who has been bewitched, my lord. You once said that I was not afraid of you, but I think I am."

"Because I made you cry once," he said, spreading his fingers and pushing them into her soft hair.

"Nay," she murmured, her eyelids closing at the pleasure of his hand upon her, "'tis because I dream of you. I have never dreamed such things before."

"I do not believe you." His mouth lowered toward hers. "Why should you dream of me, Amica of Lancaster," he whispered against her lips, "when I am the one who is so beset?"

"Please." With her hand she sought to bring him down even farther, even as she lifted herself up to meet him.

"Amica . . ."

"Lady Amica!" the lord of Reed's voice sounded loud in the silence, and Thomas jumped up from the bench, standing fully upright. Sir Eric didn't seem to notice his harsh breathing as he strode toward him. "Here you are! I have been searching you out, my lady. Ah, Tom, well met."

Thomas swallowed so loudly that even Amica could hear it. "My lord," he greeted.

"My good lady wife has just announced that Sir Stevan returns to Reed within the hour. That is cause to rejoice, is it not? It will be good and more to have him back."

Glancing at Amica, Thomas said, "Aye. He has been gone longer than I could have imagined."

Sir Eric nodded, looking from Thomas to Amica and back again. He suddenly seemed to realize that he had intruded. "Aye, well, you will want to prepare for his arriving, Tom, and I must speak with Lady Amica." Clearing his throat, he added, "Uhm . . . privately."

"Yes, my lord. As you will. Good day, then." Stiffly, he cast a bow toward Amica. "Good day, my lady."

"Good day," she murmured, watching as he walked out of the courtyard in the direction of the soldiers' quarters.

Sir Eric moved to sit beside her, and the smile on his face made Amica wary. She had grown quite easy with the giant lord of Reed during the past month; indeed, knowing now what a charming, gentle man he was, she could not even remember why she had ever feared him. He had been as kind and good to her as if she had been one of his own daughters.

"My lord . . ." she said accusingly at his happy grin.

"My Tom has fallen in love at long last, I see." He chuckled. "God be thanked, I have prayed often enough for such as that."

Amica shook her head, feeling unaccountably sad and lost, for she knew very well that Thomas held no such tender emotions for her. "You and your lady wife are more than a little fanciful, I fear. Sir Thomas bears me no love. He seeks only to please his master in suffering my presence."

"He is an obedient lad," Sir Eric agreed, "but that does not make him a fool, my lady, or blind, forsooth. If he had not fallen in love with such a beautiful maid I should have taken him by the neck and beaten some sense into him."

With a sigh, Amica took up her needle and set to work on the tapestry once more. "Thomas of Reed has no care for my beauty, my lord, just as he bears me no love. And I am no longer a maid."

He ignored her words and said, "I would be most glad to see you wedded with Tom. He is stern, I know, but a more loyal man does not live, and he would make a fine husband, I vow. Your cousin, King Henry, agrees that he would make a very good match for you, for Tom will one day be the lord of Reed, and so is acceptable for one of your lineage."

Frowning, Amica gazed up at him and, seeing that he was in earnest, she chided, "My lord, how can you make jest of such things? You know that I am already wed. To Duncan Selwyrn."

Sir Eric's smile softened. He reached out and gently took her hand, stilling her work. "No longer, my lady," he said. "A messenger from our king arrived only an hour past, bearing good tidings."

Amica felt, quite suddenly, as if her body had stopped working. She could not move, nor draw in enough breath.

The lord of Reed turned her hand until the palm faced upward, then drew a rolled piece of parchment out of his tunic. Setting it in her hand, he folded her fingers around it.

"This," he murmured, "is the proof of what I say. You are free now to wed any man whom the king approves, for you are no longer wed to the lord of Sacre Placean. Your marriage to Duncan Selwyrn has been irrevocably annulled."

A dull roaring, like the thrum of sea waves, sounded in Amica's ears. She didn't even realize that her gaze was fixed upon the document in her hands until she saw the edges of the parchment trembling like dried leaves caught up in a breeze. The breath she finally drew in caused a sharp, tight pain in her chest. She closed her eyes, squeezing her hand into a fist and feeling the thick, waxy parchment twisting against the flesh of her palm.

She thought, for one confused moment, that she was falling, but Sir Eric held her up, one huge hand warm on her back, the other clutching her arm.

"He will never touch you again," she heard him saying, near her ear, against the throbbing sound. "You are free of him, Amica. You are safe here. Always."

The world was blurred when she opened her eyes; each breath she drew made a terrible squeaking sound, just as if she were weeping and could not control her sobs. Memories of Duncan, of Alys, of her chamber at Sacre Placean, flew through her thoughts.

"Do you understand me, Amica? He cannot touch you now. You are free."

16

 "*'Tis a sad thing, Tom,*" Derryn Thewlis said with a sigh, crossing his arms over his chest. "We left him at Belhaven a peacock, and he comes home to Reed even more magnificently arrayed. What can we do with such a fellow, I ask?"

Reclining on his sleeping pallet, watching as Stevan put his things away in his clothing chest, Thomas suggested, lazily, "Dunk him in the fish pond?"

Stevan turned from his chore only long enough to give his friends a look of disdain. "If I seem grand in any way, 'tis only because the two of you are so poorly attired. As ever." He went back to folding his clothes. "A toad would look well next to the two of you."

Derryn chuckled and Thomas said, "I believe the stable would be a better place to drop him."

"Aye," Derryn agreed, still laughing. "And I can think of just the right spot. Where the muck is piled."

Stevan let the lid of the chest drop shut, then he turned and sat on top of it, smiling widely.

"'Tis good to be at Reed again," he said. "I have dreamed of this day."

Derryn and Thomas exchanged amused glances.

"I have never seen him so happy," Derryn remarked. "What can have him in such a state, I wonder?"

"Aye, he does, indeed, look very well pleased," Thomas agreed. "Mayhap he has discovered some hidden treasure, and so can repay his debt to his father and get himself wed, as he is ever prating on about doing."

His smile widening, Stevan chuckled, looking slightly embarrassed.

"Look at him!" Derryn cried. "It must be the truth you speak, Tom, for I have never before seen the lad blush, i'faith!"

"He's as pink as a shy young maid in springtime," Thomas teased. "Will he tell us what has happened, or will he burst from holding it back?"

"Aye, Stevan, don't make us wait, for 'tis clear you bear glad tidings. Speak!"

"They are glad tidings, indeed," Stevan said, looking at each of them in turn. "I was late in returning to Reed because I traveled first to Hearn, to speak with my father. I told him that I had met the woman I desired above all others to take as my wife, and I begged him—on my knees, yet—to release me of the debt I owe him, or to let me wed and continue to repay him." He paused a moment before adding, "He released me fully, and gave me his permission to wed."

"May God be praised!" Thomas declared, rising to a sitting position.

"He returned my inheritance to me and bade me take my place there. It is but a small fief, no more than a manor house, in truth, but a goodly place to take a wife and start a family."

Both Derryn and Thomas descended on him, pounding his shoulders and speaking their congratulations.

"That is blessed news," Derryn said, clutching Stevan's arm.

"Indeed, it is," Thomas agreed, gripping his friend by the back of the neck and playfully shaking him. "I cannot believe you are finally to take a wife. It has been many years that you have dreamed of it."

"I will need to speak with Sir Eric first, of course," Stevan said, gladly accepting their good wishes. "He may not release me of my vow of fealty, though my father has said that he will pay him for whatever is left of it."

Thomas waved a hand in the air, as if that were of no consequence. "I will ask him to make a gift of it to you—a wedding gift, as a boon for all your years of excellent service. Surely he will not hesitate to do so, and to offer you all good wishes."

"Thank you, Tom," Stevan said gratefully. "If you ask him, he will do it, I know. He has never before denied a request you have made of him. Thank you."

"Do not speak such as that to me," Thomas told him. "There is no need for it, for you have served me well these many years. 'Tis I who am grateful to have had you in my command." He moved to a table set in the corner of the room, where a decanter of wine sat among several goblets. "Come, let us drink to your good health, Stevan, and to your good fortune."

"Amen!" Derryn approved. As he took the goblet that Thomas held out, he added, "Here is to Stevan, to his future, and to his bride. May God bless you all of your days."

Lifting their cups, they saluted one another and drank. "Who is the woman you have chosen for a wife, then, lad?" Thomas asked. "Did you meet some comely maid in Belhaven, while you rested there?"

Derryn nudged Stevan in the side. "Some sweet beauty who nursed you? A goodly wench to keep you warm when the snow is on the ground and the wind blows cold?"

Stevan laughed. "Oh, she is, in truth, a goodly wench. A lady most beautiful and kind. A woman a man might kill to make his own. She is more lovely than any of God's angels."

With a shake of his head, Thomas declared, "No such woman lives, I vow."

"She does," Stevan said with a sigh, looking toward the ceiling as if he could see this perfect vision there. "And you have seen her with your own eyes. Amica of Lancaster."

Derryn, who had just taken a drink from his cup, made a sudden choking sound, then spewed wine all over his friends.

"Derry!" Stevan jumped back, wiping at his tunic, while Thomas stood utterly still, even as Stevan moved forward again to pound the still choking Derryn on the back.

"Amica of Lancaster?" Thomas repeated, the words lost in the sounds of Derryn's coughing and Stevan's pounding. "You wish to wed Amica of Lancaster?"

Gasping, Derryn placed a hand against the nearest wall and tried to breathe, while Stevan continued to slap his back between his shoulders.

"Will you be all right?" he asked, just as Thomas grabbed his arm and swung him around to face him.

"Do you mean this?" he demanded. "You intend to wed Amica of Lancaster?"

"You ask me that now while Derryn is choking? God above! Help me get him over to the bed."

Thomas looked at Derryn as if seeing his distress for the first time. "Oh." But when he moved to grip Derryn's arm, he was waved away.

"No," Derryn gasped, coughing. "I'm fine. Leave me be."

"If I'd known my news would take you so much by surprise," Stevan said, bending down to peer into Derryn's face and make certain that his color was returning, "I would have given you some warning. Does it seem so strange a thing that I should wish to court Lady Amica?" He straightened and gazed at Thomas, who was scowling at him. "No other man has already claimed her hand while I was gone, I pray."

"Nay. She is yet unclaimed."

Pushing himself upright, Derryn leaned against the wall, wheezing. He set a hand against his chest and drew in each breath slowly.

"And your marriage to her has been annulled, has it not?" Stevan kept his gaze on Thomas. "'Twas not, in truth, a binding marriage, for you never claimed your marriage rights. Was it not at once annulled?"

Thomas turned away, returning to the table where the wine was set. "It has been annulled." He filled the goblet he held. When he set the decanter down, he stared at the wine in his cup. "I never realized that you harbored any affection for her. I did not know that you had even done so much as to speak with her for but a few moments' time. Do you think that she returns your feelings?"

"I cannot think she does," Stevan replied, noting, with some bewilderment, the softening of tension in Thomas's stance. "And, in truth, we have spoken very little together. But I mean to win her, if I can do so, and will make every effort toward that goal. Of course, I must speak with Sir Eric to discover if such a match can be made, for I know nothing about her, save that thoughts of her kept me sane while I sojourned at Belhaven, and that she is the most beautiful maiden I have ever before set sight upon." He glanced at Derryn, whose breathing had become normal again. "But that, in truth, is all that any of us knows. Unless either of you have learned more in the days that have passed. She was all a mystery when we parted ways, and I had thought—hoped—that she had remained so." He smiled. "I have dreamed of revealing all her secrets myself, one by one."

"She is yet a mystery," Thomas said quietly. "My lord has not seen fit to reveal any more concerning her, save that which we already knew." He drank deeply from his goblet. When he set it down, he turned to Stevan. "I cannot fathom why you wish to wed such a woman, who is nearly a stranger to you."

Stevan's expression became one of gentle pity. "You would not be able to understand it, Tom. You dislike women. I do not expect you to look at Amica of Lancaster, or another woman, in the same manner that I or Derryn or any other man would."

Standing against the wall, Derryn groaned loudly, "Stevan . . . "

Ignoring him, Stevan stepped toward Thomas. "All I ask of you, as my friend, is to be glad for me. And as the man whom I have served these many years, I would ask your blessing."

Thomas stared at the arm Stevan held out to him for a long, silent moment before finally grasping it. "Of course," he murmured. "Of course, you have that— both of those—without needing to ask for either. I have always wished you well, Stevan."

Stevan smiled. "I know, Tom. You and Derryn are the finest friends a man could have, and I praise God for both of you." He grinned at Derryn. "If Lady Amica will accept me as a husband, I hope you will act as my groomsmen."

Slapping a hand over his eyes, Derryn groaned once more, even more loudly.

"Are you going to be all right, Derry?" Stevan asked with concern.

Derryn's hand slid down his face, covering his mouth and revealing wide, distressed eyes. Silently, he nodded.

"Good," Stevan said, turning back to Thomas. "You agree then? That you'll stand as my groomsmen if Amica of Lancaster agrees to wed with me?"

"I would be . . . more than glad to do so, Stevan, as I'm sure Derryn will be. You honor us."

"Nay, 'tis you who honor me. Thank you, Tom."

"There is no need to speak of thanks," Thomas said quickly. "I must go." He moved toward the door, not looking at either of them. "I must go and . . . speak with someone." Wrapping his fingers about the handle, he hesitated as if he would say something more, but he did not, and opened the door and left.

Stevan smiled at Derryn, who still stood against the wall, his hand over his mouth.

"I am the most fortunate man on God's earth to possess such friends." Looking more closely at Derryn, he asked, "Are you, in truth, well, Derry?"

Derryn's hand dropped away, and he fixed his companion with an angry expression.

"Stevan, you—you cursed *idiot!*"

Stevan's mouth gaped. "Me? What have I done?"

"Sit down and keep quiet," Derryn told him, pointing at the nearest chair, "and I shall gladly tell you."

17

He should not be here, Thomas thought as he shrugged more closely into the hooded cloak he wore and as the tavern wench set yet another tankard of ale before him. Staring at the dull, scarred pewter, he thought to himself that he surely must tell her to take it away, for he had already drunk more this night than he could ever before remember doing. That reflection quickly became lost among his more morbid thoughts, and he dug a coin from his tunic and set it in the girl's grimy hand. Taking the tankard up, he drank from it deeply.

Gazing from beneath the hood that withheld his identity from the other occupants of the Swan and Toad, Thomas's regard fell upon a group of his own men sitting at a table not far from his. He wondered what they would think if they realized that he sat so nearby, listening to their idle chatter. They would be surprised, he knew, for he seldom visited such places as this. He had, in fact, only ever set foot inside this particular tavern, so popular with the people of Reed, for one purpose, and that was to spend a few short minutes with one of the tavern whores. On the five occasions that he had done so, he had not dallied to sit with his men and share a glass of ale or wine with them. He did not think he would enjoy doing such a thing, for he was not good at making common talk, as Derryn and Stevan were, and he doubted even more that his men would welcome it. In truth, if they knew of his presence at the moment, they would most certainly become uncomfortable. Thinking of that, Thomas lifted a hand and tugged at the hood, drawing it more securely across his face. He did not wish to sit in silence this night. He did not want to be alone. The sounds of the tavern, all the clattering of tankards and servingware and cooking pots, the talk and shouts and laughter—all of it kept him from thinking too clearly, and that was what he desired.

She had looked beautiful tonight, of course. She always looked beautiful. Indeed, each time he set eyes on her she somehow seemed more stunning than the time before; and each time his heart fell into his feet, so that he wondered why he longed so much to see her when he knew very well how painful it would be. But tonight—tonight there had been something more, something in her eyes that had naught to do with mere physical beauty. She had looked so peaceful and happy. When she had looked at him and smiled, Thomas had frozen in the place where he stood. And then, when he would have gone to her, she had smiled at Stevan, and her look had held more than simple welcome. She had gone to Stevan and lifted herself up and kissed him on his face—and Thomas still didn't know how he had kept from committing murder. He had gazed at them through a red haze of fury, while Amica had smiled and laughed and held Stevan's arm and let him escort her up to the long table. It had been the most horrible moment in Thomas's entire life. He had nearly wanted to weep.

He hadn't remained for the feast, but had simply walked out of the castle. He supposed he had done so, at least, for he found himself sitting alone in the gardens, though he could not exactly recall how he had come there. When the wind became chill enough, he went to his chamber for a cloak and then to the Swan and Toad with every intention of using a whore and leaving as soon as he was finished. But he had only walked through the tavern doors and sat down in the farthest, darkest corner. And there he had remained for the next several hours, drinking himself into a stupor.

The trouble, he thought morosely, picking up the tankard and taking a long drink from it, was that he had grown used to her. To Amica of Lancaster, with her quiet speech and manner and presence. He had become comfortable, as he had never done with any other woman, not even, in all truth, Lady Margot or Lady Elaine. When he was with Amica of Lancaster, he did not feel the need to make idle speech, for she was pleased to simply sit and be quiet or to speak of whatever matters he wished to speak of. In the past month, since they had returned to Reed, they had spent much time together in complete silence, she doing her needlework and he tending some small task, caring for his weapons or armor or reading over the lists and accounts that the castellan or chamberlain brought him. He seldom needed to explain anything twice to her, for she was possessed of a ready mind and was not given to the foolish dallying manner that other maids plied to tease a man. She liked to walk, and he had found pleasure in bearing her company during such times when, again, they were content with silence or to speak only of those things that drew the eye—the clouds or flowers or birds. Amica found much delight in such simple things, and Thomas had come to appreciate her observances of the ways of God and nature. Indeed, though he had never thought he would admit such a thing about a woman, she was very nearly a perfect companion.

She would marry Stevan. She would be very foolish if she did not, and Thomas did not think Amica of Lancaster a fool. Stevan had everything to offer her, more than a woman could want or desire. A fine home, lands of his own, an honored lineage, servants and fine clothes and a life of ease. And more, Stevan possessed a handsome face and charm and an easy manner that never failed to draw out a woman's smile. And he had certainly gained a favorable reputation as a man who pleased women, both in bed and out, Thomas thought angrily. There would be no clumsy embraces if Amica were in Stevan's hands, no ignorance and awkwardness. She would never know what it was to be subjected to the unskilled touch and manner of a man who had never even begun to fathom the ways of women.

Bowing his head, Thomas contemplated the top of the table at which he sat, staring at the rough, grainy wood until it grew hazy.

Steven would take her away to the land that his father had given him. She would no longer be at Reed. She would not be there, always comfortingly somewhere, as she had been for the past month. She would not be in the garden, where he always went first each day to seek her out; or in the castle, where he looked second, helping Lady Margot with the children or overseeing the servants in Lady Margot's stead; or in her own little dwelling, where he looked third, and to where he accompanied her each night after the evening meal so that he could be certain she arrived safely. She would not be there to smile at him, to speak to him, to give him comfort. He tried to be glad, to believe that she was naught but a troublous female well to be rid of . . . but he couldn't. He couldn't think of anything, save what his days would be like when she had wed Stevan and left Reed. And those thoughts were dark, at best.

He emptied the tankard of its bitter ale and set it down, thinking for the hundredth time or more since walking in that he must make himself leave, and knowing full well that he wouldn't.

His men, sitting at their table, began to laugh all at once, very loudly, and, more out of instinct than interest, Thomas lifted his head and listened.

"She's a prime bit, that's all I know," one of them said. "A riper beauty I've ne'er seen in all my days."

"Aye, she is that," another agreed. "And Sir Eric's more the fool if he isn't having some of her while his lady wife cares for the babe."

"Nay, never," protested another. "'Tis a madman he'd be and more to betray our good lady's trust, for Lady Margot is a rare beauty, and not to be treated with any manner of contempt."

"He keeps Lady Amica out of the castle, does he not?" the second one argued. "If he goes to all that trouble, 'tis not merely for her comfort, I'd vow!"

They all began to laugh again, save the one who'd protested.

"You're fools, one and all," he muttered. "Our lord of Reed has never even gone near the priest's lodgings, where Lady Amica is housed. I have served guard there some few days, and have ne'er seen Sir Eric."

But this only served to make the other men laugh more heartily.

"You're the fool!" the first said gleefully. "Sir Eric is

no green lad to make his way so bold through her door in the clear light of day."

"Or to linger long when he has gone through," one of his fellows added.

"Aye," said the first, chuckling and lifting his tankard of ale. "How long do you think it would take him to get done, once he'd gotten his sweet mare ready to receive him and mounted? Why, he'd—"

The table shook and its wooden top gave a loud crack. The men sitting there leapt up in surprise, spilling their ale onto the table and floor.

Thomas saw them staring first at him, then at their insensible friend who lay across the table and whose head Thomas still held by a fistful of hair. To a man, they drew their swords, and the boisterous noise in the tavern fell to a deathly silence.

"You'll die!" one of them shouted, just as Thomas pulled the cloak from his head and said, "Be still."

Their swords dropped to the floor with a loud clattering; each man straightened at once.

"My lord!"

"Sir Thomas, we meant no harm."

"We didn't realize it was you, my lord."

Thomas stared at them solemnly. Relaxing his fingers, he released his captive, allowing the man's head to fall forward to the wood.

His voice, when he spoke, seemed strangely calm to him, given that he felt such a murderous rage in his heart. "You," he said to the man who had protested his companions' words, "take your sword and go. Return to your quarters and speak of this matter to no one. You have done well this night, and I will not forget you in future."

When the man had gone, Thomas stood before the remaining men for several long, silent seconds.

"You have forgotten yourselves," he said slowly, quietly, "to speak thus of your lord, moreso to speak of one whom he has made a guest in his home, a gentle lady who resides under his protection. You are no better than swine—nay, worse. You are dirty, faithless creatures, for you have said these things before the citizens of Reed, in a place that is public, where every ear may freely hear the lies you speak. I should turn you out of Reed this moment—indeed, would you not be fortunate to go with your lives in your hands?—save that it would only serve to spread your filthy lies.

"Therefore, take your fellow here and report to Sir Evrain, telling him that I have required you all to be jailed for a fortnight, in the manner of the most common criminals. In the morn, you will be allowed to speak with Sir Eric, to confess your misdeeds and beg his forgiveness."

One of them held out a hand toward Thomas, pleadingly. "But, my lord, Sir Eric will kill us!"

"For giving such insult to his good lady wife and to one who is an honored guest at Reed?" Thomas asked. "Mayhap. You must spend what hours remain this night in prayer, upon your knees, making supplication to God that it will not be so. Go now. I am sickened by the sight of you. Do not be so foolish as to try to leave Reed. If you run, I will surely kill you when I have found you."

He stepped back, allowing the men to gather up their limp friend, and he watched as they carried him out the tavern door.

The Swan and Toad remained in silence. Thomas stood in the middle of the room, every eye upon him. Turning about, he sought the tavern wench whom he had used on his previous visits and moved toward her, each booted step loud in the quiet hush of the room. The girl stared at him wide-eyed as he approached, and he knew that she understood what his intent was when a brief expression of revulsion crossed her features. Obediently, she put down her tray and, walking before him, led him up the short stairway that led to her customary chamber.

Following, Thomas tried in vain to recall what her name was. She was a pretty enough female, with long red hair that curled around her shoulders and a large, healthy figure that he had always found attractive, certainly enough so that he had responded to it, though his body had been in a state of such need for so many days that Thomas believed even the ugliest whore could, at this moment, easily arouse him.

Once inside the chamber, the girl crossed the small room to her bed, and as Thomas closed and latched the door, she climbed up onto the thin mattress, knelt at the edge of it and, with a loud sigh, drew her skirts up around her waist.

Bewildered, Thomas stared at her for a moment before saying, "Oh, no. Not like that. I—" He felt wretchedly unable to say what he wished, and he realized, with an even greater sense of discomfort, that he had never before spoken to the girl during one of his brief visits. "I wish to do something . . . different."

Still kneeling, the girl swung her head around, an expression of surprise on her face.

"Will you lie down?" Thomas waved downward with one hand. "Down. As you normally do it."

She sat, seeming very uncertain.

"You want to do it on top, then?" she asked.

Growing hot with embarrassment, Thomas began to untie his cloak. "Yes. Lie down."

Casting a wary glance at the closed door, she said, "Should I take my things off?"

Having spent the past month and more fighting his

memory of how Amica's breasts had felt beneath his hands during those crazed moments at Belhaven, Thomas felt his body coming alive at the girl's words, and with a surge of relief, said, "Your chemise. Lower it. I would see that part of you." He awkwardly patted his chest. "Here."

The girl seemed equally relieved, and her expression softened with a slight smile. Keeping her eyes upon him, she slowly unlaced her top, and even more slowly drew her arms out of their sleeves. Lowering the cloth to reveal large, pink-tipped breasts, she ran her tongue across her lips, and noted, with satisfaction, that Thomas did the same. Lying down, she pulled her skirts up once again and began to spread her legs.

"Not yet," Thomas murmured, and she let her knees fall together.

Carefully, he sat beside her, his gaze moving slowly over her face and breasts.

Lifting her hands, the girl touched his face. "You never were a nice one," she said, smiling, drawing him closer so that he felt the heat of her. "But you're going to be nice this time, aren't you? Touch me, my lord."

Thomas suddenly, horribly felt every muscle in his body turn into iron; he could not make himself move even when he tried, and he stared at the girl with alarm.

"Here," she whispered, taking one of his hands and pulling it to her breast. "Touch me." She molded his fingers around herself, arching so that she filled his palm. "Oh, yes, my lord. You're so fine and big. I always liked your face and wished you'd do it to me this way, so I could see you and those pretty eyes."

Thomas's gaze dropped to his hand, and he stared at it dumbly. He could see that it was wrapped around her breast, that she writhed beneath it, but he couldn't feel a thing. Nothing. Indeed, his entire body began to feel numb, as if he were sickening.

"Kiss me," she begged, setting her free hand around his neck and pulling him down to her. Her lips, clearly more experienced than his own, moved gently, enticingly, and her tongue, when it probed into his mouth, caressed and teased in a manner that Thomas found more than a little agreeable. Encouraged, he closed his eyes and strove to participate in the kiss, tasting her with his own tongue and copying the movements of her lips. She was clean and sweet, he discovered with pleasure, and he wondered, dimly, why he had spent so many years denying himself such an enjoyable undertaking.

Long moments passed, the girl moaned loudly and touched his leg.

"Oh, Sir Thomas," she murmured, sliding her fingers upward and causing Thomas to groan aloud. "You're so big and strong and—" Groping, she searched through his leggings to find the large bulge she'd noticed earlier. "So big and fine and . . . and—" sitting up slightly, she looked at the place her hand caressed, "and so . . . uh . . ." Thomas sat up, too, and gazed down as the girl patted her hand thoroughly over his groin. At last, she rested her fingers atop that part of him that had only moments before been so painfully aroused, and which now appeared to be dead to any and all persuasion.

Lifting her eyes, she met Thomas's angry expression with her own bewildered one.

"That _cursed_ female!" Thomas said in a rage-filled voice. "Not only has she laid siege to my wits, she's damned well turned me into a eunuch!"

"Oh!" The girl pulled her hand away at once, sitting up and away from him. "My lord!"

Standing, Thomas stalked to the chair where he'd

left his cloak and snatched the garment up. Turning as he put it on, he pinned the girl with a hot glare.

"She might as well have *gelded* me! The witch!"

"Oh no, my lord!" She stared at his groin with horror.

Pulling a leather pouch from beneath his tunic, Thomas dug out a few coins and slammed them on the table next to the bed. Leaning closer as the girl cowered away, he declared, "I will not allow it, do you hear? No woman will unman me in such a way, especially not *her!*"

She shook her head in obedient agreement, but Thomas gave no notice. He strode out of the small chamber, leaving the door open behind him and the girl, wide-eyed and sitting on the bed with a blanket pulled up around her neck, staring after him.

18

"Stand aside."

The curtly spoken order received immediate obedience, and the two soldiers who guarded Amica's dwelling silently stepped back to allow their master entrance.

Maida, who stood stirring the fire, started with surprise at Thomas's sudden appearance.

"My lord!"

He walked past her toward the stairs. "Is she abovestairs?"

"Yes, my lord, but—"

Ignoring her, Thomas took the stairs two at a time. Reaching the top, he flung open the chamber door and strode directly inside. Amica, sitting on a stool dressed in nothing more than her chemise, stood, and Margaret, who had been busy combing out Amica's long hair, stared at Thomas with an open mouth.

"My lord—" Amica began.

"Leave us," Thomas commanded, jerking his hand impatiently at Margaret.

The comb clattered to the ground as the maid lifted her skirts and hurried out. Not looking behind him, Thomas reached out and shut the door.

Amica let out a breath. "My lord, what is amiss? Nothing has happened to one of the children? Or to Lady Margot or Sir—"

"They are well, as best I know." He began to remove his cloak. "You would know better than I, having feasted with them this night."

Watching as he tossed the hooded garment across a nearby chair, Amica replied, uncertainly, "Yes, that is so. And they did, in truth, seem well. We missed your company, however. Sir Eric was not a little displeased to find you gone."

Thomas looked at her with scorn. "Missed my company? When Sir Stevan was there to charm and entertain? That does not seem likely."

"It is true, nonetheless."

He moved toward her. "You did not find any lack in my absence, I'll vow. Surely Stevan kept you well and happily occupied."

Amica backed away from him. "Thomas, you are in a strange mood. Why are you here? What have you come for?"

"Because I am maddened. I am crazed."

"I have done naught to you, my lord. I have not even seen you this night, until now."

"The spell is cast," he muttered, "and I am bedeviled. It does not matter where I am, where you are. It does not change. My mind is not my own, nor even my body. I left the village whore but half an hour past, unable to use her as I wished to ease my need, yet I come here, to you, and my body aches with wanting. Can you not fathom how it is for me?"

She came up against a wall, pressed against it as

Thomas set his hands on either side of her, imprisoning her with the large cage of his body. "I have done nothing," she said once more. "If you are driven by lust, my lord, it is of your own doing, not mine. I will not accept the blame for it."

"Are you going to wed Stevan?"

Surprise mastered her features. "Nay, I am not. Why should you ask such a foolish question?"

"He has not yet asked you to wed him, then," Thomas said. "But he will, and you will agree to do it, will you not?"

She laughed. "He will not ask me. How fanciful you are and, I begin to think, drunk."

He moved closer, so that she felt the heat and hardness of him.

"You will not wed him. You will not do so, Amica."

Her breathing grew more rapid. "Nay, I will not."

"I do not care if you wish to do so. I do not care whether you want him as you want life."

It was difficult to lift her hand in the slight space that separated their bodies, but she did, sliding it upward until she could touch his face, gently.

"I do not want him."

He whispered her name as he lowered his head to kiss her, putting his mouth against hers with great care, afraid of himself and of what she did to him, afraid that he might do something to make her cry as she had when he had last held her.

She stiffened when he pressed fully against her, making a tiny sound of surprise into his mouth when she felt his sex like a hard knot against her belly, but the next moment he touched her with his tongue, so tentatively and fearfully that her heart leapt within her, filling with a tenderness that pushed every other doubt aside.

"Thomas," she murmured. With a groan he opened his mouth wider, kissing her more deeply. She touched her tongue to his, hoping that her trembling and ignorance would not disgust him. She felt his hands stroking over her hair and cheeks as they explored and discovered one another's mouths.

Long minutes later he pulled away. Amica moaned and followed his lips upward, trying to recapture their kiss.

Bending, he took her up in his arms and carried her to the bed. Placing her upon it, he said, "I would lie with you."

Amica lifted her arms and tried to pull him down to her, but he resisted, pressing up on his elbows. Setting his fingers to the laces of her chemise, he untied the top of the garment. Slowly, he spread each half apart, revealing her breasts.

"Amica." Her name came out on a breath. "God save me."

Suddenly shy, she tried to cover herself, but he grasped her fingers and laid them on the mattress. "Nay, let me look at you . . . touch you, else I die from my need." He caressed her with slow, careful touches, hesitantly at first, and then with growing sureness. Wonder lit his features. "So soft," he murmured. "Warm. My dreams were untrue; I never knew you would be so warm." Lowering his face to the valley between her breasts, he breathed in deeply. "The scent of you is enough to make a man lose his wits." Groaning, he pressed his mouth to her flesh. A fine trembling ran through him as his lips moved, exploring, tasting. His hands slid beneath her back, smoothing over the naked skin, lifting her up as his mouth closed over one taut nipple.

Amica gasped aloud, and the hands she had pushed deep into his hair fisted and unfisted. Thomas at once lifted his head, gazing at her with worry.

"I hurt you?"

"Nay." Shivering, she shook her head, saying again, "Nay."

Thomas lifted himself higher, looking into her flushed face. Touching her cheek, his fingers confirmed the tears that his eyes saw.

"Why do you weep, then? I have made you weep again."

"It is not sorrow," she whispered. "It is because . . . you make me feel things that I have never felt before. Such good things that I never dreamed I would know."

The tension that had gripped him melted away, and Thomas released a breath. He brushed the hair back from her forehead with a gentle hand.

"I, too, never dreamed that I would know anything such as this." He kissed her mouth, hovering over her, then, uttering a sorrowful sound, suddenly buried his face into the hair that twined about her neck. "Have pity on me, Amica of Lancaster. I am not myself, nor have I been for a long while."

"Thomas." She stroked her hands through his hair. He lay almost fully on top of her, pressing against her needily. She had thought he would do what Duncan had always done to her, and had prepared herself to receive such intimacy, but as his body relaxed moment by moment, Amica understood more fully what it was that he craved.

She continued to stroke his hair in a soothing rhythm until his breathing grew soft and steady, falling warm upon the skin just beneath her ear. Only when she was certain that he was fully asleep did she stop. Sliding her hands over his large shoulders, she held him, content. She gazed at the shadows dancing in the fire-lit chamber until her own eyes grew heavy with weariness, and then she drifted into slumber.

19

"You ask my consent for what?"

The words sounded slightly amazed. Sir Eric stared at Thomas, who was scowling at his feet.

"To wed with Amica of Lancaster. I would like your permission and your help to get the deed accomplished."

Sir Eric collapsed heavily into the chair behind him. "This is very sudden, Tom. Yesterday, when I spoke with Lady Amica, she seemed to believe that you bore no tender feelings toward her."

Thomas looked at his master with some bewilderment. "She spoke such things to you?"

"Aye. Well, 'twas not so strange a thing, for we spoke of her finding a husband, and I told her that I should be glad to see her wed to you." Sir Eric lifted his hands. "After all, Tom, 'tis time and past that you had a wife, and Lady Amica would make a most pleasant one, I vow."

The expression on Thomas's face was shuttered, as if he was not certain this sentiment was true or not. "Did she seem agreeable to the idea?"

Sir Eric laughed. "We never got so far in our words. She believes, most firmly, that you bear her no love."

"Does that matter so much? I did not think most marriages required such feelings."

The lord of Reed's smile died slowly away. "You hold no affection for Lady Amica in your heart? Why, then, do you wish to wed her? I will not have her trifled with, Tom."

"And neither would I, my lord," Thomas replied in a tone of offense. "I am no such man, to dally foolishly with any maid." He flushed hotly, as if embarrassed.

Sir Eric rose from his chair and paced toward the chamber's fire. "I know that, lad. Forgive me for misspeaking. But, if you do not care for the woman, why—?"

"I do not know why. It is as great a mystery to me as it must seem to you. I only know that I must have her, and I alone. The thought of any other man touching her makes me want to—" He clenched a fist as he searched for the proper words. "It makes me crazed. I feel that I might kill any man who so much as gazes upon her. Or speaks to her. Or even *thinks* about her, should I ever know of it."

Sir Eric was staring at him with amazement again. "I see," he said, setting his hands behind his back. "Well, if that is verily how it is with you, Tom—"

"It is," Thomas assured him bluntly.

"Then you must certainly seek Lady Amica's hand. You have not spoken with her yet, 'tis clear."

Thomas frowned. "Nay, I have not. Must I do so?"

Sir Eric chuckled. "Aye, I think you must. She cannot be made to wed you by my command, I fear, but must agree to do so of her own free will."

Thomas was fully disappointed. "I thought it might be so," he admitted, "though I had prayed it would not be." An idea came to him, and he looked at Sir Eric hopefully. "Could you not at least ask her to wed me? I do not think she would deny any request you made of her, my lord."

"Ah . . . no. I cannot do that, Tom, nor would I, despite the love I bear you. If you would win Lady Amica's hand in marriage, you must do the deed on your own." The lord of Reed moved toward his working table, setting a hand upon it. "I will, however, write her kinsman on your behalf, seeking his permission for her marriage to you."

"Her kinsman?" Thomas asked. "Do you mean Duncan Selwyrn? Is he not her guardian?"

"Nay, he is not," Sir Eric said. "He has naught to do with Lady Amica any more, and never will again. She has a kinsman who has accepted the right of authority over her, though I may not reveal his name to you. The king has not yet given his permission to speak of Lady Amica's circumstances, and so I will not do so, even if you should wed with her. You must be patient to learn about such matters."

Thomas shrugged. "I have no care for who her people are, or as to whether she be rich or poor."

"Nor should you," Sir Eric said approvingly, "for you possess more than enough to make up for any lack, and will one day possess more, and yet, for Lady Amica's sake, I will ask a goodly bride's portion of her kinsman, for I would not have her shamed on the day of your betrothal. If such a day arrives," he added with a smile. "Women count such matters heavily, i'faith."

"As you see fit, my lord. I only wish to be certain that we are wed fully and legally this time."

Sir Eric nodded. "When I have had a reply from Lady Amica's relative, if it is agreeable, and I am sure it will be, you may formally request her assent to wed with you. Until that time, you have my permission to court her in a manner that is fitting and proper."

Thomas looked at his master warily. "Fitting and proper? What do you mean by this?"

Sir Eric pointed to a nearby chair. "Sit, Tom. I would speak with you more fully on this matter."

Obediently, Thomas sat, and waited in silence while Sir Eric paced in front of the fire.

At last the lord of Reed stopped, faced his waiting heir, and said, "Tom, in all truth, you are not very good with women."

"Aye," Thomas agreed without offense. "This is so."

"Aye, well," Sir Eric cleared his throat uncomfortably, "I realize that you have never cared to know much about the ways of the fairer sex, but before you court a lady of gentle birth, such as Lady Amica is, you must strive to understand them."

"How so, my lord? It would seem to be a great waste of time."

"Aye, so it would," Sir Eric said readily, "but in truth, 'twill save you much trouble in future if you will but undertake to grasp the workings of the female mind. Women are never so troublous as when they've become wives, but, as with a good steed, if you learn how to handle the creatures beforehand, you will find your life to be much simpler."

"Very well," Thomas said. "I will listen to your words of advice, my lord, and will be obedient to follow them."

"Good lad. I would have you bear in mind, always, that women must be treated very gently, with all care and concern. You must strive not to speak harshly, nor ever to let your hand fall upon your lady with anger. Always remember that women are vain creatures, and in constant need of praise. Each day, as you court Lady Amica, think of some small manner in which to speak well of her manner of dress, or of her beauty, or wit and charm."

"But, my lord!" Thomas protested. "What purpose should it serve to feed her vanity? It does not seem godly or fitting."

Sir Eric smiled at him with pity. "Tom, lad, there are few things more unpleasant in this life than a wife who does not feel herself appreciated by her own husband. And if you would make Lady Amica your wife, you must certainly flatter her, and often."

"But, Sir Eric—"

"Often," Sir Eric repeated. "Make certain of it each day, unless you wish some other fellow to come along and charm her away from you."

Scowling, Thomas sat back in his chair. "Yes, my lord."

"And make certain to refrain from looking at other women when you are in Lady Amica's company," Sir Eric continued. "She will bear you no love should she see you admiring another female. And try to remember to give her some small token of affection each day. A flower or a pretty trifle that will amuse her."

Thomas stared at him with disbelief. "My lord, you jest, surely."

"Nay, I do not. The more I think on the matter, it might be best if you asked Jace to teach you a song or two. Or perhaps some poetry that you might recite to Lady Amica when you are alone with her."

"Poetry!" Thomas said with awful horror. "God's mercy!"

"Aye," Sir Eric agreed thoughtfully. "It is quite foolish, but women do love such things. I believe a poesy will suffice. You must take her on an outing and recite one to her. I will tell Jace to choose something especially appropriate."

Thomas groaned loudly.

"And Thomas." Sir Eric's tone became more serious.

"My lord?" Thomas replied fearfully. "There can be no more, I beg you!"

"Aye, there is," Sir Eric said, moving to stand in front of him. "I would have your solemn vow that you will not embrace or fondle Lady Amica in any lewd or unseemly manner. Seek out the village whore, if your need overcomes your ability to contain it, but do not consummate your vows with Lady Amica before you take them."

Thinking of what he had shared with Amica the night before, Thomas stiffened. "My lord . . . "

"Your vow, Thomas. Once you have given it to me, I know that you will not turn away from it. You have proven yourself more than trustworthy when keeping your honor."

"Yes, my lord," Thomas replied reluctantly. "I do so make you my vow."

"Good lad." Sir Eric patted him on the shoulder, chuckling at Thomas's grim expression. "'Twill not be so bad. If all goes well, we will have the betrothal ceremony within a month's time, and you shall be wed the following week. After that, you may enjoy your marriage bed as often and as wholly as it pleases you to do so."

"I will not live long enough to do so," Thomas muttered. "A month and a week!"

Sir Eric laughed more heartily. "So that is the way of it? I had thought it must be so. But that is understandable, for Lady Amica is the loveliest of creatures. You will be content and glad to have such a wife, and Lady Margot and I will rejoice to have you wed, for you know that we have ever loved you as surely as if you were our own son. Your children will be as our grandchildren, and so we shall believe them to be."

Thomas's mouth softened into a rare smile. "'Tis strange to think of a child. Or children."

"Stranger yet to have them," Sir Eric teased. "Though

they are God's greatest gift to any man. Now, come. 'Tis not so early that we may not share a drink to celebrate this fortunate event. When we have done, you may seek out Lady Amica and say that you wish formally to court her. She will be well pleased by such news."

"My lord, there is another matter I must speak of first." Thomas stood and set a hand on Sir Eric's arm, holding him still. "Let us not drink until this eve, for I think Lady Margot, when you have told her that I mean to wed with Lady Amica, will make yet another feast. And, in truth, when you have heard what I must say, you will not wish to celebrate."

Sir Eric gave way to the pressure of Thomas's hand. "Sir Evrain sent me word this morn that there were certain men in the jail—who were there at your command. Is this what you wish to speak of?"

"Yes, my lord. I fear that it is."

He found Amica in the gardens later that afternoon, snipping twigs off a large costmary shrub. The herb's pungent fragrance filled the air as Thomas neared her.

"Amica." He spoke her name in his usual sharp manner, as if she were one of his men.

She twirled about with a gasp, dropping the basket and sending costmary twigs flying everywhere. Setting a shaking hand over her heart, she said accusingly, "Thomas! You gave me a fright!"

Seeing that she trembled, he put his hands on her arms, rubbing up and down in a brisk, comforting manner. "I forget too often the terrors that possess you. I did not mean to take you unawares."

Both her shaking and her angry expression melted away, to be replaced by a look of concern as she lifted a hand to touch his swollen cheek.

"What has happened? Did someone strike you?"

"What?" For a moment he was confused. "Oh, aye. Sir Eric did, but half an hour past."

"Sir Eric!"

"'Twas not me he intended to strike, but another man. I was foolish enough to get in the way and so justly received my master's blow. It does not hurt overmuch."

Amica looked doubtful of that. "When one is struck by a giant, the blow will certainly hurt. I cannot imagine Sir Eric so angered as to strike another man. What has this poor man done?"

"Not one man, but several. Sir Eric beat each one senseless, and had every reason to do so. He is a just man, as are his punishments. These men deserved all they received from their lord's hand, and more. They are fortunate to have their lives, for Sir Eric might well have required that of them as recompense for their wrongs."

Her hand stilled upon his cheek. "What have they done? What crime have they committed?"

"I did not come to speak with you of that. And if you would know, you must ask Sir Eric. It is for him to tell you, if he will."

Nodding, Amica pulled her hand away. "Very well, my lord. I would not wish you to betray your master's confidence." Kneeling, she began to gather up the scattered costmary.

Thomas knelt beside her. "Here." He shook the dust from a handful of twigs and tossed them into her basket.

"Thank you, my lord." Amica added her own handful to the basket. "What did you wish to speak to me about? If it concerns last night, there is no need for you to make apologies. I was as much to blame as you, and I was not angered to find that you had left without a word before I awoke."

Thomas scowled at her. "I did not come to make

apologies. If anyone should apologize, 'tis you, for having made my life a very hell."

"I have done no such thing!" she declared, lifting her head. "You are the one who has sought me out, time and again."

"Only because I was driven to distraction from the day that I set eyes on you," he said, standing and pulling her up by an arm. "'Tis clearly all your fault. And as that is verily so, you will now make recompense."

She gaped at him. "You're mad! How can I possibly make recompense for something I've never even done!"

"Easily," he replied. "You will give yourself to me in marriage."

The basket dropped to the ground once more.

"Marriage?"

He nodded. "Aye, marriage. You will wed with me, and become my lady wife. Only then can I assuage my need for you, and only then will my life return to what it once was and to what I would have it be again."

Every bit of color drained from Amica's face, and for a brief moment, Thomas was afraid she might faint. Setting a hand on her arm, he steadied her. "Is the thought of being my wife so terrible?"

"You jest, surely," she said. "How can you wish to wed me?"

"I do not wish it, i'faith, but I can see no other way to keep from being overcome by want of you. After last night, even you must see that this is so. And the idea did seem to please Sir Eric, who has wanted to see me wed for some few years now."

"But, Thomas . . . "

"He gave me his permission to court you, and has agreed to write your kinsman for his agreement."

"But . . . Thomas . . . "

"We will begin courting this afternoon, when I have finished attending my duties. I will take you for a walk in the gardens before the evening meal. Wait for me in your lodgings, and I will come for you there."

"Thomas, I cannot think. You have surprised me, and I—"

"You may have all day to think on the matter," he said, gathering her stiff body into his arms and pulling her close. "For now, I must go and speak with Stevan and try to assuage his anger. I can only pray that he will forgive me, for he did desire to wed you. Much as I value him, however, I would kill him before I would let him set a finger to you."

"I'm sure Sir Stevan has never even thought of me, Thomas, and I wish you would—"

"He's done more than thought, but that will be the end of it, if he wishes to continue living. I will kiss you before I leave. Now that we are courting, it is acceptable."

"But—"

His mouth descended, cutting off her speech. Then, as he gently and thoroughly kissed her, Amica gave way, putting her hands up around his neck and holding him. When he lifted his head, she sighed and smiled.

"I will allow you to court me, Thomas of Reed."

"I do not ask for your permission," he replied with a soft smile, setting her away, "when Sir Eric has already given me his." He bent and picked up the basket. "Make certain that you are ready to receive me when I come for you this afternoon." He put the handle in her open fingers. "I will not court you in an untimely or disorderly manner. No battle was ever won in such a way."

Amica's eyebrows lifted. "You think courtship a battle, my lord?"

He turned and began to walk away, calling back, "Only a fool would think otherwise, my lady."

20

Sacre Placean was a wild place, and like all wild things, its beauty and worth could only be discerned by one who observed the land with understanding and vision. Duncan Selwyrn knew this very well; he understood perfectly why so many people found the land surrounding his castle ugly and lacking; to the ready eye, it was. He did not let himself be distressed by such opinions, however, or by anything that others felt or thought. He could see the beauty of the land. He treasured its history, its meaning and worth. He believed, with absolute faith, as his father and his father's father and as every Selwyrn who had ever breathed upon the earth had done, that it was sacred. Holy. Powerful.

Standing now near the open window of his bedchamber, gazing upon the birthright that was his, Duncan felt the same surge of pride that he ever felt at beholding Sacre Placean's spartan, rocky hills and barren plains. The wind that was the land's constant companion swept over his body, through his hair, causing

Duncan to close his eyes and smile as he enjoyed the pleasure of its chilly caress. *Yes,* he thought. This was his. His home, his life, his destiny. Here was the ground that had given him life, that had succored him all his days, that would receive his body when his life's course had come to an end. And the power in the land would keep him safe, as it always had, when he made his stand against the king who now ruled over Britain.

He had not thought it would come so soon. He had thought, believed, truly, that Amica would be with him, giving life to his children before he would have to depose Henry and set the heirs of Sacre Placean on their rightful throne. But it was not to be.

Amica.

The thought of her gave him pain. He had loved her as much as he was capable of loving any woman, certainly more than he had ever loved her sister, but he had been cruel, and Amica must have hated him with every breath she drew. It was because he loved her that he had been so unkind. Indeed, more than once he'd been tempted to kill her, just to bring an end to his cursed fixation, to the power she wielded over him, for he had never been able to accept any form of domination. But how could he have made a finish of such perfection and beauty? To do such a thing would have greatly displeased the spirits of the earth, who cherished every form of natural beauty. How much simpler it had been to take Alys's life. She had been possessed of a fierce soul, which he had much admired, but her beauty had been as naught compared to her sister's perfection. It had amused him to let Alys think that he cared for her, even preferred her to her timid sister, for it was a sweeter form of pain than anything he had ever visited upon Amica. To watch the changes in Alys's face as the days went by and as she realized, slowly, that he had never cared for her, save as a source upon which to sate his needs and as a fool upon whom to visit his scorn, was most satisfying.

"My lord?"

Duncan didn't turn from the window. "Sit down, Alfred. You will find a document on the table. Read it."

The chamber fell into silence once again; the wind gusted and Duncan smiled in pleasured response. He thought of his son, who would grow to love this land as he loved it, and in his mind began to form plans for all the adventures they would have together, just as he and his father had.

"My lord, this is beyond belief," Alfred said at last. "I cannot fathom how the king has come to do such a thing, or how he discovered the truth of Lady Alys's death."

"But he has," Duncan said. "You see the proof of it before your own eyes. Amica surely told him. Or Andrew Fawdry did."

"But, Lady Amica—"

"Is no longer my lawful wife," Duncan finished. "The king has had our marriage annulled, with the Church's approval. I am to leave her be, else Henry will make his displeasure known." He chuckled. "His *displeasure*, by the rood. What a great idiot our king is, verily. He is no more threatening to me than a tiny bug. I shall flatten him beneath my heel."

"The time has not yet come for that, my lord," Alfred said.

"Not yet." Duncan at last turned from the window. "But soon. This matter with France occupies Henry's thoughts, more and more, and when he is more thoroughly occupied, his throne shall slip out from beneath him. On this I make my solemn vow."

Moving to the table, he took up the document and

looked at it. "Until that time, Alfred, we must devote ourselves to getting Amica back."

"That does not seem a likely task, my lord. King Henry states that she has already been promised to another in marriage, to the heir of Reed."

"Aye, to Sir Thomas of Reed," Duncan said tightly. "Who must have leapt eagerly at the chance of possessing a woman so beautiful, without care of her fearful nature. He will be rutting upon her every moment of the day and night, I vow." The parchment was crushed in Duncan's fist. "*Despoiling* my wife. I will kill him with my own hands, and when Amica has been returned to her rightful place, she shall endure a ritual of purification to remove the filthy stain of his touch. I can only pray that she does not conceive a child of him."

"You cannot kill the heir to Reed, my lord," Alfred warned. "Sir Eric Stavelot is no man to be dealt with in such a manner. You will never win the loyalty of the nobles if you incur his wrath."

Duncan's fingers relaxed, and the parchment dropped to the table. "You are right, of course, Alfred. I must not let my reason become muddled by rage. There is only one matter of import, and that is to have my wife returned to me, for she is my wife and ever shall be. No man on this earth may naysay what the gods have ordained. She must be returned to Sacre Placean without fail. I must keep my mind upon it."

"The king has annulled your marriage, my lord. She is no longer your wife in the eyes of either the throne or the Church, and if you take her, 'twill be as if you had stolen another man's wife."

"Aye," Duncan agreed thoughtfully. "Every noble house in England will see it thus, will they not? I must find a way to get her back without causing enmity. I must find a way to make this Thomas of Reed wish to be rid of her, so that I may take her from Reed with his blessing. But it will not be easily done without knowing what Amica or the king may have told him."

"He is not the problem, so much, my lord, as Sir Eric is. The lord of Reed is one of the king's closest advisers. 'Tis certain that he knows all of what the king suspects. There is naught that would convince him to let Lady Amica leave Reed until he had first gained the king's permission."

"Then Sir Eric must be taken out of the way when I arrive to claim my wife," Duncan told him.

Alfred's face drained of color. "My lord, you cannot mean to kill Sir Eric Stavelot. It means certain ruin for you, for all of Sacre Placean."

Duncan made a scoffing sound. "Don't be a fool, Alfred. I only wish to get my wife back, not take on every cursed Stavelot in Britain. I will find the way to have Amica returned to me, without force and without bloodshed. Indeed"—he waved away Alfred's expression of disbelief—"that is not what concerns me. The real trouble will be secreting Amica back into Sacre Placean without any of my people or servants discovering that she has ever been gone. There will be rumors throughout England as to what has taken place, but if my people will say, believing it to be so, that their lady has been here in the castle, any who doubt will soon come to think it true."

"And King Henry?"

"Henry may do as he pleases," Duncan said. "Once Amica is in my hands again, he will not find it so easy to remove her. I will make it plain to him that if he should dare try it, I will take his cousin's life, not caring what may befall me. If he wishes her to live, and he does, I think, else he would not have gone to so much effort on her behalf, then he will let the matter alone. He cannot risk murmuring amongst the nobles when he requires all their support to war with France. He is not such a fool as to throw that away for nothing more important than his bastard cousin, or to let any of his men die trying to rescue her."

"And what if Sir Eric should require some manner of satisfaction?"

Duncan was thoughtful, rubbing his chin. "That would be unpleasant, assuredly. I shall have to make certain that Thomas of Reed has no desire to reclaim Amica as his own, once he gives her over to her rightful husband. Sir Eric will not seek to rescue a wife whom his heir does not want." He walked toward the fire, staring into the flames as he pondered the matter. "Sir Thomas must be made to hold Amica in great disgust, that is the way of it. He must feel naught but relief to have her gone, as if she had done him some grievous misdeed, or would do such, one day."

Alfred was unconvinced. "I cannot see how that may be done. Lady Amica is sweet and gentle, also very beautiful. What man would give her up easily, when she is certain to have given him no cause for distrust?"

Duncan glanced over his shoulder. "It does not rest so much on Amica, whose behavior I understand and will anticipate. It is Thomas of Reed who will supply the cause of her guilt, for each man embraces his own secret fears. If I can but discover a one of them, Sir Thomas will be like clay in my hands. But—" he moved back to the table, his hands clasped behind his back "—this is not a matter I will worry on at present. For now we must prepare to deal with Sir Eric. You see that I did not break the king's seal when I opened the document?"

Alfred picked up the piece of wax that Duncan pointed to. "Aye. 'Tis one of the best kept I have yet seen. Shall I set Beltern to plying his craft?"

Duncan pressed his hand upon his steward's shoulder. "Aye, Alfred, that you shall. Tell him that this must be his finest work, and that he will be well rewarded for both his skill and silence. And when you have finished with that, come back here to me." Leaning down, Duncan spread the wrinkled parchment flat upon the table top, smoothing it with both hands. "You will practice your own peculiar skills this night, until the king himself would not know the difference, and shall prepare a document that will send Sir Eric Stavelot hurrying on his way to London like the most obedient of Henry's hounds."

21

"My lady, you must hurry! Sir Derryn and Sir Stevan have become most impatient."

"They will have to wait, Margaret," Maida told her, glancing up at her cousin from where she sat, brushing Amica's hair. "She's not yet ready."

"But the whole village is waiting at the church," Margaret said in despairing tones. "And our lord, Sir Eric, sent a messenger saying that Sir Thomas is ready to do something terrible if Lady Amica does not arrive at once!"

Amica turned in her chair, her face set with worry. "Mayhap I should go now, Maida. If you would but cover my hair—"

"Indeed I will not!" Maida declared. "I'll not have my lady covered, when her purity must be shown to one and all. You know full well what people will think if your hair is not uncovered on the day of your betrothal."

Amica nearly groaned. She already felt guilty enough for not being able to tell Thomas the truth, despite having tried to do so more than once, but to go to her betrothal in the manner of a virgin, with her hair uncovered, was the worst sort of lie.

If only Sir Eric had relented! She had begged him repeatedly in the past month either to speak with Thomas himself or to let her tell him of Duncan, but the lord of Reed had refused. Her cousin, King Henry, had forbidden her former marriage to be spoken of, even to Thomas, and Sir Eric would not go against the command of the king.

"He will not realize the difference on your wedding night," Sir Eric assured her when they had last spoken of the matter. "I promise you, my lady, Tom hasn't enough knowledge of women to discern such a thing."

"But how can I keep such as that from him?" she'd argued. "The knowledge of such deception will ever be in my heart, burning there. 'Tis wrong to wed him without speaking the truth!"

"He would want you for his wife whether he knew of it or not," Sir Eric insisted. "I like it no better than you, my lady, yet I have vowed on my honor that I would speak of it to no one, and so I will not. If you cannot make peace with yourself, then you must not agree to wed Tom until the king declares that he may be told the truth. Though I do not believe Tom will wait any longer."

That had proved to be more than true, for when Amica had suggested, very gently, that perhaps it might be nice to wed in autumn, after the harvest, Thomas had looked at her as if she were completely mad and said that if he had to spend the entire summer courting her he would be an old man by the time the harvest arrived. Then, when she would have argued, he pulled her into his arms and kissed her, just as he had been kissing her since the day he had announced they were to begin courting, and, as Amica had long since discovered, Thomas's kisses proved most effective in driving every bit of sense from her mind.

"Hurry, Maida!" Margaret pleaded, standing outside the chamber door and glancing down the stairs. "They are both staring up at me. I fear they will come to fetch Lady Amica whether she is ready or no!"

"Let them, if they will," Maida declared, standing back and eyeing Amica with approval. "She's ready, and God alone would know if a more beautiful lady lives on His earth."

Amica stood, and Margaret made a sound of awe. "Oh, 'tis the truth you speak, Maida. You look as lovely as one of heaven's angels, my lady."

Smiling, Amica gazed down at the heavy damask surcoat that Lady Margot and Sir Eric had given her for the betrothal ceremony. It was a dark purple, intricately patterned in glimmering gold thread, and cuffed and hemmed with soft brown fur. Sir Garin and Lady Elaine, who had traveled to Reed for the important ceremony, had gifted her with a thick gold belt ornamented with rubies, pearls and diamonds, and with a delicate gold circlet that now rested atop her head, gleaming with diamonds.

"Sir Thomas will be the happiest man in the kingdom," Maida declared.

Amica wondered if that would be true, and felt her face growing hot with the hope that it would be. During the past month she had come to hope many things of Thomas, but that he might one day come to care for her was the greatest among them. She cared for him, more deeply than she ever would have thought possible, and she thought—believed—that their marriage would be a good one. She would be happy with her stern knight. He was calm and constant and trustworthy, and the home they made together would be a refuge for them both. The only question that troubled Amica was whether Thomas would be content once his man's needs had been assuaged. He wanted her now, aye, but would he continue to want her once he had taken his fill? For him, a man who had never desired a wife, would marriage to such a weak and timorous female soon become unbearable? What if, one day, she looked into his eyes and saw nothing but regret there?

"I'm ready then." Drawing in a breath, she went out the door and started down the stairs. "I'm sorry to have made you wait," she said as she descended, directing the words toward the two men who stood staring up at her.

"Ah Stevan," Derryn said in a tone filled with awe, "I have never felt such sympathy for you as I do at this moment."

Stevan let out a loud sigh. "Do not. If 'twere any other man but Tom, I should never have stepped aside. I have lost a great treasure, s'truth, but 'tis glad I am that Tom gained it. My lady," he reached out a hand to take the one Amica extended, "you are beautiful."

Amica smiled first at him, and then at Derryn, whose expression radiated his approval.

"I am a little fearful," she told them. "Will there be many people?"

Tucking her hand beneath his arm and drawing her toward the door, Stevan said, "Many, I fear, my lady. A betrothal such as this would not be missed. Has our lord not declared the day to be one of great celebration?"

"S'truth," Derryn agreed on her other side, patting her hand. "There will be much feasting and dancing. After the ceremony, of course."

As they stepped out of the dwelling's door, Amica

was greeted by the sight of a company of Thomas's men, all dressed in tunics that bore the emblem and colors of Reed. Their captain saluted Amica and then, at Derryn's nod, they stood aside to make a path for Stevan and Derryn to escort her through.

Walking dutifully in the direction that Stevan and Derryn led her, Amica gripped their arms more tightly. The loud, even steps of Thomas's company marching behind them seemed to match the throbbing of her heart in her ears.

"I am sorry to be so foolish," she said, wishing that she could make her wretched trembling stop.

"No one will take notice of it, my lady," Stevan said, pressing his fingers over her hand in a comforting gesture. "They will be too occupied gazing at your beauty to notice anything more."

"I pray that you speak the truth, my lord," she murmured, concentrating on making her feet move one in front of the other in a steady manner, ever forward, "for I feel as if I will collapse at any moment."

Derryn laughed lightly. "Good lady, if you do, be pleased to know, at least, that you have given the people of Reed much to gossip upon."

"Tom, I wish you will cease pacing. You make me feel most weary."

Thomas stopped his movement long enough to glare at his master. "She is not here. She should have been here long since. I sent Derryn and Stevan to fetch her, as is their duty, but she is *not* here."

Sir Eric smiled at him gently. "Women are curiously lacking in their ability to attend any important event in a timely manner, lad. 'Tis a lesson best learned quickly and well by any man who takes a wife, for, whatever the occasion may be, a woman will find a way to arrive late."

"Not my wife," Thomas replied. "I'll not allow it."

Chuckling, Sir Eric glanced to where his father, Sir Garin, stood grinning. "'Twill be a pleasure watching my Tom tame his lady wife," he said.

"Aye, indeed," said Sir Garin, "though 'tis he who will be tamed, I vow. Lady Amica is meek, s'truth, but she's a woman all the same."

Lady Elaine, standing beside her husband, made a small fist and punched him in the side. "And what would you know of a woman's taming, my lord?" she charged. "You're no better mannered now than you were when first we met."

Hooking an arm about his wife's slender waist, Sir Garin pulled her close. "Verily, this is so, madam. I'd even kidnap the little shrew I'd taken such a fancy to again, if need be." Laughing, he kissed her on the mouth.

Thomas observed the loving embrace with a dark scowl. Impatiently, he turned toward the porch steps. "I will go and fetch her myself."

"Nay, lad." Sir Eric put out a hand to stop him. "You will stay here at the church doors and await your good lady in the proper manner."

"But, my lord—"

Lady Margot touched his arm. "Look, T-Tom. She is arriving. Now b-be still and remember yourself."

Thomas looked in the direction she pointed, toward the village's main thoroughfare. Derryn and Stevan marched in front of the men he had sent to escort them, fulfilling one of their most important duties as his groomsmen and leading his intended bride to the church. The sight of Amica, walking between them, beautiful and pale and frightened, made Thomas clench his teeth. He silently cursed the need for so public a ceremony, and prayed that the wretched thing would be done with quickly. Indeed, he would be more than a little glad when all of the foolishness required for marriage was done. He could not fathom why any sane man would suffer such things unless he were driven to it by need.

Courting had proven to be a much less organized matter than Thomas had imagined, despite the fact that he had striven to conduct it in an orderly manner.

Each morn, after he had risen and dressed and readied himself for the day, he attended the morning meal, sitting beside Amica and speaking to her only of spiritual matters, for the morning was, he felt, the proper time for such contemplations. Her mind in these matters was excellent, as ever, and he was well pleased that she had such a full understanding of both the accepted scriptures and of Church doctrine. Afterward, they attended morning Mass together, where they knelt side by side in the chapel so that Thomas felt the heat of her body next to his, and where he strove in vain to keep his thoughts on God rather than on what he wished he were doing with Amica at that very moment, which was, in all truth, something not in the least bit ideal or spiritual.

Having suffered through Mass in a state that could only be thought miserable, Thomas bade his intended wife farewell and accompanied his soldiers to battle practice. Here he participated in hard activity until he had achieved a thoroughly blessed state of weariness. He had been used to doing so long before he met Amica, but of late it had become essential, for he could not trust himself even to set eyes upon his future wife until the hard edge of his desire had been dulled. Derryn and Stevan had begun to tease him for such fervent daily exercise, for they claimed there were rumors among the men that their master was not content simply to practice, but that he fought each battle as if it were real. Thomas was pleased that Stevan had forgiven him enough to take up once again the jesting that both he and Derryn had forever plagued him with. Yet, even so, he never would have admitted to either of them just how much truth was in those rumors. He feared that they already knew too well how harsh the battle was that he fought each day, and vowed that he would reveal nothing more of his weakness for a certain golden-haired, blue-eyed woman who already dominated his thoughts, both waking and sleeping.

Later in the afternoon, when he had bathed and dressed in a more courtly manner, he sought Amica out to escort her to the midday meal at Castle Reed. The remainder of the day followed the pattern that Thomas, mindful of his master's admonitions, had decided upon. When the meal finished they would walk together in the gardens for an hour, discussing common matters, such as the harvest or the weather or how pretty Lady Gwendolen was proving to be. Then Thomas would make his daily declaration of admiration, commenting on either her dress or hair or good sense. It was the moment when he felt most foolish in his courting, but as Sir Eric had told him to do, so he did, and Amica suffered through it with what Thomas considered to be admirable fortitude. He would then pick the most convenient flower and give it to her, and, with much relief at having finished these tasks, he would kiss her, very briefly, as a reward to himself for enduring such humiliation.

Once he tried to learn a poem that Sir Eric had told Jace to tutor him with, but it had proved to be an impossible undertaking. Jace had laughed so hard that he'd actually taken ill and been made, at Lady Margot's command, to keep to his bed for an entire day after.

Out of fear for Amica's health, Sir Eric had at once abandoned the idea of Thomas reciting poetry to anyone, most especially to her. Thomas, in truth, had been fully relieved.

In the evenings, having spent the remainder of the day tending to more common military matters, such as the purchase of healthy horses and the condition of the armory, Thomas would once more escort Amica to Castle Reed to attend the evening meal. It was important, he believed, that they be seen in one another's company as often as possible, for he wanted it understood that Amica was his, and that any man who so much as gazed upon her with appreciation would be readily dealt with.

It was the hours after the evening meal that Thomas most anticipated and feared. Taking Amica to her dwelling and being alone with her there was something short of torture. It seemed miraculous to him that he had not once strayed past those boundaries Sir Eric had set for him, moreso that he had not yet expired from the aching need that accompanied him back to his solitary bed each night. Tossing upon his pallet, striving to thrust away images of Amica lying on her mattress only a short distance away, he spent long, sleepless nights praying that the days left until his marriage would fly by with the swiftness of the king's hawks.

Today, at last, the betrothal ceremony had arrived. In one week's time he would take Amica to wife and then, please God, his life would return to that calm, orderly thing it had once been.

Amica kept her eyes on the road, not daring to look up at the church doors until they were quite near, lest her shaking knees give way and she stumble. The entire village must be present to watch the ceremony, she thought, for the sound of the crowd murmuring was loud in her ears. Tears of fright filled her eyes and she decided that she would probably faint out of fear and make a complete fool of herself.

"Look, now," Derryn whispered in her ear. "There is Tom, coming to get you."

She did look, wanting to see Thomas's face, wanting to tell him that she could not do this thing in front of so many people, that she was afraid. He would understand, as he always did. He would find a way to keep her safe.

Blinking, she saw his tall, broad figure, clothed in the colors of Reed, moving down the church steps. Gasps rose up all around, for she was the one who must go to him to prove obedience to her future husband. Yet his purposeful stride never faltered.

He said her name, "Amica." When his fingers curled around the hand she had unknowingly held out to him, she lifted her eyes to meet his. He was scowling in his usual way, and the sight of it gladdened her as nothing else could have done. Squeezing his hand, feeling the strength of him, she said, "My lord."

"Come." He pulled her toward him, setting his other arm about her waist and hoisting her up against his side, nearly lifting her off the ground. "We will have this thing done between us."

"Yes, my lord."

"You see how it is," Derryn murmured to Stevan as Thomas led Amica away. "It could not have gone any other way for either of them."

"Nay, it could not," Stevan agreed, watching as the couple ascended the stairs together in perfect union. "She loves him. I admit the truth of it, and pray that Thomas will understand how fortunate a man he is."

Derryn chuckled lightly. "He is too blinded at the moment to understand anything at all. Give him a month after he weds her to see more than his lady wife's beauty. By then he'll have bedded her enough to think clearly."

Stevan grinned. "Two months, more likely. Tom has ever been a thorough lad."

Sir Garin met the couple at the top of the steps, lightly touching Amica's elbow and directing her toward the place where his wife, Lady Elaine, stood on one side of the church's massive oak doors. Thomas, with a nod at Sir Garin, went to stand near the other door beside his master and Lady Margot. At a signal from Sir Eric, Father Baruch, dressed in his most splendid robes, ascended the stairs and stood directly at the center of the doors, between the two groups.

When the crowd had grown quiet, Father Baruch lifted his voice and declared, "We are gathered this day to witness the intention of Lady Amica of Lancaster and of Sir Thomas of Reed to wed with one another. If there is any man or woman present who knows of a reason why they may not be joined together as man and wife, it is now your duty before God to speak."

Silence pervaded as Father Baruch's gaze moved over the assembled, and then he said, "Each of you who bear witness this day are required to come forward and attest to the truth of what you know should any question regarding this union arise in time to come. A written record shall also be made." He pointed to a young monk who sat at a small table near the foot of the stairs, parchment and ink spread out before him.

He turned to Thomas and asked, "What is your intent toward this woman who is called Amica of Lancaster?"

"I would take her as my wife," Thomas replied.

"Before God, in truth, vowing to keep and care for

her according to the laws of heaven, of the Church, and of that earthly king whom God has ordained to rule over all of England?"

"Aye, that is my intent. In truth, so do I vow it before God and man."

Father Baruch turned to Amica.

"Amica of Lancaster, will you accept this man, Thomas of Reed, as your intended husband, in truth and in faith, to agree to be a godly wife to him in every fitting manner, in obedience and service, in the bearing of children, to succor and uphold him, to accept him as your head and master, as God has ordained?"

Master. The single word had the power to steal Amica's voice away. She stared at Father Baruch, filled with memories of Duncan, and could not make herself speak even a word. Sir Garin set his arm about her waist; she heard Lady Elaine, her voice filled with concern, murmur, "My dear?" Ahead of her, Thomas's mouth curved into a frown, and Amica knew that she would very shortly burst into tears.

Sir Eric muttered a curse and stepped forward, grabbing Thomas by one arm and dragging him to Father Baruch. They spoke in hushed whispers while the crowd below murmured, and then, with much nodding, Sir Eric and Thomas resumed their places. Father Baruch looked at Amica once more and said, simply, "Amica of Lancaster, what is your intent toward this man who is called Thomas of Reed?"

Her hands were shaking so badly that Amica clenched them, pressing them deep into the folds of her dress.

Staring at Thomas, who unwaveringly held her gaze, she whispered, "I would take him for my husband."

"You will agree to care for him and tend to him in every manner befitting a godly wife?"

"Yes," she said. "I will do so. I make my vow before God and man."

Father Baruch turned back toward Thomas. "Who is the kinsman who speaks for this man in the matter of the bargain?"

Sir Eric stepped forward. "I do so, Father. Thomas of Reed is my lawful heir, and thus I claim the right of kinsman."

Father Baruch turned to Amica. "Who speaks for this woman in the matter of the bargain?"

Sir Garin stepped forward. "I have claimed the right of kinsman to Amica of Lancaster. The king has given consent to this by his own hand."

Amica glanced gratefully at Sir Garin, thinking of how glad her grandfather would be to know that his dear friend had given her his care and protection. It had not been an easy thing to do, for her cousin, King Henry, had been unwilling to relinquish his right as kinsman. Yet Sir Garin had held fast in his demand, declaring that his right was one of honor, which in this matter was greater than blood ties, for Amica's family had not proven themselves worthy of the right to oversee her future. Her cousin had given way in the face of this truth, not without some shame, which he admitted to Amica in a missive he sent her, explaining that she would no longer be under the hand of her father's family, and that he, personally, would inform them of this when the time came for all the mysteries surrounding Duncan Selwyrn to be revealed. She had not realized, until she had read his missive, that she was believed to be still living at Sacre Placean, and that she had been accounted as having given birth to a child, Duncan's son and heir. Alys's sudden death had been attributed to some form of contagious disease and, as was always done with such victims, she had been buried at once without benefit of a public funeral. No one in their family realized that aught was amiss. No one realized that Amica was, at this moment, about to be betrothed to a man whom they had probably never even known of.

"What does this man bring to his marriage?" Father Baruch asked.

Sir Eric glanced first at Thomas, an expression of pride possessing his features, then answered, "Apart from the lands and monies that belong to Reed which he will one day inherit as lord, he brings his own property, which is called Lansworth. It is a fief owing loyalty to Reed, residing not more than ten miles apart, consisting of one hundred and fifty acres of land, a fine manor house, with its own serfs and vassals. The number of these persons is thirty-two, and their names, ages, occupations and state of health have already been written down and given to my father, Sir Garin Stavelot, for his approval on behalf of Lady Amica. There are presently forty-five head of cattle at Lansworth, including six milking cows, also six horses, thirty sheep, including five rams, twenty-two laying hens, seven pigs and six goats. All of these animals have been accounted as being in good health and without disease. This estate, in its entirety, with all its possessions, including those that have been stated, is offered as a widow's dower to Lady Amica, if she does, in truth, wed with Thomas. It is to be held solely by her in the event that she be found a widow, for herself and for any children she may bear, either in this marriage or any other. Her rights in this matter will be made certain, and shall in no way be assailed."

It was a widow's dower almost too grand to believe, and the crowd took up a loud, excited murmuring.

Over the noise, Father Baruch asked Sir Garin whether Thomas's offer of a dower was acceptable to Amica.

"It is," Sir Garin replied.

"What does this woman bring to her marriage?" Father Baruch asked.

Sir Garin cleared his throat and stood very tall. "Lady Amica brings to her marriage a portion of the estate of Lestonshire, to be held by Sir Thomas for as long as Lady Amica lives, or by Lady Amica herself if she is widowed, for the remainder of her life, to include one hundred acres of arable land and all the rents thereof, also one hundred acres of forest land and all the rents thereof, to be overseen as Sir Thomas sees fit and by a manager of his choosing. She also brings many chests filled with fine materials, including heavy cloths, silks, velvets, furs, also spices, medicines, wax candles, various colors of dye, sewing needles, many spools of waxed thread, a goodly quantity of parchment, writing quills, sealing wax, several pots of ink, and finely milled soap."

Again, murmurs of approval rose from the crowd. From across the width of the church doors, Thomas met Amica's shy smile with a look of resignation, for he had not cared whether she brought anything to their marriage save herself. It was clear, however, that the fine dowry Sir Garin and Lady Elaine had so kindly provided made her happy, and for that, also for peace on the matter, also because he knew Sir Garin would be fully insulted if Thomas did otherwise, he was grudgingly willing to accept it. To that end, he had prepared himself accordingly, but Sir Garin surprised him by speaking again.

"Also, our majesty, King Henry, has added to Lady Amica's dowry twelve finely crafted goblets made of gold, set with matching rubies, and twelve large platters made of gold. These she also brings to her marriage."

The announcement was a surprise even to Amica, who turned to Sir Garin while gasps went up from the crowd.

"My lord, is this true?"

"Aye." He smiled at her. "It is so. I had a missive from him only a few days past. He is well pleased with your marriage."

Father Baruch turned to Sir Eric. "Is Lady Amica's dowry acceptable to you?"

Sir Eric cast a smile at his father. "It—"

"Is *not* acceptable."

There was a frozen silence, and everyone turned to look at Thomas.

"What?" Sir Eric asked, as if he couldn't believe that he'd heard correctly.

Thomas scowled darkly. "It is not acceptable. The goblets and plates—whatever King Henry gave her. That is not acceptable to me, and I will not have them."

"But, Thomas . . ." Amica began.

He gave her a furious look. "I will not have them, and that is final. I will not speak of the matter further."

"You damned well *will* speak of it." Sir Eric grabbed his arm and dragged him over to the far edge of the porch, where Sir Garin joined them and where the three men stood muttering and cursing and shaking heads for several minutes. Although Sir Garin's and Sir Eric's voices rose often during the discussion, Thomas's only once grew loud enough for others to hear it, and then only the words, "Nay! Not from one of her admirers, I won't!" were clearly understood.

Sir Garin stepped back. "He is under your hand, Eric. Make him obey you. I will not have Amica further humiliated this day. Indeed, I am sore tempted to withdraw the bargain and take her home to Belhaven."

Thomas looked at the older man directly. "Amica's home is not Belhaven," he said, the words crisp, adding, respectfully, "My lord."

Sir Eric smothered a dark curse and turned to look at

his wife. She smiled at him sweetly, her expression peaceful, and lifted her delicate shoulders in a tiny shrug. Sir Eric gazed at her for a full minute, thoughtfully, and then, having calmed, turned back to speak again to Thomas. Leaning close, he spoke too quietly for anyone, even Sir Garin, to hear. The only indication of what passed was the expression on Thomas's face, which went from angry to furious to bitterly cold in a matter of seconds. He said something to his master in turn, in a tone tight and unhappy, but Sir Eric only chuckled and set an arm about Thomas's rigid shoulders and hugged him, which shattered the coldness in the younger man's face so that he looked, for the briefest moment, as if he might weep. The next moment, however, Sir Eric had hauled him back to the church doors, where Thomas stood, his ready scowl back on his face, looking very much as if he would rather be anywhere else in the world.

Sir Garin returned to Amica's side, and nodded at Father Baruch, who asked Sir Eric once more, "Is Lady Amica's dowry acceptable to you?"

Sir Eric spoke loudly and clearly, for one and all to hear. "It is."

The crowd broke into loud cheers, which Father Baruch at last managed to quiet.

"What will you give, Thomas of Reed, as assurance of the pledge that has been made, and of the bargain that has been agreed upon, between yourself and Amica of Lancaster?"

Thomas turned to Lady Margot, who pulled a small object out from beneath her surcoat and set it in his waiting palm.

"These, Father." Thomas showed the priest the two gold rings that a village craftsman had joined together with a thin band of silver. On the top of each band was a large, shining diamond, set deeply into the gold.

Father Baruch took the united rings and held them high for all to see. "Let us pray for God's blessing on the proposed union between this man and this woman."

The prayer was not a long one, and when it was over, Father Baruch handed the rings to Thomas again, with one command. "Break the seal."

Looking at Amica, Thomas took the two gold rings in his fingers and pulled. The silver band melted away as though it had been made of butter, and fell near his booted feet.

"Come forward," Father Baruch told Amica.

She moved toward Thomas, who, taking her right hand, folded the larger ring into her palm.

"With the exchange of these rings, Thomas of Reed and Amica of Lancaster hereby declare their intent to wed, and their agreement to all that has been promised in the matter of their betrothal this day. All you who attend, bear witness."

Amica's hands had never seemed so tiny to Thomas as they did at that moment. He was trembling, unaccountably, and when he reached down and grasped her left hand and looked into her blue eyes, seeing the trust and gladness in them for what they were about to do, he felt, for the second time in one day, as if he might weep. Pushing the foolish feeling aside, he looked down at the little hand clasped in his, so small and white against his own large, dark paw, and lifted it so that he might slide the gold band marking his possession of her onto her third finger. On their wedding day, this ring would be moved to her right hand, and he would place another band here, one wider, made only of gold, intricately engraved but with no rich stones to decorate it. A ring of completeness, of permanence. But the ring he slid over her slender finger now just as surely made her his, and let every other man on God's earth know that Amica of Lancaster was betrothed.

When he had finished, Amica took the ring she held and, with more difficulty than Thomas had had, pushed it over his large, bony knuckle and all the way onto his finger.

"Clasp hands," Father Baruch told them. They did, and the crowd fell hush.

"You have exchanged these rings as a bond of good faith in your intent to wed with one another. To this end, make your pledge before God and man."

"I do so vow it," Thomas said.

"I do so vow it," Amica repeated more softly.

Setting his hand over Thomas's and Amica's clasped ones, and lifting up his voice, Father Baruch made a short benediction. When he had finished, he announced, "As they have each made their pledge, in honor and in faith, before God and man, and as they have made acceptable exchanges to seal this pledge, and as no man has come forward to gainsay the proposed union between them, therefore, in seven days' time, with God's blessing, Thomas of Reed and Amica of Lancaster will be joined as one in holy wedlock."

The crowd gave out a great, boisterous cheer, while everyone standing at the church doors thronged around the now betrothed couple.

"You're as good as wed," Sir Eric said happily, thumping his heir on the back. "Kiss your lady to please the crowd and we'll begin the celebration."

The crowd cheered even more loudly, demanding that the kiss be given.

Thomas, obedient as ever, pulled a gasping Amica into his arms and did his master's bidding.

22

The celebration lasted nearly six hours, which was, in Thomas's opinion, five and a half hours too long. The entire week, unfortunately, until the wedding was finally done with, would be one filled with celebrations. There would be feasting and dancing and much merrymaking. It was enough to make Thomas grind his teeth with aggravation.

"How does it feel, Tom?" Derryn asked, sauntering toward him with a tankard of ale in each hand.

Keeping his eyes on the center of the great hall where many of the feasters danced to a merry tune played by Jace and two fellow musicians, Thomas took a tankard and drank deeply. He didn't need to ask what Derryn meant. "It feels, thus far, like torture. If I begin to howl like a beast shortly, do not be overly amazed."

Derryn chuckled and patted his friend's shoulder. "Patience, Tom. A week, no longer, and your misery will be finished."

"Or just beginning, mayhap."

"S'truth," Derryn said thoughtfully, his gaze wandering to the same place that Thomas so intently watched. "You will have a wife to plague you, as women are given to do. But such a wife, my lord. Only look at her! She is as beautiful as an unearthly sprite, dancing there with our lord."

Thomas made a low rumbling sound.

"Why do you not go and dance with her?" Derryn asked. "It seems unfair that she must dance only with Sir Eric and Sir Garin."

Thomas gave him a look of disdain. "Derry, we have known one another for many years. In all that time, have you ever known me to do anything so asinine as to dance?"

Derryn's smile was gentle. "Indeed, I have. You've been especially odd since you've known your betrothed lady wife. Come—" he lifted a hand in a placating gesture "—dance with Amica. There is no harm in it, and no one will think you foolish. In sooth, they must wonder why you have not yet done so."

Thomas kept his gaze on Amica, watching as Sir Eric twirled her about in the spirited dance. Her face was damp from her exertions, her hair had come loose of the circlet that had already done little to confine it, she was laughing and smiling and having a wonderful time, just as Sir Eric was. Thomas's palms felt damp, too, and he twisted them about the cold tankard he held.

"I cannot do so," he said. "If I set so much as a finger to her, I will—" He let out a harsh breath. "I will not be held accountable for what happens thereafter."

"Ah." Derryn nodded. "I thought that might be the trouble. S'truth, I can see the worry, for it did seem, when you kissed her at the church doors, as if you were about to lay her down and make your claim upon her certain and irremediable. Before witnesses, yet."

"You're crazed," Thomas muttered.

"Nay, it did seem so, and Lady Amica looked more than ready to oblige. In truth, I can't decide which one of you might have pushed the other to the ground first. If Sir Eric hadn't picked you up and carried you down the stairs, the need for a wedding ceremony would have shortly been a vain one."

The music stopped and Thomas saw Amica turn in his direction, searching. Quickly, he pushed his empty tankard into Derryn's hands. "That, in all truth, would have been a blessing. If I survive these next seven days, Derry, it will be nothing less than a miracle."

Without giving Amica another glance, without seeking out either Lady Margot or Sir Eric to ask permission to take his leave, and in full view of all those present, Thomas stalked to the great hall's doors, opened them, and left.

Amica sent Maida and Margaret to their beds the moment she returned to her dwelling. She was too exhausted from the ceremony and the following celebration to put up with their fussing, and too muddled to answer the prodding comments they would make about why Thomas had so strangely and suddenly walked out of the festivities. She did not know why he had done it, though she had an idea. If anyone did ask her what she thought, however, she would reply honestly that Thomas of Reed was a strange man, and that no one who knew him well would let themselves be surprised by anything he either said or did.

Sir Eric had certainly been angered at his heir's behavior. While he and Sir Garin had escorted Amica to her dwelling he had done much muttering and grumbling about what he would do and say to Thomas when at last he found him. Sir Garin had chuckled and said something about Sir Eric at last understanding what he'd put his own father through, but that had only made Sir Eric mutter louder.

When the two men finally discharged their duty and bid her a good eve, Amica had gladly collapsed before her waiting fire, thankful that the day was over.

"Two unwed men escorted you to your betrothed," Maida remarked as she and Margaret doused the lamps, "and two married men escorted you home. 'Twas all done just as it should be, and there'll be no cause for any worries."

Thinking of those words as she sat on her bed, brushing out her hair, Amica smiled faintly. Maida clearly put a great deal of faith in the strict adherence of rituals and customs. It was a shame that such things could not promise that a marriage would be a happy or prosperous one. Duncan had believed in following rituals and customs, too, and through him Amica had learned how futile such things were.

She looked down at the ring Thomas had placed upon her hand. The diamond glittered prettily in the firelight, and the sight made her heart constrict. She had never had a betrothal ring before. Duncan had not given her one, and shortly after their marriage, he had removed the ancient gold ring that he'd put on her finger during the wedding ceremony and taken it away. He had only referred to it once after that, saying that she was not worthy to wear the ring that had belonged to his mother and grandmother and every lady of Sacre Placean until she gave birth to an heir.

An heir. Children. She pressed the hand she had been looking at against her belly. Thomas wanted children. He had told her so many times during the past month, and there could have been no mistaking the hopefulness in either his tone or his expression. What would happen if she truly was barren? If it had not been Duncan's fault that she had not conceived? Thomas would be more than disappointed if her womb never quickened. Mayhap so disappointed that he might even set her aside, as was his right, and take another to wife.

"Amica."

Startled, Amica nearly fell off the bed at the unexpected sound.

"'Tis only me. Do not be afraid."

His voice was coming from just beneath her open window, and the next moment his head popped into view.

"Thomas! What do you do there? How—?"

"I climbed up," he said simply, pulling his large body through the window opening and into the chamber with as much ease as though he were merely walking through a door.

"Yes, I see that, my lord," she said, standing. "I did not, however, expect to see you entering my chamber through a window."

Standing full height, he took her in from head to toe in a slow perusal. He was no longer dressed in the fine clothes he'd worn for their betrothal, but wore only a plain tunic and leggings. His feet, Amica noticed with some surprise, were bare.

"I have seen you in that before," he said. "Do all women sleep in such thin garments?"

Amica realized what he meant, and flushed heatedly. She crossed her arms over her chest, knowing that, with the aid of the firelight, he could see very well through the white cloth.

"I do not know," she told him angrily. "Do all men scale dwellings to climb into ladies' chambers?" She looked at his feet. "Barefooted?"

His eyes upon her, he moved toward the heat of the fire. "I have no knowledge of it, if they do. 'Tis certainly not a difficult thing, if one knows how."

"Which you clearly do," she said. "What have you come for that could not have been brought through the front doors, in daylight?"

Thomas frowned. "I must speak with you. I will not be able to rest until I have done so, and now that we are betrothed, if anyone should see me crossing your threshold at such a late hour, whether it be in innocence or no, 'twill be assumed that I—that we—"

"Oh." Amica's face burned. "Because we are so nearly wed."

He nodded. "As good as wed. We could embrace our marriage rights if we so pleased and no man could naysay us." He looked into the fire. "But the gossip in the village would be noisome, indeed, and I promised my lord that I would not take you to wife before we were wed. God save me."

"As you wish, my lord."

He uttered a humorless laugh. "As I wish? It is not at all what I wish. And what of you? Are you so eager for the marriage bed, my lady?"

His scoffing tone made Amica wary, but she replied, truthfully, "I do not know, my lord. I think I am a little afraid . . . and a little eager, too."

She took a step toward him, and Thomas promptly moved back to the window. "Do not come so near to me, Amica. I am not made of stone. Speaking of such things does not make it any simpler to keep from touching you, and if I touch you I will have you. On that very bed."

"I did not mean to speak in an unseemly manner," she told him. "It is simply that, just as I never realized how pleasant kissing would be until you taught me, I have also wondered what the rest of it could be like."

Thomas released a loud, tense breath. "I have been thinking on the matter a good deal these past weeks and have decided that, as with the kissing, skills used in the marriage bed require much practice if one desires to become accomplished in them. I believe—hope—that we will one day become accomplished." He glanced at her sideways. "That will be our aim, anywise. If we do not achieve it quickly, perhaps we shall at least succeed in conceiving a child."

Amica hugged her arms more tightly to herself. "Thomas, there is something I must tell you."

"Nay, I must speak of something first," he said, agitatedly running a hand through his hair.

"What I must tell you is very important," she insisted.

"Not as important as what I must say," he countered.

They both spoke at the same moment after that, and said, in unison, "You may not wish to wed with me."

Silence reigned for a full ten seconds while they stared at one another.

"What?" Amica asked, just as Thomas demanded, "Why?"

"Well— I . . ." Amica looked more closely into his face, trying to see whether he was enraged or simply astonished. "Shall I speak first?"

He nodded.

"I meant to tell you before today. I've tried to tell you before, in so many ways, but the words never came out as I wished."

He reached out a hand toward her arm, then just as suddenly dropped it. "Tell me," he said in a thick voice.

"I do not know if I can bear children. I may be barren."

There, she thought. She had told him the truth, she had spoken plainly. Surely he would realize what she meant, and that she was not the virgin he thought her to be.

But instead of the fury she expected to form on his

features, Thomas only looked relieved. A faint smile tilted his mouth up at the corners.

"I thought that you . . . were going to say something very different," he said, though he never would have admitted that for one horrible moment he'd expected her to say that she had given her heart elsewhere, mayhap to the king, and could not bring herself to wed another. But that was foolish. Had she not said often that she wished to wed with him? He was not forcing her into this against her will.

"We will not worry over the matter of children," he said, waving her words away as naught but typical female fears. How would she know whether she was barren or not? She probably didn't even yet fully understand how children were created. "We will leave that in God's hands, as is right. If he sees fit to do so, we will give life to as many children as he blesses us with. If he does not, we will devote ourselves to the care of Reed and to Sir Eric's and Lady Margot's daughters."

"But, Thomas, you have said often that you wish to have children of your own. What if I cannot give you any?"

She made too much of the matter, he thought. She was healthy. He was healthy. They would most likely have the first of a dozen or more children birthed before they'd been wed a year.

"You will not set me aside?" she asked, annoyed.

He gazed into her beautiful, angry face with surprise. "Set you aside? After all I've suffered to get you? I'd rather be tortured by heathen Turks first. Now, come." He led her back to the fire. "Be quiet a moment," he said, pushing her into a chair, "and let me speak. If either of us has cause to set the other aside, 'twill be you."

"I cannot believe that is so," Amica told him.

"Hear me out," he said. "I should have spoken of this

to you long ago, but it is not so simple a thing for me."
Agitated, he moved toward the fire, then away from it,
then back, as if he could not decide whether he wished
to be warmed by the flames or chilled by the air coming
through the open window. At last he stopped somewhere between the two, looked at Amica and said, "I
killed my father."

The words struck Amica dumb, they were so totally
unexpected. She sat staring at him, and Thomas went
on very quietly, "I will understand if you wish to annul
the betrothal. I will speak with Sir Eric in the morn and
tell him to—"

"Nay. Do not."

Thomas clenched his hands behind his back so that
she wouldn't see how badly they shook.

"You do not mind about it, then?" he asked, thankful that he at least had the power to keep the raging fear
he felt out of his voice. He had been ready to plead with
her, to go down on his knees and beg her to keep him
despite the terrible thing he'd done. Her calm response,
however, left him suddenly unprepared. "It will not
trouble you to be married to one who murdered his
own father?"

"I do not believe it. Thomas," she rose from the
chair, "how did you ever come to believe such a lie?"

"Amica," he said in a warning tone as she stepped
toward him, "do not come near me."

She fell still. "You did not kill your father. It is
impossible."

"I wish, please God, that it were. As many years as I
have spent denying the truth of it, so must I now accept
what I have done. It is one kind of sin to deny the truth
to myself, but 'tis another kind, much worse, to keep it
from you. A woman should not be made to wed a murderer, thinking him something else."

"You are not a murderer," she insisted. "Obstinate, you are, and thick-skulled. Coarse, aye, on occasion, and sometimes unkind and ill-tempered. Stubborn and foolish, s'truth, and certainly quick to judge, but you are not a murderer, my lord."

"I am not obstinate," he said, scowling. "Nor stubborn. I am a reasonable man."

"You are the most contrary, unyielding man I've ever known. Only see how foolishly you are thinking now, calling yourself a murderer."

Angry, he strode toward her, staring down. "If I am contrary and unyielding, then you are a forward, over-bearing female. I killed my father. I am a murderer. What more can I say to make the matter clear to you?"

Amica set her hands on her hips and glared up at him. "Much more, I fear. I will not be convinced by mere declarations. I would have an explanation, my lord. In full."

A little of his bluster fled. He ceased looming over her, and straightened.

"I told you once that I did not remember much of what happened that night when my father died."

"Aye, you did." She lifted an eyebrow. "You did not speak falsely then, did you?"

"Nay, I did not," he muttered. "But I have thought long on the matter since we left Belhaven and can only find one solution, no matter how I approach it."

"He beat you," she said, ignoring his look of surprise. "He almost killed you."

"How did you—?"

"Lady Margot told me. It does not matter, though I am sure you are angered that she should have done so. But I know the truth, you see, and so cannot be swayed by what you now say. Your father would have killed you if he'd not fallen and hit his head. And he must have done so, for you could not have pushed him or hit him with anything when you were already so near death."

With an expression of anguish, Thomas turned away. "I did push him, Amica. It is the last thing I remember. I wanted to kill him, and did not care whether I, myself, died."

Amica moved around his big body to look into his face. "Thomas, tell me what happened. Everything that you can recall."

He lowered his head. "I was ten and four years of age, and had been living under Sir Eric's hand as squire for two years. I did not live with my father, but was ever at my lord's side, either at Reed or at Belhaven, wherever he might be. When we journeyed to Belhaven, however, I made myself go to my father, though I did not wish to do so. I thought it was my duty as his only child to see how he fared. Even then, I did not stay with him long, for he was ever angered at the mere sight of me.

"That night, I left word at Castle Belhaven for Sir Eric that I would return as soon as I had made certain of my father's health, that I would return before the evening meal, for it was my duty to attend my lord and his lady during meals.

"My father was not glad to see me, just as I told you. He had seen me riding into Belhaven beside Sir Eric that morn, with all the townspeople cheering, and had decided that I thought too highly of myself. It angered him, for I was naught but the son of a whore, he said, and should not be allowed to put myself above others who were better than I. And certainly not above him, who had given me life in the first place."

"He was drunk?" Amica asked.

"He had been drinking, but he was not yet drunk.

Perhaps that was the cause of his anger," Thomas mused. "He had no more wine in the dwelling, and no money to buy more. He told me to give him whatever coins I had, and I did. I wanted to leave then, but he barred my way. He was a big man, and strong, despite his love of drink. I could not have gotten past him on my own.

"He told me that I was to return to Castle Belhaven and find more money, or gold, or wine, and bring it back to him. Sir Eric had refused to pay him for the loss of his son, and he felt, very strongly, that he deserved some recompense. If I did not do as he said, I would never leave his dwelling again."

"God's mercy," Amica murmured.

"I should have lied to him, I think. I should have told him anything that might have gotten me out into the village streets and away from him, but I was stubborn." He looked at her. "As a lad, I was *perhaps* more stubborn than is right."

"You told him that you would not do as he asked?"

Thomas nodded. "I had seen him angered many times in my life, but none of them as he was then. He said that Sir Eric would not have me, then, for he was going to kill me as he had killed my mother. It was the first time he had admitted killing her, though I had long wondered if he had. It was that, the thought that he had killed my mother, that made me so crazed. I was no longer afraid of him, and as much as he wished me dead, so much more did I wish the same of him. I did not care what happened to me, I decided that I would kill him, for my hatred in that moment was a white hot fire."

Amica touched his arm. "But desiring to kill him does not make you a murderer, my lord. In truth, he is more to be blamed, for he nearly beat you unto death."

"He did," Thomas agreed, "yet I killed him. It has

taken me many years to remember it, but I do. I pushed him at the last moment, when he had beaten me almost into senselessness. Somehow I found the strength, and I pushed him and he fell and hit his head on the table. I was barely aware of anything, yet I remember it now as if it had just happened. I killed him, Amica."

"You were defending yourself. If you had not pushed him, he would have killed you. You are not a murderer."

He frowned down at the hand she kept upon his arm. "You speak these words with conviction, when I had thought you would take me in disgust."

"Never you, my lord. Your father fills me with loathing and disgust, aye, for he would have so brutally killed his own child. He deserved death, though not one so mild, but his soul is in God's hands, and God will deal with him justly."

She moved closer, bringing the warmth of her body near his. Lifting her other hand, she touched his cheek. "I will never hold you in disgust, my lord, for in truth, I hold you most dear."

He seemed to stop breathing altogether, and stared at her, so that after a moment, Amica said, with worry, "My lord?"

He rigidly stepped from her, pushing her hands away and heading for the window.

"If I remain in this room another half minute," he said, sticking one leg out the window, "I will break my vow of honor to Sir Eric. You are worse than the plague, Amica of Lancaster. Come here."

He was not, Amica thought fondly, a man given to the ways of romance.

"I am worse than the plague, and yet you bid me come?"

"Aye, come here. No, wait." He held out a hand to stop her. "There is one thing more I must tell you."

She looked at him warily. "We are going to be wed, are we not, my lord?"

"We are," he stated, "but I wish to speak to you of the king's gift."

"Oh, Thomas, I do not care about that. You may throw the goblets and platters in the river, if it pleases you to do so."

He blinked. "That is exactly what Sir Eric said this morn. But I do not wish to be so foolish. We will put them aside for our eldest daughter, at once, without so much as looking at the cursed things."

"Very well, my lord." She smiled. "Is that what made you change your mind this morn? What Sir Eric said?"

"Nay, it was not that. It was the rest of what he said, that if I did not wish to accept the king's gift, he would give Stevan the opportunity to do so."

Amica laughed and Thomas held out a hand. "Come here," he said once more.

She went, and let him pull her into his arms and kiss her, one leg out the window, one leg in her chamber. It was a deep feverish kiss. He ran his hands over her slender buttocks and gently cupped her breasts. Abruptly, with a groan, he set her aside and swung his other leg outside.

"I have never before cursed my master, or ever wished to do so," he said as he hefted his body off the ledge, "but that is very like to change before this week is done."

23

One week later, much to Thomas's relief, he and Amica were married in a brief, succinct ceremony that suited him very well. Because the betrothal ceremony had satisfied the legal aspects of the marriage, the wedding itself was little more than a short formality giving testament to the fact that neither side involved in the union had, in the seven days between betrothal and marriage, raised any disputes regarding the exchange of lands or gifts. Within a matter of minutes, Thomas gave up his solitary state for that of a man responsible for a wife. Nothing, ever, had given him such blind satisfaction. He almost squeezed Amica's hand off her arm when Father Baruch pronounced them to be wedded, and he had to bite his tongue to keep from declaring aloud that Amica of Lancaster was his and his alone, and that every man who'd been slathering over her like a sickened dog had best gather his wits unless he wished to find himself facing the sharp edge of Thomas's sword.

The celebration that followed was another matter. It was neither brief, nor succinct, and it didn't please Thomas at all. He allowed his wife to dance with Sir Eric, also with Sir Garin, also with Derryn and, in a fit of generosity which he still couldn't fathom, with Stevan. Jace made an attempt to dance with her once, but Thomas had stormed into the midst of the dancers and dragged her away to the banquet table, muttering loud invectives about troubadours in general and about Jace in particular.

"He's very nice," Amica had begun, to which Thomas had replied, "He's fathered more children off of more unsuspecting women than any other man on God's earth! And *you* aren't going to be the next one!"

But that had been unkind of him, he thought now as he watched his wife being twirled about by Sir Eric, who had very promptly arrived to take her back to the dancing despite Thomas's insistence that she stay in the chair he'd thrust her into. She had looked as if she might weep after he'd said the words, and he'd wanted to cut out his thoughtless tongue. He had no reason to distrust Amica. She could hardly even look at another man without fainting—he would not be so foolish as to expect her to actually dally with someone else. He was the only one she felt truly comfortable with. *Him*, and no one else. Not Sir Eric, nor Sir Garin. No one but him. And he was dear to her. She had said the words herself, of her own free will, and they had burned in him since. He'd not even been able to speak to her in the days following without fear of making an idiot of himself. For an entire week, he had managed to avoid her altogether, though God alone knew how hard it had been, and what it had cost him. He'd nearly gone mad.

"Will this cursed dancing never be done with?" Thomas muttered when Stevan and Derryn came to stand beside him.

The two men exchanged glances and laughed.

"You are impatient, Tom," Stevan said. "That is not like you. Whatever can be so troubling, I wonder?"

"Now, Stevan, don't tease him," Derryn advised with a wide grin. "He's suffered enough this past month."

"A month and a *week*," grumbled Thomas.

"A month and a week," Derryn agreed. "'Tis no great mystery that he's little patience left. I'd not, if I were him."

"Nor I," Stevan admitted.

Thomas scowled. "Has all been made ready? I do not wish to delay any longer than I must."

"All has been made ready," Derryn promised.

"But why must you go to such lengths, Tom?" Stevan asked. "Would it not have been simpler to tell Sir Eric and Lady Margot that you did not wish to spend your wedding night in Castle Reed?"

"I did speak with them, but our lord and lady would have none of it. A great spectacle must be made over Amica being led to the bedchamber, and I must endure a public conduct as well. It is very foolish, but my lord said if he had to endure, so then must I."

"Look!" Derryn pointed toward the dancers. "Lady Margot and Lady Elaine and their ladies have gone to fetch Amica. 'Twill not be much longer now, Tom."

Stevan eyed Thomas consideringly. "Must we carry you up, then? On our shoulders?"

Thomas never took his eyes from Amica, who docilely followed Lady Margot and Lady Elaine up the stairs while all those below burst into loud cheers. "I would not attempt such a thing, Stevan. You wish to live long enough to see your own wedding night, do you not?"

"Sir Eric and Sir Garin are looking at you in a very odd manner, Tom," Derryn told him. "You know how troublous they can be when they've a mind. Worse than children, I vow."

Frowning, Thomas turned his gaze to where Sir Garin and Sir Eric stood smiling at him. "God save me. The last time I saw Sir Garin with such an expression was on my lord's wedding night." He began to look about for the nearest way of escape. "I'd best hide until 'tis time to go abovestairs."

But it was too late for that. Stevan and Derryn each hooked a strong hand around either of Thomas's arms, and, laughing and ignoring his struggles and curses, held him fast while Sir Garin and Sir Eric made their approach.

Amica heard the commotion long before the door to the chamber burst open. The sound of men's laughter filled the room, followed by a shaking *thud* on the floor and Thomas's angry curses. Lying naked in the large bed that Lady Margot and Lady Elaine had put her in, she pulled the covers up to her chin and listened as all those in the chamber, save Thomas, joined in the laughter.

"God's feet!" she heard Sir Eric saying. "He's heavier than I e'er thought!"

"Eric! Surely you d-did n-not carry him all the way! Over your shoulder? Up every s-stair? You m-might have h-harmed yourself!"

"'Twas not so bad, my love, and there was no other choice. He wanted to walk to his bride on his own two feet. As if such a thing would be allowed."

"Years of my life I've given you," Amica heard Thomas mutter. It sounded as if he was lumbering to his feet. "*Years* of devoted service. This is how you repay me."

"You may be the only son I ever have a chance to

carry to his marriage bed," Sir Eric replied. "A father has his duties, is this not so?"

It was Sir Garin who said, "Indeed, this is true, as I'm certain Thomas will remember. I still bear the bruises on my neck from his efforts to defend you on the night of your own marriage, Eric, when you were carried up to your lady against your will. Be glad that Thomas has no such fierce squire to fight on his behalf."

"Very well," Thomas said irately. "I have endured the humiliation of being lugged up the stairs before all the people of Reed. May I now be left in peace with my lady wife? Or is there something more?"

"Tom, lad, have you no knowledge of how this is done?" Derryn asked with amazement. "We have to put you into bed with your lovely lady. We must make certain that she is . . . ah . . . prepared to receive her lord."

Feeling herself turn crimson, Amica pulled the covers over her head and wished she were anywhere else but where she presently was. It was bad enough to be worried about what was shortly going to pass between herself and Thomas, worse to have to spend a night in a castle chamber, though she knew she could endure it as long as Thomas was with her, but to be stared at while in such an exposed state by a roomful of onlookers made her shake badly.

There was a short silence in the room, followed by more laughter, and then Amica heard footsteps moving toward the bed. She peeked out from beneath the covers just in time to see the curtain part and Thomas stick his head inside. Their eyes met and held, and then Thomas scowled. The next moment his head disappeared and he jerked the curtains tightly shut.

"I will be damned to Hell and back before I'll allow such a thing. I didn't marry the woman to let everyone on God's earth have a look at her lying unclothed. Be pleased, my lords and ladies, to *go away*." His voice was low, calm. Anyone who knew him at all would have understood the danger they were in. All of those in the room clearly understood. The door to the chamber opened and Amica heard people moving toward it.

"We've teased you and your good lady enough this night, Tom," Sir Eric declared. "Now you may enjoy what you have waited so long for. You look as impatient as Jacob must have been after his many years of waiting for Rachel."

"S'truth, my lord, I understand very well how he felt. He wasn't allowed any privacy, either, I'll vow."

More laughter, and the lord of Reed said, "We will leave you in peace. Good eve, lad."

"Good eve, my lord," Thomas replied, the words whooshing out of him as Sir Eric evidently hugged him. This was followed by the sound of a kiss, and Lady Margot said, more softly, "Good eve, T-Thomas. Remember all that I have t-told you."

"Aye, my lady, I will do so. She'll be unmarred in the morn, hale and hearty, I promise you."

The door closed after that, the chamber grew quiet, and Amica released a long, tight breath. The bedcurtains were pulled aside once more and Thomas looked down at her.

"Are you well?" he asked.

Still holding the covers up to her nose, she nodded.

"Good. Then rise and clothe yourself." He tossed her chemise onto the covers. "I will wait for you by the window."

A few minutes later, Amica stood by the window, staring at Thomas in complete disbelief.

"My lord, have you gone mad?"

He checked the security of the rope he had tied

around a heavy clothing chest before saying, "Aye, since the day I set eyes on you. By tomorrow morn, however, I pray that I'll have recovered some of my senses. Even a little, if not all of my sanity." Standing, he surveyed the rope with satisfaction. "I thank God that Derryn and Stevan are men of honor. I worried that they might have thought it a merry jest to say they had made all ready when they had not."

Amica backed away from him a step. "Thomas, I am not going out that window. I do not wish to die."

"We must all die, my lady. One day or another, it makes little matter. But you may rest easy on the matter, for I have no mind to die this night, or to let you die. Not after all the misery I've suffered just to get wed." Moving to the open window out of which the rope hung, he swung a leg over the ledge and held out a hand to her. "Come now, Amica. We will go."

She gulped, then looked down at herself, dressed in nothing more than a thin chemise. "I'm not decently clad, my lord," she said, hoping he'd show the same concern for her modesty that he'd expressed only a short while ago.

Instead of concern, he made a face of impatience, insistently extending his hand. "'Tis dark out, and no one will see you."

Trembling, she shook her head. Thomas mistook her fear, for he dropped his hand and said, "Amica, I am not going to hurt you."

"Hurt me?"

"I am not skilled with females," he said. "I have admitted this to you. But I am not such a dullard as to ever harm a woman while bedding her. Have I ever caused you pain before? You have no reason to fear me, now or ever. All I am going to do to you this night is remove your clothes and touch you with my hands, very carefully, and perhaps with my mouth, very carefully, and then I shall put part of myself inside of you—I shall explain more of that later, though it is certainly nothing for you to be frightened of—and then it will all be done. The entire matter is very simple, and you will soon become well used to it. Now," he said calmly, holding out his hand once more, "come."

Amica already knew what the "matter" entailed. Duncan had forced himself upon her often enough that she was quite expert, and her heart sank when she realized that Thomas still thought her to be an untouched maiden.

"Thomas, I—"

"Come, Amica," he said, holding her gaze. "I have waited long for you, but I will wait no more. I will not let you fall, and I do not speak false."

"Nay, my lord," she whispered, putting her hand in his. "You do not. Where are you taking me?"

His fingers closed over hers and he gifted her with one of his rare smiles. "I know how much you hate such places as this, and I will not have my wife suffer when there is no need. Did I not promise this day to care for you, for all of my life?"

She nodded. He pulled her closer, wrapping one strong arm firmly about her waist.

"I am taking you to your—our—dwelling, and when we are there, we will become man and wife in whole. Put your arms about my neck and hold tight."

The next moment they were flying, as easily as if they were birds. Amica gasped, then laughed, and Thomas whispered for her to be quiet.

"I do not think my lord will be glad to find us disappeared in the morn," he told her, descending down the side of the castle as simply and quickly as if he were merely walking down a road. "But I would delay his wrath as long as we may."

The cool breeze tickled its way beneath Amica's chemise and fluttered her unbound hair. She felt weightless, her legs dangling free, safe in Thomas's grip. She never would have thought that hanging from a rope outside a castle window could be such fun.

"I had not realized that you possess such talents, my lord," she said. "Indeed, I had not realized that *anyone* could so easily climb up and down the sides of castles and dwellings."

"'Tis not so hard as it may seem," he told her, coming at last to the ground and setting her on her feet. He wrapped the rope around a nearby bush, then turned and swung Amica up into his arms. The next moment he was striding through the darkness in the direction of the priest's lodgings, which Sir Eric had bidden Thomas and Amica to use as a dwelling for as long as they wished. "I had cause to use such skills often when I was a lad."

Amica set her hands about his neck. "Sir Eric told me of the time you snuck past the guards at a well-fortified keep called Beronhurst, where he and Lady Margot were being held prisoner."

Maintaining his brisk stride, he asked, "Did he?"

"He did. He was very proud to speak of it. The men who had come to rescue them could never have passed through the gates without many of them being killed, but the guards paid no heed to a young boy, and that night, in the darkness, you slipped about, opening all the gates to let the others enter. Sir Eric claimed that he and Lady Margot would not have been delivered if it hadn't been for you. Indeed, he himself was shortly to have been killed before the keep was overtaken by surprise."

"Aye, he's ever had a way of finding trouble," Thomas said. "I have often had to toil greatly on his behalf, to keep him safe and thus to keep my lady Margot from distress. 'Tis bad enough when he's alone, but when he's in the company of his brothers . . ." He shook his head dismally. "I have, on occasion, been sore tempted to tie him up."

Amica smiled. "You are verily long suffering, my lord. Will you be so with me?"

He made a scoffing sound. "I have already been. Never have I suffered more than because of you, Amica of Lancaster."

"Nay," she murmured. "'Tis Amica of Reed, now. Is that not how I shall be called?"

"If it pleases you."

"It does." She leaned forward and placed a gentle kiss beneath his ear, felt his arms tighten about her and his pace quicken. "Thomas," she whispered, "I am pleased to be your wife. I shall strive to make you happy."

Reaching the dwelling, he took the steps to the door two at a time. "You are about to make me thoroughly happy," he told her, opening the door with one hand and closing it by hooking a foot around it as he walked inside. He did not stop to put her down, indeed, he did not stop at all, but carried Amica directly up to the chamber they would now both share.

"Where are Maida and Margaret?" she asked as he bent to open her chamber door.

"Gone." He took her into the room and set her down before the hearth, in which a warm fire glowed. Amica looked about as Thomas closed and latched the door. "It is all prepared," she said with some amazement. "'Tis just as if they expected—"

Turning her by the shoulders, Thomas drew her to

him and placed his mouth over hers, kissing her greedily. Almost as suddenly he lifted his head and stepped back. The next moment he had drawn his tunic over his head and tossed it aside. Moving close to her again, he found her hands and drew them up. "Do I frighten you?" he asked, his labored breathing giving testament to his urgency.

"Nay," she replied softly. "You do not. Never, Thomas . . . "

When he pressed her hands against his bare chest, she spread her fingers wide, feeling his heat and hardness. She had touched Duncan hundreds of times, in many different ways, and had hated every moment. Touching Thomas was an almost painful pleasure. He was very beautiful, she thought as she looked at him. His skin was darkened from the sun, silky and warm to touch. He was muscular and wide; she ran her fingers over his shoulders, across his chest, slowly downward, brushing over the curling hairs that made a slender arrow above his belly. He sucked in his breath when she smoothed her hands over his sides, as she pressed and felt the bones there.

She realized, for the first time, how easily she could wound him, how easily she could please him. Duncan had scoffed at her, and had laughed and called her every name there was for insufficient, but Thomas shivered beneath her hands. She was powerful. He wanted her touch, craved it. Needed it. Duncan had demanded pleasure of her, and she had given it out of fear. To Thomas, she would give freely, gladly, because she loved him.

Sliding her hands to his back, she lowered her head and kissed his chest, once, twice, softly. He shuddered and groaned, and the next moment he grasped two handfuls of Amica's chemise and dragged the garment upward, over and off her body.

"Oh." The word of surprise came out of her unbidden, and, shocked to find herself so suddenly exposed, she tried to cover her body with her hands.

"Nay, Amica." He picked her up in his arms before she could step away. "Let me see you, my lady."

Carefully he set her on the bed, and carefully pulled her hands away, pressing them on the bed.

"Please, my lord . . ." She squeezed her eyes shut against the sight of his gaze moving over her.

"Amica." He spoke her name in a hushed, reverent whisper. When she felt him stand, she opened her eyes. In a matter of seconds he had shed his leggings and shoes, and stood naked before her. She stared at him, unable to keep her eyes from widening at the sight of his fully aroused manhood.

Thomas let out a shuddering breath. His hand moved as if he would cover himself, then fell away.

"This is what men are like," he said in an apologetic tone. "Not always, of course," he added quickly. "Only in times such as this. Does it— Is it—" He sat beside her. "Are you frightened?"

He was much larger than Duncan, Amica thought, still staring at him. She wondered just how much this was going to hurt.

The touch of his hand on her bare stomach caused her to look into his face.

"It—this part of me—must go inside of you." His hand slid slowly downward, and he touched her gently. "Here. Do you understand, Amica?"

Amica could hardly think, let alone understand him. His fingers stroking lightly over her woman's place was unbearably pleasant. She'd never known anything like it before.

"Amica?" His voice was closer to her, and she opened her eyes without realizing she'd closed them.

"Yes?"

He lay down on the bed, pressing full against her.

"Are you well?" he asked with concern.

"Yes." She couldn't hold back the moan that escaped her lips. Her whole body tingled with sensation, and when his hand strayed up to touch her breast she grasped it, pushing it downward. "Please do that again, my lord. It feels very good."

"This?" Thomas asked, clearly astonished. He set his hand against the place between her legs.

With another moan, she pushed against his palm. "Yes."

"I can wait no longer, else I spill my seed on the covers. I must be inside you, Amica. Later, I shall touch you anywhere you please, for as long as you please, I vow."

She spread her legs wide as he moved atop her, knowing what to expect. He positioned himself to enter, and then, gazing into her eyes, hesitated.

"I will try not to hurt you," he said, worry heavy in his voice. "I promised my lady Margot that I would not do so. You must tell me if I do."

Amica smiled gently, and reached down to stroke his heavy member. "Come into me, my lord," she whispered, guiding him until he slid deeply inside and letting out a breath at how easily it was managed. Her body had never accepted Duncan so readily, with such pleasure. "Thomas," she murmured in a voice filled with wonder.

It was over almost before it began. With a loud groan, he pressed heavily, thrusting strongly and quickly for only a few short moments before giving out a low, exultant cry.

"God save me," he beseeched as he collapsed on top of her. "God save me." This was followed by a long sigh.

Beneath him, Amica squirmed. She ached, everywhere, from head to toe, and she felt, strangely, as if she would shortly burst into tears. Her body was hot, tingling, as if she'd contracted some manner of pox and no amount of scratching could make the itch go away.

He lifted his head, smiling lazily.

"You are well?"

She felt almost more furious with him than she ever had with Duncan. What had he done to her, she wondered, to make her body ache so? But she was determined to be a dutiful wife, and so she lied, "Yes, my lord."

He rolled off her and gave another relaxed sigh. "That is good." He put his hands beneath her and pulled her body easily up against his own. "I did not wish to harm you."

"You did not," she told him, releasing a hissing breath as he lifted her higher and set his mouth to one of her breasts, suckling on the tip of it suddenly and deeply. The itching feeling grew worse.

"Hmmm," he murmured with contentment while he suckled. Releasing her, his mouth traveled a path to her other breast as his hands lifted and moved her about as if she weighed less than nothing. "That bodes well for the remainder of this night," he said. "As you had no troubles the first time, there should be none with the rest." He rolled her over onto her back once more. "I have never truly kissed a woman's breasts," he said, running his tongue over one hardened nipple. "'Tis most pleasant. Derryn says a woman may be kissed in many places." His mouth moved lower, over her belly. "I had never heard of such as that before."

Amica clenched and unclenched her hands in his hair, while his mouth moved over her flesh, torturing. She heard herself moaning and wanted to weep with mortification, but there was naught she could do to make herself stop. She was as much his prisoner, in that moment, as she had ever been Duncan's, and as she moaned and moved beneath him, she wondered if a person could die from pleasure.

It was a thought that was to occur to her often throughout the long night as Thomas sated his needs, over and over and in various ways. He was as happy as a curious boy with a fascinating new amusement, exploring and discovering and delighted with each find, while Amica suffered what she believed must be the fate of the damned, burning and aching for something that she couldn't begin to fathom and praying that it would come to an end.

In the early hours of the morn, after Thomas had fallen into an exhausted slumber, Amica lay awake, still burning, still aching, and wondered whether she was going to survive this marriage any better than she had survived the first.

24

"*By the rood, Tom,* give us a moment to rest," Derryn begged, pulling his helmet from his sweat-soaked head. "'Tis too hot this morn to work so hard." He leaned against a nearby tree and closed his eyes.

Dismounting Maelgwn, Thomas said, "You would think it much hotter if this were a real battle, I vow." But he nodded at Stevan, who was mounted beside him. "Relieve the men, Stevan. Tell Sir Edward that they will spend the afternoon in the practice of archery. Tomorrow morn we will march to Lansworth and take our midday meal there before returning to Reed. Tell the men, save those who are set to guard, to be ready to depart at first light."

Stevan rode away and a servant set a large bucket of water in front of Thomas. A moment later, both he and Derryn were refreshing themselves.

"You're going to kill us with so much practice," Derryn complained, pouring a dipperful of water over his head and scrubbing his face vigorously.

"You will find this as naught compared to what we will shortly endure in France," said Thomas, washing his own face.

Derryn straightened to full height, stretching. "It will come to that, then, you think?"

With the hem of his tunic, Thomas dried his eyes. "Aye, I do, and sooner than we may think. The king grows impatient, and will not wait forever to claim his rightful place there. When he goes, you may be certain Sir Eric will follow, and where Sir Eric goes—"

"Thomas will surely go," Derryn finished, chuckling. Removing his sword, he sat down at the base of the tree.

"Aye," Thomas said, removing his own sword and sitting beside him. "And so we train and work hard, for I will not suffer losing my men on foreign soil for lack of skill. They will be ready to fight and they will make any Frenchman who sets sight upon them quake with dread. So I make my vow, and so God may judge me."

"Your good lady wife will miss you sorely if you leave her for long."

Thomas pushed strands of his wet hair off his forehead as he leaned against the tree. "Every woman whose husband goes to fight misses him. Amica will be no different from Lady Margot or Lady Elaine."

"Aye," Derryn admitted, "but Amica will suffer more greatly, for she requires your presence to be at ease. Is this not so?"

Thomas gave no reply.

"She has clearly grown more content in these days since your marriage. Everyone who sees her remarks upon the change. She is no longer the timorous mouse we found so many months ago."

Thomas picked at a speck of dirt on his armor. "There is still much that frightens her."

"But she is easier of late than she was before. And she is ever in a merry mood, smiling and easily pleased." Derryn nudged Thomas with his elbow. "Though why such as that should surprise me, I cannot fathom. You spend your every spare moment locked away in your dwelling together, while the servants patiently wait without to be invited inside once more." He laughed. "'Tis certain and more that marriage agrees with you, Tom, and with your lady wife."

Not looking at him, Thomas frowned. "I do not know that what you say is true, Derry. Sometimes, I wonder . . . "

"What?"

"I should not speak of it."

"Nay, speak," Derryn said. "Something troubles you? Is aught wrong with Lady Amica? She is not ill—"

"Oh nay," Thomas said quickly. "I do not think it is an illness, anywise. It is that I— On occasion— I wonder if I am not somehow displeasing her."

"Displeasing her?" Derryn repeated. "Because you are so obstinate?"

Thomas's head came up. "I am *not* obstinate."

Derryn grinned. "You have a head thicker than the trunk of this tree. Now, tell me, plainly, how are you distressing your good lady wife? Do you argue every little matter with her?"

"Not always," Thomas said grudgingly.

"You are cruel, then, and will not let yourself be pleased and so make her weep?"

"Nay! I am not cruel to her, nor should I ever let anyone be."

"Hmmm." Derryn looked at him thoughtfully. "You do not overuse her in the marriage bed? Women are not always given to as much need as men."

Thomas reddened all the way up into the roots of his

hair. "I do not think so. She always seems more than willing, at first. Indeed, she is always most eager. It is only after that she seems so . . . displeased."

Derryn stared at him. "After? You have given her no pain, I pray."

"Nay. Never," Thomas insisted. "I thought, at first, that I had, but I have asked her, many times, and she has always promised me that it is not so."

"Ahh, so you have asked her," Derryn said approvingly. "But she has not given you reason for her displeasure?"

Thomas scowled. "She does not wish to speak to me, much, after we have done with one another. In truth, she seems more than a little vexed, and once she went so far as to strike me."

"To strike you?" Derryn said with disbelief.

Thomas shrugged. "'Twas as though a fly had struck me, it was so little. That it gave me no pause seemed to make her only angrier."

"This is most odd, Tom. I cannot see Lady Amica doing such a thing without being truly vexed."

Thomas leaned his head back on the tree, shutting his eyes. "She *is* vexed, and that is the trouble. When we are in the midst of—" he waved one hand about, "*that*, she is all that I could desire. Eager. Wonderful." He opened his eyes and stared at the sky. "But afterward, 'tis as if I have done some grievous wrong. She will not even let me touch her, but flies about the dwelling in a fury. She says I make her itch, everywhere, but I cannot understand how this is so. I have never seen proof of it. There are never any pox, or a rash, and it goes away shortly, so that she is all that is desirable again. And when she is like that," he said guiltily, "so sweet and loving, I cannot help myself, and take her back to our bed again. But afterward she is vexed anew, more than before. I hate it."

Derryn blinked several times. "But, Tom . . . you said that you had done all I had told you of. All that women enjoy so greatly."

"Yes," Thomas said, "and 'tis truly pleasant, though Amica twists about in a way that is most distracting. But what has that to do with the matter?"

"Everything. She does not twist about after you have finished pleasuring her, does she?"

There was a short silence, and then Thomas asked, "Pleasuring her?"

"Aye. Once she has been pleasured, she cannot require more. Or is that the trouble? She is insatiable, perhaps?"

"I do not understand," Thomas replied, sitting up a little straighter. "What do you mean, once she has been pleasured?"

More silence, more blinking. Derryn stared at him and made an odd sound.

Thomas frowned. "You are not sickening, are you, Derry? I cannot spare you just now."

Muttering an oath, Derryn sat back against the tree. "God save me. Between Stevan and you, I shall shortly be made into an old man. Now be quiet, my lord, and listen well. I am about to explain exactly why your good lady wife has been so vexed with you of late."

"That looks fine, Margaret. It is straight enough, I think. What do you say, Maida?"

Maida looked up from where she stood by the fire, pouring hot water into a large wooden tub. "Higher on the right, m'lady."

Amica pulled on the rope she held with both hands, hefting the heavy tapestry an inch higher. "By the rood," she muttered. "'Tis heavy."

"Aye, 'tis that, my lady," Margaret agreed as both she and Amica secured the ropes to iron rings set in the walls. "My lord, Sir Thomas, will be full angered when he sees what we've done. He dislikes it when you work overmuch."

"He may be as displeased as he wishes to be," Amica replied as she climbed down from the chair she had been standing on. "I will do as I like in my own home. And it does look so handsome, does it not?" Standing back, she admired the outcome of more than three months' labor, not only her own, but Lady Margot's and that of several of the castle ladies. The large tapestry depicted a hunting scene in which Sir Eric and Lady Margot were most prominent. Lady Elizabeth was also there, shown riding the spirited black mare her father had gifted her with on her last birthday, and Thomas, riding Maelgwn, and several of Sir Eric's highest ranking knights. Lady Margot had insisted that Amica be included, though Amica had never been a member of a hunting party in her life, nor had she wished to be. She thought, in truth, that she looked rather foolish, shown mounted beside Thomas on her own mare, a small bow clutched in one hand as if she actually knew how to use the weapon. But she liked the rest of it, how she was shown glancing at her husband with a tiny, secret smile. Thomas was not looking at her, of course, for he was intent upon the hunt, but Amica thought that if the tapestry had told a real story, that was just how she might have looked at her magnificent husband.

"Is my lord's bath ready, Maida?" Moving to the window, Amica looked up at the sky. "You know how impatient he is to bathe when he arrives home."

Margaret chuckled. "Aye, m'lady. He is most impatient, s'truth."

"Hold your tongue, Maggie," Maida chided. "My lord's bath is ready, my lady Amica, and there is more hot water over the fire so there'll be plenty if that in the tub grows too cold ere he arrives." She set a small pot on a nearby stool, along with a drying cloth. "Here is soap and his cloth, and here are his shaving things." She put a sharp razor and a bowl on the mantle beside another cloth.

"Thank you, Maida, Margaret. You are very good to Sir Thomas and me, for we seldom have to think of anything before you've already taken care of the matter. Go and enjoy the rest of this fine day as it pleases you both."

The girls made a slight bow, smiling at one another in a knowing manner. "Thank you, my lady."

A moment later they were out of the dwelling, turning to wave at Amica as she watched them from the window. Sighing, she waved back. Maida and Margaret knew very well why she relieved them of their duties so early each day, before Thomas arrived home. It would have been impossible for anyone not to know when, after Thomas arrived, the door to their dwelling was shut and locked and neither of them emerged until the next day's sun had given light to the sky.

After one month of marriage, Amica had come to a conclusion about her husband. Thomas might have spent the years leading up to their wedding in avoiding women as much as possible, but he was now striving to make up for all that he had missed.

The man's need for physical union could seemingly not be slaked. Every time she set sight upon him no more than a few minutes passed before he was undressing her, and then himself, and then fitting their bodies together. Amica could not say that she disliked his needy behavior, exactly, for he was always so tender and gentle, yet, each time, when he had finished, he left her feeling wretched, tormented. Worse, he left her thinking of—nay, hoping for—nothing more than that moment when he would next require the use of her body. Even now, when she knew what would happen shortly after he came through their door and that she would be just as miserable as she ever was after it was done, Amica stood by the window and waited with anticipation.

He came striding into view a few minutes later, glancing up as he came nearer. Amica smiled and waved, but he only kept walking. She heard him opening the door and entering the dwelling, and then his heavy footsteps were on the stair. He strode into their chamber unhurriedly, closing the door behind him with quiet care.

"Good day, my lady," he greeted, not looking at her as he moved to set his helmet and gauntlets on a nearby table. "You are well?"

It was much the same as every other day, Amica thought. He was very dirty, damp with sweat, his long, white hair unruly.

She stood where she was, and said, with equal calm, "I am well, my lord. And how does this day find you?"

"Well," he replied, moving to sit upon the bed. "You will help me out of my armor?"

He didn't really need to ask; she had helped him with the task each day since they'd been wed, after he'd realized that neither Derryn nor Stevan were present to lend him aid. It was not too difficult a chore, and Amica was glad to be of more use to him than just a ready body with which to quench his need. With a few tugs, also with his help, she at last drew the chain mail over his shoulders. It was too heavy for her to carry, but Thomas easily lifted it and set it on the bed. Then

Amica knelt before him to draw off his boots. This left him barefooted, wearing naught but a padded tunic and a pair of leggings, and for a few moments Thomas sat, eyes closed, wiggling his toes in relief, while Amica carried the boots to the same table where his helmet and gauntlets lay.

"You will take water, my lord?" She was already filling a goblet from a pitcher. He was always very thirsty after a day of training with his men. He took the cup and drained it, passing it back to her waiting hands. "Would you have more?" she asked.

"Nay." He was looking at her now, just as he did each afternoon at this time, and Amica knew exactly what was going to happen as soon as she returned the pitcher and the goblet to their places. She would turn to face him and he would stand and come to her, and take her in his arms and kiss her in his fierce way. Then he would pull the clothes from her body, and kiss her . . . everywhere. He would put her on the bed and remove his own clothes, and then come into her body and take his pleasure. It would happen exactly as it did every day. Afterward, as she lay on the bed, wanting to weep, he would enjoy a leisurely bath, calling her, after a while, to come and wash his back. And even when she was so miserable that she would much prefer bashing him on the head, Amica would rise and do as he bade, because she loved him and wished to please him. She wouldn't bother to don any clothes, for the moment he was finished bathing, or sooner, he would be ready to use her again. Later, they would dress and go downstairs to eat and then to sit beside the fire, and he would tell her about his day and ask about hers, and when they had done, they would go back upstairs and prepare themselves for bed. Sometimes he would take his pleasure of her once more before falling into slumber, and sometimes they would lie awake, talking before they fell asleep. But always during the night he would wake her, needy, and would mount her at once and finish very quickly. Moments later, he would be soundly asleep once more, while Amica would lie, eyes open, staring at the ceiling.

"Amica?"

"Yes, my lord. I am here."

She waited for him to stand and come to her, but he didn't. Instead, he silently held his hand out.

Surprised, she moved toward him, putting her own hand out. He pulled her close, between his legs, and wrapped his arms about her waist. With a sound of contentment, he pressed his cheek against her stomach. He was silent, simply holding her, and Amica at last set her hands on his shoulders.

"You are a very troublous female," he said quietly. "I spend all day thinking of you, when I should not be doing so, when I should be keeping my thoughts on my duties." With a sigh, he slid his hands over her buttocks, then further down to slip under the hem of her surcoat. "I wish always to be here with you, wasting the sunlight hours in idleness." His hands moved slowly up and down the backs of her silk-clad legs and thighs.

Amica drew in a shaking breath as his fingers smoothed over her bottom, caressing, gently kneading. "Such idleness is a sin, my lord."

"Aye." He kissed her stomach and nuzzled the underside of one breast. Beneath her surcoat, his fingers found the laces of her undergarments. "'Tis a very grave sin, Father Baruch says."

Amica shivered as he pulled the silk garment down, past her hips and knees and finally, with his mouth still nuzzling lazily over her belly and with Amica willingly lifting one foot at a time, all the way off her body. When his hands slipped back under her skirt again, touching her bare flesh, she uttered a low moan.

"I hope you do put the blame on me, my lord," she murmured, gasping when his hands suddenly slid higher, beneath her chemise, to cup her breasts.

"But I do," he said, moving his hands to her back and bringing her forward so that his mouth could more easily reach her breasts. "I must punish you, I think, for causing your lord to harbor such sinful ideas." Ignoring her incoherent protests and her hands pressing against his shoulders, he wet the cloth with his tongue until her nipples thrust out rigidly. "Ah, yes," he whispered, pulling away to gaze at her. "Beautiful."

"Please, my lord." She tried to move forward, to push him upon the bed. "Do you not wish to use me?"

One hand slid higher beneath her dress, to cup her neck and draw her down to him. "Oh, yes, lady wife. I do, indeed."

He kissed her gently, pulling back when she strove to deepen the embrace. "Nay, not yet," he said, and took his hands out from beneath her clothes.

Amica attempted to climb onto his lap, to kiss him again, but he took her shoulders and held her. "Nay," he repeated. As he began to unlace her surcoat, he added, "I want you very badly, but it has been explained to me that I have not been a dutiful husband to you. Now I will make recompense."

"My lord, I do not desire recompense," she insisted, her own hands undoing the laces of his tunic. "I only wish to have you inside of me."

"Such an impatient wife," he teased. "You shall have your wish, I vow." He pulled the surcoat over her head and tossed it aside. "But first I shall bathe you."

Amica's hands fell still. Breathing needily, she

straightened and stared at him. "Bathe me? I do not need to be bathed. I need—"

He captured her mouth and kissed her thoroughly. "To have me inside you," he said when he pulled away. With a grin, he unlaced her chemise. "I cannot believe I once thought you shy and meek. You are very demanding."

"If I am, it is because *you* make me feel crazed." She lifted her arms as he tugged the garment over her head.

Picking her up, cradling her, Thomas replied, "Indeed, this is so, but I will make amends. I have only recently come to understand what the trouble is, and also the cure for it."

"There is no cure." She glared at him as he set her in the tub. "You only wish to torment me."

Ignoring this, Thomas stood full height and stripped off his tunic. Bare chested, he knelt beside the tub. "'Tis well that the fire is lit, else we should become chilled." He dipped a hand into the water. "Is the water warm enough?"

Amica crossed her arms over her breasts. "You are foolish, my lord. I do not wish to be bathed."

Gathering her unbound hair in his hands, he squeezed it as dry of water as he could and set the lengthy mass over the side of the tub. "You once complained that I would not aid you in your bath. At Belhaven. Do you not remember?"

With a huff, she looked away.

Thomas poured handfuls of water over her arms and shoulders, letting it trickle before using his fingers to smooth the droplets over her skin. Her tension, beneath his hands, was a palpable thing, but knowing at last what the source of it was, he smiled.

He scooped some soap from the nearby pot and, leaning closer, gently rubbed the slippery substance over her shoulders, massaging. He murmured near her ear, "You are very beautiful, Amica. I do not think I have told you since we have wed how much you please me." His soapy hands slid to cup her breasts, to rub slowly over them.

"You did not need to . . . to speak of it. Your pleasure has been clear."

His hands moved lower, over her belly, and she pulled her legs up as if she would keep him from going further. Thomas kissed her ear, touching it lightly with his tongue and delighting in the shiver she gave. Insistently, his hands moved lower. "Aye," he admitted, "you have given me much pleasure, and will give me much more in the years to come." The fingers of one hand dipped into the sensitive place between her legs, and Amica set her hand against his to stop him.

"You will make me mad," she told him. "Nay, please, Thomas . . . I cannot bear it."

"Shhhh." He kissed her ear again, softly. "Do not be distressed." He withdrew his hand, sliding it to her knee. "There. I will do nothing to displease you this night." He continued to wash her as she sat, trembling. "I have no one to blame but myself," he said, rinsing the soap from her skin. "Never again will you be left to suffer so long, my lady."

He dried her as gently as he had bathed her, then, setting his chain mail tunic on the floor, he put her upon the bed. She lay, watching him as he shed his one remaining garment, and whispered, "You are strange tonight, my lord. I am a little afraid of you."

"Nay, you are not." He climbed onto the bed, kneeling over her. "You are never afraid of me, Amica." He kissed her, tasting and caressing her with his tongue, pulling forth a fervent response. He did not wait any longer, knowing how great her need was, and pushed her legs apart and put himself deeply inside of her. Her low moan, the expression of pleasure on her face as he began to move spoke fully of her relief.

"God's feet," he said, groaning as his own pleasure beckoned him. "What a hard siege I have laid. But I have given my vow and will not turn from it."

He made his body obey and concentrated on Amica. She writhed beneath him, her hands clutching his arms, her head tossing upon their pillow, her mouth moving, pleading with him, uttering every kind of meaningless sound. Thomas spoke to her as best he could while moving in her slowly and deeply, murmuring what he thought was some form of encouragement, though he found it very difficult to think. And then he could not speak at all, but gritted his teeth against his body's painful demand for release. He heard Amica saying his name, felt her own body meeting the rhythm of his, and what happened after that was so strange that he could never thereafter put it into words. Something came to life within him, some instinct long buried but suddenly so clear it was as if he had always known it. He realized what was happening the moment it happened, and his own body responded without the need for conscious thought. Their movement became perfect, and everything save their union grew dim, vapored, as if the room, the bed, the entire world, for all Thomas knew, went away. His mind could grasp onto nothing else save Amica, and when she shuddered beneath him and cried out, his own body answered fiercely so that he, too, for the very first time, helplessly shouted his pleasure.

Afterward, Thomas strove to put his senses into order. That he was still breathing was his first clear thought. That he was able to open his eyes and focus them was the second. That he was still in his bedchamber at Reed was the next, and that he was lying, collapsed, upon his wife was the last. He felt utterly weary, as if he had no strength left, and with a loud groan and much effort managed to lift an arm and roll off of Amica and over onto his back.

He gazed at the ceiling and realized that the room had grown dark. Had it taken so long? he wondered. Or had he been insensible for such a long time after?

"Amica." He turned his head to look at her. Her eyes were closed and she made no response. "Amica?" Rolling quickly onto his side, he touched her cheek. "God's mercy, did I crush you? Amica?" He shook her.

"Mmm," she murmured contentedly, snuggling against him. A moment later she pressed a hand to his chest, sighed, and began lightly to snore.

Chuckling, Thomas gathered her close, kissed the top of her head, and waited. Several minutes later she stirred.

"Do you awake at last?" he asked, letting her push from him to lie on her back. She blinked, an expression of confusion on her face. "Should I be offended that my efforts to please you put you to sleep?" he teased.

"Nay," she replied, perplexed. "My lord, what did you do to me? That has never happened before."

He stroked her cheek. "It has not, but it should have. I was far remiss in not seeing to your needs before now, but from this day on, that will not be so. A husband should see to such as that, and so, I vow, I will."

"Is it what you feel when you take your pleasure? I felt, for a moment, as if I were dying."

"Aye." He smiled. "Something like that, though it has never happened to me that way before, either. 'Twas much better. I think I must practice often to become more perfect in the matter."

Her expression brightened visibly. "Aye, my lord, I think you must. I begin to understand that you have much to repay me. When I think of what I have suffered this past month!" She shook her head. "'Tis grievous, I fear. You must pay well and fully."

He laughed, capturing her hand and kissing it. "You will be a hard task master, I think."

"If I was demanding before," she said, "I shall be more so now. Indeed, I should very much like it if you pleasured me again."

He kissed her mouth. "I shall," he promised. "But first 'tis your turn to attend your good husband in his bath. Then we shall go belowstairs and take our sustenance, for we shall need it," he added quickly when she opened her mouth to protest. "And then, my lady Amica," he kissed her more deeply, "I shall most certainly pleasure you again."

25

"*It does seem odd,* but here is the missive. You may read it for yourself."

Sir Eric set the unfolded piece of parchment into Thomas's outstretched hand, then waited in silence as his heir gave all his attention to it.

At last, with a shake of his head, Thomas gave the document back to his master. "It makes no sense, my lord. Why should the king call you to London without giving good cause? And to tell you to bring Lady Margot and the children . . . "

"And a portion of the household," Sir Eric added. "Aye, 'tis worrisome, I vow. It is clear that Henry will keep us in London for a goodly length of time if we must set up our own dwelling there." With a sigh, he dropped the parchment onto his working table. "I cannot like being away from Reed for so long."

"I cannot like it that the king asks you to bring so many of Reed's fighting men to London. He will have no need of them there, and 'twill leave Reed without sufficient protection. It is not like him to ask you—any of his nobles—to do such a thing. Would it not be wise to send a missive in turn, asking him to make the matter more clear?"

"Nay, I must believe that there is some just cause that he will explain to me when we have arrived at court. He has not been pleased with Elizabeth's unhappy reception of Kenric Willan, and it may be that he wishes them to spend more time together to persuade her to accept him as a husband."

Thomas gave a snort. "She hates the lad. He should be less stubborn in his choice of wife."

"S'truth, but 'twas Elizabeth he decided upon and Elizabeth he asked Henry for and Elizabeth that Henry has promised to give him."

"He would be better served to promise Willan the moon. And, in truth, it does not seem likely that Henry is so concerned with marriages, just now. 'Tis France that occupies his thoughts."

"Aye," Sir Eric agreed. "And that may be why he requires soldiers from Reed. Mayhap he requires an escort to France, and who better than my army? There are none in England, anywhere, who are better trained or more capable."

"I fear you speak the truth of the matter, my lord," Thomas said grimly, "and if that is so, then I must go with you."

Sir Eric smiled. "And leave your wife of three months? Is this the same man who nearly drove me mad with his impatience to wed? Have you so quickly grown weary of your beautiful lady?"

"Nay, of course I have not. I have no desire to leave Amica, but if my men are going into battle, I must go with them."

The lord of Reed's expression filled with amazement.

"You doubt my ability to lead my own army into battle? I would have you bethink who it was taught *you* to fight so well, impertinent whelp."

Thomas looked at him patiently. "Be serious, my lord, I beg you. Your father and brothers will all be going to fight in France, save Sir Aleric, who is the only male in your entire family whom God saw fit to bless with any reason, and you know very well that when you are all together your behavior borders on the lunatic. The French will begin to think that King Henry emptied all the asylums in England to form his army, and I will be worn thin trying to keep all of you alive as well as to tend to my men. Mayhap," he said thoughtfully, strolling toward the fire and ignoring his master's outraged effort to speak, "I will take Amica to London with me. She would enjoy seeing something other than what's inside the walls of Castle Reed."

"Ha!" Sir Eric exclaimed. "What she needs is to be let out of your dwelling more often, or out of your bed-chamber, rather. We've seen so little of either one of you at mealtimes that we've begun to worry that you will shortly take ill."

Thomas scowled. "Is that not the reason that men take wives?"

"To make them ill?"

"Nay, to make use of them," Thomas said, tossing one hand up into the air in an irate gesture. "And Amica does not seem to mind it. Indeed, I can promise you that she does not. And she is never ill."

"Not yet," Sir Eric agreed dryly, "though with the vigor with which you've been using her that state should not be far off."

It took Thomas a moment before understanding dawned. "That form of illness I will gladly welcome," he said, "and will give praise to God."

"Hmm." Sir Eric moved to stand beside him. "That is another fitting use for wives. The getting of children."

"Aye, and the more, the better. I should be glad to have many children."

"You will have an opportunity to pursue the matter at your leisure, then, for you will remain here at Reed with your good lady wife—"

"Nay, my lord!"

Sir Eric held up a silencing hand. "You will remain and oversee the management and safety of Reed. I will take Derryn Thewlis and Stevan of Hearn to London to command my army."

"Nay," Thomas repeated sternly. "That will not suffice. Leave Derryn and Stevan here, if you will, but I must lead my men. Have I not given them my solemn oath, my lord, that I would not fail them? Shall I let them go into battle while I remain in comfort at Reed, doing little more than bedding my wife?"

"It shall be as I have said," Sir Eric told him. "Reed will be left weakened and vulnerable with so many soldiers gone from it. Every care must be taken to make certain that no threat bears fruit. You know this as well as I."

"Aye," Thomas admitted grudgingly.

"There is no one else to whom I may trust my lands and people. I like it no better than you, Tom, but there is no other road to travel. Derryn and Stevan are good soldiers, capable fighting men, and they will take all care with my army, but they cannot safeguard Reed as you can. Is this not so?"

"My lord—"

"Is this not so?" Sir Eric demanded.

Muttering a curse, Thomas replied, "It is so."

Sir Eric moved toward his working table. "Very well. I will want to leave for London in five days' time. Make certain that the number of men Henry has requested are ready to leave by then. I will leave the selection to you."

"I would ask a favor of you, my lord."

"Of course, Tom."

"Take Derryn to London, as you wish, but be pleased to leave Stevan here at Reed. His knowledge of estates is helpful, and as I think you must take your chamberlain, Sir Lowell, to oversee your household in London, I will have a great need of him. Derryn can care for the men with the help of Sir Evrain."

"Very well," Sir Eric said. "Stevan will stay behind. And I shall also leave Jace, although my lady will miss him sorely. I know that you bear Jace little love, but the servants obey him and he knows more of the ways of Reed than any other living person, I trow. His service has been estimable to me these many years."

Thomas gave no response to this, but stared thoughtfully at the fire. After a time he said, quietly, "I do not like this, my lord. There is naught about it that makes sense."

"Nay, there is not," Sir Eric agreed. "But I do not readily question the king's commands. Not without good cause."

"I suppose you do not," Thomas agreed reluctantly. "I will do as you have said, my lord, and will remain at Reed. And I will do what I can to endure Jace's aid in certain matters, but I would have you speak with him before you depart and forbid him to father any more children on the serving maids while you are not present at Reed. If I catch him dallying with any of the women in the castle I will probably strangle him."

Chuckling, Sir Eric patted Thomas on the shoulder. "Don't worry yourself over Jace, Tom. Fix your thoughts on your wife and on fathering your own children."

His mouth set in a grim line, Thomas replied, obediently, "Yes, my lord."

*   *   *

"Sir Eric *commanded* you to father children?" Lying in her husband's embrace, Amica had to squirm away slightly to look up into his smiling face.

He chuckled. "He did not, in all truth, command it. His suggestion was made most strongly, however."

"Then, as you are ever obedient to your master, my lord, you must surely do his bidding."

"You have become more than demanding, my lady. You are now a tyrant. May I not be allowed to rest for a few moments?"

"A very few," she teased, yelping when he tickled her. "Cease, my lord!" she cried, laughing and pushing his hand away. "Tormentor." She held his hand captive. "Cruel and wicked tormentor, you will make me crazed."

"Aye, indeed I will." Thomas kissed her, freeing his hand to wrap it about her neck and hold her still while his mouth moved over hers. When he lifted his head, he murmured, "What do you think of this manner of torment?"

"'Tis most effective. I am more than ready to do your bidding."

He made a *tsk*ing sound. "You are a very easy conquest, lady wife."

He was smiling, and Amica could hear the teasing in his voice, yet a sudden sadness filled her. "Nay, I am not. I never believed I would know such happiness, my lord. Sometimes I am afraid that it is not real, that it will all go away."

He stroked the hair from her face. "It will not."

"It might. You do not know much about me, or of my past, or even who my family is. One day the king will decide that the truth may be revealed, and when it is, mayhap you will come to despise me."

"Amica," he said, gathering her close, "that I will

never do. I have no care for what is in the past, or for who your family may be."

"But—"

He kissed her again, adamantly, until they were both breathless. "I do not like to speak of these things. You are my wife, Amica. Forever. Nothing will change that."

"You do not know that, my lord," she whispered.

"I do know it. You wed me, knowing that I killed my own father, that I am the vilest manner of murderer. Yet you have not set that sin as a barrier between us, indeed, you have never spoken of it at all, so that I begin to believe it truly does not matter to you."

"It doesn't."

He cradled her face gently in one large palm. "Just as your past, your family, makes no difference to me. We will not look back farther than the day we were wed, but will begin from there and go on."

Amica pressed her face against his chest. "I'm so glad that you will not be leaving Reed," she said fiercely. "I will thank God upon my knees every day, for I love you."

Thomas stiffened, and for the space of a minute or more the only sound in the room was that of the fire. Amica lay very still, her heart thumping loudly in her ears, and waited for him to speak. At last he said, softly, "Father Baruch says it is a grave sin to love one's spouse. Only our holy God is worthy of love, and we must give all that we possess to Him. I think, then," he whispered, pressing a kiss into her hair, "that I am guilty of sin. Does it trouble you to be wed to such a man, Amica?"

"Nay." He had said as much as he was capable of, and she was content. Pulling him down to her, she murmured, "If we will be guilty of sin, my lord, then let us be guilty together."

26

"What is all the noise about?" Amica asked, setting another rose in the basket Maida held.

"I do not know, my lady. It comes from the village, I think."

Both women fell silent, listening.

"It sounds as if there are many horses," Amica said softly, tilting her head. "It cannot be that Sir Eric and Lady Margot have returned already. They only left Reed four days ago."

"Listen!" Maida held up a hand. "The village gates are being closed. What can it mean?"

"I do not know, Maida. Here." She set her clippers into the basket. "We will return to the dwelling and I shall change my surcoat and go to the castle to speak with my lord."

"Oh, my lady!" Maida cried fearfully. "You do not think Reed is under attack?"

"I do not," Amica told her firmly, taking the younger woman by the arm and guiding her out of the garden.

"And even if we were, my lord Sir Thomas would be more than able to keep us safe. No sane man would willingly face him in battle."

"But the fighting men are gone with Sir Eric."

"Not all of them," Amica reminded, quickening their pace in an effort to keep her own thoughts from being overtaken by fear. Thomas had been worried over the possibility that some lawless baron might know of Sir Eric's departure, and might realize just how vulnerable Reed was at present. The troublous, wandering armies of such men had never been a worry while Reed was fully manned, for Sir Eric's army was too large and well trained to be easily overcome. But now, with more than half of that army gone to London, the wealth of Reed was truly a most enticing prize. As long as his body held life, Thomas would not let anyone take that prize, and it was that truth, more than the fear of Reed being under attack, which filled Amica with dread.

The two women were nearly running by the time the dwelling came into view, and a few moments later Amica was in her bedchamber, nervously unlacing the tattered surcoat she always wore while tending the gardens.

"The blue and gold surcoat, Maida," she directed the maid. "I will not go to my lord poorly clothed while he sits as lord of the castle."

Maida had only just finished lacing Amica up again before the door to the dwelling noisily burst open.

"My lady!" Margaret screamed from below. "My lady!"

Amica ran to the landing. "Here, Margaret! What is amiss."

"My lady, you must run!" Margaret cried wildly. "*Run!* Now, before they come for you!"

Duncan.

It had been long since Amica had known her old fears, but at the realization that Duncan had at last come to find her they rose up fresh and sharp, robbing Amica of all her senses save one. Terror. She stood upon the landing, staring down at Margaret, watching as tears streamed down the girl's red cheeks, as her mouth moved, shouting the same word over and over. Run. *Run!*

Her body obeyed before her mind told it to, before Amica could even think, and she was suddenly down the stairs, pushing past Margaret and out into the bright open warmth of late summer. Momentarily blinded, she ran toward the direction of the gardens and, unseeing, right into the arms of a tall, strong man who held her tight even as she screamed and struggled to be free.

"My lady." His voice was stern, sharp. He took her by the shoulders and shook until Amica looked into his face and realized who he was.

"Stevan!" she cried with relief. "Thank God." Weeping, she clutched the front of his tunic. "Thank God."

"Sir Thomas has sent me to find you," he said, sounding, to Amica, very unlike himself.

"Thomas?" She looked up at him. "He's all right? What is amiss? We heard the commotion in the village, and Margaret came into the dwelling and . . . "

Her voice drifted away as she saw that several soldiers of Reed surrounded her. Wiping her face with the palm of one hand, she looked at each one of them in turn, and then, with a growing sense of dread, faced Stevan again. "Thomas is all right, is he not, Stevan? You must tell me the truth."

"Sir Thomas is well," Stevan replied. "He has sent me to escort you to the castle, my lady, where you are to attend him."

He spoke coldly, distinctly, all the while gazing at

Amica as if he did not know who she was. The dread
inside of her turned into something hard and heavy; she
heard Margaret and Maida weeping loudly from somewhere behind her and remembered what Margaret had
so frantically cried. *Run. Before they come for you.*

She stepped away from Stevan and swept her gaze
once more over the soldiers. Their expressions were
hot, angry, and she realized all at once that she had
somehow become their enemy. Thomas had sent them
to find her, to bring her to him.

"I have done nothing," she whispered. "Nothing."

Stevan's hard expression never wavered. "You must
convince your lord of that, my lady, not me."

"Stevan, I beg you . . . "

He stepped away. "Only those who are guilty beg.
Will you come of your own free will? I will have you
chained and dragged, if I must."

Her limbs shook badly as she followed behind him.
Twice, her legs gave way completely and she collapsed,
only to be roughly pulled back up to her feet and
shoved in the direction of the castle.

The great hall was silent as Stevan pushed open the
doors and led Amica through them. Thomas, she saw at
once, sat in the room's highest chair whence Sir Eric, as
the lord of Reed, issued judgment. Standing beside him,
smiling, stood Duncan, surrounded by several of his
most trusted men.

For one fearful moment Amica believed she would
faint. She felt hot and numb, and she stood where she
was, trying to cause Duncan's much hated face to
become more clear. The old feeling she had always
experience when setting sight upon him came to life—a
sharp, knife-like thrust of fear accompanied by a duller,
more constant desire to kill him—and Amica acknowledged it like a long known acquaintance come back

from the dead. She recognized the look of triumph upon that hated face; she had seen it often enough after he had bent her to his will. Her gaze moved upward, to Thomas. She recognized the expression he was directing at her, as well. She had seen it whenever he had heard his master, Sir Eric, slighted, or when she, herself, had been subjected to insult. Cold, hard, angry. Merciless. She saw it now and her heart turned to stone.

Duncan had given him lies, and Thomas had believed him.

For the first time in her life, Amica's fears fled as quickly as they always came upon her. For the first time in her life, she felt absolutely nothing. When Stevan prodded her forward, she went without trembling or hesitation. She stopped in front of Thomas, her eyes held firmly upon his.

"Is this the woman?" Thomas asked.

"It is," Amica heard Duncan reply. "This is my wife, also known as Amica of Lancaster."

"She is the granddaughter of John of Gaunt? The bastard daughter of John Beaufort, earl of Lancaster?"

"She is, as well as cousin to King Henry. You have the statement sent by her uncle, Henry Beaufort, the Bishop of Winchester and the king's own chancellor, but if you will not believe what he has said, ask her for yourself if this is not the truth."

Thomas's eyes narrowed as he held Amica's gaze. He was very pale, she saw. "If you know how to speak the truth, lady, then do so. You are the granddaughter of John of Gaunt?"

"I am." Her voice was so clear and steady that Amica was almost surprised. How strange, she thought, to not be afraid.

"And you are this man's wife, as he has claimed?"

"Nay," she answered firmly, not so much as glancing at Duncan. "I am not. I am your wife, my lord."

"So I believed," he said, standing, several documents clutched in his hand. "Before I saw this." Thomas lifted up a particular piece of parchment, one bearing the king's official seal. "This is the document recording your marriage to the lord of Sacre Placean. It is signed by Henry Bolingbroke's own hand. Do you say it is false?"

"Nay, it is not," she admitted. "But my marriage to Duncan Selwyrn has been annulled. The king found good reason to do so."

"Your uncle, the Bishop of Winchester, states otherwise. S'truth that the king considered having your marriage annulled, but, with the good counsel of the rest of your family, he changed his mind." He moved toward her. "You have given your family much trouble, it seems, running away from your husband and spreading every manner of foul lie about him to convince your cousin, the king, that Sir Duncan was cruel to you. Because of those lies, Henry lent you aid in escaping the man to whom you lawfully belong."

"Nay!"

He thrust the papers before her face. "You would deny it when I have the proof of it here in my own hand? Deceiving *witch!* Henry believed you, just as my master believed you. Then you decided to practice your lies on *me.* Will you deny it?"

"Yes!" she cried furiously. "I deny it!"

"Is your uncle a liar then? Is that what you claim? That a bishop of the holy Church has written me naught but lies?"

"My uncle was glad to be rid of Alys and me," Amica told him, "for he did not want the care of us when our father died. He would say anything Duncan asked him to, especially if enough gold was offered."

"Then what of this?" Taking her hand, he slapped one of the documents into it, a small piece of parchment, badly wrinkled. Breathing hard, speaking from behind clenched teeth, he commanded, "Read it. Aloud."

Confused, Amica unfolded the single sheet. Her own handwriting greeted her eyes, and she gasped. "I did not write this!" She looked at Thomas. "You know that I did not write this!"

"Read it!" he shouted loudly, so that everyone in the hall could hear.

Drawing in several breaths to steady her voice, Amica bent her eyes to the document in her hands.

"To Sir Duncan Selwyrn, lord of Sacre Placean. My dearest husband," she threw a look of disdain toward Duncan, who merely nodded, "do not be angered when you receive this, I pray, for I regret having left you as I did and desire above all things to be reconciled to you. I admit my foolishness in all that I demanded, for I know now that you did all you could to please me, though I refused to be content. Henceforth I vow to be a dutiful wife, obedient and satisfied in every way, and I beg that you will let me return to you, despite all the wrongs I have done. I have suffered greatly since I have been gone from Sacre Placean, and have been made to endure the crude embraces of a simpleminded knight who believes himself to be my husband. He is so clumsy and lacking that he even thought me a maiden when we first lay together, which amused me for a time, but now I can no longer endure his unwelcome touch, and wish to return to you, my husband, who have never failed to bring me such great pleasure. As a sign of my good faith toward you, I will place the wealth of Reed into your hands, thusly: the lord of Reed and his family will be leaving for a long sojourn in London, and at the king's command will be taking with him more than half his army. The fool who thinks himself my husband will be left in command, and I can easily dispose of him. 'Twill be but an easy matter to take from Reed all that you wish, my beloved. Come quickly, my lord, to conquer, and to receive the embraces of your devoted wife. I long for you, Duncan, as I long for Sacre Placean. Come quickly. Amica."

A rumbling of voices had begun while Amica read the missive, and now there was a loud chorus of those who stood in the great hall, every one of them shouting for her immediate death.

Amica lifted her eyes to Thomas, who stood glaring at her, his chest rising and falling with each breath he drew. There was nothing in him now to suggest the man she loved so well, who would never have believed such lies of her.

"I did not write this," she said quietly. "You cannot believe this of me."

"Why should I not?" he asked harshly. "Sir Duncan brought me these documents when his army easily could have overrun and destroyed Reed. All he requires in return for this act of good faith is that his wife be returned to him. Can you think of any good reason why I should not do so, save that you deserve to be kept at Reed and executed as a traitor?"

Shouts went up in the great hall, "Traitor!", and grew deafening as many demanded her death.

"Silence!" Jace's voice roared above the din. "Silence, all of you!"

The troubadour stood on the dais beside the lord's chair.

"Who is this man?" Duncan demanded.

"He is no one," Thomas replied tightly. "Nothing more than my master's fool. Ignore him."

"Do as you please," Jace said aloud. "For I will most

certainly do as I please. And it pleases me, my lords and ladies, to declare that Lady Amica speaks the truth. She is no traitor. These documents are falsely written, just as she is falsely accused."

"Then you are a fool in truth," Duncan told him. "This Jezebel is my wife, and has been for many years. Think you that I would not know her? That I should have no understanding of her devious nature?"

Thomas held up a hand. "It does not matter, my lord. He is the only one present who believes her lies, and as he is a fellow with a lusty nature, I can only believe that she has seduced him in some manner, just as she seduced me and many others. Stevan, come forward."

Stevan moved to stand beside Thomas, his face rigidly set.

"Stevan, speak what you know of this woman," Thomas commanded. "Did she not deceive you with sweet words and promises? Did you not declare that you wished to wed with her?"

"Aye," Stevan replied readily. "She did so deceive me, and I, falling prey to her wiles, did wish to wed her. I can only thank a gracious God that such did not come to pass. And for you, my lord, I feel naught but sorrow, for you did wed her, aye, and in good faith, as all who are here can attest."

The loud shouting began again, going on until Thomas raised a hand and brought the crowd to silence.

"What shall be done to Amica of Lancaster, then?" he asked. "What say you, Stevan?"

Amica shook her head, murmuring Stevan's name.

"Death to all traitors," Stevan replied.

"I say she is innocent!" Jace cried from the dais. "You are wrong to believe this man, this stranger, when Lady Amica has been among you for so many months, proving her goodness to one and all." He leapt to the ground and went to stand beside her. "Your own lord and lady took her into their hearts," he argued. "Can you think them so dull-witted as to be so easily fooled?"

"Nay," Thomas replied hotly. "They are not dull-witted, they are merely too good-hearted. Is it not so?" he demanded of the crowd, which replied with fervent agreement. "They were as taken in by her wicked beauty and false manner as we all were. Verily, she must be of the devil to have so easily deceived us." He looked at Duncan. "If you want her, then take her. Do whatever you please with her, but get her out of Reed. I would not have the sun set upon her shadow here. She is foul and evil. Take her away."

"Nay!" Amica shouted, knowing a strength she had never been able to imagine. "If you believe this of me then kill me now! By your own hand."

Boldly, she strode to him, and boldly, as he stood staring down at her in complete surprise, she pulled the dagger from his belt and thrust the hilt into his hand. Forcibly curling his big fingers around it, she hoisted both hand and knife up to her throat and held them there. Then, looking directly into his face, she said, "I gave you my love, which I have given no other man, and you have made it as naught. Now I know that no man is worthy of trust, and I wish to die. If you believe me guilty of the crimes you have accused me of this day, then you must kill me, for I will *not* go with Duncan Selwyrn."

His gray eyes were very dark, and what she saw in them confused her. He whispered her name so softly that it sounded like a breath rather than a word, and his hand relaxed so that she felt his fingers pressing against hers. She began to draw away, to speak to him, but a sudden, sharp blow fell on the back of her head, and she descended into darkness.

27

Amica could not see when she at last awoke, and for a moment she lay still, pondering the weighty darkness that enveloped her until she realized that she was wrapped, head to toe, in a blanket and that her throbbing, aching head was covered with something else. Dragging her hand slowly upward, she touched her face, feeling, instead of her skin, a soft cloth. It was some kind of sack, she thought as her hand traveled over her mouth and nose and eyes. It was tied loosely, though securely, with a cord around her throat.

"Are you awake, my lady?"

She recognized the voice only a moment before a hand touched her shoulder, pulling the blanket away.

"My lady?"

"Aye, Jace. I am awake."

"God be praised," he murmured, uncovering her and slipping a hand beneath her shoulders to pull her into a sitting position. "How do you feel? Does your head ache?"

She felt his hand move gently over a tender knot on the back of her skull.

"Forgive me," he said when she winced. "'Tis not as bad as I had feared, though I should like to look at it without this mask covering you."

"Duncan required me to be covered?" she asked softly, blindly moving one hand in the air until she found where Jace was sitting. "Where are we? I can hear others nearby."

"We are at the place where we will sojourn for the night, several miles from Reed, for we have traveled long. And, aye, we are well guarded, I fear. We are not alone in this tent, nor will we ever be alone. Your lord has declared that we both be constantly guarded. He has been sent word that you are awake, and will be here shortly, I think."

She nodded her understanding of this. "Why are you here, Jace?"

His hands squeezed her shoulders in a comforting gesture. "I would not let them take you without a fight, and so Sir Thomas bade the lord of Sacre Placean to take me with him. He was not pleased, but he would have had to kill me before I would let you leave Reed."

"Lady Margot would be afraid if she knew you were here," Amica murmured, "for she loves you better than a brother, but I am so grateful . . . so grateful."

"Now, now." He put his arms about her. "No good will come of giving way to fear and grief. I have never been so amazed as I was this day, to see you standing before Sir Thomas, speaking as if you were a new creature, so brave and bold." With a sigh, he added, "Would that you were not already wed. I should gladly throw my heart and life and self at your feet."

She gave a small shake of her head. "That is why you came?"

"Nay. I came because I believe you are innocent, and because Sir Eric would strike my head from my shoulders for letting you go alone."

"You believed me, when no one else did? When Thomas did not, nor even Sir Stevan? Why?"

"Perhaps because I am a fool," he told her. "Perhaps out of love for my lady Margot. It is hard to say."

Amica gingerly felt the sore spot on her head. "Duncan struck me?"

"Nay, Sir Stevan did. With the hilt of his dagger."

"Stevan," Amica repeated. "I cannot fathom it. He was ever so kind and gentle. Am I to wear this all the way to Sacre Placean?" She tugged at the dark hood.

"I do not know. Sir Duncan put it on you before he carried you from the great hall. Sir Thomas asked what he meant by it, but the lord of Sacre Placean only said that it pleased him to carry his wife back to his home in such a manner."

"I see," she said, and with a sigh dropped her hands into her lap. "You cannot stay, Jace. He will kill you at the first opportunity. 'Tis the truth I speak, for I know him well. You must flee, for he will never let you set foot upon Sacre Placean."

She heard his low chuckle. "My lady, you cannot see them, but there are four large men occupying this tent as well as us. Not only do they hear every word we speak, they would most certainly stop me if I dared to leave. I believe that I would rather stay near you than take my chances with them."

"Staying near me will do you no good. Duncan enjoys killing anyone who is dear to me. It would give him great pleasure to observe my horror by killing you in my presence."

Jace lifted her hand and kissed it. "Then if I must die, at least I will know that someone other than myself cared about it, and to have the concern of the most beautiful lady I have ever seen will make the knowledge that much sweeter."

The tent flap opened, letting in a gust of cold air.

"You are indeed a fool, sir," Duncan said as he entered, "if you believe whatever lies this witch is telling you."

"I was speaking of my lady's beauty," Jace replied easily, "and even a fool can see that her beauty is no lie, my lord,"

She heard Duncan moving closer.

"Beauty that covers a heart filled with sin is the gravest lie known to every power that exists, be it in the earth or otherwise. And she is not your lady. She is mine. Guard your tongue, fool, else you'll have no tongue to guard. I have no care that you belong to the lord of Reed."

"I do not, as it happens, belong to the lord of Reed," Jace said calmly, "but to his lady wife, whom I have served since I was a boy. She would be unhappy to know that you have threatened her favorite, and Sir Eric, whose might you will have heard tell of, does not suffer his lady to be made unhappy. By anyone."

Amica could feel Duncan's tension, though he was not touching her. The tent grew very still, the air taut with silence. There was nothing Duncan would wish more in that moment, Amica knew, than to put Jace's life to an end. He had never tolerated being spoken to in such a manner. But he was not so foolish as to ignore the importance of what Jace said. It was one thing to insult a great lord, quite another to insult that lord's wife. Killing Jace would win Duncan the eternal enmity of the lord of Reed, and that was a thing not lightly won.

"Get out," Duncan said in a low voice. "I will give

you a horse and you may return to Reed with my blessing. You would never have come save that I wished to be
on my way to Sacre Placean as quickly as possible. There
was not time to argue the matter with a simple fool."

"There is naught that is simple about me," Jace said
with a laugh. "And I will return to Reed when I have
seen that the Lady Amica arrives safely at Sacre
Placean. I do not believe that you mean to treat her
well, or even to keep her alive, as you have said."

"Then you will learn differently, for Amica is my
wife, and I, more than any other, know how to treat her
as is fitting. Now go, all of you. I would speak with her
alone."

Jace squeezed her hand before rising. In another
moment, after a great deal of noise, the tent fell into
silence.

It was new and strange to Amica to not be afraid, so
much so that she marveled at her ability to fold her
calm, steady hands in her lap and to wait, breathing
normally, for whatever was to come.

"You have made that idiot's death certain, Amica,"
Duncan said, and she felt him kneeling beside her. "I
need only devise a way to make it appear natural to satisfy Sir Eric's wrath." His fingers tugged at the hood
around her neck, and the next instant a knife cut the
cord. With one swift movement, the hood came away,
and Amica blinked in the candle light. "You may be
pleased with yourself," he said, standing.

She drew in a slow breath, filling her lungs with
clean, cool air, then lifted a hand to rub at the sore flesh
on her neck.

"Let me look at you," he said more softly, tossing the
hood into her lap. "I have dreamt of your beauty these
many nights. Lift your face to me."

Silently, Amica looked up, and was surprised anew

that she felt nothing beyond the recognition of his dark hair and handsome features. She gazed at him with indifference, and then rolled her head from side to side, stretching her stiff muscles. The next moment his hand fell hard against her cheek, sending her sprawling to her side.

"*Whore*," he murmured. "I should kill you outright for the insult you have given me. Instead, I will make you regret what you have done for the rest of your life. Not a day that you draw breath shall pass when I will not repay you for what you have done. To *me*. The master of Sacre Placean."

Pushing herself up with one hand, Amica looked at him with all the cold, calm fury she so magically, gratefully felt.

"Nay, Duncan, it will not be so. There is nothing more that you can do to harm me. You have killed everyone, everything, that I have loved. You may do as you please, whatever you please, but you have no more power to cause me pain. I am *free* of you."

He struck her again, and again, and when she did nothing more than look up at him with the same calm expression, he struck her once more, at last throwing her back to the ground. But she only pushed herself upright and turned her face, red and swollen, up to gaze at him.

With a gasp he backed away, as if she might cause him harm, as if she posed a horrible danger.

"You do not tremble," he said, his own voice shaking. "What has happened to you, Amica?"

"My heart has turned into stone and can no longer feel." She smiled. "You must kill me, Duncan. You know that you must." She stretched a hand toward him, watching as he took another step away. "Come," she coaxed. "Do it. You must be braver than Thomas of

Reed was. Do it now, for I will surely drive you to it, if not now, then later."

Eyes wide, he shook his head. "Nay."

Amica lowered her hand. "If you will not do it now, then it must be later. But it will come, one way or another. You will not long abide a wife who can give you no pleasure because of the pain you give her."

"You loved him, then."

"Yes, I loved him. As much as I hated you, thus did I love him. I did not think anyone could hurt me more than you have done, but I was wrong." She frowned. "You will not kill me?"

A slow smile started on his lips. "You know me better than that, Amica. You believe you can withstand my punishing, but you cannot. And I think I like you this way, so fierce and angry! You remind me of Alys, in the days before I broke her spirit. I much enjoyed the game I played with her, just as I shall enjoy what I will do to you."

With a sigh, Amica looked away. "'Twill not matter," she said in a quiet voice, as if she were speaking to herself. "I am all dead within."

He drew nearer. "Then mayhap I shall bring you to life again." Kneeling, he touched her hair, gently. His breath fell warm on her cheek as he spoke. "Mayhap I shall court you sweetly, and pleasure you, and cause you to love me as you loved him." Pushing her hair aside, he kissed the side of her neck. "I could do it, so easily. I could make you beg for whatever I might wish to give you."

Amica made no response, even as his hands covered her breasts, caressing, or as his mouth traveled over her neck and upward to her ear, which he licked, and across her cheek and eyes and at last to her mouth. He pushed her onto her back and kissed her fully, thrusting his tongue deeply inside.

"Amica," he murmured, his fingers working frantically to unlace her surcoat. "How I have missed you . . . wanted you. God's mercy, you are more beautiful than I remembered. Your breasts . . ." With a rough tug he exposed them. "Beautiful. I am going to kiss you everywhere. I am going to pleasure you as that young idiot you took for a husband never could have done." He lowered his head to take a nipple into his mouth.

Amica lay beneath him, wooden and unresponsive, gazing at the roof of the tent and enduring Duncan's efforts to arouse her in silence. Long moments passed and at last, over the sounds of his impassioned moaning and murmuring, she stated, "There is a small tear in the cloth."

He lifted his head, breathing harshly.

"What?"

"There." Amica pointed upward. "If you do not have it fixed soon the tent will leak when it rains."

Duncan sat up, staring down at her in disbelief. Amica lay before him, relaxed and calm and clearly unaffected.

"You see, Duncan," she said, not a spark of emotion in her tone, "I am beyond you now, just as Alys is, and as my grandfather is. Just as anyone who is dead is."

"Nay, Amica. Not for as long as you draw breath. I am your master and well you know it."

She smiled, displaying her first sign of emotion. "Mayhap I am not all dead, for this thought does give me great pleasure, that I shall never name you master again, Duncan Selwyrn."

"You will," he promised, standing. "I vow it on the name of all that I hold holy, even on the souls of my ancestors, you will bend to me again. Now cover yourself before my men return, unless you mean to play the whore and try to seduce one of them into lending you aid."

Amica sat and wordlessly laced her surcoat. When she had finished, Duncan approached her with the black hood.

"You will wear this from now until the time that we return to Sacre Placean, for you left in secret and must return in secret. None of my people will ever know that you have been away, save these few men whom I trust for their silence."

She sat quietly as he replaced the hood and while he tied another cord around her neck, shutting Amica in a darkness that was to last, day and night, for the next several days until they arrived at Sacre Placean. Even when she was given food or wine, the hood remained, though the cord was loosened enough for her to eat and drink.

Duncan did not attempt to speak with her again until the day before they reached Sacre Placean and Amica, in turn, spoke only to Jace, who stayed with her every moment, serving as her eyes, helping her to mount her horse, to eat her meals, to find the pallet where she slept with Jace beside her. So it was with some surprise, and a sinking of heart, that Amica awoke on the last day of the journey to find that Jace had somehow managed to escape during the night.

"I should have killed him the moment we left the boundaries of Reed!" Duncan shouted at Amica, who stood unmoving before him, having been dragged from her bed the moment Jace's absence was discovered. "Where has he gone? What did he tell you before he left?"

Amica answered truthfully that she did not know, which only caused Duncan to strike her, repeatedly, until she lost consciousness. When she next awoke, it was to find herself in her old chamber at Sacre Placean, chained to the bed.

28

The next morning Alfred the steward arrived and led Amica to another chamber not far from her own. Here several maids whom Amica had never seen before stood waiting beside a large tub. They undressed her and put her into the uncomfortably hot water; a few moments later the door opened and Duncan entered, followed by two men whom Amica did recognize, one a priest and the other a physician.

What she endured for the following several hours, which Duncan explained was a ritual of purification necessary to remove Thomas's touch from her body, left Amica exhausted and weak. Her skin was first scrubbed until it was raw, then massaged with a mixture of oil and herbs. She was made to drink a strong purgative that, on her empty stomach, made her violently ill. Her mouth and teeth were cleansed with a pungent soap and her hair was washed with lye. Lastly, having been rinsed and dried and placed, naked and only partly conscious, on a bed, she was examined by the physician. Half asleep, she felt his hands moving over her.

"Is she with child?" Duncan asked, sounding as if he were very far away.

The physician's reply seemed even more distant. "It is possible, my lord. I cannot yet be certain. We must wait a few more days."

She was not returned to the chamber that had always been hers but, for the next four days, was kept in the chamber with the tub. She was tended to by the same maids who came and went and saw to all her needs, but was otherwise left to herself. It was a pleasant room, with finely made furniture and a fire that was always kept fueled. Alfred brought her material and goods so that she might keep herself occupied with sewing and made certain that there was enough candle-light by which to work. There was one window in the room, but it was nailed shut—the only sign Amica had that Duncan truly understood that if she had had the opportunity, she certainly would have risked her life in an attempt to escape.

On the morning of the fifth day the physician arrived to examine her again, although Amica could have told him what it was that he sought to know. She wondered, at times, whether Thomas might have kept her at Reed if he had known about the child she carried. But what good would have come from it? He had faith in Sir Eric and in Lady Margot, in Derryn Thewlis and Stevan of Hearn and even in Duncan Selwyrn, but not in her. He would have suspected that the babe was not his, and both she and the child would have lived beneath his constant scorn. It was better this way, she thought. She knew what it was to live without love; she could not bear to cause an innocent babe, her own child, to suffer such a life. Neither could she remain at Sacre Placean and allow Duncan to bring the babe harm. Somehow she would find the way to escape again. Alys was not there to help her now, yet Amica vowed that she would do it all the same.

If only she could get a message to either Sir Eric or the king! They knew she was innocent of the wrongs Thomas had so readily believed, and would at once send men to rescue her. Indeed, Duncan would be fortunate if King Henry did not demand his life for what he had done. The thought brought a grim smile of satisfaction to Amica's lips. If Duncan were dead she would at last be able to live in peace—she and her child. The pain of Thomas's rejection would be there, aye; she knew that would last for as long as she lived, but it would not touch her child, his child, whom she would love with every breath she drew.

The next morn Amica's maids arrived laden with clothes, bearing a message from Duncan that she was to accept the garments as a gift from him. They dressed her in the fine silk undergarments and a grandly ornamented, dark blue surcoat, then plaited her hair and placed a gold circlet atop her head. A short while later, Alfred arrived to lead her to the grand chamber that had always belonged to the lord of the castle.

Duncan rose to greet her at once, a soft smile upon his lips and a hand outstretched to pull her further inside the room.

"My love." He bent to kiss her cheek and Amica saw, with a frown, that he was clothed in a tunic made of the same cloth and of the same color as the surcoat she wore. "There are no longer any bruises, may God be praised," he said, holding her chin and turning her face from side to side. When he saw, for the first time, the faint scar on her cheek, he fell very still. "What is this?" he whispered. "I did not do this to you."

"I did it to myself," she stated plainly. "To rid myself of beauty."

With a finger he traced the nearly invisible line. "I see. Well, it has not marred your perfection, and will fade in time, so it is of no matter to us. But, come, my lady, for this is a very great day in our lives." He led her toward the large, curtained bed in the midst of the chamber. "Come and see your son."

Pulling one curtain aside, he revealed a slumbering child. Amica moved closer, eyes wide, to gaze at him. He was perhaps seven months of age, plump and healthy and very beautiful. Golden hair curled thickly on his head and dark lashes covered what Amica knew would be blue eyes.

"God's mercy," she murmured, reaching to touch the soft, sleep-warm cheek. "Alys's child."

"Nay, love." Duncan captured her hand and put it to his mouth, kissing it. "Our child. Is he not becoming? Today he is going to be baptized."

For the first time since Thomas had so unjustly accused her, Amica felt a clutch of pain constrict within her. Tears stung her eyes, and she blinked at them.

"May I hold him?"

"Of course, my love," Duncan said, kissing her hand once more before he carefully took the child up and set him into Amica's arms. "Of course you may hold him, as often as you wish, whenever you wish. He is your son, and has needed his mother very badly."

The tears were streaming down her face now as she gazed at the sleepy, angelic countenance, but she did not feel them. She felt only the heat and heaviness of his sturdy little body, and the way he snuggled against her, turning his nose into her breast, nuzzling, and the sharp, aching pain in her heart for all Alys had lost.

Weeping, she sat upon the bed, cradling him in her

lap so that she might touch his soft hair with her fingers.

"What is his name?"

Duncan sat beside her, smiling down at the child.

"Conall, for he will one day be a mighty ruler. It is fitting, do you not think?"

"Conall," she murmured. "Poor little boy. He is so innocent. May God have mercy on him." She pressed a kiss to his forehead, wetting his face with her tears.

"And why should God not do so?" Duncan asked angrily, snatching the babe from Amica so suddenly that the child woke and began to whimper. "Come, we must go belowstairs, where all await to attend the baptism of their future lord."

Amica realized at once what it was that Duncan wanted her to do, and shook her head. "Nay."

"Aye," he said impatiently, handing the unhappy child to Alfred. "Do you want my people to know he is a bastard? Do you think Alys would have wanted that? After all that you both suffered because of your illegitimate birth?"

No, Amica thought. Alys would have spared her son such as that, if she could have done so.

"Only a few trusted souls in Sacre Placean know that Conall is Alys's child," Duncan went on more calmly. "Everyone else, all of my people, believe he is yours, my legitimate heir. If he is not my legitimate heir, Amica, then I have no use for him." He met her furious gaze steadily. "You understand what I mean. Sacre Placean will never have a base-born ruler. Never."

"Yes, I understand you," Amica said hatefully, rising. "You would kill him without care, without a twinge of remorse." Taking a step closer, she glared up into his face. "You are surely the vilest creature on all God's earth." Turning abruptly, she strode to where

Alfred stood, attempting to calm the child. "Give him to me," she commanded, taking Conall protectively into her arms. "There now," she soothed, unwittingly imitating Thomas, whom she had so often seen holding and comforting Lady Gwen. "There, there, love."

The babe quieted, gazing up at her with solemn blue eyes.

"Conall," Amica murmured, stunned by the fierce love she felt for him, as if he were, in truth, her own. "What a fine lad you are." Gently, she wiped the tears from his soft cheeks. "Fine and handsome. How greatly your mother would have loved you."

She could hear the relief in Duncan's voice when he spoke behind her. "You will do this, then?"

Amica lifted her chin. "For Conall and for Alys. Not for you."

"Of course, my love." He dropped the hand he had held out when she jerked away from it. "That is all I expected, nothing more. Let us go."

The ceremony was unfortunately a long one. Amica was exhausted by the time it was over and was grateful that Duncan did not require her to continue with her pretense throughout the celebration that followed. Conall, who had fallen asleep midway through his baptism, was heavy in her arms as she climbed the stairs with Duncan on one side of her and Alfred on the other.

"Here," Duncan said, his tone oddly gentle as he pushed his chamber door wide, standing back for Amica to enter. He lifted Conall from her arms and pressed the boy into Alfred's ready hands. "Take him to his nurse and await word from me. I will speak with my wife alone."

Amica watched as Alfred carried Conall from the chamber, then turned a wary gaze upon Duncan, who had moved to fill a goblet with wine.

"What do you wish now, Duncan?"

He brought the wine to her. "Only to speak with you, Amica. It will not take long, and then you may rest. Drink, please, and sit." He motioned to a chair. "I would have you be comfortable."

"I will stand," she said. Glancing at the goblet he held, she added, "I do not trust you, my lord, and I do not wish to be in your company any longer than I must. Say what you will and then send me away."

Anger possessed his features, but he nodded. "Very well, Amica. Do as you please. Will you have none of this?" He lifted the goblet a little higher. "It is not poisoned, I vow, though I can see it is what you think. I offered it because you are pale and look weary. I thought to be kind to you."

A slight smile touched her lips. "Did you, Duncan? That is strange in you. If you wish to be kind, in truth, you will give me my freedom."

"We may speak of that yet," he replied with a frown. "I have thought long on all that has passed, and have much to say to you. It is not easy to do, however, when you refuse my hospitality. I do not wish to be cruel to you, Amica, but you try me sorely."

"Very well," she said, taking the goblet. "I will drink your wine and sit in your chair, but only because I wish to be finished with you." Suiting action to word, she walked to the cushioned chair and settled into it. "Speak and then let me alone."

Duncan stalked to the nearest window and gazed out of it, silent for several minutes.

"Amica," he said at last, "this is not easy for me, and I pray that you will strive to understand."

He turned to her, and she was stricken anew by what a handsome man he was. It was something she had thought on often during her years of imprisonment at

Sacre Placean, that a man so pleasant to gaze upon should be so evil.

"I have not been kind to you," he stated. "In truth— and I will be truthful to you this day—I have treated you most cruelly. It is a sickness with me, and whether I was born with it or learned it from my own father, I do not know. The suffering of others has always brought me great pleasure, and I cannot seem to stop myself from the practice of inflicting harm, even to those whom I love. I know that you will neither believe nor understand when I say that I love you, but it is true, nonetheless. As much as I can love any woman, any being, thus do I love you, Amica."

Amica gazed at him blankly, saying nothing.

Duncan pushed from the window. "You do not like the wine? Have you even tasted it yet?"

Grateful to turn her attention elsewhere, Amica lifted the goblet and drank deeply. The wine was horribly bitter, and she coughed.

Duncan sat in the chair beside hers, pulling the cup from her stiff fingers and setting it aside. The next moment he gathered her cold hands in his. "Amica, I want you to become my wife again. Not as you were before, but in truth. There will be no more chains, no more suffering, I vow it on the souls of my ancestors, whom you know I hold most dear. Indeed, you need not even suffer my company. I will leave you in peace, to do as you wish, to go where you wish, with all freedom, so long as you will be a mother to Conall."

Against her will, Amica's eyes widened.

"I will not set a finger to you again, nor make any demands, not even for children or to share my bed. You may have any chamber in the castle that you wish to occupy, any servants of your own choosing. You may come and go as you please, anywhere, even to stay at another dwelling if you desire it. All I ask is that you claim Conall as your own, that you be a mother to him, as you would be, for I can see that you love him already, and that you tell your cousin the king that you choose to remain my wife of your own will."

Amica pulled her hands free. *"Never."* The only man she would have chosen of her own free will was forever lost to her, and the very thought of Thomas made her want to weep.

"Is it so hard?" he asked.

"You are a liar, Duncan. You cannot exist without causing others pain and grief. You could not let me live unless you were able to visit every manner of torment upon me."

"Nay, that is not so," he insisted. "I will leave you in peace, just as I have promised. And you must think of Conall. If you refuse me, then you leave the boy without a mother to love and care for him. You do not wish to let me have the raising of Alys's child, do you?"

His words struck Amica sharply. Conall was indeed in Duncan's hands, to do with as he pleased, to mold as he pleased. Without thought, she lifted a hand and protectively covered her stomach. Duncan's eyes followed the movement.

"Ah yes," he murmured, setting his own hand over hers and pressing hard. "There is this to consider. Thomas of Reed's child growing in your belly. Another man's child. It is the only thing that I cannot accept, as you already knew."

"You would make me give it up?" she asked anxiously.

"I will not even let you give it life. But that does not really concern us. Whether you agree to be my wife again or not, the babe will be destroyed." Seeing her sudden paleness he added, reassuringly, "There are many ways to be rid of a child in the womb without harming the mother. You will be perfectly fine in the morn, love."

"In the morn?" she whispered, horrified. Pulling away from him, she stood. "I am not going to let you take my child."

He gazed at her calmly. "It is not a matter of letting, Amica. You will no longer be with child by tomorrow morn. What concerns us now is your decision. I would send the king a missive on the morrow, written by your own hand, that you freely wish to remain at Sacre Placean as my wife." He stood, attempting to take her hand even as she backed away from him. "Once that is done, my love, we will begin our marriage anew."

"Nay, Duncan," she said, distressed to hear the old tremor in her voice. "You cannot ask me to give away the life of my child. I— I will stay with you, just as you wish, in whatever manner you wish, but let me give the child life."

"Nay, I cannot, even should I wish to do so. It would be an abomination to the spirits of the earth."

"It is Thomas of Reed's child," she said desperately. "He will take it away once it is born. You know that he will do so, if you would but tell him of it."

"Ha!" Duncan scoffed, following as Amica circled the chamber. "You cannot believe that. Thomas of Reed despises you. Any child born of your body would be greeted by him with naught but contempt. *If* he even deigned to believe that the child was his, which he most likely would not."

The truth of his words only served to make Amica furious. "There was a time when Thomas would have been glad—when he would have rejoiced to know that I held his child within me. I wish before God that I had told him what I suspected the moment I did, for then he might never have believed your lies!"

Duncan flushed angrily. "But he did believe me, Amica, and quite readily. How can you think he cared for anything more than the lust that he satisfied upon your body? I have shown more love for you than he ever did!" He thumped his chest with a fist. "I have shown more faith in you, for I have always known what lay within your heart. Did you think it not so?" he asked, moving quickly and grabbing her by the arms, shaking her. "I have understood you better these past many years than Thomas of Reed or any other man could have done," he insisted, pulling her near, "and in my own way I have loved you. You do not know how to believe the things I say, for I have never given you cause, but in this you will know, for I have offered you a free choice."

"To be your wife or your prisoner?" she countered angrily. "That is no choice, Duncan. Not when I must pay for it by letting you kill my child!"

His expression grew faintly amused. "You misunderstand me, Amica. I do not mean to make you my prisoner again if you refuse to become my wife." He chuckled. "If your answer is no, then I will kill you. Either way, you see, the child dies."

"Nay," she insisted, shaking her head. The slight movement made her feel strangely dizzy.

"Aye," Duncan countered, smiling.

His face, though close to her own, grew blurry, and Amica blinked to clear her vision.

"You are beginning to feel the effects of the wine," Duncan murmured. "You will sleep for now, my love, while the leech rids you of the babe. In the morn, when you are feeling better, we will speak on these matters again. Without the child to cloud your judgment, you will realize more readily what your decision must be."

Gathering her waning strength, Amica pushed free

of him, swaying on her feet. "You said it was not poisoned!" she accused hotly, struggling to think clearly against the odd buzzing in her head.

"I lied," he said simply, reaching out to steady her. "Be still now, Amica."

His hands felt heavy on her arms, like steel, and she was encompassed by a thick sense of sorrow, mixed with fury, both of which were directed fully at Thomas. It was all *his* fault, she thought angrily. His fault that she was here, in this impenetrable fortress, with this crazed madman, about to have their child, perhaps her own life, taken from her. She wished with all her heart that she were back at Reed, simply so that she could have the chance to beat some sense into Thomas's thick skull.

"Come, love," Duncan said, pushing her toward the bed. "You must lie down."

Amica didn't realize what she was doing until she had already done it. Her hand closed over the handle of the small dagger in Duncan's belt, her arm flew upward and then, with surprising strength, plunged down, hard, into his chest. His shout of surprise spurred her into movement, and she shoved him away.

"Amica!"

She was out the chamber door before she heard his furious scream. Breathing harshly, she stumbled in the direction of the stairs, toward the sound of the ongoing celebration taking place in the great hall. In the midst of the confusion she might be able to make her way out of the castle unnoticed, then to the stables, and if she could but steal one of the horses . . .

"Stop her! *Stop her!*"

Duncan's voice filled her head like the dull roar of thunder. She put her hands up to cover her ears, to keep the sound of him out. Somehow she had stopped moving, and another voice was speaking.

"I have her, my lord."

Alfred's expressionless face swam before her eyes.

"What shall I do with her?"

"My baby," she murmured, striving to speak as clearly as her muddled mind would allow. "Do not let him take it."

"Take her to her old chamber and chain her to the bed." Duncan was suddenly looming over her, his face set with a mixture of fury and pain. "Amica of Lancaster has made her choice."

29

The attack on Sacre Placean was so sudden and fierce that both the villagers and Duncan Selwyrn's soldiers were quickly overwhelmed. The fact that almost everyone who lived in the land was either drunk or weary from the day-long celebration that had followed Lord Conall's baptism served to keep the loss of life low. Very few villagers, at the sight of the massive army approaching at a thunderous speed, rose up to defend themselves, and not many more soldiers gave resistance, especially when they caught sight of the king's own colors preceding the attackers.

Thomas was too impatient to fight, however, or to wait until the castle gates were finally forced open. Knocking both Derryn and Jace aside when they tried to stop him, he tore off his boots, secured his long-roped grapple over his shoulders, and dove into the moat, swimming as deeply as he could to avoid the arrows aimed at him. By the time he emerged on the other side, he could hear Sir Eric on the bank, cursing loudly even as he and Derryn sent arrow after arrow in an effort to buy Thomas some small measure of safety while he scaled the castle wall. He climbed quickly, having secured the grapple on a high, unmanned arrow loop, stopping only long enough to decide which window he should use for entry. The one directly above him would be easiest, Thomas thought, but two men were presently hefting a large, steaming pot to its edge, preparing to douse him with something quite hot, either oil or water. The window to his left was higher up, also manned by two armed soldiers, but when an arrow struck one in the chest, sending him to his knees, Thomas decided the extra effort would be worthwhile. He swung to his left only moments before the pot's boiling contents were sent flying at him. Sir Eric and Derryn clearly understood his intent, for a flurry of arrows showered the farther window as he neared it, stopping when he was too close to the target. The soldier at the window had drawn his sword and, leaning out as far as he dared, tried to hack the rope from which Thomas dangled. Thomas tried to reach his own sword, which flapped against his thigh, but it was impossible without risking a fall. Muttering a curse, he lifted his face and shouted hoarsely at the man.

"I fight with the army of King Henry! Cease your efforts and help me into the castle and I shall make certain that you live and go free! If you kill me you shall surely die!"

The man stilled and their eyes met and held. Thomas could see the indecision in his face.

"The castle will not hold much longer," he added, bellowing above the roar of the battle. "Save your own life!"

Gritting his teeth, he pushed himself higher and lifted a hand. The man stared at it, clearly realizing that this was his moment to kill Thomas if he wished. With a curt nod, he put his sword away and reached down to pull Thomas all the way into the window.

Still wet from his swim, and exhausted from the strenuous climb, Thomas sat in the dark chamber into which he had fallen, breathing heavily. The man whose heart had taken the arrow lay nearby, dead, and the one who had helped him stood in the farthest corner, watching him carefully, ready to bolt if Thomas should suddenly attack.

"I do not speak falsely," he told the man as his breathing calmed. "You have saved my life, and so I will make certain of yours. What is your name?"

"Leofson," the man replied.

"I am Thomas of Reed," Thomas told him, laboring to his bare feet and taking up the sword that Leofson had dropped. "Nay, I mean you no harm," he said when the other man stepped toward the door. "The lord to whom you have sworn fealty will soon be dead. I will give you the chance to swear loyalty anew to my master, who is Sir Eric of Reed. If you do so, you will fight beside me this very hour, and when the battle is over you may return to Reed with my lord's army and I will make provision for you there. If you would remain loyal to Sacre Placean, I will lock you in this chamber until the fighting is finished, and then I will release you and let you go on your way unharmed."

"I will swear fealty to Reed," Leofson said without hesitation.

"That is well," Thomas said. "Tell me, then, if the army of Sacre Placean will hold fast to the end for their lord, or if they will give way."

"Some will hold fast," Leofson replied, "and some will give way. Only a fool will hold fast against the army of the king."

"Or a mad man," Thomas agreed. "A woman was

returned to this place a short time ago, one who was called Amica of Lancaster."

"The lord's wife?"

"Once his wife," Thomas told him, "but now mine. Do you know where she is chambered?"

Leofson shook his helmeted head with confusion. "Nay, my lord. She was seen this day for the baptism of her son, but otherwise she is always kept abovestairs. In all truth, I have but seen her twice since she came to Sacre Placean more than four years ago, on this day and on the day she wed our lord."

"You do not know where she is, then?"

"Nay, I do not."

"Can you take me to Duncan Selwyrn?"

"I can try, my lord."

"Then take your sword, son of Leof," Thomas held the weapon out to the man, "and guide me to the lord of Sacre Placean, for I am going to kill him."

The great hall of Castle Sacre Placean was curiously empty. The attack had come so suddenly and unexpectedly that there had been no time to gather the villagers into the castle for safety, and Duncan had at last sent the few remaining soldiers in the hall out to the battlements when word came that the castle gates had been breached. He had told them to go and surrender, to lay down their weapons and give themselves over to the king's army. There was no sense in fighting when the gods had abandoned the land, and him, Duncan knew. No amount of bloodshed would make things right again. It was finished.

Duncan stood alone, gazing at the table where the most precious of the Selwyrn treasures lay, sometimes touching them, caressing them gently.

He had committed an unforgivable act and had displeased the spirits of the earth, and in doing so he had forfeited his life, his lands, and all that had been sacred to every one of his ancestors.

He should not have killed Amica, he thought. In the moment that he had done it, he had known how grave a sin it was to destroy such beauty, how great an insult it was to the gods who had created it, yet he had been unable to draw back, as he now wished he had done. It was Amica's fault, really, for she had goaded him into it with her foolish attempt to kill him. His anger had been white hot, there was nothing else he could have done to assuage it. How different she was from the timorous girl Duncan had once known her to be. He had not realized until that moment how powerful a thing love was, to break her heart so thoroughly and forge such changes. She was like a whole new being, and Duncan had grieved the loss of her while she was yet still alive, before her heart had stopped beating forever. In her own way, Amica had visited her revenge on him, a revenge that was complete and all encompassing. She had repaid him in full for all that he had done to her, for now he would lose everything.

"Selwyrn."

Duncan lifted his head toward the sound of the voice. When he took in the man who stood at the other end of the hall, wet and barefooted, his eyes filled with disbelief.

"I had thought you might be the one, Thomas of Reed, but I did not think you would come to me in such a state."

Sword in hand, Thomas advanced upon him. "My state has naught to do with the manner in which I kill you."

"But it does," Duncan protested, hefting the sharp

bladed javelin from the table and ignoring the pain in
his shoulder, where Amica had stabbed him, "for I will
not be killed by a man who does not even wear shoes."

The javelin stilled Thomas with caution, for not only
was it a deadly weapon, but Duncan Selwyrn clearly
knew how to use it. He had not come so far to save his
wife only to be killed before he could do so.

"Where is Amica?" he demanded, taking his steps
with measured care.

"I suspected," said Duncan, aiming the javelin at
Thomas, "when I took her from you, that you but
played a part in your sudden hatred. There are many
things Amica is capable of, but willful deceit is not one
of them. Anyone knowing her even for a short period of
time would realize that. I was a fool to believe that you
would so quickly take the side of a stranger over hers.
And the troubadour, Jace, was your spy, was he not?"
He advanced slowly as he spoke, circling Thomas even
as Thomas circled away.

"Where is she?"

"You did it to keep Reed safe, is that not so?"
Duncan asked, jabbing sharply at Thomas, who easily
jumped away. "But you had no care for what your rejection did to Amica, of how great a harm you visited upon
her. I am glad that I took her from you, for at least I
loved her."

"God damn you!" Thomas shouted furiously. *"What
have you done with her?!"* He charged his opponent.
With a flash Duncan thrust; the blade sliced through
Thomas's tunic and as he leapt away blood welled
bright and red from the wound.

"What have I done? I have given her peace," Duncan
said, breathing more quickly, advancing upon Thomas,
who, stumbling and grimacing with pain, moved to put
the distance of a table between them. "She was

unhappy, for you had made her hate her life and the life of your child, which she carried."

Thomas's mouth fell open. "Child?" he repeated. "God's mercy!" The next instant the shock was replaced by renewed fury. "You beat her senseless after Jace escaped," he said in a tight voice, lifting his sword again. "If you have harmed her, or the babe . . . "

"She loved you," Duncan said, lifting the javelin and advancing once more. "You are the one who brought her harm, not I. I gave her the choice between life and death, and because of you, Thomas of Reed, she chose death!"

"Liar!" Thomas shouted, lunging so suddenly that Duncan lost his balance and fell to the ground. Snatching the javelin in one hand, Thomas threw the weapon aside. "Now," he said, standing over Duncan and setting the point of his sword at his throat. "Where is my wife?"

Duncan smiled. "You must ask God that question, my lord. I can only say that she no longer graces this world."

The tip of the sword pressed sharply. "You lie."

"I do not. I killed her by my own hand."

Thomas's hand began to tremble. "You *lie*," he insisted.

"I loved her better than you ever did," Duncan told him softly. "I loved her enough to kill her when you had made her life a misery. I have given her peace."

Thomas stumbled back as if he'd been struck by an invisible blow. Coming up against the table, he stared at Duncan in horror. "Amica . . . dead?"

"Aye, she is dead," Duncan replied, sitting up. "I opened the veins in her wrists more than an hour ago. Her life's blood has drained from her. She is long dead, and so is your child."

The sword clattered to the ground, and Thomas sank down on his knees beside it. "God," he murmured. "God. Amica." Sudden tears streamed down his cheeks, and he closed his eyes and bowed his head and wept soundlessly. He heard Duncan approaching, heard his sword being taken up off the floor with a loud scraping sound.

"Now I will give you peace, Thomas of Reed," Duncan promised, "just as I gave it to Amica."

Thomas waited for the blow to come, for darkness to fall, but a moment after he heard his sword slicing upward into the air the doors to the great hall flew open, and Sir Eric's furious shout filled his ears more loudly than a thunderclap. It was only one word, his name, but it sent Thomas springing away just as the blade descended, striking the table instead of his head.

Thomas lay on the rushes, breathing harshly and blinking with confusion. Both Duncan and Sir Eric were shouting, and then Sir Garin's voice joined in.

His eyes finally focused to see Derryn and Leofson gazing down at him.

"Tom," Derryn said. "What's happened?"

The next moment both Derryn and Leofson disappeared, having been picked up and easily tossed aside by Sir Eric.

"Tom! God's mercy. You've been wounded."

The sight of his master's face shattered every wall of self-control that Thomas had ever erected. Uncontrollably, he began to sob, and blindly reached a hand toward Sir Eric.

"Amica's dead," he managed. "Dead . . . dead . . . "

He felt himself being crushed in strong arms, as if he were a child again; he could hear Sir Eric saying his name, over and over, dim against the force of his sorrow.

The violent wave of emotion stopped as suddenly as it had started. In the space of a minute Thomas mastered himself, and pushed free of Sir Eric and onto his feet. "I am going to kill him," he said, swaying and wiping his wet face with his forearm. "Give me my sword. I will hack him to pieces."

Sir Eric set Thomas's sword in his hand. "My father has claimed the right to kill him," he said, holding Thomas steady. He motioned to the lord's chair, where Sir Garin had dragged Duncan and in which Duncan sat, waiting.

"I have vowed to kill the man who caused Andrew Fawdry much suffering," Sir Garin said, "but if this dog has killed Lady Amica, I relinquish my claim. Thomas's is by far the greater one." He stepped away from the dais. "Do as you will, Tom. No man on earth, nor God in heaven, will judge you harshly for the deed."

"I have no care for that," Thomas said as he moved unsteadily toward the dais. "I killed my own father. Duncan Selwyrn will never prick my conscience as he has. I will only regret that I did not kill him at Reed, for at least Amica would still be alive."

"Lady Amica is yet alive, Sir Thomas."

The statement drew the attention of everyone present in the hall.

"Alfred!" Duncan cried, standing as his steward walked slowly toward him. "What is it that you speak? You saw me kill her with your own eyes!"

Alfred was not able to reply, for Thomas grabbed him by the tunic and lifted him off his feet, shaking him. "My wife is alive?" he demanded.

"Aye," Alfred squeaked, struggling to breathe. "She's alive!"

Thomas set him on the ground again. "Where is she?"

"Abovestairs, my lord," Alfred answered quickly. "She but sleeps, I vow it."

"I killed her!" Duncan shouted. "She is dead!"

Alfred looked at him with contempt. "You opened the veins in her wrists, but that is all you did. Then you left me there to watch as she died, but the moment you shut the chamber door I made to bind the wounds. She lost very little blood, Duncan. You did not kill her."

"But . . . Why, Alfred?" Duncan murmured, slumping down into the chair. "You are the only person on this earth whom I fully trusted. How could you betray your own brother?"

"Aye, my brother," Alfred said, fingering the dagger at his waist. "My own dear brother, who has made me naught but his lifelong slave because I was bastard born and not worthy to claim my rights as a true Selwyrn."

"But you understood that," Duncan protested. "Father explained it to you, just as he did to me."

"Oh yes, time and again, he did. My blood is tainted with that of the whore who gave me life. I must be grateful for that noble part which I did receive, and because of that gratitude I must live as nothing more than a servant to you, the true heir. I have been as your dog, Duncan, and worse, all of my life. You tried to take everything away from me, even the right to be a whole man."

Duncan paled. "I did not do that to you, Alfred. You know I am not the one to blame. It was Father—"

"Who had me gelded when I was a boy?" Alfred finished. "Aye, it was Father who decided that I must be made into naught, so that the precious Selwyrn blood should never again be tainted as it had been by my birth, but it was *you* who taunted me, Duncan. You who have never ceased to remind me that I can never please a woman, nor gain her love. But you were wrong, brother, for I did have a woman of my own, a beautiful woman who loved me as fully as I loved her. Alys of Lancaster." He smiled as he drew nearer, pulling the dagger from its sheath. "Since the day she died, I have waited and prayed for this moment."

Duncan shrank back in the chair, holding up a pleading hand. "Nay, Alfred, not you—"

"Aye, me, brother," Alfred whispered, lifting his hand. "One more thing I shall tell you before I send you to Hell. Conall is not your son."

He gazed into Duncan's face, waiting until the moment that understanding came and the expression there grew horrified.

"No more Selwyrns," Alfred murmured, and brought the knife sharply down.

30

"*You see, my lord,*" Alfred said. "*She but sleeps.*"

Thomas hardly heard him. He dropped his sword and crossed the chamber in three strides, setting one knee on the bed where Amica lay and leaning across it until he touched her with his own hand, setting his palm against her cheek, and feeling her warmth.

"God be praised," he whispered, lowering his head to kiss her. "God above be praised." He stayed there a long time, murmuring apologies, alternately pressing his beard-roughened cheek to hers and kissing her, and all the while she slept peacefully.

He didn't realize that Alfred had left, nor that he had returned, until he heard his name. Twisting, Thomas sat all the way up and stared.

"I did not wish for Lady Amica to be returned to Sacre Placean," Alfred said, moving further into the room and setting the squirming child in his arms on the floor, "but it was necessary that she come back so that she could care for her sister's child. I promised Alys that I would not kill Duncan until the babe was safe with Lady Amica. I did not realize that he would attempt to kill her else I might have secreted the child out of Sacre Placean before encouraging Duncan to recover his wife."

"Who is the boy's father?" Thomas asked, watching as the sturdy, crawling youngster took interest in his bare feet. "You said he was not Selwyrn's, and you, surely, could not sire a child."

"Nay, I cannot, for I have not the means to do so," Alfred admitted. "In truth, I do not know who the child's father is. Alys was desperate to conceive, and I loved her." He shrugged. "I brought several young men to her, then paid them well afterward and sent them far away. I can hardly recall even a one of their faces, and the boy takes almost wholly after Alys."

The child had crawled over to the edge of the bed and, sitting on the ground, began to inspect Thomas's toes, which Thomas was wiggling at him.

"He is a fine lad," Thomas said.

"Aye, my lord. Your own babe may look much as Conall does. Indeed, he could be Lady Amica's child, so much does he resemble her."

The babe gripped Thomas's big toe in his tiny fist, squeezing and pulling so that Thomas laughed. "He is strong. What a warrior he will become one day! None of that, now, lad." He bent to pick him up when the child sought to taste the prize he held. "Are you so hungry that you'd eat my foot?" Thomas asked, bringing their faces close together. Gazing with grave bewilderment at the stranger who held him, the babe set his plump hands on Thomas's cheeks, patting as if to see what the stranger was made of.

"You will raise him and care for him as the child of

your wife's sister?" Alfred asked from where he stood across the chamber. "It is your duty to do so."

"I will raise him as my own," Thomas replied, his eyes held on the child's. "He shall be my son, and I will love him well, as Amica already must." Setting the boy on his lap, Thomas glanced at Alfred. "Amica does know of him?"

Alfred nodded. "She does." He seemed to relax. "I believe that you will do as you have said toward the boy, my lord. Now that he is secured, I have done all that I promised Alys I would do. Her death has been avenged, and Lady Amica will be a mother to her child. My beloved may rest with contentment, and I may find my own peace."

"You need not do so," Thomas said. "Why should you not live and enjoy what is left of your life? The king will not charge you with any crime and, indeed, you are now the lord of Sacre Placean."

"I do not wish to be," Alfred said, "and I do not wish to live without Alys. She was the only woman who saw beyond all that I am, or all that I am not, rather. And that she should turn to me . . . to *me* . . . out of every other man in Sacre Placean when Duncan spurned her . . . you will not be able to understand what that meant to me, or of how I grieved when Duncan had her poisoned. If it had not been for the child, I should have killed my brother long before he could have harmed her, but she knew that his men would put us both to death, and the child with us. She pleaded with me to live long enough to make certain that the child was in her sister's hands. How could I deny her anything when I loved her so?" He lifted his hands in a helpless gesture.

"You did well, Alfred of Sacre Placean, and I am wholly indebted to you for saving my lady's life. If you grieved for your Alys as I grieved when I thought Amica gone, then your suffering has truly been great. I would ask you to choose life, to let me repay you for what you have done."

"I do not desire it," Alfred said. "I would only ask that you do as you have said toward the child. Also that, when my body is found, you will not bury me beside my brother, nor by my father. I would rest in the place next to Alys's. If you will do that for me, then I have been repaid tenfold."

"It shall be done."

Conall began to squirm and whimper, and Thomas spoke to him soothingly.

"I will send the nurse, my lord, to feed him. Is there anything else I may do for you before I go?"

"Accept my thanks," Thomas said, hugging the child to comfort him.

"I do, my lord." He made a slight bow and left the chamber. Two hours later, as Thomas sat in a chair beside Amica's bed, rocking the recently fed babe to sleep, Derryn brought word that the steward's body had been found at the foot of Lady Alys's grave, where Alfred had fallen upon his own sword.

It was dark when Amica opened her eyes, though the chamber was illuminated by both the fire and several candles. She was confused for a few long moments as she strove to clear her thoughts, to make sense of where she was and what had happened. Her wrists ached badly, and she realized, dimly, that they were heavily wrapped.

A familiar voice spoke her name, twice, "Amica," and a hand touched her cheek.

"Baby," she said weakly. With an effort, she lifted one hand to press against her belly.

"Our babe was not touched," he answered softly. "Duncan is dead. He tried to harm you, but Alfred the steward kept you alive, and also our child. You must not fear for anything, Amica. You are safe."

She tried to turn away, but he made a soothing sound and, with gentle fingers held her still. The next moment a damp cloth was pressed against her dry lips.

"You have slept many hours," he said. "Try to drink, if you can."

She tried to focus her gaze on him. "Why are you here?" she asked, her voice thick and dull.

Thomas loomed over her, one hand sliding beneath her neck to lift her up, the other holding a goblet which he put to her mouth.

"I know you are angry," he murmured, "but drink, first. When you have done you may curse me as much as you wish, for as long as you wish."

Thirsty, Amica sipped at the cool water, pushing his hand away when she was done. The action caused her to see the heavy binding on her hands, to feel the deep slashes that she realized Duncan had made, and she winced.

"I am sorry that he harmed you," Thomas said, carefully grasping her hand and holding it. "Unlike the one upon your face, you will bear the marks of these scars for the remainder of your life." He gently pressed her arm back down onto the mattress. "Each time I see them, I will curse myself. It is a fitting punishment, and one that I well deserve."

"Why are you here, my lord?" she asked again. "Is it because of the child? You learned of it, somehow, and decided to keep a traitor—a liar—as your wife because of that? If I am all that you believe me to be, how can you even be certain the child is yours?"

His expression filled with pain. "I am certain, for you

truly are all that I believe you to be. You are good and honest and loving, and I trust you more than I trust another living soul. Aye, even more than I trust Sir Eric. I never believed any of the lies Duncan Selwyrn said of you, and I knew at once that the documents he produced were false. You will not wish to forgive me for handing you over to him, for speaking such evil falsehoods of you before the people of Reed, but if I had the choice again, I would do everything exactly as I did. I sacrificed you for the good of Reed. I would have sooner taken my own life than do so, but there was no other way."

She gazed at him warily. "No other way to keep Reed safe from Duncan, you mean?"

He nodded. "He arrived with all of his army, ready to destroy Reed to have you if he must. It is not something that he could have done if all of my men had been present, but with more than half of Reed's army gone to London with Sir Eric, there wasn't any way to protect the castle from an attack such as Duncan Selwyrn's forces could mount. The village surely would have been destroyed and many of my lord's people killed. I had an early warning of his army's approach, and when he sent word within the castle walls, asking for entry, I had already determined what I must do. There was only enough time to make certain that Stevan and Jace understood what parts they must play when the lord of Sacre Placean arrived."

Amica's brow creased with confusion. "Is that why Stevan behaved so strangely?"

"Aye, that is why. He hated to do so, but it was necessary if Selwyrn—and those in the castle—were to be convinced that we believed the lies given us. If Stevan had had his way, he would have killed the lord of Sacre Placean for the charges he set against you."

"I find that difficult to believe, my lord," Amica said. "Indeed, Sir Stevan found it a simple thing to strike me as he did."

"He was sickened at having done it," Thomas told her, "but he felt it necessary. He saw how I wavered, that I was nearly ready to give way, for I could no longer bear to harm you. Indeed, Amica, you did not do as I had thought, with the fear that I had believed would possess and overwhelm and keep you silent. How did you suddenly come to be so bold?"

With a sigh, she turned her head on the pillow, away from him. "I do not know. I felt as if I had died within, knowing that you had no faith in me, no trust. I had given you my love, but it was as naught to you, just as I was naught."

Thomas leaned over her, touching her face. "You are everything to me! Can you think I let you go so easily? It was as if I had cut off one of my own limbs, as if I had taken the soul from my body. I do not ask you to forgive me, Amica, but I beg that you will not go away from me forever." He pressed his face against her neck, hugging her tightly. "What will my life be if you are gone? How should I make myself rise each morn when there would be naught but the emptiness that I have endured while you were in Selwyrn's hands? I love you." He lifted his head. "My love is not something of great value, for I know that I am not a worthy man, but I give it, nonetheless, and you may do with it what you will, only do not leave me, I pray. I can abide anything, even your hatred, as long as you are near."

Blinking back tears, she uncertainly touched his cheek. "You survived without me these past many days. You do not seem harmed by the lack of me."

He pressed his hand over hers, turning his face to kiss her palm. "You were not out of my sight for long,

beloved. I left Stevan to protect Reed until Sir Eric
could send my soldiers back from London, and I followed behind the army of Sacre Placean, keeping you in
my sight as often as I could. Only the knowledge that
Selwyrn would at once kill us both kept me from going
to you. There was no way that I could have saved you
and kept you safe, but I vowed that Selwyrn would die
by my hand. He would have, if Alfred the steward had
not killed him first."

"Alfred killed him?" she asked with surprise.

Thomas told of what had passed between Alfred and
Duncan, and between Alfred and her sister. Thinking of
Alys, Amica suddenly remembered the child, and strug-
gled to sit. "Where is Conall?" she demanded.

"Nay, rest." Thomas pressed her back down upon
the pillows. "He is well. He sleeps there by the fire." He
pointed at a cradle set near the warmth of the flames.
"Do you see?"

"I will not return to Reed without him," Amica told
him.

"Nay, and neither will I," he promised. "He will be
our son, if you will allow it. If you will stay with me," he
added more quietly. "Say that you will do so, Amica.
Tell me what you desire, whatever it may be, and I shall
do it if you will not turn me away."

She was silent, gazing at him, seeing the fear in his
eyes and knowing that it was there because of her. He
had given her over to Duncan and the pain of that was
yet fierce, but he had done it only to save Reed and for
that, she knew, he would even have sacrificed Sir Eric.

"I want to return with you," she said at last, "but I
do not know how it will be." Her voice was filled with
all the sorrow she felt. "Something has died within me.
I do not know if it will ever come to life again."

He seemed to understand what she meant, for his

expression filled with a matching sorrow. "I will make no demands of you, Amica. Everything will be just as you wish, for your comfort. If you do not want me to live with you in the dwelling that we shared at Reed, I shall abide in the castle. I will not force my presence upon you in any manner. I will not even speak to you unless you have given me leave."

"Thomas—"

"You need not answer now," he said quickly. "You are weary and ill from all that has happened. Rest, and think on the matter." He stood. "I will send a serving maid with food and drink, and will take the babe so that you may rest more fully."

"Oh, nay, leave him," Amica protested even as Thomas bent to scoop the sleeping child carefully into his arms. "He will be no trouble, and I would have him near."

Cradling the babe close against his shoulder, Thomas looked at Amica's thickly bound wrists. "You cannot even lift him until your wounds have healed." He took a blanket from the crib to wrap it around the small, sleeping body. "Let me care for him, and in the morn I shall bring him back to you. You may tell me then what you wish to be done, and if you would rather have his nurse care for the boy, I will allow it."

He left then before Amica could speak again, and a few minutes later Sir Garin arrived, dragging in the same physician who had examined Amica before. At sword point, he caused that reluctant man to tend her wounds and make certain that all was well.

"You will treat her with all care. One tear from my lady," Sir Garin warned, "and I will exact a hundred like tears from you."

It was the most gentle handling Amica had ever received from Duncan's physician.

Servants came after that, bearing food and drink, though Amica could not partake of either. She wished that Thomas would return, that he would simply be there, beside her.

Her wrists ached and she was miserably unhappy, furious with herself and with Thomas and with all that had happened to destroy the goodness they had known with one another. Sleep evaded her, though she longed for the small peace it might bring.

The chamber door opened and Sir Eric entered.

"My lady? You do not sleep?"

"My lord," she murmured, grateful to see his huge, familiar person.

Closing the door, he moved to the bed, sitting upon it so that the mattress sagged beneath his tremendous weight.

"I praise God above to find you alive and well," he said, bending to kiss her cheek. "My grief was immeasurable when I thought you gone, and Tom was like one gone mad. You know that Duncan Selwyrn is dead?"

"Thomas told me that Alfred killed him, also that Alfred took his own life."

"Aye, he did do so. I would have stopped him if I had known, but there was no warning. Amica," he said more softly, lightly touching her hand, avoiding the bindings at her wrist, "if there is any fault in what has happened, it is mine. I was deceived by the false missive that Selwyrn sent under the king's seal, and left Reed unprotected so that he, or any man with enough power, could enter and make whatever demands he pleased, even to carry away one to whom I had given my solemn oath of protection. There is naught I can do or say to be forgiven."

"Oh no, my lord," Amica assured him. "It was not your fault. Duncan deceived you, just as he has

deceived many others, even as he once deceived Alys
and me. How could you have known that the missive
was a false one?"

"I should have," Sir Eric countered grimly. "Thomas
asked me to send a missive to the king, to make certain
that the document was what it appeared to be, but I
would not. If I had listened to his advice, Selwyrn never
should have been able to take you away, to cause you
such suffering. It is my fault that he did do so. None of
the blame can be laid at Thomas's feet."

Amica felt her color rising. "I know that, my lord,"
she whispered. "I did not know it at the time, or for a
long while afterward. Indeed, only this day have I
learned the truth."

"He is sitting out on the battlements, more wretched
than I have ever seen him because he is certain that you
will never forgive him for handing you over to Selwyrn."

"It is not a matter of forgiveness," she said, struggling to keep the tears that threatened her at bay.
"There is no need to forgive when he had no choice in
what he did. But, I . . . I do not know if I will ever be
able to be with him again and not remember all that he
said, all that I felt. I loved him," she said, drawing in a
sobbing breath, "and when I thought that he had turned
from me, I wished to die. Can you not understand how
it is?"

"Aye, most surely I do." He lowered his head to gaze
at the hand he held. "It is what anyone who loved
deeply would feel, and you must not distress yourself
over what is fully natural. But Thomas has suffered,
also, for you know as well as I that not every surprise he
expressed on the day that Duncan Selwyrn came to
Reed was feigned. He wed you, thinking you a maiden,
and gave his heart to you never realizing that you had
been another man's wife or that you are of such noble

birth. I have known Tom for all of his life, my lady, and can promise that it goes hard with him to think himself such a fool, even though he understands why the king found it necessary to withhold the truth."

"Thomas is not a fool," Amica insisted. "Never that. Never."

"Nay, he is not," Sir Eric agreed, "but he tells himself that he is. He finds no value in himself and so does not think others will find any. Even as a child Tom could not believe himself worthy of either love or honor. You know that his father treated him most cruelly?"

"Aye, but he cannot blame himself for what his father did."

Sir Eric toyed with the edge of her blanket, his expression inscrutable. "Oh, my lady, you must not think the matter so simple. Children take on the sins of their parents quite readily. I did so, when I discovered how evil a man my natural parent was, and you, I think, have taken your mother's guilt in bearing bastard daughters upon your own shoulders time and again. Can you not imagine my Tom as a lad, striving to win his father's love and setting the blame upon himself when he could not do so?"

She nodded.

"I will tell you something of Tom, when he was a lad," Sir Eric said, gently wiping the tears from her cheeks. "He was very stern, just as he is now, and solemn. Hard as rock, he was, possessing about as much feeling. He was so thin and starved one could see his bones pushing sharply at his flesh, and his feet were ever bare. What a scourge he was to the village of Belhaven! He stole every bit of food that he and his father ate and made no apology for it. 'Tis a wonder that the villagers didn't drown him, but they may have thought he was punished enough, for the beatings his father gave were loud and frequent.

"I cannot recall when he first became my shadow, or why. I showed him a few small kindnesses, I suppose, though I can scarce remember now what they were. I gave him a pair of shoes, once, and that may be what began his devotion, though he was so hungry for any amount of kindness that even a pat on the head might have done it. Whatever it was, it was enough to spur him into climbing the castle walls at night so that he might steal into my chamber."

"Into your chamber!" Amica exclaimed.

"I would wake and find him there, curled up in a chair, soundly sleeping. The first time I caught him he would not so much as speak to me, but fought wildly when I tried to hold him and ran away, down the halls and out the castle before he could be caught. He hid from me during the day, but that night he climbed back through the window again. It went on like that for more than a week before I got him to speak, and that only because I had kept a plate of sweets ready to bribe him with."

"He told you why he kept coming to your chamber?"

Sir Eric smiled. "He said he wished to guard me, which was the only way in which he could repay me for whatever I had done for him, though I think mayhap he longed to be away from his father, as well."

"His sense of honor was strong, then, even as a child."

"This is so. I quickly grew to love my fierce protector, for even his childish ways were clear and true. I have never known a man or child more honest than Tom. No guile exists in him whatever. Who could not love him, knowing him?"

"I do not know," Amica replied softly.

"I made him my squire when he was but ten and two years of age, and a finer squire a man could never know. Always he put my life before his own, my needs before his own. I could not make him stop even when I tried. He was always there, whenever I needed him, exactly when I needed him. It was then that I came to love him so dearly, as if he were my own son, and determined to make him my heir.

"I said nothing to Tom of this at first, but went to his father when we visited at Belhaven and told him that I wished to adopt Tom. The wretch demanded money, and I refused to pay it, for I valued Tom too dearly to barter for him like a simple possession. In all truth, I bid the man go to the devil, and vowed to keep Tom far from him for the remainder of his life. It was unwise of me, for Tom went to him later, as was his habit, and by the time I discovered that he had gone, it was too late to save him from harm, and nearly too late to save him from death."

He looked at Amica and she stared back at him.

"You will have guessed already that I am the one who killed Tom's father. I have never been ashamed of the fact, for when I entered the dwelling the fiend had recovered from his fall and had taken up a knife, ready to finish what his fists had begun, save that I knocked him down before he could. I would do it again to save Tom's life, but I should have spoken of what happened ere now. I was silent not for my own sake, for no honorable man would judge me guilty, but because I was afraid Tom would hate me for what I had done, and I could not bear to lose him. Not for the sake of a man who would have killed his own flesh."

"He thinks he is the one who killed him," Amica murmured.

"He did think it," Sir Eric admitted, "but no longer. I told him the truth before I came here to you, and would have told him long ago if I had but known that he believed himself guilty." He closed his eyes as if he were in pain. "Now I, like Tom, am afraid that I have lost the love of one whom I hold dear."

Amica touched his arm. "Surely you know that he would never hold anything against you, my lord. Not even the gravest of sins, for he loves you better than his own life."

Sir Eric shook his head. "It is not so easy a thing, and now he believes that I only made him my heir as a way to atone for what I did. He has said that he will renounce every claim to Reed and will only become my vassal again, a servant instead of the son I would have him be. I have pleaded his forgiveness, but I think I must be patient before I gain it. It is hard, my lady."

"Aye," she whispered.

Sir Eric rose to leave. He stopped at the door. "You have no cause to grant any request that I make, for I have brought you much pain, though I never wished to do so. Yet even so I would ask that you be kind to Tom. Not for my sake, nor even for yours, but for his. He is not capable with words, but surely he has shown, time and again, all that he feels for you. Do not leave him to suffer simply because he has no skill with the pretty words that a more confident man might use. Tom has never hidden what he is, and though he thinks it a poor gift, he has offered all that he can—aye, even his heart—freely and honestly. I beg you, Amica, consider long and well before you turn such as that away. Tom is a man of strength, but the heart he harbors within is easily assailed, and there are some wounds, my lady, that, once made, can never heal."

31

The sun had not yet risen in the sky when Amica at last pushed her way onto the battlement where Derryn had told her Thomas was.

Cold, damp air greeted her as she pushed the door wider and walked out onto the open roof. Shivering, she hugged the heavy cloak she had donned more closely to herself and gazed about. She saw no sign of Thomas, but the sight of the smoke rising from the village drew her closer to the protective half wall that ran the length of the castle.

"God's mercy," she murmured, stunned at the destruction Sacre Placean had suffered. Surrounding what was left of the village, tents flying the colors of Reed, Belhaven, and the king formed an almost complete circle, and the small figures of several hundred soldiers and horses moved about, gathering in groups around the several fires blazing in the camps. The smoke of these joined the smoke that drifted in great black columns from the village, turning the visible sky dark and gray.

"'Tis not a cheering sight, is it, my lady?"

Amica turned and saw Thomas sitting behind her on a long bench, a blanket over his shoulders. He looked weary, as if he had not slept in days, and the stubble on his face had grown into a visible beard. His long white hair tangled messily about his shoulders, strands of it sticking damply to his neck.

"Nay," she said. "It is not. Will you come below, my lord, and warm yourself by the fire?"

He rested his head against the wall behind him. "Not yet." Then, after a moment of silence, he added, "You should not be here, Amica. 'Tis cold and damp, and you are yet weak from your wounds. You should be abed."

"I would not sleep, even if I were."

He looked at her, troubled. "I forgot your dislike of such places. I should have sent a maid to bear you company while you rested."

"It would have made no difference. I would not have slept."

His expression grew bleak. "You have decided what you will do, then? You have come to tell me?"

"Aye. But there is something I must know from you, first, my lord.

"Anything," he said. "Ask, and I will answer as best I can."

"Very well." She took a step toward him. "I wish to know why you seem to think I should forgive you."

His already pale cheeks grew paler. "I . . . do not think you should, Amica. I only ask it, knowing that I do not deserve such mercy."

"Nay, you do not," she told him, "and I could not pretend to give mercy where it is not due."

"Nay," he whispered. "Amica."

She saw the tears in his eyes as she neared him, and

the surprise, also, when she knelt and placed her hands upon his knees.

"You do not deserve mercy because you have done naught that requires forgiveness. I am the one who must beg you to be merciful, and to forgive."

He began to shake his head. "No . . . "

"Aye," she murmured, trembling. "I love you, Thomas, and yet I held the truth from you."

"Only because the king commanded it."

"Not because of Henry," she said. "Because I was afraid that you would hate me and turn from me. Because I could not bear to lose you. My cousin's command was a welcome excuse, and Sir Eric made it easier still by being so ready to obey the king, but I should have told you. You had a right to know the kind of woman you took to wife."

"I knew full well what kind of woman I took to wife." He slipped one hand from beneath the blanket and pressed it against both of hers to warm them.

"I was not the maiden you thought me. You never would have wed me if you'd known. 'Twas not fair to keep it from you!"

He frowned. "I would have wed you still, Amica. It would have made no difference."

"I do not believe you," she said miserably. "What man would wed such a woman? So used and defiled? How you must have hated me when Duncan told you the truth."

"I will never hate you," he said, "and I knew the truth before Selwyrn spoke it."

"*What?*"

"I did not know that you were of such high birth, certainly, or that had been wed before, but I realized, only a few weeks after our marriage, that you had not been a maiden."

She stared at him.

"It was a simple matter to discern. There were no signs of a maidenhead on our wedding night, for you expressed no pain. And there had been no blood. But 'twas my own learning that eventually showed me the truth, for when I thought on the matter it became clear that you had already known what to expect, much moreso than I, with all my ignorance of women."

Shocked, she sat back on her heels. "And the thought did not anger you?"

"It did, at first," he said slowly, "for I hated thinking that another had touched you as I touched you, but when I bethought myself, it did not seem so grave a thing, for you were my wife and mine alone. Indeed, I was more worried in those days that you had taken me in distaste, for it was before that time when I discovered how to pleasure you, and it was upon that which my mind fixed. Not the other."

"I do not understand you, my lord," she said. "Any other man would surely have turned his wife away if he had learned such a thing."

"Why should I? 'Twas your love I craved, not your hatred. Above all things that I have ever hoped or dreamed of . . ." He did not seem to know how to speak the rest. "I crave your love," he repeated, reddening.

"You must know the truth," she murmured, "all of it, before you speak of such a desire. I must tell you of the ways in which Duncan used me, for you must know how defiled a creature I am."

"Nay, Amica. I do not wish to hear such things. I think I know already, for I saw the foul chamber in which you were kept, with all its chains and horrors." Grimacing, he lifted his other hand out from beneath the blanket. "I went a little mad, I think, when I saw it."

"Thomas." She sat up on her knees again, closer to him so that she could touch the wrappings that covered his hand. "What did you do?"

"I tried to pull the chains from the walls. When I thought of you shackled there by him, and of all that you must have suffered," he lifted his eyes to meet her gaze, "I went mad."

"We are a pair, my lord," she said tearfully, lifting up her bound wrists.

"Aye, we belong together."

"How could you want such a befouled creature for a wife?"

"How could you have ever wanted a murderer for a husband?"

"You are no murderer!" she countered angrily, wiping at her tears with her fingertips.

"And you are in no way foul," he said gently. "Ask what you will of me, and I will give it to you, but I beg you, Amica, do not leave me."

Grasping his good hand, she brought his fingers to her lips and kissed them fervently. "I wish to stay with you, Thomas, for I love you. There is only one thing I will ask, and it is not to have that love returned."

"Anything," he vowed.

She gripped his hand more tightly. "You must forgive Sir Eric and let him adopt you as his son. Fully and completely." Ignoring his darkening scowl, she pressed on. "You must take the name of Stavelot as your own, and in turn gift Conall with it."

"No," he stated in a hard voice. "I cannot."

"You are so angered with Sir Eric that you cannot forgive him?"

"I am not angered with him at all. He dealt justly with my father, who killed my mother and also meant to kill me. But I cannot let Sir Eric make me his heir because of that . . . because he feels guilt and thinks he must somehow make recompense."

"You let him make you his heir before you knew that he had killed your father."

"Aye, but only to silence him on the matter, also because I thought that I, better than another, would be able to keep Reed and all its possessions safe for my lord's daughters. I do not mean to have any of it for myself, or for Conall. You and he must be content with Lansworth."

"I am content to live with you anywhere," she said. "Even if it be no more than a tent. I do not ask you to do this thing for me, or even for Conall. I ask you for the sake of Sir Eric, because he loves you and because he worries that you will never forgive him. If you love me as you have claimed, my lord, then you, above all others, will understand how your master suffers with worry."

Thomas lowered his head, looking a little guilty.

"Is it so hard a thing?" she asked. "You love your master, and he wishes to make you his son. It is the only thing that I ask of you."

"I am not worthy," he murmured. "'Tis not fitting that such as I should name a man so fine as Sir Eric his father. 'Tis not right."

She touched his cheek with her fingers, lifting his eyes to meet hers. "It goes hard with you, Thomas of Reed, and so I will not press the matter. I ask it of you, but I will not turn aside from you if you will not do it, for you have neither asked nor required anything of me, save that I not leave you, and that is a request I will not . . . cannot deny. I pray that you will crave my love forever, for you shall always have it."

With a sound of relief, he reached down and pulled her into his lap, holding her closely. She hugged him, and then, disbelieving what she heard, touched his face and felt the wetness there.

"Surely you do not weep, my lord."

"It is very foolish," he said, sniffling, "but it is so. I am most weary, I fear, else I would not do such a thing."

"I love you," she said, pressing her head against his shoulder as he wrapped the blanket around her chilled body. "I have loved you since I knew of you, I think. Although perhaps not when you called me a stupid girl."

His kiss fell firmly against the top of her head. "Did I ever say a thing so foolish and untrue?" he asked, and the next moment hugged her so hard that she squeaked. "I have been afraid," he said in a voice thick with emotion. "I cannot think of what I must say, save that I love you, and that I wish you had told me before that you still loved me, so that I would not have spent the whole night making every possible supplication to God, who must now think me the most foolish of all his creatures."

"Thomas," she murmured, taking his face in her hands and bringing his mouth down to hers to kiss, tasting his tears and vowing that she would keep him from such suffering for as long as she lived.

His bandaged hand banged against her belly, so that she laughed and pulled away. "The child, my lord. He will not be glad of such attentions, I think."

He gazed at her with reddened, tear-filled eyes. "Child," he repeated, dragging the blanket away to look at her belly, as if he would make certain it was still there. "Our child."

"Aye. Ours. I meant to tell you days before Duncan arrived at Reed, but I could not think of the way to do so, and I wished to be certain."

"Our child." He reverently touched the unwrapped tips of his fingers to her slightly rounded stomach. "When will he be born?"

"Next spring," she answered. "Perhaps near the time when we first met."

A slow smile started on his lips. "When I called you a stupid girl, do you mean?"

Returning the smile, she nodded. "Even so, my lord."

"I called you that because you frightened me. Because you affected me as no other woman had done before. And I was afraid, then, because I knew that you would be the end of me. And so you have been."

"The end?"

"Of all my emptiness, and of all my wanting. I had dreamed so long of love that I feared it when it came at last. But no more, my wife," he murmured, kissing her. "No more. Now my dreams have come to life, and I am content."

Epilogue

"She'll be fine, Tom. Stop pacing or you'll wear Conall down to naught."

Thomas stopped midstride, causing the tiny toddler who followed his every step to stop as well. "Are you deaf, my lord? She is *not* fine! Can you not hear all that screaming?"

Ignoring Conall's duplicate babble, which sounded just as angry as his father's, though much less distinct, Sir Eric stooped to pick the child up into his arms. "Everyone in Reed can hear it," he said, "though I vow that my own lady has shaken the walls just as well while birthing all of our children."

"With you there beside her," Thomas charged hotly. "I want to see my wife!"

"Now, Tom," Sir Eric said patiently, bobbing Conall up and down in his big arms, "you know full well that Amica doesn't wish you to be present. She told you quite clearly that she wanted you out of the room."

Thomas raked both hands through his hair. "She bid

me to the devil, is what she did," he said. "She's never spoken to me in such a way before." He began to pace again, a worried expression on his face. "I vow I cannot think what's come over her. You would think birthing a child to be a simple matter. She's always been a very gentle lady before now."

Sir Eric chuckled, setting a hand over his mouth when Thomas glared at him. When the lord of Reed next spoke, he addressed the child he held. "I believe I will take my grandson for a ride in the fields. He enjoys the horses so greatly, as the heir to Reed should do. What a fine warrior he will make one day."

Thomas stared at his adopted father with horror. "Indeed he shall," he said. "But not this day. If Amica thought you had taken Conall up upon a steed she would—"

"The babe has arrived!" Lady Elizabeth called loudly into the great hall. "Thomas! Father! Hurry!"

All of the other occupants in the hall cheered as Thomas and Sir Eric, holding Conall, bolted up the stairs.

They argued over who would hold the newborn Andrew Stavelot first.

"I am his father," Thomas declared with much affront.

"I am his grandfather, and also his lord," Sir Eric stated.

"I," said a smiling Lady Margot, snatching the child from a grateful Amica, who was fully exhausted, "am his grandmother. And if either of you m-men think you shall t-take him from me before I am ready to give him up, you have m-much to learn."

Lady Margot carried the babe out of the chamber, followed closely by Sir Eric and Conall, and Thomas collapsed upon his knees at Amica's bedside, holding her hands and gazing worriedly into her weary face.

"Thank you," he said, kissing her hands, "for my son."

"You're welcome," she murmured. "Stay with me for a time. I wanted you so badly while the babe came."

Thomas's expression was fully astounded. "But you told me . . . You called me . . . "

"I was in much pain," she said, yawning. "I would have said anything. Please stay, Thomas. I do not wish to be alone in this castle."

He climbed onto the bed covers that the maids had newly laid and put his arms about her.

"Even now, love, you think of the time that you spent at Sacre Placean?"

"I think of it sometimes," she whispered, her eyes closed, "but never when you are with me. Stay, my lord. If you say you will, I shall rest easy, for you do not speak falsely."

Thomas kissed her pale cheek and pulled the covers up about her warmly. "Then know that I am here, Amica. Always here, beside you. So do I make my vow, and I do not speak falsely."

Let HarperMonogram
Sweep You Away!

❦❦❧❧❧

Once Upon a Time by Constance O'Banyon
Over seven million copies of her books in print. To save her idyllic kingdom from the English, Queen Jilliana must marry Prince Ruyen and produce an heir. Both are willing to do anything to defeat a common enemy, but they are powerless to fight the wanton desires that threaten to engulf them.

The Marrying Kind by Sharon Ihle
Romantic Times *Reviewer's Choice Award–Winning author.* Liberty Ann Justice has no time for the silver-tongued stranger she believes is trying to destroy her father's Wyoming newspaper. Donovan isn't about to let a little misunderstanding hinder his pursuit of happiness, however, or his pursuit of the tempestuous vixen who has him hungering for her sweet love.

Honor by Mary Spencer
Sent by King Henry V to save Amica of Lancaster from a cruel marriage, Sir Thomas of Reed discovers his rough ways are no match for Amica's innocent sensuality. A damsel in distress to his knight, Amica unleashes passions in Sir Thomas that leave him longing for her touch.

Wake Not the Dragon by Jo Ann Ferguson
As the queen's midwife, Gizela de Montpellier travels to Wales and meets Rhys ap Cynan—a Welsh chieftain determined to drive out the despised English. Captivated by the handsome warlord, Gizela must choose between her loyalty to the crown and her heart's desire.

And in case you missed last month's selections . . .

You Belong to My Heart by Nan Ryan
Over 3.5 million copies of her books in print. As the Civil War rages, Captain Clay Knight seizes Mary Ellen Preble's mansion for the Union Army. Having been his sweetheart, Mary Ellen must win back the man who wants her in his bed, but not in his heart.

After the Storm by Susan Sizemore

Golden Heart Award–Winning Author. When a time travel experiment goes awry, Libby Wolfe finds herself in medieval England and at the mercy of the dashing Bastien of Bale. A master of seduction, the handsome outlaw unleashes a passion in Libby that she finds hauntingly familiar.

Deep in the Heart by Sharon Sala

Romantic Times Award–Winning Author. Stalked by a threatening stranger, successful casting director Samantha Carlyle returns home to Texas—and her old friend John Thomas Knight—for safety. The tender lawman may be able to protect Sam's body, but his warm Southern ways put her heart at risk.

Honeysuckle DeVine by Susan Macias

To collect her inheritance, Laura Cannon needs to join Jesse Travers's cattle drive—and become his wife. The match is only temporary, but long days on the trail lead to nights filled with fiery passion.

Harper Monogram

ONE OF THE FEW BY GP. CAPT. J. A. KENT

He became the leader of one of the most successful fighter squadrons in World War II . . . Group Captain Johnny Kent – the man whose skilful leadership helped the famous 303 Squadron to play such a decisive part in the Battle of Britain, and won him the highest Polish military award, the *Virtuti Militari*.

This is Captain Kent's own story of his life in the R.A.F. – it is a story of triumphant achievement in combat and of a man whose air force career certainly picked him out as *One of the Few* . . .

'J. A. Kent's story is told modestly and without heroics, yet it gives a genuinely vivid impression of the way the work was done and many sound technical explanations.'

0 552 09692 X   50p

COMBAT REPORT BY BILL LAMBERT

1914–1918 were years of crisis. For the first time in history war was being fought in the trenches, at sea *and* in the air. Aviation was still in its infancy, and to the pilots of World War I each flight was an adventure – a far cry from the computerized safety of today . . .

COMBAT REPORT

is Captain Bill Lambert's story of the time he spent in the famous 24 Squadron. His unshakeable love of flying helped him to become one of the most outstanding fighter pilots of the war and in this, his own personal 'combat report' he describes his most dangerous and exciting aerial victories . . .

0 552 09742 X   50p

A SELECTED LIST OF WAR BOOKS THAT APPEAR IN CORGI

All these books are available at your bookshop or newsagent: or can be ordered direct from the publisher. Just tick the titles you want and fill in the form below.

CORGI BOOKS, Cash Sales Department, P.O. Box 11, Falmouth, Cornwall.

Please send cheque or postal order. No currency, and allow 10p to cover the cost of postage and packing (plus 5p each for additional copies).

NAME (Block letters) ....

ADDRESS..

(MAY 75) ....

While every effort is made to keep prices low, it is sometimes necessary to increase prices at short notice. Corgi Books reserve the right to show new retail prices on covers which may differ from those previously advertised in the text or elsewhere.